Usurper

Paul Finch is an ex-cop and journalist turned best-selling author. He first cut his literary teeth penning episodes of *The Bill*, and has written extensively in horror and fantasy, including for *Dr Who*. He is also known for his crime/thriller novels, of which there are twelve to date, including the Heckenburg and Clayburn series. Paul lives in Lancashire with his wife and business-partner, Cathy.

P.W.
FINCH

Usurper

CANELO

First published in the United Kingdom in 2023 by

Canelo
Unit 9, 5th Floor
Cargo Works, 1-2 Hatfields
London SE1 9PG
United Kingdom

A CIP catalogue record for this book is available from the British Library.

Print ISBN 978 1 80436 205 1
Ebook ISBN 978 1 80436 204 4

Cover design by kid-ethic

Cover images © Shutterstock

Look for more great books at www.canelo.co

Printed and bound in Great Britain by Clays Ltd, Elcograf S.p.A.

1

For my parents, Brian and Margaret, both of whom instilled in me an abiding fascination for the past

FOREWORD

A TALE OF TWO KINGDOMS

It's no secret that the period of history during which England belonged to the Anglo-Saxons ended on Christmas Day, 1066, with the coronation of Duke William of Normandy as King William I, later known as William the Conqueror.

Even now, it remains one of the most tumultuous events in British history, not just because one dynasty replaced another, or because the reins of power passed from one nation to its deadly rival, but because, unofficially at least, it signalled the end of what we now call the Dark Ages, and the commencement of the Middle Ages.

There is no hard and fast rule about that of course and, doubtless, historians of other nationalities will give me an argument. But in England, at least, the arrival of William the Conqueror was transformative. The old, archaic world of earls, thegns and long-halls was superseded by a physically very different one filled with barons, knights and castles. The English language, once spoken across the whole of society, was replaced by Norman-French at the higher levels, while the imposition of harsh penalties for the pursuit of game, fowl and fish – and even for the unlicensed collection of firewood – turned a vast landscape of woods, moors and mountains into a hunting park reserved exclusively for a cruel and foreign nobility.

And yet, English civilisation did not end in 1066. A previously happy people might well have been reduced overnight to a state of ongoing pain, sorrow and impoverishment, but the hardy island race survived, and in due course adapted; and though there was much fighting, bitterness and further loss on both sides, it finally resumed a settled way of life. If the English never exactly came to admire their new masters, they were at least, in time, able to tolerate and eventually serve them.

The aim of The Wulfbury Chronicles is to tell exactly that story. Not as a schoolroom lecture, but as seen through the eyes of a single individual, whose own personal journey mirrors these events.

For this reason, the tale must be told via two books rather than one, because it's a story of two very different kingdoms. In the first instalment, *Usurper*, our hero travels through a Saxon England in its death throes. In the second novel, *Battle Lord*, he ventures through a Norman England struggling to survive even at the very dawn of its creation.

Needless to say, a journey from light to darkness can be just as torrid as a journey from darkness to light. I therefore trust that each one of this duo of novels will be an epic in its own right. Massive sacrifices are baked in, death and violence par for the course, but only alongside endurance, redemption and, maybe, even a kind of victory.

Yes, The Wulfbury Chronicles are a two-part voyage out of necessity. But I hope it's one that you'll enjoy keeping me company on.

P. W. Finch, January 2023

PROLOGUE

He was lying on his back in a world of abyssal darkness. Pain transfixed every part of him. His eyes were gummy orbs trapped under lids sealed shut by a gritty, sticky substance that coated his entire face. But his ears worked at least, because as he lay there, shifting about awkwardly, trying by instinct to twitch life back into his deadened limbs, he heard voices approaching, speaking a language he didn't understand and yet somehow reviled.

Sluggishly, sick to his guts, hands weak and shaking, he reached up and scraped the filth from his eyes. And found himself gazing into a beaked, feathered visage no more than an inch from his own.

It was sleek and black, its beak curved, bloodied like an axe, its eyes unblinking blots of reflected flame. The boldest raven he had ever seen, it filled his entire vision as it sat there on his chest, peering down at him for what seemed an age, before suddenly lofting upward on its tar-black wings. Circling lazily, it finally perched on the bough of a nearby tree that was twisted and leafless, bristling with arrows, gashed by blades, spattered crimson in the flickering firelight.

He couldn't make sense of it, nor of anything else. That firelight was dim, cast by many sources, though most were distant from him and moving slowly back and forth. It was sufficient, though, to reveal the heaps of men lying hacked and dismembered on all sides. The sight might have jolted him with horror had he not by some means expected it; had he not already known they were there, smelled their opened innards, sensed their gaping mouths, slithered in the lake of blood they'd shed as it mingled and clotted with his own.

The voices grew louder. They were coming this way.

He turned his head leftward, though it hurt his neck abominably. Three hefty figures approached in a pall of smoky torchlight. Their mail clinked, their leather creaked, but he saw that they'd removed their helmets. One of them carried a spear, the others were armed only with staffs. They wielded these implements liberally as they shoved and rummaged through the gory, butchered remains.

He risked a glance to the right, and saw other lights in the darkness, heard more foreign voices. One of them laughed cruelly.

He snapped his eyes closed as the first group came upon him. The haft of a quarterstaff tapped against his ribs, or rather against the ring-coat that clad them.

His heart sank.

Even in this abattoir from Hell, they'd spotted the quality of his armour...

PART ONE

THE DARK VEIL

CHAPTER 1

The two warriors faced each other across a stretch of sun-dried grass. Nearby, the grove of apple trees called Gonwyn's Orchard basked in the afternoon heat, the River Swale rippling close by. It was a scenic spot, but the warriors saw nothing of this. They were tightly focused, clad in ring-mail coats and helmets with face-guards, carrying broadswords and circular shields.

The weapons were nicked and scarred from extensive use in many bouts, though when the twosome finally joined, few contests could have been as fierce. The blades sang together with fury, sparks flashing, splinters flying as blows hewed into linden wood. The taller fighter soon had the better of it. They clashed repeatedly, grunting and gasping as they smote at each other, breaking apart to get their breath but always re-engaging, the taller one's strokes increasingly swifter, surer, harder. With a deft uppercut and a vicious backhand, he sent his opponent's weapon twirling from his grasp.

A third fellow stood by, watching. He was young, no more than seventeen, with golden hair and a compact body. He bore no arms and wore only a loose tunic, breeches and felt boots. He bit his lip nervously as the shorter combatant scrambled after his sword, retrieved it and spun straight back into battle, striking hard at his opposite number's helmet, at his torso, even at his legs, but always finding only his shield or his deflecting blade. He cursed as he swept down with a high slash, only to be parried with ease, then as he aimed for the neck and shoulder joint, to be effortlessly blocked, edged steel clattering his nosepiece, his blade again sent spinning.

'What troubles me, Cerdic,' the taller of the two sneered, 'is that you're built for this. You're no weakling. You have the physical stature, and yet you never seem to improve.'

'Bastard,' his opponent, the one called Cerdic, muttered, breathing hard in the dusty air.

He wafted his sword back and forth as he returned to the fray. They fought even more fiercely, dancing around each other, steel shimmering, shields shuddering with each biting impact, and now, the taller one, whose name was Unferth, wasn't quite as quick to disarm his adversary.

They broke apart again, gasping, streaming sweat.

'That's better,' Unferth said. 'But if I go in more brutally...' He drove at his opponent with a sudden frenzy of cross-cuts and overhead hacks, Cerdic's blade knocked down with such force that it stood quivering in the grass. Unferth pushed him against the nearest tree, sword-tip at his pulsing throat. 'It ends swiftly, does it not?' He stepped back, pulled off his helmet and his leather coif and shook out his sweaty blond mane. 'Which, somehow, is even more pathetic.' He seemed saddened as well as frustrated. 'You can handle it when I'm playing, but when it's real...?'

Stung by the dismissive tone, Cerdic flung off his own helmet and swooped up his blade. It was not untrue that he had the stature for swordplay. Unferth stood an impressive six foot two, but Cerdic, his younger brother, was six feet himself, and though not massive in shape, still lean and agile.

He banged his sword on the iron rim of his shield. Unferth, who'd sheathed his own weapon and turned away, glanced back.

'What... I've upset you now? Called your manhood into question?' He drew his steel again. 'Then show me. Put me right.'

Cerdic attacked. Unferth fended him off, then counter-attacked. They circled, swords ringing. Before Cerdic's, inevitably, was dashed from his hand.

'The sad truth,' Unferth panted, tossing his shield aside, then reaching out and ruffling Cerdic's hair in the manner he knew had annoyed him since he was a child; Cerdic slapped his hand away. 'The sad truth… is that I think you've learned as much as you're capable of.'

The lad watching, Letwold, now spoke. 'How much does he need to learn if he's going into the Church?'

Unferth snorted. 'You think churchmen don't fight? It's plain as mud that you young fools have never seen a battle.'

'Neither have you,' Cerdic replied irritably.

Unferth bared his teeth. 'I've ridden to war, you little whelp!'

'There was no fighting.'

'Whether *I* can hold my own on the field of honour is not in question here.'

'Most priests use maces, anyway,' Letwold said. 'Don't they? Cudgel their enemies?'

'That's because most priests are of ignoble blood,' Unferth replied. 'Use a mace, you might as well use a lump of stone. And hard though I am on my little brother, he's too good for that.'

'You see, Cerdic,' Letwold grinned. 'There's hope for you yet.'

'Let's not overstate it,' Unferth said, though something else now distracted him.

For several minutes, a girl had been approaching along the nearby valley road. Now, almost level with them, she diverted toward the orchard. Her name was Eadora, and she was sister to the blacksmith's boy in the village of Brackley-on-the-Water. At eighteen, she was already a vision of loveliness: pink-lipped, with blue-near-violet eyes, hair that hung in long flaxen ropes, and a shape like Freyja herself. She saw them watching, and puckered her lips in a small, coy smile as she unslung the basket from her back, hitched the hem of her kirtle to her left hip, exposing a smooth brown leg, and commenced climbing.

Unferth slid his sword into its scabbard again. 'There ends today's lesson.'

'I've time yet,' Cerdic said, though he too was mesmerised by the comely young creature now moving lithely between the boughs as she purposely picked only the rosiest apples.

'No, that's it for today.' Unferth unbuckled his ring-mail as he walked slowly over there.

'Aye,' Letwold agreed, looking at Cerdic. 'That's it for today. For *you* at least.'

Cerdic watched as his brother halted under the first apple tree, clasping Eadora's waist to help her down again. They spoke together out of earshot of the younger two, the peasant girl uncommonly relaxed in the company of a young lord-in-waiting, even giggling at some jest he made. Arm-in-arm, the basket and apples forgotten, they ambled away under the trees.

Cerdic grabbed up his helmet, brushing grass seeds off it, unbuckled his sword-belt and with quick, jerking movements, opened the front of his ring-coat.

'Earl Rothgar's second son, and she doesn't even know I exist,' he grumbled.

'That's because the earl's first son got there ahead of you,' Letwold replied.

It wasn't an exaggeration. Unferth had been bedding the village beauty for most of that summer, in barns and stables, out among the hayricks. Anywhere, in truth, where they could find privacy.

'Besides,' Letwold said, 'should you really be thinking that way?'

Cerdic sighed as they walked back along the road, his war gear bundled under his arm. 'I suppose not.'

In the early part of his vocational instruction, Aethelric, his tutor, had advised him that it wasn't in itself sinful to look on a woman and desire her. It was part of Nature, and one had no control over that. However, one was expected to exercise restraint, and apparently, when temptation came, there was power and solace to be found in prayer. For his part, Cerdic wasn't so sure. He was a God-fearing lad and he prayed a lot, for

8

all sorts of things. But as yet, there'd been no divine intervention to avert his lusty gaze from Eadora. Partly, he suspected, this was because he didn't pray very hard for it.

'We can all dream,' he said.

'Unferth's right about the training,' Letwold replied. 'I mean... that you may still need it.'

Cerdic threw a lingering glance backward. Already, Unferth and Eadora had vanished from view, blending into the orchard's green, shadowy heart. The lads trudged on. Beside them, the river ran clear and shallow, gurgling over rounded stones. Brown trout darted beneath the glinting surface. Above it, swarms of midges danced like specks of gold.

'Is he right that I'm a useless clod?' Cerdic wondered. 'That I'd be better with a darning needle or cooking spoon in my hand than a sword?'

'He didn't quite say that.'

'And what do *you* think? You'll be a housecarl at some point.'

Letwold shrugged. 'I think you held your own well. Unferth's a dangerous opponent. He knows his business with sword and axe. He's strong, and he uses that strength.'

'He's used it all my life against me.'

'That's what older brothers do. It's part of their job.'

'Some throw themselves into it more than others.'

Letwold shrugged again. 'Does Athelbere comment on your progress?'

'He says I'm "doing well".'

They mulled that over. Athelbere, Earl Rothgar's hoary house-marshal, wasn't just an experienced campaigner, but a stern taskmaster who wasn't for wasting words. If he'd said that Lord Cerdic was 'doing well', he'd have meant it truthfully. But the fact he'd added no more than that told its own story.

'He doesn't concentrate on me one-to-one, the way he did with Unferth,' Cerdic said.

'Because you're bound for the priesthood?'

'What else?'

It was a painful truth. Athelbere even preferred it when Cerdic sparred with wooden weapons rather than actual steel. Hence this afternoon's session being held by Gonwyn's Orchard, far from the burh and the drill-yard. Sparring with real blades led to injuries and death. Not regularly, but it was a risk the earl's housecarls had to take every day because that was what they'd face in real war. But it wasn't a risk the marshal of the house deemed necessary for Cerdic, because the lad would shortly be attending the Minster School at York. Though if, in due course, he rose to prominence in the Cloth he would indeed need a basic knowledge of combat, it would never be his actual profession.

'Are we for The Corn Mother?' Letwold asked, rubbing his hands together. There were sounds of celebration just ahead of them. 'There're lots of luscious lasses around when there's no work to be done, and on a day like today the drink will be flowing. There'll be dancing, the dancing might turn to tumbling... you know what I mean?'

'I'll need to see you there later,' Cerdic replied. 'I'm late for my studies.'

'During Harvest Ales?'

'The only days I'm not required to study are Good Friday, Easter Day and Christmas.'

'God help us!' Letwold grimaced. 'That must be unbearable.'

'Aethelric says it's improving me as a person.'

'It's a hard road you've chosen, my lord.'

'If only I *had* chosen it.'

Brackley-on-the-Water appeared around the bend, where it straddled the river close to the foot of the Keld Brae. It was one of numerous farming settlements straggling east to west along the Swale, all offering rights and services to the tenant-in-chief of that region, Rothgar Aelfricsson, Earl of Ripon and ring-giver to many thegns in the north-central Danelaw, but it was easily the largest of them, the shallow ford at its heart allowing travellers to wade from one side to the other even when the river was in spate.

Today, to celebrate Harvest Ales, the village was filled with jugglers, minstrels and acrobats. Dales folk wearing sprigs of herbs and flowers cavorted among them, relieved and delighted that the days of backbreaking toil were over for another year. In gratitude, Earl Rothgar had provided two hogs as a gift to each village. Brackley's pair were roasting on spits in the square. Nearby, stalls sold bowls of pottage and hot fish soup, while the Lord of the Harvest, armed with his sickle and hidden behind a heavy mask woven from summer grass and wheat husks, wheeled his cart around, crying, 'Hooky, hooky!' as he distributed warm, freshly baked loaves. It was a jovial scene that would likely turn riotous as the evening descended.

Cerdic and Letwold parted ways in the village centre, Cerdic oblivious to the frivolity around him, Letwold assuming his companion's downbeat mood was because he had several hours of grammar, theology and mathematics ahead. This was partly the cause, but not wholly.

Cerdic could hardly tell Letwold how jealous he was of Unferth. He knew he ought not to be. Unferth was the larger of the two brothers, the more handsome and imposing, the wilder and brasher. On top of all that, he was their next commander. It was natural law that he'd have first pick of all prizes. But Eadora was more than just an everyday prize. At least, she was to Cerdic. Queen of the May each spring, Maiden of Misrule at Yuletide, she had many rivals among the local lasses, but no equals, and Cerdic, who'd fumbled with and kissed the odd girl, but had never lain with one outside his feverish dreams, felt she was unobtainable for that reason alone, never mind because she was Unferth's lover. It was ridiculous, of course. Beyond the pale even. Her older brother, who worked at the village smithy, was a cottar, or freeman, but still a ceorl. In that regard, it was worse than demeaning to entertain such fantasies, especially the way Cerdic's future had been mapped out for him. Even Letwold, a persistent if mostly unsuccessful pursuer of well-built lasses, had pointed this out. Of course, it was all a bawdy joke at this stage, nothing more than banter, but Cerdic knew that he should consider his position, and the position he'd shortly occupy. Letwold might be a loyal confidante, but at some point the earl's second son could return here in priestly robes, and how damaging to his dignity would it be if even one person, no matter that it was a former friend, knew he'd harboured such earthy desires.

The heat beat down as he ascended the track to Wulfbury, as it had for most of that long, dusty summer. Little wonder this year's Harvest Ales was turning raucous, though merely thinking about the fun and frolics to be had at village festivals was itself torture. In a month's time he'd be in a stone cell in York, a novice with head shaved, wearing a habit and sandals, working every hour God sent on scraps of parchment and calligraphic squiggles that would test the eyes of an eagle.

In so many ways, the Year of Our Lord 1066 was proving worrisome.

CHAPTER 2

Wulfbury burh was Earl Rothgar's citadel and the heart of his great estate. It sat at the east end of Swaledale, atop the Keld Brae, a high plateau jutting out from the range of hills enclosing the dale from the north. It occupied a commanding position, but a range of even higher fells, a rocky massif known locally as the Devil's Brow, towered above it a little further north, though this was separated from the burh by aprons of scree and broken limestone, placing the homestead far out of bowshot from those higher places.

As for the brae itself, a forest of sharpened stakes protruded from its lower slopes, while a mighty palisade circled its upper rim. Within, the burh was crammed with timber buildings arranged around a central paved square. Just west of this was the great dragon hall: an immense structure nearly eighty yards long, its roof of heavy thatch. Over its great front doors – two massive slabs of oak studded with brass-headed nails – a magnificent beast with multiple coils and a terrifying roaring head had been cut into the wood; a menacing legacy of the days when pagans held this place. Earl Rothgar had seized upon the device with joy, his artisans painting its eyes red, its teeth white, its multiple scales blue, green and gold.

A much humbler abode – very humble indeed, considering that it housed the Lord of Hosts – stood, almost unseen at the mighty structure's rear. It was a squat, stone chapel, very basic and simple, with just a stone dais and wooden table for an altar. Currently, there were two persons ensconced in the window-less cell screened at the rear of this. The first of these, Father

Aethelric, Earl Rothgar's chaplain, was elderly, with a shock of white hair and a weathered face. He was also tall and rail-thin, an impression enhanced by his habit of black burel, which only came down as far as his knees, revealing pale, stick-like shins. At present, he stood at his bookstand, squinting as he sought to assess a number of documents by flickering candlelight. The other person, Cerdic, sat at his desk, quill in hand, a fresh sheet of vellum in front of him.

'Before we start today,' the lad said, 'I have a question.'

'Go ahead,' the priest replied. 'But be brief; we are already running far behind.'

He glanced up, noting again that Cerdic's sunny hair was a mop, his tunic damp with sweat. Clearly, the lad had been up to some horseplay or other when he should have been here. But there was only so much you could do to chastise the son of an earl, even an unusually enlightened earl like Rothgar.

'Do churchmen automatically go to God?' Cerdic asked. 'I mean, when they die.'

Aethelric straightened up, puzzled. 'Well... not automatically. We are prone to the same temptations as everyone else. Sometimes we surrender to them.'

'So... if I take the Cloth, it's no guarantee of anything?'

Aethelric laid down his quill. 'Cerdic, what's this about?'

'Nothing.' Cerdic shrugged. 'I suppose I'm trying to decide whether or not it will be the right thing for me.'

'That's already been decided.'

'Not by me.'

Aethelric sighed. All too often they'd had this conversation. He assessed his pupil carefully.

For a seventeen-year-old, Cerdic was not a displeasing individual. He might not have Unferth's physical bulk, or his best friend Letwold's sense of humour, but he was handsome enough in a rugged, Saxon sort of way, with metal-blue eyes and an old scar on his left cheek where an adder had once bitten him. He had an affable air most of the time, but his lineage showed through on occasion; he could be curt and frosty when the mood was on him. He was no bully, but his was a world where orders were issued and compliance expected. In all ways, he was part of the ruling elite. But unlike so many, Unferth for example, he had a lively and enquiring mind, and he enjoyed broadening his knowledge. And to Aethelric's eyes, to waste all that would be a pitiful failure on both their parts.

'What do you want in life, Cerdic?' Aethelric asked. 'What do you *really* want? To be a warrior? You have passable skill with sword and axe; I've seen you training. But you aren't your brother. By the same token, though –' he came around the bookstand '– Unferth isn't you.' The priest tapped the side of his head. 'Your strengths lie *here*. You read and write exceptionally well for your age. You have a good grasp of geometry and mathematics. Your Greek is excellent, you're fluent in Latin already. You have great gifts, Cerdic. But they're not of the martial kind. Why disown them by ignoring the scholarly path?'

Cerdic sat back. 'Father is no priest, and he's made his education count.'

'Cerdic... you can't be an earl any more than a warrior. Unferth is ahead of you in that line, too. But you could wield equal power and influence, maybe more, when you rise in the Church.'

Cerdic huffed. 'There are so many limits in that life.'

'So, this is why you ask if sin is permissible?'

'I didn't ask it as bluntly as that.'

'Let me rephrase it. This is why you wonder if you'll go to Heaven when you die whatever you've got up to in life, simply because you wore a cassock? There are some who behave that way, certainly. But the answer is *no*. Very firmly... *no*. However, that doesn't mean it can't be a fulfilling existence. Why do you ask this now, anyway? Haven't we talked about it before?'

Again, Cerdic hankered after the dream that had nagged at him more and more as the year had worn on and his date with the Minster School had approached: a heroic life in the midst of able-bodied friends; song; celebration; battle honours; beautiful girls yearning for his caresses.

Again, it was too ludicrous for words.

'Is it because the time is near?' Aethelric wondered aloud.

Cerdic shrugged.

'And you're worried that your life will change for the worse?'

'Won't it?'

The priest gave a rueful smile. 'If you're concerned about hunting and hawking and the like, maybe even feasting and drinking... I know many bishops and archbishops who fill their free time with exactly that. I can't say I approve – there are always spiritual matters that need attending to – but if it was good enough for Saint Wilfrid, I see no reason why it won't be for you, so long as you also attend to your duties. Which we must both do right now.'

He shuffled back behind the bookstand, but, turning, saw again the dejection in his pupil's face.

'Cerdic, Wulfbury is not the world. Neither is Swaledale. Your father has created an oasis here in a desert of harshness. Whatever route fate chooses for you, however your – what's that word I hate so much because it's so irredeemably pagan? – however your *wyrd* is woven, you'll have to go out there and sample it for yourself at some point. And you won't like it. Nobody does. But if you go out there, not just as a man of God, but as a learned man, you'll have advantages over most of the rest of the people of this kingdom. You may not believe that now, but you will... and in return for that, you will use your intellect, which you so obviously possess, to improve the lot of others. And you will enjoy doing that, because it will be a key part of your calling. And *that*, nothing else, will guarantee you a place in Heaven.'

'And yet there are clerics who commit sin. Or so you said before.'

Aethelric shook his head. 'We are not scheduled to study philosophy this afternoon. The rules are simple enough. Love

God, love your fellow man. An episcopal ring will not protect you from celestial wrath if you fail in that, but it *will* grant you the authority to do these things more easily. Now, shall we begin…?'

Cerdic watched him, waiting, quill in hand. But his face was written with displeasure.

'And still he is unhappy,' the priest said.

'I'm not unhappy. We should work.'

'In other words, let's get this damn thing over with?'

'If I'm attentive to my lessons, does it actually matter what I think about them?'

'Not if you don't mind leading a miserable life.'

'But I *do* mind.'

Aethelric harumphed. 'Let's get on, shall we? After all, the Harvest Ales festival is calling you.'

–

It was early evening when Cerdic entered The Corn Mother. The low-roofed tavern was noisy and sweaty, crammed to bursting with shepherds, ploughboys, fowlers and drovers. Ribald song rang under the smoke-stained beams, but Cerdic was in a non-celebratory mood when he forced his way through and sat down at Letwold's table. Letwold, who'd clearly been drinking thirstily, was in a semi-slump, his pink-tinged face written with a lazy smile.

'So,' he said, 'is your head aching with all that new inform-ation?'

'It's numb,' Cerdic replied. 'Like the rest of me.'

Letwold's grin downturned into a concerned frown. He signalled to the serving maid. 'Agnetha! A pot of ale for his lordship, here.'

'Did Unferth come back?' Cerdic asked.

'If he did, I haven't seen him. There's a feast tonight at the hall, is there not?'

'Aye.' Cerdic looked thoughtful.

'You're not still worried that he bested you? He always bests you.'

'Thank you for reminding me.'

'What kind of servant would I be if I didn't lay honest truths before you?'

'The kind who isn't asking for a cuff behind the ear,' Cerdic replied.

Agnetha, who was buxom and apple-cheeked, nudged up to them, a frothing tankard in either hand. Skilfully, without spilling a drop, she laid one on the table.

'Nicely done, my love,' Letwold laughed. 'Now...' He grappled with her, wrapping both arms around her waist, trying to pull her onto his knee. 'It might be warm in here, but I've got a warmer spot for *you*.'

'If it's all the same to you, sir.' She struggled free, doing everything in her power not to spill the other tankard. 'I'm working.'

'Bring me another ale, too, will you?' he shouted, tossing her a coin for Cerdic's drink, which she caught smartly and slipped into the money pouch on her girdle.

'So long as you keep your hands to yourself,' she retorted. 'I haven't got time for such nonsense.'

'I'm wearing that one down, I think,' Letwold said cheerfully, which sent an elderly villager stumbling away, laughing into his hands.

Then the tavern door hurtled open, crashing so hard into a couple of drinkers that it sent them stumbling. The jolly atmosphere in that place rapidly changed as a group of five young men thrust their way in, pushing aside those who wouldn't willingly move for them. Their leader, who was head and shoulders above the others and almost as broad as tall, wore a stained leather apron, but his arms and chest were naked and corded with sinew, a product of his occupation. This was Haco, assistant to the village blacksmith, and Eadora's older brother.

His eyes, black pebbles under his heavy brow, roved the cowed congregation, finally falling on Cerdic and Letwold. He elbowed his way through to them, throwing an empty purse onto the table in front of Cerdic.

'You! Your bloody lordship! Fill that, if you please, and you'll hear no more about it!'

The cramped room fell deathly silent.

Haco's cronies were exclusively the rougher fellows of the village, thin and wiry with muscle, ingrained with the dirt of their various trades. None of them smiled.

Letwold lowered his mug. 'What's your game, turd-breath?'

'I'm talking to the arse,' Haco replied, 'not the rag he rubs it with.'

Letwold made to stand, but Cerdic grabbed his arm.

'Are you seriously threatening Lord Cerdic?' one of the others present said.

'It's no threat to invoke the law,' Haco replied. 'Someone in your family needs to pay up, or your brother will be called to the shire-moot for ravishing a maiden.'

Cerdic jumped to his feet. 'Unferth would... he would never...' was all he managed to stutter.

'Oh, no? Then ask my sister. He took her by force this afternoon. In the orchard near Brackley Beck, while she was there to collect apples.'

'She told you that?' Cerdic said, astonished.

'She didn't need to. Your brother was seen humping her as she wept and begged him to stop. An otter-man working the river with his nets was witness to it.'

Cerdic fought to stay calm. More than anything, he wanted to smash his ale mug into the brazen, brutish grin in front of him. But that would have been madness. To everyone else around here, the complaint sounded legitimate. Violence would only compound it. The problem was that he felt certain Unferth had *not* raped Eadora. Cerdic had seen her playful coquettishness when his brother had led her into the greenery. He also knew that this was only one of many assignations between the young lovers. But he could hardly announce that, could he? What would that do to Eadora's reputation? The flower of the dale… a nobleman's whore, a village slattern.

And yet, Unferth's reputation was also at risk here.

'You'd take the word of an otter-man?' Cerdic said. 'Against the word of the earl-in-waiting of Ripon?'

'It's not just him,' Haco replied. 'I've had the truth from Eadora too. The *full* truth.'

Cerdic looked at Haco's hands. A pair of dirty hams bristling with thick, pig-like bristles. One of his knuckles had split and was oozing fresh blood.

'You beat her, did you?' Cerdic said.

'As her elder, it's my right.'

'And as *your* better, is it my right to beat you?'

'That would be amusing,' the assistant blacksmith said.

'You addled, lad?' an elderly shepherd whispered, taking his arm. 'You mock the earl's son?'

Haco shoved the fellow back, rounding on Cerdic again. 'You and your brother lord it through the villages with your fast horses and your yelping pack, but you're not above sin and you're not above paying for it. And pay you will, one way or the other.'

'I'd mind my manners,' Letwold warned him. 'This could go hard for you.'

'Manners, is it? When you assault our girl-folk? Do manners come before justice in Wulfbury?'

Letwold stood up, tossing the empty purse back. 'You've no interest in justice. If you want that filling, go to the cots. There're rabbit droppings a-plenty.'

Haco's lip curled; there was thunder in his brow.

'Landlord,' Cerdic said, edging around his table, passing another coin across the serving-top, 'my apologies for this unpleasantness. We'll be leaving now. It's not my intent to spoil the festival.'

The landlord nodded. Letwold drained his mug and hurried to follow, but Haco called after them. 'Apologies, Lord. For saying you terrorise from the saddle. It's your brother who does that, with his wild, swaggering ways. While *you* tag along at the rear. Scampering in his shadow. More a pet than a terror.'

Haco's friends grinned. There were sniggers from crowded corners.

Cerdic swung back, cheeks aflame. But he knew the peril he was facing here. Both his father and Aethelric had drilled it into him.

'My brother *does* swagger,' he said, when his rage had abated sufficiently. 'He *does* ride hard to the hunt, he does cause fear and maybe damage with his arrogance and his thoughtless roistering. But I'd have him over you any day. I pity Eadora, working all hours on the land, then coming home at night to cook and skivvy for a boorish, buffoonish oaf, a petty tyrant who for all his muscles, only wields power over a tired and frightened girl.'

Again, there was silence. Again, Cerdic and his friend made to leave.

'At least she had a good mother,' Haco hissed. 'Not some Mercian strumpet who'd open her legs for the first Viking dog that came sniffing!'

'You village idiot!' the landlord shouted.

Cerdic spun around again. With studied insolence, Haco turned his back and moved to the serving-top. Cerdic lurched after him and rammed bunched knuckles into the nape of his neck.

'Cerdic!' Letwold warned.

Haco tottered forward, but Cerdic took him by the belt and dragged him backward across the tavern and out through its door, throwing him onto the road. There were gales of laughter from the drunken revellers outside but when they saw the combatants an amazed silence fell. Haco grovelled where he lay, stunned – perhaps unnaturally so. He made no effort to regain his feet, though his eyes were wide open. Cerdic dropped onto his back with a knee, pinning him down, took his mop of hair and banged his face against the ground, over and over, grinding it in the dirt.

'You dare insult my mother!' he spat. 'My dead mother! Whose soul even now prays for the folk of this shire!'

Eadora appeared, bustling through the crowd, hair tousled, mouth bloodied. She squealed in fright, and ran first to Aescher, the burly miller.

'Aescher... stop this, please.'

'Why should I?' came the curt response. 'Seems like you're the cause of it.'

She ran to Gerlac, the blacksmith, who mopped his hands with an oily cloth.

'Gerlac, help your apprentice, I beg you.'

Gerlac smiled. 'My girl, your Haco can help himself any time he chooses.'

Letwold, meanwhile, grappled with Cerdic, trying to restrain him. But Cerdic threw him off, pummelling Haco again and again before lugging him over onto his back. The blacksmith's boy was dirtied and bruised, but his lips had curved into a crimson, sickle-shaped grin.

'You deepen the offence, my lord.' Blood bubbled between his teeth. 'Now you'll *really* pay.'

Sweat prickled Cerdic's brow. He wanted to strike that impudent face till it was a mask of gore. But his anger ebbed as understanding set in.

Shaken, he got to his feet. He regarded the circle of watching faces. They were grim to a one. Not necessarily with disapproval, but, knowing their overlord's rules, curious about the outcome of this one-sided affray. At last, his gaze fell on Eadora, who ran forward and cradled her brother's head. Her eyes filled with hurt as she stared up at Cerdic, but also with bewilderment.

'You beat him like that when he can't hit you back?' she said. 'When you know he wouldn't have dared...?'

Cerdic was stumped. She was completely right.

He was the master here, Haco the serf, and yet in response to one moment of impertinence he'd abused that position badly, had become a brute, a raging beast. He glanced again at the faces around him: still blank and inscrutable, never having seen this bestial side of their overlord's youngest son, perhaps wondering if his educated manner and affable air were nothing but facade.

'I…' He hesitated. Attempting to explain might reduce him further in their eyes. He looked down at the blacksmith's boy, still grinning through his blood and spittle. A moment of impertinence, yes. But calculated impertinence all the same. And he'd lost control over it, a mistake even Unferth wouldn't have made.

Weary and shamefaced, Cerdic allowed Letwold to lead him away.

'You didn't need to do that,' Eadora wept behind him.

'No,' he chided himself, 'I certainly didn't.'

CHAPTER 3

The interior of Wulfbury Hall was vast and airy, reinforced with rock at its four corners, but vaulted along its ceiling with a hundred pine logs. Six great crossbeams were decked with variously coloured battle-shields, the sloped inner walls were clad with flax, animal hides and woven cloths. Its floor was paved with slate and carpeted with rushes, but narrowed by two inner rows of pillars, tree-trunks cut square and carved all over with runes and interlacing images of flowers, elves, toads and winding Icelandic serpents. A long hearth, stacked with wood for the approaching autumn, ran down the centre, tables and mead-benches ranged adjacent to it. Despite the scene of riotous merriment it had hosted the night before, this morning the air in the hall hung heavy.

Earl Rothgar sat at the far end of it, on his seat of judgement, a high blackthorn chair upon a stone dais. A large crucifix was suspended above it, the figure of Christ painted white, his arms spread as though imparting wisdom rather than suffering death.

The earl was in late middle age, but still a tall, robust man. Not given to flamboyance, the only glint of gold on his person was the chain of office across his chest. Aside from that, he wore a tunic and breeches of black wool. His thick beard and long hair had run much to grey, which was near enough the colour of his face, for even by normal standards the nobleman was troubled.

'And what does the girl say?' he asked.

There were five others present. To the right, Athelbere, the ear's house-marshal, stood in thoughtful silence, his massive, be-ringed arms folded. To the left, Aethelric, Unferth and Cerdic made an awkward, uneasy group. Facing the earl was Godric, his reeve, an elderly man who kept his feathered cap in hand and shifted from foot to foot as though he yearned to urinate.

'My lord, she is silent on the matter,' Godric replied. 'Apparently too ashamed to give her side of the story.'

'Too frightened, you mean,' Unferth said. 'Fears she'll get another walloping off that lummox of a brother of hers. I notice he didn't confront *me* in The Corn Mother.'

'Of course not,' Aethelric said. 'Much better to seek redress from *two* members of the earl's family.'

The earl focused on his eldest. 'Unferth, did you force the girl against her will?'

Unferth shook his head. 'I told you, Father. I've lain with her several times already.'

'So, there *was* intercourse?'

'Yes, but we both of us wanted it.'

Rothgar glanced at Cerdic. 'And you were present when the girl arrived at the orchard?'

Cerdic's mouth was almost too dry to swallow. All gazes fixed on him, his brother's as intently as his parent's. 'Yes, Father.'

'She was there to gather apples, I understand?'

'That was my impression.'

'And when she went off with Unferth… was she willing? The truth now, Cerdic.'

Rothgar's eyes were deep, grey pools. He was a picture of studied calm, but the lad knew he could call on fury when he needed to.

'She didn't seem to be unwilling,' Cerdic replied.

'Didn't *seem* to be?'

'I wasn't privy to their conversation… but she wasn't forced. Not as I saw.'

Unferth grunted with affirmation, throwing a satisfied look at Reeve Godric.

'So, the girl's family claim she was raped,' the earl said, 'but the girl herself will not testify. And I now have witnesses who claim the contrary.'

Godric looked abashed. It wasn't every day that his office called him into conflict with his lord and master. 'The girl's family don't want this case to reach the shire-moot. It will only bring further disgrace on them. But they do seek restitution.'

'Restitution!' Unferth interjected. 'It's nothing but blackmail.'

'How much are they asking?' the earl said.

Godric shrugged awkwardly. 'Well… there's also the not-insignificant matter of the fight afterwards. Lord Cerdic brutalised the girl's brother.'

Athelbere sniffed. 'The way I hear it, he allowed himself to be brutalised.'

'Nevertheless,' the earl said, 'to outrage a village girl and beat her family when they remonstrate… It's hardly the way I desire these lands to be governed.'

'Father, these charges are fake!' Unferth snapped. 'I've been humping the lass for weeks—'

'And are you proud of that?' the earl retorted, his tone harder. 'Just because she didn't bite and scratch, that doesn't excuse you. You outrank her a dozen to one. How could she even say no?'

Unferth's eyes flashed defiance. 'It wasn't like that. Eadora's—'

'What?' the earl demanded. 'What are you going to tell me? She's your intended? Your betrothed? Dear God, it's shameful enough you spend so much time in the barracks whorehouse. Your mother would turn in her grave at that. Now you debauch the village girls, too?'

'It wasn't rape,' Unferth said through tight-locked teeth. 'You've asked Cerdic. Now ask Letwold. He was there too.' He glared at them all, Cerdic included, and then stormed from the hall.

'I'll ask him,' Rothgar called after his son, 'be assured of that.' He rounded on Cerdic, who stood with head bowed. 'And now *you*. Unferth's offence is questionable. Yours is undeniable. In fact, *your* offence makes it impossible for us to wave this business away.'

'If I may, my lord,' Aethelric intervened. 'There were many witnesses to this second incident, and most of them seem to agree that Lord Cerdic was severely provoked.'

'Look at me, boy.' Rothgar's face remained graven in stone. 'Are you telling me that you, of all people, the supposed brains of our family, didn't realise what this village lout was up to?'

Cerdic hung his head again. 'I was too angry to think straight.'

'Too angry to think straight? Was that Alfred's response when driven to hide in the marshes of Athelney, while the Danes roistered in his halls, drank his mead, paraded the corpses of his slaughtered thegns along every country lane, proclaiming there was no king in Wessex and that the God of the English was dead?'

Cerdic's cheeks burned. 'No, Father.'

'No, indeed! The exact opposite, in fact!' The earl sighed long and hard. 'Either way, whatever the rights or wrongs of it, I can't have my two sons dragged to the shire-moot. The scolds and prattles would have a field day.' He nodded to Athelbere, who handed him a purse. It was small but it clinked with silver. He passed it over to Godric. 'Take this to the family with my blessing and heartfelt apology. Assure them this will never happen again, and that both miscreants will be punished.'

Godric took the purse, bowed and backtracked away. 'My lord, you are wise—'

'Just do it, Godric.'

Godric bowed again, and was gone, hurrying down the hall.

'Unferth's right about one thing, Lord,' Athelbere said. 'You've been blackmailed.'

'It's the way of things,' the earl frowned, 'when one's scions run wild like bucks.' There was a brief, pondering silence.

27

'Follow Unferth for the rest of the day,' he told the house-marshal. 'The news will soon reach the hearth-men, especially his. If there are any reprisals against the village of Brackley, I will be extremely displeased. Impart that message to Redwald personally.'

Athelbere nodded, and also went out.

Rothgar turned to his chaplain. 'Any words of advice?'

'You handled it well, my lord,' Aethelric said. 'I congratulate you.'

'It's best to resolve these minor matters as quickly and conveniently as possible. Believe it or not, there are worse things in the wind.'

'So I hear,' Aethelric said. 'You're waiting on letters, I take it?'

'I am.'

The priest nodded soberly then, sensing that Earl Rothgar wished to be alone with his youngest son, took his own leave from the hall.

'Worse things, Father?' Cerdic asked.

'Nothing for you to concern yourself with.'

Cerdic looked away.

'Now we are alone,' the earl said, 'tell me the truth: did Unferth force the girl? Remember, Cerdic, you're shortly for the priesthood. Telling lies to protect a rapist would not be the best way to start.'

'It wasn't rape, Father. Eadora... the girl was glad when Unferth went over to her. They went into the orchard together, willingly. And it's true what he says. They've lain together a number of times since spring. Always with both parties' consent.'

Rothgar nodded. 'I would that your brother was half as quick with his wits as he is with a sword.'

'But shouldn't...' Cerdic shrugged. 'Shouldn't the ceorls know their place? I know that you're always for a peaceful and contented realm, but this... I mean, *this...*'

'Of course they should know their place.' Rothgar arched an eyebrow. 'As should we. Don't be one of these noblemen, Cerdic, who believes that others only live to give them rank. Not when the truth is that we only have rank so that others might live.'

'But, Father, *we* are still the masters. We guard and enforce the law.'

'A law that applies to us equally. A law in which it is nowhere written that a man may beat his neighbour half to death in response to harsh words and no fine be imposed.'

Cerdic shook his head. 'He insulted Mother. I couldn't let that pass.'

Rothgar's gaze became flinty. 'You think that isn't something I have to live with, too? It's the family weakness, the chink in all our armour. But, Cerdic, men must be stronger than that.' He paused, knuckling at his brow. 'I mentioned King Alfred before. You understood that reference?'

The lad nodded.

'Of course you did,' Rothgar said. 'You're an excellent student of history, or so Aethelric tells me. Alfred resisted the taunts of the Danes so he could stay hidden in the marsh until a time came when he was strong enough to fight them on an equal footing. You think he did this purely to save his own skin?'

'If all he'd wanted was to save his own skin, he could have fled the kingdom,' Cerdic replied.

'Exactly. A hundred other princes in lands over the sea would have given him succour. He could have had lordships elsewhere, vast estates, wealth. But he refused all that to remain in Wessex and live like a beggar.' The earl sat back on his chair, which creaked audibly. 'And he did that because his duty called him to it. Not just duty to his kingdom. A kingdom on its own is no more than a name. But to his subjects. He could have fled into a comfortable retirement, but he would not abandon his people to the pagan tyranny of Ragnar's sons. Instead, he moved from one hiding place to the next, always hunted, always hungry, and yet scheming, plotting, slowly drawing plans against them until the time was right to fight. You understand what I'm saying?'

Cerdic nodded again. 'That duty can be onerous.'

'And complicated. Much more so than simply leading a battle-charge. It can force you into difficult decisions, into making sacrifices that many advisors will say can never be worth it. But Cerdic… this is the duty the average man faces. The duty of *lordship*, when there are so many dependent on you… that can be infinitely more challenging.'

'Father, if I'm for the Church—'

'It's not *if*, Cerdic,' the earl said. 'You *are* for the Church. But a lad of your breeding will rise to rank there too, and then you'll be protecting souls as well as bodies. Imagine how much more important *that* duty will be. But…' Suddenly, Rothgar looked weary, dispirited. 'Before that time comes, and certainly before you are ordained, which will be years from now, it's entirely possible that occasions will arise when both Unferth and I are away from Swaledale at the same time. Far away. When that happens, you will need to be the stand-in Earl of Ripon. In fact… it's my *command* that in our absence, you stand in for us.'

'Of course, Father.'

'Don't treat this lightly, Cerdic. Think on everything I've said. About duty and what it may entail. No kingdom is ever safe from threat. It would be gross self-deception to pretend otherwise. Our response to that, however, will never be to rage and panic, to unleash all our weapons at once.' Rothgar regarded his son gravely again, before sighing out loud. 'But it wasn't my intent to lecture you endlessly. You seem to have learned a hard lesson today. Now, you should go. We all have things to prepare for.'

The lad nodded, and trudged toward the main doors.

'Cerdic.'

Cerdic glanced back. Strangely, his father didn't look at him this time.

'Everything I've just said notwithstanding, and even though your studies are good... work harder in the drill-yard. You may need those skills too, and sooner than you expect.'

CHAPTER 4

Three days later, Earl Rothgar received the summons he'd been expecting. Or rather, he received *a* summons – it was not quite the one he'd been expecting.

'A Viking army marching on York?' Aethelric said, shocked. There hadn't been a major Norse assault on England for fifty years, but there was still no word a churchman feared more than 'Viking'. Even though Christianity was spreading among their ranks, the majority of the Northmen remained stubbornly pagan, and their willingness to attack Christian churches with fire and sword was a tradition undimmed by time. 'But where have they come from?'

'They've sailed down the Humber and into the Ouse. Their leader is Harald Sigurdsson.'

'The Hardraada?' Aethelric said, appalled. 'The King of Norway?'

Rothgar nodded grimly. Aethelric crossed himself.

There was probably no warrior in Christendom more notorious, both for his innate ferocity and his vengeful nature, than Harald the Hardraada. In addition to that, if there was any Northman whose infamous exploits alone could summon a great host of adventurers to his banner, this was he.

'His army will be vast,' Aethelric said.

Rothgar nodded. 'He has a whole fleet of longships. Not to mention Earl Tostig and his usual horde of mercenary scum.'

Aethelric blew out a long, unsteady breath; the arrival of Earl Tostig was to have been expected. A bitter and ruthless man, he was King Harold of England's brother, and a former earl of Northumbria now in exile for the savagery he'd shown to his own people. For the last year, he'd sought any number of devious ways to return.

'Do you have to go yourself, my lord?' Aethelric asked. 'It's not as if you've anything to prove.'

Rothgar sighed. 'You know my views on that. A true leader must always be seen on the field. I can't ask my soldiers to do something I wouldn't do myself.'

'Is it not Lord Unferth's time?'

The earl smiled grimly. 'Unferth is a warrior through and through, but he lacks combat experience. And trust me, this will be a *real* fight. It's no time to blood him with a full command. And yet, because he needs that experience, I can't leave him behind either.'

Aethelric frowned. 'But if both of you go...'

'I know, I know... but even the most careful planning can be thwarted by events one never saw coming.'

The silence hung tense between them.

'My lord,' Aethelric said quietly, 'Cerdic is very young to be put in charge of affairs here at Wulfbury.'

'Not as young as King Edgar was when put in charge of the whole kingdom, and those were golden days, were they not?'

'They were also days when the Viking menace was relatively slight.'

'Then Cerdic's baptism may be harder!' the earl said forcefully, a hint of his inner angst showing itself, though just as quickly he regained control. 'It may even be that Cerdic is all you have.' He sighed again. 'We can't know what will happen in the coming weeks, Aethelric. No man can. But we must ready ourselves for all outcomes.' He eyed the priest carefully. '*All* outcomes, you understand?'

Aethelric did, of course, even if he hardly dared think it. 'I suppose it will do the lad good to hold some responsibility.'

'Consider it another part of his education. Even if we all return safe and well, it won't have been wasted.'

'But with regard to the Minster School? Because all things considered, my lord, that still remains your second son's best hope to make a name for himself in the world.'

By his aspect, Rothgar didn't disagree, but he remained thoughtful as he sought to balance these rival priorities. 'We can delay Cerdic's start there, I imagine?'

'Under these circumstances, I believe so, yes.'

'A month should be sufficient to tell us what the future holds.'

'And if it doesn't, Lord?'

'If it doesn't?' Rothgar shrugged. 'If it doesn't, I rather fancy there'll be no schooling of any sort at York Minster, seeing as that is likely to be Harald Hardraada's first target for desecration.' He paused to mull it over. 'Prepare some documents, if you would. We need to formalise these matters.'

Aethelric nodded and strode away, halting once before leaving the hall. He looked back. 'My lord, I'd expected the main invasion to come from the south.'

'It will,' Rothgar replied. 'This is a completely different invasion.'

—

'Unferth!' Cerdic shouted as he entered the barracks yard. 'Unferth!'

This was actually a sub-yard reserved for Unferth's personal hearth-troop. As such, it wasn't a large area, though at present it was crowded with helmed and armoured figures, who, with the assistance of numerous grooms and scurrying thralls, were busy loading their war gear and other supplies onto skittish steeds. There was a chaos of neighing and shouting, hooves kicking through heaps of weapons or clashing loudly on the gritty, straw-covered earth.

'Unferth!' Cerdic pushed his way through.

'Well… if it isn't my favourite brother,' Unferth replied.

He seemed to be in fine fettle. Like the rest of his twenty-five-strong command, he was sheathed head to foot in gleaming ring-mail. Over the top of that, he wore the uniform white surcoat and cloak of his father's household, the former emblazoned with Earl Rothgar's ancestral symbol, a blue boar's head equipped with huge, curving tusks. Item by item, he too was loading his mount, though his broadsword was already buckled at his waist, his helmet hanging from his saddle. Like most of the rest of his troop, he'd shorn his blond locks down to bristles.

In the face of such martial prowess, Cerdic felt inferior simply because he was wearing civilian clothes. It left him stammering. 'I hear... I hear the Viking you ride against is Harald Sigurdsson.'

'Yes.' His brother continued with the task at hand. 'I've heard a rumour to this effect.'

'Isn't he one of the fiercest warriors in Europe?'

'I'm sure he thinks he is.'

'They...' Cerdic made an effort to steady himself, to prevent his voice turning querulous. 'They say he's brought an armada of longships.'

'We know all this, Lord Cerdic,' came the voice of Redwald, Unferth's most senior housecarl. A stout older man with hefty bushes of red-grey hair on both his head and jaw, he was fully armed and mailed, and now came forward, belting a broadsword to one hip, an axe to the other. 'We've prepared accordingly.'

Cerdic felt left out as the two soldiers now conferred, Redwald updating his master on the mood and fitness of the men, and adding that his own horse, which had thrown a shoe that very morning, would be ready anon. In truth, the lad barely heard any of this. His head was still spinning with the news that Harald 'the Hardraada' Sigurdsson had invaded the kingdom. Not only that, but he'd landed not less than sixty miles from where they now stood, and with what, by all accounts, was a colossal force. Even without that, though, the Hardraada was a name to invoke nightmares.

After fighting at the battle of Stikelstad as a mere boy, he'd fled his native Norway with a price on his head, making his way wounded and barefoot over forest, mountain and plain to Kyiv and thence to Constantinople, where he'd joined Byzantium's elite Varangian Guard. Rising to a senior command, he'd gone on to wage over eighty successful campaigns against Saracens and sundry rebels and corsairs, butchering every man that fell into his hands, but had later turned on his own paymasters, personally tearing the eyes from the head of Michael Kalaphates, Emperor of the Greeks, before fleeing the East with the wealth of Mikelgard stowed in his ship, a fortune he'd then used to reconquer Norway.

The Hardraada was nominally a Christian; during his time in the East, he'd supposedly built a church on the grave of Jesus Christ. But his reputation for brutality travelled far and wide. He had a wagon train of wives and concubines, and, according to rumour, whenever he sat to feast, he still followed the sign of the cross with the sign of the hammer. In Aethelric's own words, and he was not given to exaggeration, 'a more fearsome opponent could not be imagined'.

'I asked Father if I could come with you,' Cerdic blurted out. 'But he said no.'

Unferth didn't even look round. 'Of course he said no.'

'I know you don't consider me a useful sword, Unferth, but Athelbere says I'm close.'

'This will be an arduous campaign, Cerdic. We've only got room for trained and competent men. Not boys learning on the job.'

'Don't be offended, Lord Cerdic,' Redwald put in. 'You'll note that your friend Letwold is staying behind too.'

Cerdic *had* noted this, though it was no consolation. Letwold's father was a seasoned housecarl. Letwold himself was training for that status. So, even though it made sense that a lad bound for the clergy might be left behind, it seemed a wasted opportunity for someone headed to the military. But for all his liveliness, Letwold was not the most healthy lad; in winter, he sickened, and whenever he ran or rode hard, he coughed. So it was hardly a surprise.

'You're in the way,' Unferth said irritably.

Cerdic stepped back to avoid being shoved. '*You* can speak to Father. Tell him I can be useful.'

Unferth still didn't look at him. 'That won't change his mind.'

'If you and Athelbere put a word in for me together—'

Unferth swung around. '*Cerdic!*'

They locked gazes and suddenly there was a sternness of purpose in the older lad's face, rather than the usual overconfident sneer, which Cerdic had never seen before.

'Someone must hold the fort,' Unferth said. 'You understand that? You're not being left behind because you're neither use nor ornament. Nor because your future weapons will be prayerbook and crozier. It's because an Aelfricsson must remain *here*, in Wulfbury... in command. And I'm sure Father's already told you this. Look, this is a serious war we embark on. The king himself will likely come north to fight. But even then, we can't second-guess the outcome.'

Cerdic was shaken to hear it put in such blunt terms.

'Well... well, *that's* the other thing I wanted to talk to you about,' he ventured. 'For the last two days you've avoided me—'

'You didn't hear my captain-at-arms?' Unferth indicated Redwald, who still stood close by. 'We heard a rumour a war was coming. We had to prepare.'

'Then it's all the more important we speak now. If there's a danger that—'

Cerdic's words dried in his throat, as if he couldn't give voice to his fears.

'Danger of what?' Unferth asked him. 'That we'll never meet again?' He sighed. 'This is what I do, Cerdic.' Half a foot of shining steel caught the sun as he part-drew his sword from its scabbard. 'It's my purpose, what I'm *made* for.' Re-sheathing the blade, he turned terse again. 'But you're my brother, not my sweetheart… So don't you dare stand weeping in a doorway when I ride off.'

'Unferth… why are you so dismissive of me? What have I done to infuriate you?'

Unferth nodded to Redwald, who discreetly ambled away. 'Let me think,' the older lad said, 'perhaps you could have spoken on my behalf a little more assertively. I mean with Father.'

Cerdic was shocked. 'I *did* speak for you. I told Father you were innocent.'

'And yet we paid a fine to that wretched girl's family.'

Cerdic was stung. But not on his own behalf. 'Wretched girl? You've been tumbling her for months, and now she's a wretched girl?'

Unferth threw him a puzzled frown before checking his saddle straps.

'Is that all she ever was to you?' Cerdic asked. 'You must have known your relationship with her would emerge at some point.'

'Relationship?' Unferth chuckled.

'What if you'd got a brat in her belly?'

'But I didn't. You know why?' Unferth scowled. 'Because I'm not stupid. And now this thing has happened anyway. Here I am, going off to war, maybe facing death, and everyone thinks I'm a rapist.'

Cerdic understood his frustration about that. 'I told Father it wasn't rape. Even though it could have meant Eadora carrying a mark of shame for the rest of her life.'

Unferth frowned. 'And what's Eadora to you… just out of interest?'

'Well… nothing.' Cerdic shrugged. 'She's a ceorl. But she has feelings, she can be hurt.'

Unferth smiled, at first with disbelief, then with pity. 'You *like* her, don't you? You want her for yourself.' He chuckled again, before reaching out and ruffling Cerdic's hair with even more vigour than usual. 'You lustful little pup. Well... now's your chance. At the very least, I'll be gone several weeks, but it might be forever. Either way, *you* can't waste time. Very soon, you'll be taking vows of chastity. Then it'll be awkward.'

Cerdic's cheeks burned. 'It's not like that...'

'Of course not. My lust is sinful, but yours isn't. Don't worry, I've heard that before. From priests, mainly. You're going into the right career after all.'

Cerdic was discomforted to hear such irreverence, even from Unferth, who spouted it freely. Who knew what price his brother would have to pay? But he was disquieted for himself too; it reminded him brutally that, of all the disadvantages a future in the Cloth would bestow on him, a life without any kind of female contact was the most difficult one to contend with. 'Unferth, I...'

Unferth summoned a thrall, who hurried forward, carrying his shield.

'Unferth,' Cerdic said, 'if nothing else, we should part friends.'

'We're hardly enemies.'

'We shouldn't even part as rivals.'

Unferth smiled to himself. 'How can we not be rivals when we're siblings?'

'I'm serious, Unferth. Especially if this campaign will be as hard as you say.'

Unferth slung the shield onto his back and pulled his helmet into place. He glanced at his younger brother, taking in his pale features and moist eyes. 'Christ Almighty, give me your hand!'

Cerdic did so, warily. Unferth grabbed it, clutching it in a strong, soldierly grip.

'I know you spoke for me,' he said. 'And I'm grateful you did. I'm also sorry I was harsh about it... well, we're all a little on edge.'

'I understand,' Cerdic replied.

'But whatever's said in the heat of the moment, Cerdic, we're brothers. Kindred. That's closer than any friendship can ever be.'

'Which is why I need to go with you.' Cerdic tried not to sound as if he was pleading.

Unferth broke away from him. 'Haven't you been listening?'

'You and Father go off to fight… and I stay behind. How will it look?'

'It doesn't matter how it looks. You have a job to do.'

'I'm leaving for the Minster School next month. What do I do then?'

'Aethelric will resolve that, I'm sure.'

'Damn it, Unferth! There's a war raging… a serious one, you say. And I'll be a novice, a nobody, locked away in a cell, studying theology…'

'Before then you have an even more important task.' Unferth picked up the last of his kit. Behind him, many of his carls were now mounted and moving out of the barracks yard. 'You were man enough to admit to me that you have an eye for Eadora… so I must be man enough to admit that I do, too. More than an eye in my case.' Briefly, his cheeks coloured, as if this was something he really hadn't wanted to divulge. 'She's a village lass, yes, a ceorl… but she's special.' He eyed his brother again. 'You already realise that, clearly. So, watch out for her, yes? Keep her safe.'

'My lord!' Redwald called, reining his horse up alongside them.

Unferth swung into the saddle. His own mount pawed the ground nervously and he wrestled to control it. 'Do your job, Cerdic. And I'll do mine.'

CHAPTER 5

Cerdic and Letwold watched as the housecarls gathered in front of the dragon hall.

Earl Rothgar had ninety such troops in total, but their numbers were supplemented by the carls of his leading thegns, who had ridden in from their estates all along the dale. Unferth's twenty-five were also present. In total, they were over four hundred strong, and made an impressive sight.

The housecarls had been selected because they were among the strongest and hardiest men in the earl's realm. Each one was taller than average, but all were now flat-bellied and huge at chest and shoulder from long hours of practice in the drill-yard and on the hewing block. Again, they all wore heavy ring-mail, their white cloaks and surcoats bearing Earl Rothgar's Blue Boar sigil. They carried an assortment of weapons: mattocks, flails and daggers, as well as broadswords and battle-axes. Each man had a brace of throwing spears beside his saddle and wore his circular shield on his back.

'I should be with them,' Letwold said sullenly.

Cerdic didn't comment, though he knew that his friend was at least as riddled with jealousy and shame as he was. Maybe more. As the only young freemen in Wulfbury remaining behind, they felt conspicuous even standing to one side of the main square. But Letwold suspected he'd been left behind because his father deemed him inadequate.

'Father says I still have soft flab where muscle ought to be,' he murmured, as much to himself as to Cerdic. 'He says my skill with arms is mediocre.'

'At least your time will come eventually,' Cerdic replied.

Earl Rothgar and his leading thegns now came from the chapel, where Aethelric had sung a mass and heard their confessions. They too were girt for war, their ring-mail polished so that it dazzled in the noonday sun. The earl, also in his household white-and-blue, mounted his steed, named Sleipnir after Odin's great horse, pulled up his leather coif and donned his helmet. It was elaborately engraved and embossed with gold, covering his nose and cheeks. When his Blue Boar banner was unfolded, it billowed in the breeze.

One by one, his thegns' standard-bearers unfurled their own pennons, each one different, though Cerdic recognised them all: the Green Hawk of Easingwold, the Red Claw of Tollering, the Crossed Black Daggers of Skelthorpe.

With their overlord in front, the war-band set out along the main thoroughfare to the burh gates. They said nothing to the silent crowd of women watching, though, just before Unferth passed, he raised a gloved finger in salute to Cerdic, who could only make the vaguest gesture in response. His brother had warned him not to stand weeping like some lovelorn sweetheart, but how else were you supposed to feel when your family was heading out to war and you were not? Cerdic tried to dismiss any notion that he might never see his father or brother again, but it was impossible. What good was he doing here, seriously? Maybe he wasn't the finished article when it came to combat, but surely he could do more to help than this? He could polish weapons, perhaps. Mind horses. Even collect spent arrows on the battlefield. Instead, though, he'd be feigning command here at the burh while in reality studying *grammar*.

When the last of the riders had gone, and Osbert, the earl's steward, had closed and barred the gates, Cerdic threaded between the cramped outhouses and climbed to the palisade gantry. Letwold followed him.

Down in the valley on the south side of the burh, the whole of the landfyrd was also on the move: a great mass of common men streaming eastward to join with Earl Rothgar and his housecarls in Brackley-on-the-Water. Carts laden with bushels of arrows and heaps of sling-stones trundled with them, drawn by oxen. The land-troops themselves trailed back along the valley road for as far as the eye could see. Some of them wore mail shirts, others leather jerkins and iron caps. All were armed, though for the most part their weapons were poor quality. Instead of swords and axes, many carried scythes, mallets, threshers. There were plenty of hunting bows on view, but more quarterstaffs than spears, more slings than javelins. In Brackley, meanwhile, Brithnoth, the village priest, stood atop an upturned barrow casting blessings on the men and boys trudging past. Even from this distance, Cerdic saw that one of them was Haco, walking among his ferret-faced friends, a maul at his belt, a sledgehammer at his shoulder. It might have been Cerdic's imagination, but for half a second, he could have sworn that he'd heard the smith's boy say something like 'brother's pet' and his companions laugh in response.

'Even the peasants go to war, but we do not,' Letwold said glumly.

Cerdic said nothing. It was a pointless complaint. They both knew the old laws of muster laid down by King Alfred, namely that, in addition to the private forces held by his nobility, every hide of land in the kingdom must maintain at least one soldier to serve in times of emergency, and that these men must be personally responsible for provision of their own weapons and equipment.

Letwold chuntered on. 'Much good they'll do. Bunch of clodhoppers armed with sickles and thatching knives, while men trained at arms like us are left—'

Cerdic whirled around. '*Letwold... enough!*'

Startled and abashed, Letwold drew back.

'Stop talking... just for a minute,' Cerdic said. 'You're only making yourself feel worse. Not to mention me.'

Letwold shrugged. 'Apologies, Lord. I'm... just...'

'I know. We both of us know. And there's nothing we can do about it, so it's best not to brood.'

Which was a hopeless ambition, of course, as both of them knew full well. Even as Letwold decided it best to beat a tactical retreat, and descended the ladder, Cerdic remained there, staring into the valley.

—

Cerdic was still on the gantry a good hour later, the valley road now bare of all except normal traffic, when someone else ascended the ladder to stand alongside him. A gently cleared throat revealed the presence of Aethelric.

The lad looked round, his features wan. 'Just the man I need to see,' he said.

The priest shrugged. 'Then why not attend your lessons?'

Cerdic looked back into the valley. 'There'll be no more lessons.'

'There won't?' Aethelric's tone remained neutral.

'I won't be attending the Minster School.'

'Your father mentioned nothing of this to me.'

'Father wishes me to command here. In his stead.'

'Which is as it should be. But that's a temporary arrangement, is it not? Your father will return.'

'Hopefully, but I may as well tell you now... because you'll need to know at some point –' Cerdic swallowed the lack of conviction he knew was evident in his shaking voice '– I can't... I can't face this humiliation any longer.'

'Humiliation?'

'This should have been my first battle.'

'Many men are glad to reach old age having never seen a battle.'

'People will say I'm a coward.'

Aethelric tutted impatiently. 'This is becoming foolish.' He turned to the ladder and climbed down. 'People know why you are not going.'

'I don't.' Cerdic descended after him. 'Bishops lead men into battles too. Priests must know how to fight. I must have *some* experience.'

Aethelric crossed the burh, but called back, 'I thought you'd decided you weren't going to be a priest.'

Cerdic scampered down and ran in pursuit. 'You know it's not in my power to make that decision... but *you* can speak to Father when he returns, tell him I'm not right for it.'

Aethelric gave him a disbelieving look. 'Lie to my lord and master? Never.'

He went into the chapel. Cerdic waited at the door, eyes downcast as he struggled to get his emotions under control. When he finally entered, Aethelric was in the cell behind the altar. Standing at his bookstand, he shuffled documents, folding each one carefully, smearing it with wax and sealing it with the earl's boar-head signet ring.

He didn't look up as he spoke. 'All youngsters want to be warriors, Cerdic. Until the reality of war confronts them. Then all but the bravest of the brave wish they were somewhere else.'

'I can never know how brave I am until I am there,' the lad replied.

'Your father would spare you the agony of that moment. And so would I.'

'And yet I'm expected to guard Wulfbury in Father's absence?'

Aethelric eyed him. 'Only for a short time.'

'We can't possibly know that. It's the King of Norway who's invaded, not some Viking vagabond with a couple of ships and a crew of rapscallions.'

The priest signed and sealed another document. 'Earl Rothgar has made provision even for the King of Norway. Among these documents there is a letter for the prefect of the Minster School. The situation is explained in full and a request made that commencement of your studies be delayed by a term of one month. If that term proves insufficient, you shall attend the school anyway, and Osbert will take charge here at Wulfbury.'

There was a stupefied silence, then Cerdic stuttered: 'You're... you're lying! Father ordered *me* to stand in for him. He told me to my face.'

'He told me too, but this is a sensible compromise.'

'A compromise *you* suggested, no doubt!'

Aethelric gave him a hard look. 'The final decision was your father's. This way you exercise leadership, which will be a valuable experience, but your studies will not be put off indefinitely.'

'But... *Osbert*? In command of Wulfbury?'

'Osbert is one of your father's most trusted servants.'

'But still a servant!' Cerdic spread his hands. 'Why would anyone even listen to him?'

'They'll listen to him because he'll have your father's authority.' Aethelric pushed a document he hadn't yet sealed across the stand. Cerdic snatched it and read its contents. Unlike most of his father's more important missals, it was written in English, though Aethelric's elegant longhand would render any piece of scripture easy to read. As the priest had said, it conferred full licence on Osbert to manage all the estates and properties appertaining directly to Wulfbury. It commenced in November, but only in the event that neither Earl Rothgar nor his son, Unferth, had returned from the war.

Cerdic shook his head. 'Why would Father do this?'

'Because it makes sense,' Aethelric replied. 'Similar arrangements have been made with other underlings for those holdings of the earl's lying further afield.'

'Why would he shame me so?'

The priest rolled his eyes. 'You're not listening, Cerdic. Mostly, it's not about you. But where it *is*, it's because your father is determined that, whatever else happens, the plans he's made for you will hold good.'

'Why is he so bent on that?'

The priest looked at him long and hard, perhaps wondering if he'd overestimated his pupil's intelligence. There were almost fifty years between them, yet Aethelric felt like a second parent to this boy who had grown up without even a memory of his mother. Countess Eallana had died during his difficult birth, so, while Cerdic's father was occupied with matters of state, Aethelric had been the one to find a nurse for him in the village: the matronly Oswalda, whom even now Cerdic was close to. It was Aethelric who'd baptised him, tutored him and, where possible, introduced him to higher things. It was Aethelric who'd wielded the stick when his father had been away. It was Aethelric who'd heard all his confessions and counselled him accordingly. It was Aethelric who'd given him his first Eucharist, Aethelric who'd said the Last Rites over him when, as a six-year-old, he'd lain shivering and sweating from an adder bite. Cerdic had responded well to such loving care. He was every inch a child of his class, convinced that someday he would, or should, be lord of all he saw, but most of the time he was affable and even-tempered, he didn't brutalise the thralls and he lacked his brother's swaggering boastfulness. And for all these reasons, the priest loved him like the son he'd never had.

But sometimes, of course, a love like that meant imparting hard truths.

'Your father won't divide his earldom between you and Unferth, Cerdic. It's small enough as it is, and King Harold won't permit it. He wants strong governance in Ripon, to check the powers of Mercia and Northumbria. In short, you have no future unless you don the purple. That won't just give you purpose, but position too. Not to mention a very lucrative career.'

Pointedly, Aethelric busied himself now with the other documents, strongly implying that the audience was over.

'What are these?' Cerdic asked.

'These refer to your father's private business.'

'Too private for me?'

'You'd find them very mundane.'

'Are there many?'

Aethelric sighed again. 'I shall be busy for quite some time.'

'So… no lessons today after all?'

'I doubt you're in the most receptive state of mind.'

Cerdic hovered, puzzled. This didn't seem like Aethelric, to whom learning and study took priority over all. If anything, he felt his tutor seemed a little tense, his mouth set firm as his quill scratched across various parchments, worry lines furrowing his brow. This set the lad wondering about other things. The unfolding war, for example. How unusually stern and humourless his father had been this last couple of days. How subdued the hearth-troop. The unexpected affection Unferth had shown that very morning. And then, when a fleeting breeze set the candle guttering, eerie flickers of orange light rippling around the walls of the narrow cell, he recollected something even more disturbing.

The crimson, longhaired star that had briefly burned in England's skies the previous Easter.

Oswalda and the other village gossips had crossed themselves and called it 'the Firedrake' – a sign of doom, a portent of evil.

'I keep pointing out that priests and bishops fight,' Cerdic said. 'And no one denies it.' Aethelric scribbled determinedly on. 'And Father has trained me for war, not just for the Cloth. The other day he even told me to intensify that training.'

'Your father has to keep his options open.'

'You mean in case he and Unferth are killed?'

Aethelric wrote on, eyes averted downward, 'All possibilities must be considered, no matter how remote.'

'And how remote is that one?' Cerdic asked. 'We all know the Hardraada. His shadow travels before him like an oncoming storm. And then there's Earl Tostig… who hates no man in the world more than Earl Rothgar of Ripon. Should Tostig triumph, my father would do well to flee England, never mind Northumbria. That's assuming his flayed corpse isn't already nailed to a tree next to the battlefield—'

The priest jerked upright. 'If you know this already, why do you ask these questions?'

'Why does God not serve the righteous?'

Aethelric arched a bushy white eyebrow. 'God may smite any nation at any time. His ways are not for us to question. *But* – and listen to this, Cerdic, because it's very important – your father trusts the king. Harold Godwinson will come. Of that, he is certain. And these interlopers will yield or perish. You think he'd have held you back from the Minster School for one month only if he expected a more terrible outcome?'

'One month only. Yet a month during which the most dramatic events in all our history may happen. And I will miss them... because I'll be hiding *here*.'

'Not hiding. Doing your duty.'

'A duty deemed so important that Osbert, a servant, will take it over in one month's time!'

'Cerdic, you are perfectly capable of thinking more clearly than this—'

'Well, if it's a duty fit for a servant, it's a duty that servant can undertake right this moment!' Cerdic snatched up the letter authorising the household steward his extra duties and tore it end to end, scattering the pieces. 'I know that Father signs these parchments in advance of you writing them for him. It must be wonderful to be trusted so implicitly. Well... now you can write another, giving Osbert full authority from *today*.'

Aethelric regarded him stonily.

The young man's eyes blazed with defiance, but his lips trembled.

'I understand that you're upset, Cerdic—'

'*My lord!*' Cerdic stated flatly. 'I understand you are upset, *my lord!*'

'But anguish often leads to unwise action,' the priest said patiently. 'I suggest you take some time to reflect on our current predicament... and then maybe, we can talk again.'

'*My lord!*' Cerdic said again, though inside he was horrified to be addressing his tutor so.

'We can talk again, *my lord.*'

Cerdic shook his head as he backed away. 'Write the letter. Let me know when it's done.'

CHAPTER 6

'You wanted me?' Letwold asked, finding Cerdic waiting by the entrance to the dragon hall.

He'd been wary on first receiving the summons. Though Cerdic had just about resisted losing his temper the previous morning, when his father and Unferth had departed, he'd been in such an ill mood ever since, speaking only to himself, moping about the burh with a face torn between thunder and despair, that everyone had steered well clear. Even now, he looked pale and tousle-headed, as though he'd recently been asleep, though Letwold knew that wasn't the case. More likely, it was because he *hadn't* slept. Not at all, which in itself was disconcerting. However, in response to Letwold's question, Cerdic merely nodded at the open doorway.

'Go inside,' he said.

Still Letwold hesitated. 'What is it?'

'Go in and I'll tell you.' If nothing else, the stand-in lord of Wulfbury at least *seemed* calmer.

Letwold entered the hall, and, aside from the usual one or two thralls assigned to cleaning duties, was surprised to find only Cuthred the gatekeeper, Osbert the steward and Father Aethelric, the earl's chaplain. The trio stood together just inside the door, but weren't conversing. They regarded him with curiosity, clearly as bemused at having been asked here as Letwold was. He nodded in greeting, to receive only grunted responses.

Cerdic now came in, walking brusquely past them down the hall. At its far end, he made no effort to ascend his father's seat of judgement, even though he was currently entitled to, but plonked himself down on one of the mead benches reserved for the earl's senior thegns.

'Thank you all for making yourselves available,' he said, indicating that they too could sit.

Slowly, still uncertain, they chose seats for themselves.

'I'm genuinely grateful.' Cerdic looked at the table rather than the men, his voice strangely lifeless. 'I know we all have much business to attend. But as you're aware, there has recently been a large and unexpected Viking incursion into Northumbria. My father and Unferth have ridden out to participate in the repulsion of these hounds. As yet, here in Wulfbury at least, the exact situation is unknown to us—'

'Excuse me, Lord Cerdic,' Osbert interrupted. 'Is this... some kind of council?'

Cerdic eyed him carefully. Osbert was a heavyset, self-important man, who kept his hair cropped and his beard trimmed, and who affected fine embroidered clothing in the manner of his superiors.

'If you like,' Cerdic said.

'Only,' Osbert stood up, 'as you've already said, I have a rather taxing schedule today, and—'

'Perhaps, Osbert,' Aethelric cut in, 'it might be worth listening to what Lord Cerdic has to say before deciding that it doesn't concern you?'

Osbert glanced from one to the other, finally noting his young master's taut, strained expression. 'I... of course. I meant no disrespect, Lord.' He sat himself down again.

'Is it important *I* be here, sir?' Cuthred wondered. 'I'm only your father's gatekeeper and—'

'You're also head of the Wulfbury Watch, are you not?' Cerdic asked him.

Cuthred half-smiled. 'Well, it's a grand term, but there's only me and a couple of lads—'

'That's not strictly true, is it?' Cerdic fidgeted on the table in front of him. 'Not anymore. My father specifically assigned ten members of the fyrd to remain on guard duty at the burh.'

Despite his age, Cuthred was a doughty fellow, still strongly built with a straggly blond beard only slightly running to grey. A fighter by trade, with much experience, now he just looked puzzled. 'You fear the Vikings will come this far north, Lord? That's what this is about? Because your father's mustering point was York. That's several days' south of here.'

'It's not what I fear, Cuthred,' Cerdic said, 'it's what I don't *know*. It's what none of us *knows*. They were several days away when last we heard. We don't know where they are now. So, we need to be ready.'

'Ready?' Osbert asked. 'Am I to understand that, if the Vikings *do* come here, you'll seek to resist them?' He seemed more troubled by this prospect than by the invaders' actual presence in the earldom.

'There are different meanings to the word "resist",' Cerdic said. 'We obviously can't go and fight them down on the valley road. But we can sit behind our palisade if we need to, and keep our gates barred.'

Osbert twitched with discomfort. 'Would even *that* be wise?'

Cerdic raised an eyebrow. 'You're suggesting we... let them in?'

'Lord Cerdic...' Osbert smiled understandingly, as though imparting a simple lesson to a confused child. 'I know it doesn't feel like it at present, but autumn will very soon be on us. And after that, winter. And you propose that we spend all that time under siege?'

'We are well provisioned to withstand a siege, are we not? The harvest has been gathered, the grain-rooms are full to bursting.'

Osbert shrugged. 'That's true, but we haven't yet started baking bread or collecting and salting meat for the winter.'

'Our outhouses are stacked with fruits and fresh-dug vegetables.'

'My lord—'

'The Vikings won't have that advantage,' Letwold chipped in. They looked at him. He reddened, unused to being the

53

centre of attention. 'Pardon me, Lord, but if the Vikings manage to come this far north, that means they'll already have got past or through your father's company. Like as not though, they'll have suffered losses. Even as victors, they won't be a huge number. They'll be spread out even if only to raid more widely. For all these reasons, it's difficult to think they'd have enough organisation to supply themselves for a winter-long siege...'

'May I ask why our young friend is even here with us?' Osbert said tersely.

Cerdic was still thinking on Letwold's words; he couldn't be too fulsome in his acceptance of them, but they made a worrying kind of sense. 'Because Letwold is the closest thing we have in Wulfbury to a housecarl.'

Osbert and Cuthred glanced at their lord with a bewilderment verging on incredulity.

Cerdic was undeterred. 'And because he's making military sense. If what you mean, Letwold, is that a Viking force coming here won't have the resources to mount a lengthy siege and thus will try to storm the burh, I'm inclined to agree.'

Letwold made a helpless gesture. 'In which case, what will we do?'

'Surrender, of course.' Osbert made it sound like the most obvious answer in the world. 'Go into captivity. They'll accept us. Why have our heads on spikes if they can have ransom payments instead?'

'They won't get ransom payments for the common people of the dale,' Aethelric said.

Osbert seemed puzzled that *this* had even been raised. 'The common people must make do as best they can.'

'Flee into the hills, you mean?'

'It's not like it isn't a time-honoured tradition.'

'With autumn coming, as you say, and then winter?'

'What else?' It wasn't a real question. Osbert was being dismissive. In his mind at least, this question was settled.

Cerdic looked to Cuthred. 'What say you?'

The gatekeeper pursed his lips. 'Oh, it's not for me to have a say on things like this, Lord.'

'I'm giving you an opportunity to tell us what's on your mind, because something clearly is.'

Briefly, Cuthred looked flustered. 'I… I was a soldier once, as you know.'

'I know.'

'I went with your father to Scotland.'

'And distinguished yourself at Dunsinane.'

'But that was years ago, Lord. And we were many then, not the few we are today. And even then, sometimes…' The gate-keeper's hard-bitten features flushed. 'Sometimes, to pointlessly resist, to kill enemies when there's nothing to be gained from it, a course that will enrage them even more… well, I'd call that ill-advised.'

Cerdic nodded. Finally, he looked at Aethelric. '*You've* been unusually short on helpful suggestions.'

The priest considered. 'It's really about the *purpose* of any resistance.'

Cerdic frowned. 'The purpose will be to save as many people as possible for as long as possible.'

'Which would be laudable if that was solely it.'

'What are you trying to say, Aethelric?'

'Excuse me, Lord,' Osbert interrupted. '"As many people as possible for as long as possible?" How would we do that?'

'By bringing them into the burh,' Cerdic replied. 'How else?'

'Offer them refuge *here*? How many?'

The lad shrugged. 'I don't know. It depends how much warning the Northmen give us. It may only be the population of Brackley-on-the-Water. It may be less than that, but it may also be more.'

Osbert looked aghast, and not without cause. Cerdic knew that if there was any type of siege here, their current resources would see them through until spring, but would be stretched to breaking much sooner should the burh be flooded with refugees. But in truth, this whole conversation felt superfluous. Even from the brief discussion they'd had, it was already clear there were too many variables, too many uncertainties to make firm plans.

'We shouldn't agonise over this just yet,' Aethelric said, apparently reaching the same conclusion. 'For one thing, the most likely outcome is that no Northmen will come here. Harald Sigurdsson seeks the throne of England, not the Earldom of Northumbria, and certainly not the fortress of Wulfbury. As Cuthred says, he is fifty miles to the south, and before he can even leave that place, he must fight the combined forces of our northern earls... and that is assuming the king himself doesn't come, which your father was confident he would, *my lord.*'

Cerdic nodded, but was reluctant to give too much ground. It wouldn't flatter his position if he backed down completely. 'I still feel we should make some rudimentary preparations. Cuthred, take charge of your fyrdsmen. Drill them a little, if you can.'

'Drill them? Lord, they're just farm lads...'

'Had they been selected to accompany the rest of the land-fyrd, they'd be expected to fight in the second or third line,' Cerdic said. 'The least you can do is drill them. In addition, allocate them watch-points around the palisade. Cover all approaches. And make sure they know they have a job to do and must stay alert.'

'Ten of them, Lord? To watch our whole perimeter?'

'It won't even be ten,' Osbert put in sulkily. 'They can't man their posts day and night. You'll need to organise shifts...'

'Then organise shifts,' Cerdic retorted. 'And make sure that at least every day from now on, one of them rides a few miles along the York road, questioning local folk and passers-by about any suspicious activity they may have seen. Don't worry, Osbert, it will be far less difficult for *you*... all you need do is source some additional accommodation for anyone seeking shelter in the burh should the Vikings attack.'

'Well, my lord, in truth, that *will* be difficult—'

'Do it anyway!'

The steward looked beseechingly at Aethelric.

'Our household chaplain has no say in this,' Cerdic added heatedly. 'And even if he did, until the commencement of November, *I* am in command at Wulfbury. And *I* am requiring you to make living space for extra people. Now, both of you… go about your new duties. Straight away!'

The pair shuffled off with attitudes of surprised but suppressed annoyance. Cerdic was also annoyed. He hadn't wanted to raise his voice, but he couldn't have them treating him like a green boy or, even worse, a simpering Church novice who hadn't had his head shaved yet. Even if he was both of those things.

'Where do you want me?' Letwold asked.

'You know our predicament,' Cerdic replied. 'Pick the spot where you feel you'll be most useful.'

Letwold seemed a little crestfallen not to have been allocated a specific duty, but he nodded obediently and departed the hall. Aethelric stood up too, his expression strangely inscrutable.

'I thought you'd approve of me making space for the villagers, at least,' Cerdic said.

The priest pondered. 'Did I say that I didn't?'

Cerdic sat back. 'No, but you didn't praise me for it, either.'

'Ah, it's praise you want?'

The lad shook his head with disbelief. Everything he said was being twisted…

'May I enquire what's brought about this change of heart?' Aethelric asked. 'Now, all of a sudden, you *are* taking charge here for the month of October?'

'You never produced the letter I requested, stating otherwise.'

'You know I never intended to. And now you *are* going to the Minster School at the start of November?'

'If that's in my *wyrd*.'

Aethelric winced at the pagan term, but shook his head. 'You can't fool me, Cerdic. I know what's going on here. You seek now to be a solid figurehead. You're no longer the proud boy who wants to run off to war to prove he can fight. Instead, you're a man of wise counsel. And you aim to impress me so much with this that I'll tell your father you'd be wasted in a habit.'

Cerdic shrugged. 'Even if that *was* my plan—'

'It *is* your plan, *my lord*.'

'Even if it was, mature governance is beneficial to all, is it not? Isn't wise counsel to be sought?'

'*Wise* counsel, yes?'

'I see. You're worried I'm looking to *pick* a fight if the Northmen come? You're concerned I'm so distraught about not going to the real war that I'll start my own?'

'Cerdic... the simple fact is, if the Norse do come here, and as I say, it's unlikely, you'll need to negotiate. And yes, it will be better to do that from a position of strength, but to get the outcome we all want, you'll need to be seeking a peaceful solution, not looking to make your mark in history. And to achieve that, it may require a significant sacrifice.'

Cerdic said nothing, but clearly this was an oblique reference to his father's treasure, the bulk of which was buried somewhere in the precincts of the burh itself, but which only Earl Rothgar and a select few knew the exact location of.

So... buy the Vikings off. That was Aethelric's cryptic advice.

It was hardly controversial. The whole concept of Danegeld, a policy approved by king after king throughout history, had been to give the invaders treasure rather than make them fight for it, thus minimising their aggression, sending them away happy rather than with blades dripping.

It never stopped them coming back for more, of course, but who was Cerdic to raise such concerns when they'd always been ignored in the past?

'You think we should dig up Father's silver,' he said. It wasn't a question.

Aethelric was non-committal. 'Your father himself made provision for a geld payment should the worst come to the worst. But my main concern is that you're so eager to prove yourself, you're confecting a risk we actually don't face.'

'So, what would you have from me?'

'Allow Osbert and Cuthred to do their jobs.' Aethelric edged his way down the hall. He had other tasks to attend to, which were clearly now pressing. 'We'll watch the York road closely, of course we will. But your main priority now should be to focus on your studies, which are almost complete, and to prepare for your new life. You have one month's stay, but trust me, that month will be gone in the blink of an eye.'

Cerdic walked along the hall with him. They halted at the top of the entrance steps.

'I don't dismiss your anxieties,' the priest said, 'but we all have hopes, desires and dreams that are... unrealistic.' Cerdic said nothing, just watched him. 'In most cases, it doesn't hurt to strive for them. But some of us have duty too. And duty must always come first.'

'Duty?' Cerdic said. 'That's all I seem to be hearing about these days. But there appear to be various ways I can perform my duty here.'

'There aren't. There's only one. And I think you already know that.'

With a vaguely sympathetic smile, Aethelric walked away. Cerdic stood in weary silence.

So, even if the Northmen came here, his options to do Earl Rothgar proud were thin. In fact, according to the wisest man in Wulfbury, there were no options at all. Except to give away the family wealth. To acquiesce to this murderous dog, Hardraada, and his traitorous friend, Tostig, without so much as a harsh word. And all in the same month that his father and brother had vanished into the inferno of war. The mere thought was intolerable, and yet on the other hand, was it truly better to fight and lose than not fight at all? Especially with such a potential cost in innocent lives?

Cerdic's head ached. He'd been leader here for one day, and already the trials and tribulations of the role were more than he could bear. In truth, it was a relief that such horrors would only come to pass if his father was defeated, which was also inconceivable.

That definitely would not happen. It *could* not.

Spying movement, he glanced up to the palisade gantry. The ten fyrdsmen assigned to the burh had taken position there. Twenty yards to their left, Letwold, now having donned his ring-mail coat and strapped a war-axe to his waist, prowled back and forth, visibly nervous, anticipating action at any moment. Every few yards, he would halt, turn and gaze stiffly to the east, determined to sight the enemy before the enemy sighted Wulfbury. Meanwhile, at ground level, life in the burh went on seemingly as normal, the thralls hurrying about their business, the household's skilled labourers working in their shops. Even the fyrdsmen seemed relaxed. For one thing, there was no sign of Cuthred, so they weren't being drilled, not yet, while for another, they weren't even keeping watch, just talking quietly together, throwing the occasional amused glance at Letwold's back.

Helpless and disconsolate, Cerdic trailed through the hall. The obvious thing now was to head to the chapel, where he could throw himself on his knees and pray for guidance, though partly because he didn't expect to receive any, and even if he did, it would likely be guidance he didn't want, his feet chose a different route, turning him into his sleeping quarters at the hall's western end. Here, he pulled a chest from under his cot, and from it a ring-mail coat, not the battered one with links missing that he used for training, but the new one that was presented to him by the housecarls on his seventeenth birthday. It was expensively wrought and gleamed in the candlelight. All he'd need do was throw it over his head, buckle it at the waist and pull on the leather, steel-studded gauntlets that Unferth had given him for his sixteenth, and at least then he'd *look* like a leader.

Or would he? Would it not be more self-defeating folly, the earl's second son, the one who *hadn't* gone to war, now strutting around the burh like some military buffoon… like Letwold?

He laid the mail-coat down, and instead, took the broadsword from under his bed. Just touching it was reassuring.

It was Danish in design, captured at Tettenhall and passed down through several generations of his family, which meant it had seen battle upon battle. Its great wood-and-iron cross hilt was bound with wolf fur, its pommel set with a sphere of emerald just under half the size of his fist. This was a fabulous gemstone, his father had always said, no doubt pillaged from some shrine in the East. The blade had originally been notched with heathen runes, which Earl Rothgar had wanted to beat out before gifting the sword to his son, though in the end his smith had advised against this for fear that it might weaken the blade. Cerdic had not been concerned by that, as he felt the ancient symbols added to the weapon's majesty, though in due course he'd persuaded Aethelric to take the sword with him on one of his journeys to York, where he'd paid a Norse trader to translate the meaning of the inscription.

'"Usurper",' Aethelric had explained on returning, with a hint of disapproval. 'In other words, one who takes power by force, invariably when he has no right to it. That doesn't speak well of its original owner… a conqueror with violence in his heart.'

'He paid the price for that at Tettenhall,' Cerdic had replied.

'One can only hope.'

Still mesmerised by the weapon's perfection, not to mention the mysteries of its past, Cerdic held the blade aloft to catch the beam of daylight spearing through the sheet of horn covering his bed-chamber's one upper window. Blue steel shimmered;

the engraved characters, pagan or not, were flawlessly done. It was the handiwork of a master sword-maker.

Usurper. His most valued possession.

Sliding it back into the fleece scabbard and clipping it to his belt, he went outside and walked to the drill-yard. If nothing else, the housecarls' absence meant there was no queue for the hewing block. He clasped Usurper's hilt, thinking to work out his frustrations by hacking wood. But almost immediately, he came to a standstill.

Perched atop the great scarred hunk of timber was the largest raven Cerdic had ever seen. Its feathers shone like black metal, and its beak was an axeblade.

'Be off!' He threw a handful of wood chips at it.

It hopped about on top of the block, unconcerned. Only when he drew his sword did it flap away, circling up to perch above the thatched eave of the barracks, from where it peered down at him with eyes that were soulless chips of jet.

CHAPTER 7

Earl Rothgar and his hearth-troop arrived outside York on the evening of the third day after their departure, halting on the riverside meadow northwest of the city, where a vast range of tents and pavilions already covered the landscape. Household pennons fluttered, spears stood in racks, pillars of smoke ascending from innumerable cooking fires. Everywhere, men in ring-mail coats stood in groups or practised with axe and shield.

The earl was greeted by a horseman wearing black and blood-red livery, and carrying a standard depicting a red bear on a black field, the sigil of Morcar, Earl of Northumbria. The horseman, a marshal of the earl's personal household, welcomed the lord of Ripon, and directed him to a corner of the meadow reserved for his company.

Checking it for himself and seeing there was adequate space for his housecarls at least, Rothgar left Athelbere to organise the encampment, while he and his son proceeded toward the city on foot.

'Earl Morcar is ready for this fight,' Unferth remarked, impressed.

'Looks can be deceiving,' his father replied.

'With all these men mustered?'

'I've no doubt his men are brave. They're fighting for their homes and families. It's Morcar himself I'm unsure about.'

'I thought we had good relations with Northumbria?'

Rothgar nodded as they strode. 'He and I have witnessed documents together, we've struck bargains, he's listened to my

63

advice. But he's ten years his brother's junior, and he often behaves that way.'

Unferth pondered this. As he'd bragged to Cerdic and Letwold, he'd ridden to war once before: the previous year, when his father had finally taken up rebel arms against the treacherous Tostig Godwinson. That had been the only occasion thus far when he'd met the Aelfgarsons, Morcar and his older brother, Edwin of Mercia, and though Earl Edwin had been gruff and opinionated, Morcar had been civil, polite and much more interested in Earl Rothgar's views. But Unferth thought he understood what his father meant. Even then, there'd been an air of indecision about Earl Morcar, as if he couldn't reach judgements unless his brother had done so first.

'I heard Athelbere talking with the carls,' Unferth said. 'The feeling is that Earl Edwin will join us.'

'Earl Edwin's interests lie south of here,' Rothgar replied. 'He'll come. He may even be here already. But it's a matter of how committed he'll be. And, therefore, how committed his brother will be.'

Entering the city wasn't as easy as they might have hoped. For much of the second half of the distance between here and Swaledale, the roads had been clogged with refugees: cottars and their families pushing carts, droving animals, all seeking shelter behind the northern capital's thick walls. Now, they either pitched their own small camps by the waterside, drawing what comfort they could from the presence of so many soldiers, or crowded at the city gates with much quarrelling and confusion.

As the two noblemen forced their way through, only their martial finery preventing the ragged folk's anger turning on them, Unferth observed the city's great ramparts. They were as indomitable as ever, the original Roman defences now mossed and eroded but reinforced along the top with more recent battlements, either the hewn log structures added by the Northmen who had once held sway here, or the more recent stonework built by the late Siward Ulfsson, the greatest of all Northumbria's earls. Ancient though they were, it was impossible to imagine that any army could breach such fortifications.

Inside the city, there were soldiers everywhere, drinking or eating in the doorways to taverns, brawling, shouting. The majority, Unferth noted, wore mantles bearing the colours of Mercia, the black eagle on an orange sun. Earl Edwin's housecarls were here after all, and present in great numbers. Their banners hung on all sides: from windows, flag-posts, the catwalks along the city walls... Earl Morcar's banners were visible too, but not in such abundance.

'Let's hope this air of swaggering self-belief is justified,' Rothgar said.

They entered the Archbishop's Palace, a large stone house in the centre of the city, and were shown into a reception chamber, where, respectful of the summer breeze still drifting from the west, only a small fire crackled in the hearth.

'Rothgar! And not before time.'

Earl Edwin approached. To Unferth's eyes, he had put weight on even since the previous autumn. His torso was hefty at the best of times, surmounted by a thick neck, a large, bull-like head, a dense tawny beard and moustache, and a wild mop of tawny hair. He was still a fearsome sight, and yet, as Rothgar had implied, there was something about Earl Edwin that failed to inspire. It was noticeable that he wore leather and worsted rather than mail, his boots and leggings muddied; he'd evidently spent the afternoon chasing stags and boar rather than preparing for battle.

'I see no sign the Norse have stormed the city,' Rothgar replied, handing his cloak to a thrall. 'If hostilities haven't yet commenced, we're here in time.'

Earl Edwin snorted with irritation.

Earl Morcar came forward to join them. 'Edwin's just uneasy, Rothgar. No slight was intended.' He was a younger, leaner, fresher-faced version of his brother. His blue eyes were bright, the handshake he offered friendly.

Rothgar nodded, and passed no comment on Morcar's own hunting apparel.

Unferth watched and listened with interest, for his father had to tread warily here. The small earldom of Ripon was an anomaly, more like a glorified shire, the complexity of its very existence dating far back into antiquity, when Northumbria had been a kingdom. Its most unusual aspect today was that the earl of Ripon, though entitled to sit on the witenagemot, held his lands from the earl of Northumbria rather than the king, and thus swore allegiance to him as overlord. Earl Rothgar might now be regarded as an elder statesman, who had many times been called on by his seniors to offer counsel and military aid, but there were limits to the familiarity any man could show with the great magnates of England.

'You know Waltheof?' Morcar said, turning and nodding behind them.

Rothgar looked round.

A man who'd been supping at a table at the far end of the room now came over, mopping his mouth with his ring-mail sleeve.

Though not much older than Unferth himself, Waltheof, Earl of Huntingdon, younger son of the great Earl Siward, had already won a reputation for courage and wisdom, personal traits that seemed implicit in his sharp, handsome looks. To Unferth's mind, it was impressive that he'd even come this far north. Like Ripon, the earldom of Huntingdon was another lesser earldom within the sphere of Northumbrian influence, though much further off.

'It's an honour, Earl Waltheof,' Rothgar said, offering his hand. 'I fought with your father at Dunsinane, where we broke the power of the Scottish wolf, Macbeth.'

'Father spoke well of you, Earl Rothgar,' Waltheof replied. 'Many times.'

'In fact...' Rothgar turned, 'I served with *all* your fathers. And at no time did I feel anything less than solid kinship.'

'That's as may be, Rothgar,' Edwin said. 'It leaves us misty-eyed. But Aelfgar and Siward are dead. And now it's *our* turn to be tested. And be warned, this won't just be a ride to the coast to find that the brigands have already fled. Our scouts report that Sigurdsson has brought five hundred longships.'

'Which gives him seventeen thousand men,' Morcar said. 'Maybe more.'

Unferth glanced at his father, who had expected sizeable opposition, but still looked shaken by such a figure.

'They've flocked to Sigurdsson's banner from everywhere,' Morcar added, 'or so we're told. And it's not just Norse. There are Danes, Shetlanders, Orkneymen...'

'The majority of them pagan,' Waltheof added.

'The Hardraada is Christian, at least,' Rothgar replied.

'Sometimes,' Edwin grunted.

'They anchored at Riccall in the first week of this month,' Morcar said, 'and already they've plundered that whole district.'

'The point is, Rothgar,' Edwin said, 'where is the king?'

Rothgar eyed him. 'How could I know, my lord? I've come from the north.'

Edwin folded his arms. 'At Northampton last year, you assured us he'd make a strong, reliable ally.'

Rothgar shrugged. 'He must be on his way.'

'We've sent gallopers along every road south,' Morcar said. 'There's no sign.'

Rothgar pondered. 'If this is all of us, how many do we number?'

'How many do *you* have?' Morcar asked.

'My housecarls number nearly a hundred,' Rothgar said. 'Between them, my thegns bring three hundred more. In addition, I bring fyrdsmen to a total of three and a half thousand.'

Morcar pursed his lips. 'Four thousand is a healthy number.'

That was a generous response, Unferth felt. Morcar himself would have brought twice as many, but then the earldom of Northumbria was twice as large.

'In that case,' Edwin said, 'all told, we can field sixteen thousand men.'

'Those numbers are evenly enough matched,' came an aged, whispery voice. 'As for the rest… we should put our trust in God.'

No one had seen Archbishop Ealdred of York enter by a side door.

He was tall but crooked with age, his emaciated form only vaguely visible under a simple white robe. A single monk assisted him into his chair, where he laid his staff aside. At eighty, he was the oldest man any of them knew, his eyes rheumy, his scraggily bearded face cadaverous. His hair hung past his shoulders in lank, white strands, though much of his scalp was bald.

They shuffled forward in order of rank, genuflecting and kissing the episcopal ring.

'These are grave times, gentlemen,' he said.

'They'll be graver still if the king and his army do not come,' Edwin rumbled.

Rothgar's cheeks coloured. The previous autumn, during the northern earls' truce-meeting with Harold Godwinson at Northampton, it was Rothgar who'd persuaded Edwin and Morcar that, once the childless King Edward had died, it should be Harold himself, the strongest fighting man in England, on the throne, rather than Edward's distant fourteen-year-old cousin, Edgar. In fact, Rothgar had gone even further, suggesting that if the northern earls could guarantee their support for Harold's succession, and maybe tie themselves to the Godwinsons through marriage, Harold might reciprocate by securing pardons for their rebellion and maybe even arrange the banishment of his troublesome brother, Tostig.

'Where is the closest Norse camp?' Rothgar asked.

'A village just south of here,' Morcar replied. 'A place we call Fulford.'

Rothgar frowned. 'That's no more than three miles away.'

'It's Sigurdsson's advance guard. But it's substantial.' Morcar drew their attention to a side-table, where a sheet of vellum had been etched with images of the roads, meadows and waterways encircling the city. 'They're about seven thousand strong.'

'Less than half their force.' Rothgar considered, but only briefly. 'We should attack tomorrow. First thing.'

'Tomorrow?' Edwin looked shocked. 'Your contingent has just arrived. They must be tired. Mine certainly are and they arrived yesterday.'

'But if you wait, my son,' Archbishop Ealdred put in, 'the Northmen will only strengthen.'

'This is correct,' Unferth said before he even realised that he'd spoken. He flushed as, for the first time, everyone turned to him. 'In, erm... my opinion.'

'And who is this?' Edwin asked.

'My lords, my lord archbishop,' Rothgar said. 'My eldest son, Unferth, who one day, though not soon, I trust, will be Earl of Ripon.'

'You've opened your mouth once, boy,' Edwin said. 'You might as well do it again.'

Unferth cleared his throat. 'Well, my lords... Harald Sigurdsson is a warrior of renown. He won't make the mistake Jarl Hastein did at Benfleet. He'll leave a force to protect his ships. But his eye will be on the main prize, which is almost certainly this city. There is nowhere in England closer to Viking hearts than York. So... well, the longer we hold back, the more men they will feel it safe to bring forward, so that at some point they'll be strong enough to assail our walls.'

They contemplated this.

'We have sixteen thousand men, Edwin,' Rothgar said. 'When King Harold arrives, he may wonder why we had so many and yet did so little.'

Edwin rubbed his bearded jaw. Evidently he'd rather engage their foes from a position of maximum strength, preferably with the king's army at his side. He glanced at his brother. 'Do we know for sure that Harald Sigurdsson would be any worse than Harold Godwinson?'

Morcar looked as though he knew the answer, but hesitated to give it.

Rothgar replied instead. 'In the Norse tongue the very name "Hardraada" means "hard king". He rules by the axe. All across Norway, dissenters are vanquished. You think you can reign unmolested in Mercia with a brute like that on the throne?'

Edwin scrubbed a hand through his hair.

'We should strike now, my lords,' Rothgar said again. 'Nothing is guaranteed. But we *must* take this half-chance that's offered to us.'

'You will beat him, my sons.' Archbishop Ealdred nodded, his eyes lidded. 'God wills it.'

The prelate seemed almost ecstatic in his conviction, but Unferth, for one, wasn't reassured. He didn't doubt the might of God, but many times in England, the Almighty had granted victories to heathen men. Unferth's place was not to question that celestial wisdom, of course. But he'd learned a lesson from it, namely that when it came to battle, he must put most faith in the leadership qualities of men like his father. And now, perhaps unfortunately, earls Edwin and Morcar.

CHAPTER 8

When Aethelric set out from the burh that morning, so early that dawn mist still cloaked the land, hurrying his old nag down the Keld Brae as fast as he dared, though it wasn't very fast as he'd never been much of a rider, he wondered at which point the firm oversight he'd determined to bring to Cerdic's decision-making in his father's absence had changed into aloof and unhelpful reproach.

Cerdic had been rude and aggressive the other day, and was quite in need of reprimand, but the lad had also been out of sorts, for a week now at least, confused about his role in the world, not just his role at Wulfbury. These last two days alone he'd been expected to absorb a number of different and challenging ideas, some at variance with each other. It had been drummed into him that he was bound for the Church, but at the same time he was instructed to prepare for the outside possibility that one day he might need to exercise a layman's duties and so should maintain his military training. He was advised that protecting the people was everything, and thus given a grave responsibility when put in charge of the burh, and yet in the same breath he was told that the household steward, a pompous but lowly servant, would take the job off him in one month's time. His scheme to resist a Viking attack had been dismissed as unworkable, one voice of so-called wisdom reckoning they should surrender themselves as hostages instead and the hell with the common folk, while another said they must pay for their safety by handing over his father's silver... and all of this when he'd been charged with *protecting* this place as an essential duty. Little wonder the lad was confused. And, of course, throughout the whole dilemma, the possibility that his father might not return must have been preying on him. What youngster wouldn't be terrorised by such a thought, even if his upbringing meant that he'd bottled it up inside himself, which also must have hurt.

Aethelric cursed as he rode, lambasting himself for allowing personal pique that his beloved student was slowly wriggling free of his influence to cloud his judgement. In a subconscious effort to keep Cerdic the youthful charge he'd always been, he'd been stern and reproving instead of offering considered support. It shouldn't have surprised him one iota that he'd risen that morning and found the lad absent from the morning service. But to then hear that he'd foregone breakfast too and in fact had sent one of the grooms for his horse, had thrown the cleric into a panic. So much so that he was now en route to York himself, with no escort, no food inside him, only his cowl to provide head cover should the sun rise again to an unseasonal fiery zenith, and no way to restrain the lad and bring him home forcibly if he even found him.

'Forgive me, Cerdic,' he said aloud, 'we are none of us perfect, and some of us don't even have immaturity as an excuse. But don't do something ridiculous, lad. Just, please… don't.'

-

'Last Christmas, my father attended the royal court at the Palace of West Minster,' Cerdic said, 'where King Edward lay on his deathbed.'

Aethelric reined up his horse. The morning mist had cleared and he was now several miles south along the York road. It was little more than a well-trodden track at this point, though the carts and wagons of the recently passed landfyrd had ploughed it deep. Dense woodland, mostly still green in its summer plumage, but flecked here and there with russet and gold, grew close to the highway's edge. A little way back into the thickets,

Cerdic sat on a grassy hummock with head hung. Aethelric might have ridden right past him had he not seen Fireflax, the lad's roan palfrey, standing by the roadside, grazing.

'I'm well aware your father spent Christmas at the West Minster.'

Cerdic still didn't look up. He wore his best ring-coat, with Usurper fastened at his waist. However, he looked anything but warlike. He seemed beaten down, demoralised.

'Just before King Edward breathed his last,' he said, 'he signalled my father to his bed and whispered in his ear.' The lad lifted his face; it was sallow and haggard. 'He told him he'd just had a nightmare in which two monks he knew from his youth, both long dead, came to his bedside. Even though he knew them, they had no faces under their hoods, which horrified him. They then told him that a dark veil was drawing over England... that before this year was out, an army of devils would sow pain and fire across the whole kingdom.'

Aethelric sighed. 'I have heard this story. It was a dream, nothing more.'

'It doesn't concern you?'

'It was a dying man afflicted by terror of the afterlife.'

'It wasn't the afterlife that terrified him.'

'It was a man whose mind was failing him, a man beset by nameless fears because he no longer understood who he was or where he was.'

'Or... it was a portent.' Cerdic spoke with fatalistic gloom.

'Portents are stuff and nonsense.'

'What of the Firedrake last Easter?'

Aethelric sighed again. 'Do you know anyone who's ever actually seen a dragon, Cerdic?'

'We all saw the Firedrake.'

'We all saw something. A strange ball of flame in the heavens. These things have appeared before... they are natural events possibly, things we've no understanding of. But they don't always herald the fall of kingdoms.'

'Taken alongside King Edward's terrifying dream, you don't think it a sign… that the doom of England is upon us?'

Aethelric considered the best way to respond. At present, he was just relieved to have found his young lord. As the morning had dragged on and he'd seen nothing but empty highway ahead of him, he'd genuinely started to fear that the tormented youngster might ride all the way to York. Of course, he still might.

'It's inevitable that you're fearful at a time like this, Cerdic. We all are.'

'I didn't say I was fearful. I was riding *toward* the fight, not away from it.'

'Forgive my poor choice of words…' Aethelric dismounted. 'It wasn't my intent to impugn your courage.' He led his beast to the side of the track, and sat himself down on the hummock, nudging the lad with his bony hips to move him along a little. 'But it's not unmanly to be alarmed by dangerous prospects.'

Cerdic peered into the distance. 'I don't know if I believe in omens and visions.'

'Well… good. For real ones are thin on the ground.'

'But… if it's true, if the Twilight of England is upon us, it's even worse than I thought… and there am I, sitting at home, apparently with no plan other than to *bribe* the enemy should they come to our door.'

'Let me ask *you* a question, Cerdic.' Aethelric gave him a level stare. 'Is a man only a man if he wields a sword? Now, you already know the answer to this. You've enjoyed being educated, you've seen its potential for changing the world. You fully understand the power of the pen. But it isn't just that. Think of those who work the land, who run livestock, who cut timber and quarry stone. Think how hard they labour so that our society may function. Are they not men too?'

Cerdic snorted. 'Many are with Father. Wielding weapons.'

'The late King Edward lived like a monk,' the priest said. 'Yet he reigned for twenty-four years, and all that time his people prospered.'

'Aye, because men like Father drew steel in his name.'

'Sparingly, Cerdic. There were fewer massacres under Edward's rule than there were under belligerents like Canute and Edmund Ironside. But again, you already know this.'

'I know only one thing for certain. That sometimes one simply can't avoid a fight. If that's the sole thing you strive for, you're likely to be disappointed. As well as enslaved.'

Aethelric pursed his lips. 'In that case, why are you sitting here by the roadside?'

'Fireflax had a stone in her hoof. I had to clean it out.'

'Which you now have done. And yet still you wait.'

Cerdic looked sullen beyond belief, but also tired and resigned. He got to his feet. 'Can we talk on the way back?'

'Of course.' Aethelric stood up too, brushing leaves from his habit.

They rode toward Wulfbury at a walking pace.

'You realise they mocked me?' Cerdic said. 'They'll mock me even more when I return.'

'No one mocked you.'

'They didn't do it to my face, but I'm sure there've been things said behind closed doors.'

'Even if that's true, you think your father's never been mocked?'

Cerdic glanced round. 'Father?'

'Oh, you hold him in high esteem, and so you should. But he's had his share of detractors.'

'The stories about mother were gutter talk...'

'I don't mean that. That tale he told you about the monks by King Edward's bedside and the portent of doom. There were many who dismissed that as a falsehood.'

Cerdic was even more stunned. 'A falsehood? My father?'

'They say Earl Rothgar lied to frighten people, because he wanted Harold Godwinson, the most powerful noble in England, on the throne.'

'He believed Harold would bring stability.'

'But there were other factions who didn't want that, and they scoffed at your father and called him Harold's lackey.'

Cerdic rode speechless. That his father could have been so disrespected over something so important to the country's fortunes was a new concept.

'Myself?' Aethelric added. 'I call it statesmanship. Harold is not a perfect man, but your father believed he was the best to be king, so he engineered it. He displayed similar statecraft four years ago when he rode with the Godwinsons against Gruffydd ap Llywelyn. He fought in that war solely to mend his relationship with Harold, and to commence turning him against his brother, Tostig, which he duly did. These were huge achievements, Cerdic. And all accomplished by talking, not fighting.'

Cerdic nodded. But then scowled again. 'I can't even be a statesman, though, can I? Because I'll be a churchman instead.'

'Churchmen can't be great too, in their own way? Tell me what you've learned about Saint Cuthbert.'

'He was Bishop of Lindisfarne, and much adored for his holiness and devotion. He once lived eight years as a hermit, surviving on almost nothing, and since his death has worked many miracles. He is the greatest saint of the north.'

Aethelric nodded. 'Saint Wilfrid?'

'Bishop of Northumbria. He established the Rule of Benedict, converted the pagans of Sussex, and fixed the dates on which we celebrate Easter.'

Aethelric nodded again. 'And what of Eric Bloodaxe?'

Cerdic looked vague. 'Bloodaxe was a Norse king of Northumbria. He created the Hold of Ripon and conferred that title upon Wulfric, a Viking supporter of his. For his new capital, that Viking renovated an old fortress of the Britons, which he called "Wulfric's Burh", or as we know it today, Wulfbury. He was driven out when King Eadred reduced Northumbria's status from kingdom to earldom, and granted Ripon to an Englishman, Sigobert Aelfricsson, my great-great-grandfather.'

'So, you know about your family's personal connection to Bloodaxe, but do you know about his actual reign? The role he played nationally, the edicts he passed?'

Cerdic frowned. 'If memory serves, it was precious little.'

'You mean in comparison to the lives of those great churchmen?'

'In truth, I mainly remember Saint Wilfrid for his love of drinking.'

Aethelric shook his head in near despair.

'Wilfrid makes it easier to bear the thought of a life in Holy Orders, Aethelric. But will I have to be tonsured? No disrespect, but it looks ludicrous.'

The priest tinged pink as he rode. 'I'm just pleased you've made the decision to turn back. It shows a maturity I wasn't aware you possessed.'

'As to that, I had no choice.'

'No?'

Cerdic was a little more his normal self now, but still seemed doleful. 'Yesterday, you nearly persuaded me that I was planning my defence of Wulfbury against a foe drawn from the imagination.'

'*Nearly* persuaded you?'

'The foe is *real*.' Cerdic said this without any particular excitement or animation. He peered along the road ahead as though seeing phantom shapes that weren't actually there, or weren't there yet. 'England is in the grip of another barbarian horde, is it not?'

'Yes, but—'

'Then you're wrong to dismiss it. Whatever you say, Aethelric... they *are* in Northumbria, and we don't *know* what the Hardraada intends. He may seek to subdue the north before he goes south, in which case Wulfbury could lie directly in his line of march.'

'And you thought the addition of one more man to the northern earls' army would prevent this?'

'No. But I still had to go.' Cerdic pondered. 'Yesterday, I was half-prepared to stay at home. But all last night I dreamed of these omens. The faceless monks, the Firedrake. And now Land Waster, the Viking Raven... that monstrous bird that always foretells Odin's coming, that means his dark spirit is abroad in the land. Don't get me wrong. I said I don't believe in visions, and I don't. But these dreams were so vivid that they enforced on me how real this war actually is. Even if it hasn't come to Wulfbury yet, even if it *never* comes to Wulfbury, the mother of all battles is now.'

'So, why,' Aethelric enquired, 'and I've asked you this question today already and still haven't had a clear answer, are we riding the other way?'

'Because I'd be abrogating my duty if we weren't.' Cerdic gave a sigh that seemed to come from his very core. 'All the way along this road today, I heard Father's voice telling me that if leadership was easy, anyone could do it. That hardship and responsibility go hand in hand, that difficult choices must be made.' He paused, his gaze narrowing. 'It also struck me that there are different forms of leadership. That buying off our enemies might also be considered buying time... time we could use to build resistance. That maybe the key to defeating the Norse is to be clever, to lure them into a false sense of victory, as Alfred did. Pay on some occasions, fight and fortify on others. Though none of those options, or any combination of them, would have been open to me had I gone all the way to York.'

Aethelric made no immediate response, though inside he was pleased and impressed that Cerdic had reached this complicated rationalisation on his own. To start with, the priest wasn't quite as convinced the risk to Wulfbury was as insignificant as he'd been letting on, but he'd seen no sense in making people more frightened than they already were. It was good though, that Cerdic, after some contemplation, had seen through this, and yet had also kept his worst fears to himself. A series of intense nightmares had finally provoked him into abandoning his post and heading south, but after a relatively short distance, he'd restrained himself again.

Maturity at last. A clear sign of budding maturity.

-

An hour later, as they rode back through Brackley-on-the-Water, the river running so shallow at the ford that their hooves clipped on dry stones, Cerdic felt very self-conscious.

'You might as well be leading me by the ear,' he muttered.

'No one cares.'

That seemed to be true. It was evening now, whale-oil lamps sparking to life in the village houses. The one or two folk out and about, mostly women, paid him no heed.

'They have other matters on their minds,' Aethelric said.

On second glance, the women looked preoccupied with worry. They wanted their men to come back to them, preferably unbroken. Even in the event of victory, not all would.

'These are trying times for everyone, I suppose,' Cerdic said as they ascended the brae track.

'Indeed,' the priest replied.

Even inside the burh, no one seemed interested that the lad had returned, if they'd even noticed he'd gone. That was hardly flattering, but perhaps it was better to go unnoticed than be thought a fool.

CHAPTER 9

The two armies faced each other across a relatively narrow front, a raised stretch of road running between the River Ouse and a glimmering expanse of marshland.

Though Harald Sigurdsson had left at least half his host to guard his anchorage at Riccall, the numbers he had with him this morning had swelled overnight, so that now they were close to nine thousand. On top of that, they were in strong formation, rank after mailed and helmeted rank wedged behind their shields, all of which were painted with vivid colours and monstrous images, and which they now beat upon with fist and pommel. In the Vikings' foremost rank, the *berzerkers*, men of colossal size and strength, whose fanatical fury carried them past all pain and reason in the heat of battle, howled like the wolves whose fur they wore over their ring-mail, and shouted their black-hearted chant, the dread *Merseburgsgaldr*.

The English numbered around ten thousand and were arrayed in similar phalanx. They could have put more on the field, but late the previous evening the earls had decided that they too should leave levies behind, mainly as a reserve, but also to guard the city and its approach roads. They made a din of their own, blasting horns and pipes, offering ecstatic prayers to Wilfrid, Cuthbert and John of Beverley, another great saint of the north.

'Last night, I didn't think the earls Edwin and Morcar had the belly for this,' Unferth said to his father, having to shout to be heard.

'It comes easier to some men than others,' Rothgar replied, watching their opponents. 'But I'd have avoided this fight, too, if I could. Diplomacy is better than war, always.'

'Of course.'

'That must be your way, too, when you are earl. But sometimes there's no option.'

Unferth also eyed the ranks of the enemy. 'They seem very confident.'

'Viking armies are famous for that. To die in battle guarantees them a place in Odin's drinking-hall. It reinforces their courage.' Unferth nodded and swallowed. 'Don't be intimidated by that,' his father said. 'We know they're fierce opponents, but that's a good thing. It means we won't underestimate them.'

He lowered his helmet over his head, fastening the chinstrap.

Unferth was relieved to do the same. He was pale-faced and nauseated, but his iron nose-guard and cheekpieces went some way to concealing it. Hands damp inside his gauntlets, he unslung the limewood shield from his back and gripped the hilt of his broadsword in what he hoped was a fearless manner, trying to draw comfort from the strength massed around him.

In the normal fashion of his people, and of the Northmen too, the decision had been taken to fight on foot, but today it was an obvious strategy. With advance knowledge of their coming, the enemy had deployed early, blocking the road from York to Fulford at a point where the hardpacked track ascended to the village's outer hovels. This gave them higher vantage, but also meant that, with unmanageable ground to east and west, only a direct frontal attack was possible, rendering cavalry useless. In fact, this was a strong position in every sense. So much so that, on first viewing it, Rothgar had been hesitant to engage. But after a quick discussion with his allies, the decision had been taken to proceed. A retreat now would give their enemy heart, while discouraging their own men, who wouldn't understand the reason for it and might assume their leaders had been cowed.

This was another complexity that Rothgar had explained to Unferth. In battle, a leader needed to be visible. He had to be with his men at the forefront, sharing both the risk and the glory. But only a fool of a leader placed himself at the spearpoint. When a leader was killed, a battle often ended; the entire cause could be lost in an instant. Even if his warriors strove on, there was nothing surer than that, without aim or direction, they too would ultimately succumb. As such, Unferth and his father were located in the midst of their housecarls, alongside the earl's Blue Boar banner and about three ranks from the front.

Their position on the field was to the left. In the middle, Morcar's Red Bear fluttered alongside Edwin's Black Eagle. Far over on the right, Unferth could just about distinguish Waltheof's Wolf. Also on the right, a burning cross indicated where a significant number of priests and monks had sallied from the city, and not just to offer comfort or spiritual succour. For too long they'd been brutalised and slain by the Vikings. Now, they wore ring-mail over their black robes and brandished maces, and when the fighting commenced, they would advance behind their fiery symbol.

Of course, the Northmen had brought heraldry too. On the highest point of ground to their rear, two immense battle-standards streamed alongside each other: Earl Tostig's Golden Lion of Northumbria, and the symbol that England had come to dread over many centuries of fire and slaughter, a gigantic black bird, its wings spread on a field of white... Land Waster, the raven of doom.

However, though all now were deployed, the wait went on. At length, Rothgar pushed his way to the right, seeking further counsel with the Aelfgarsons. Athelbere, who stood in front of his two masters, his huge frame blocking much of the opposition from view, turned round and grinned. 'How do you fare, Lord Unferth?'

'Sick as a dog,' Unferth admitted.

The marshal of the house laughed. 'It's always that way in your first battle.'

Unferth nodded. As Cerdic had reminded him, though he'd gone to war with Athelbere and his father the previous year, also against Earl Tostig, on that occasion no blows had been struck.

'Stay close to me, and don't tackle any big ones,' Athelbere advised. 'Especially don't tackle their *berzerkers*. *They'll* not be concerned about claiming ransom.'

Unferth nodded. This also had been his father's advice. If he went down and found spears at his throat, it was neither sin nor shame to yield. These Northmen were opportunists. The quality of his arms and armour would imply his status; he'd be a prize catch. But the prospect of ransom would mean nothing to those of *berzerkergang*, that crazed, fur-clad priesthood whom legend claimed would fight on with claws and teeth when their weapons were broken, who could ride out cuts and blows of every sort, who would rage on and on until all sense and purpose to the struggle was lost.

The young lord looked toward their roaring mob through an oily haze, along a rural highway now hardened to ruts. The sun had risen properly at last. Though the local fields were stripped of corn, the orchards of York denuded of fruit, that summer without end went on. His head baked inside his helmet, dust motes swam in his eyes, and yet, when he glanced left at the emerald marshes, they lay twinkling and serene. There was great depth there, he suspected, and quagmires of mud underneath. Not the ideal place to finish up when wearing ring-coat and helmet.

'Ready yourselves!' came his father's voice.

Rothgar, who had just returned, checked the buckle on his chinstrap and drew his broadsword. 'Edwin sought to tempt them from the higher ground by waiting,' he said. 'But the Hardraada's no fool. Now any delay will only advantage him further. Scouts report that additional Norse war-bands are heading this way from Riccall. The size of our force may have surprised him and he doesn't want to take chances. So we go now.'

Unferth swallowed bile as he drew his own blade. He glanced over his shoulder, seeing an encouraging nod from Redwald.

'On the signal!' Rothgar shouted.

The English host fell silent as word passed among them. They glanced to their centre, waiting expectantly, only yelling out again when Earl Edwin and Earl Morcar's banners tipped forward, inclining toward the enemy. With a new blasting of horns and skirling of pipes, they tramped forward, in looser formation than they might have liked, though their marshals insisted on it for they were advancing uphill, and likely to come under missile attack. Almost immediately, javelins, stones and throwing axes darkened the sky before clattering down on helmets and shields.

Several men dropped, clutching gruesome wounds. Unferth's own limewood was pierced through in front of his face by a bodkin-shaped spearhead, its weighted shaft soon proving an encumbrance. It took several strokes of his sword to cut it loose. Already, he realised, he was tiring, for the upward gradient was deceptive. Blood beat in his ears; sweat ran freely under his layers of linen, leather and mail. And all the while, the clamour rose. Up ahead, the Vikings hammered the earth with their spear butts, chanting ever more frenziedly.

Instinctively, the English closed ranks again, bearing through the deadly hail, gazes fixed on the eyes of the Northmen in their gargoyle helmets, on their bushy beards, their roaring red mouths.

'Easy, lads, easy,' Unferth heard his father rumble.

The gap narrowed. From forty yards, to thirty, to twenty.

The earth now shook; the air vibrated.

The shieldwalls were ten yards apart, when suddenly, as one, the Northmen's roars reached a shuddering crescendo and they launched themselves downslope, a furious elemental wave. The collision resounded like thunder, a frightful din erupting as two storms of blades engaged each other, slashing, hacking, rending through wood, iron and flesh. Blood flew in spatters. The morning rang to the clangour of shields exploding, of spear-hafts splintering. Cries of rage became shrieks of agony.

Incredible though it was to Unferth's eyes, the *berzerkers* literally leapt into battle, raised up on the shields of their comrades and springing over the heads of men like beasts, bellowing as they cleared the first line of their foes, bellowing even louder as they landed amid those behind, striking out on all sides. One wielded a smith's hammer, and struck a housecarl's helm such a blow that the metal imploded, the brains erupting through his faceplate. Another plied the infamous Dane-axe, and with a single two-handed swipe, sliced the thegn of Tollering's head clean from his shoulders, only to die himself a moment later, Redwald's sword thrust hilt-deep through his vitals.

Unferth's own first contact came quicker than expected.

Directly in front of him, amid clouds of dust, Athelbere and his housecarls were already fighting like machines, axes rising and falling as they advanced over shattered shields and broken corpses. But a gap was appearing alongside them as the next company gave ground, a wedge of open space into which the opposition was suddenly aggressively pouring. Very quickly, that whole part of the English line found itself separate from the rest and manoeuvring toward the marsh, where all formation disintegrated, the shieldwall coming apart. Before Unferth knew it, he was driven along in a huge press of men, and then was floundering in the shallows, jostled from every side by open combat, warriors hewing at each other, or rolling and biting like rabid dogs, the waters around them turning scarlet. It was the last thing they wanted, for in one-to-one chaos the more battle-hardened Vikings would always have the upper hand.

Frantic, he looked landward, and saw the tall, rangy form of his father perched on drier ground, but swapping blows with two opponents at the same time, and already staggering with fatigue. Even as Unferth watched, an axe-blow split Rothgar's shield. Shouting, the lad waded toward them, only for a Viking in steel-studded leather to come howling at him along the water's edge. He was unhelmeted, his face brutally gashed, his hair a sopping mat of blood, but he came on apace and drove his two-handed spear at Unferth's chest. The lad cut it aside and chopped him down, a backhand stroke across the side of his legs severing the right knee. The Viking slumped backward, gargling with pain. Unferth followed with a downward thrust, his sword ramming through the open mouth, a ruby fountain spurting as it sheared through bones and tissue at the back.

Fleetingly, the fact that he'd just killed his first man was incidental to the young Englishman, but as he spun around, his stomach lurched and vomit burst from his lips. Even so, he hobbled up onto dry ground, where his father had felled one of his opponents, but was struggling to fend off the other. This second one was of larger, heavier build, in addition to which Rothgar now was wounded, an axe-slash visible on the left shoulder of his hauberk. It couldn't have been deep for he was still able to heft his shield, but that entire side of his body glinted red with gore.

'Pagan dog!' Unferth shouted, closing on the Viking from behind.

The fellow turned. This one *was* helmeted, but his aventail was made from cloth rather than chain, and Unferth's sword clove through it, biting deep into the muscles and tendons of his neck. The fellow toppled sideways, dead before he hit the ground. Unferth grabbed his father by the wrist. Both were white and drenched with sweat, Rothgar's helm dented and scarred, its nose-piece bent.

'Our lines are broken,' Unferth panted.

'We can still beat them,' the earl replied. 'Where's Athelbere?'

They looked around for the marshal of the house, and saw him straight away, though it was an unexpected sight. He was far up the corpse-strewn road in front of them, Wiglaf, their standard-bearer alongside him, as he and the Swaledale carls wrought savage execution on the Northmen, who now appeared to be falling back. Just beyond him, the housecarls of Morcar and Edwin were visible, also cleaving through the Viking hedge, scything men like sticks of wheat, while close at their backs came hordes of fyrdsmen with hammer, knife and boar-spear, clubbing and stabbing out the lives of the Norse wounded.

The chaos that had embroiled the left side of the English line had been fleeting. In the fury of that first assault, they'd splintered away from the main body of the army, but the centre and the right had held.

Father and son advanced. Any Northman they met, either upright and on guard or grovelling in his own bowels, they smote. When the earl found a new shield, he grabbed it. It was gouged and dripping with other men's blood, but it was solid and hefty, and he beat his blade on it as they rejoined the fray. Athelbere bellowed a greeting as another Northman fell beneath his axe.

Unferth went in fiercely, driving his sword-tip through the broken links worn by a youthful Viking in front of him, impaling the chest, closing his ears to the shrill screams. He would leave his regrets until later, he told himself. All that mattered now was to live. But not just to live, to win. Because victory felt close. Their company continued to advance, stepping over more and more of the Viking slain, though as the gradient steepened, it became harder and heavier in their harness, and the enemy now was backing away rather than engaging. But not running, he noticed. With sudden alarm, it occurred to Unferth that this was *too* easy. And even as this thought struck him, he heard battle-horns sound anew, and a great, thundering *crash* as the retreating Northmen halted, reforming their shieldwall in a single movement. Though not in the centre, where an avenue cleared, and down it advanced a stupendous figure. With his brass-ringed coat, horned helmet and swirling cloak of white 'faerie bear' fur, it could only be Harald 'the Hardraada' Sigurdsson.

The Norse king was broad as an ox, and a full head taller than any man there. In one hand he wielded a broadsword, in the other a scramasaxe. At his heels came an entire pack of *berzerkers*, carrying Dane-axes and baying like wolves. But it was Sigurdsson who led the counter-charge. Unferth watched in awe as the giant figure threshed his way among the shields and spears of his foes, arms windmilling as he dashed out brains and sundered necks. Wulfnoth, one of his father's strongest housecarls, attempted to engage the great warrior front-on, but he was bare-headed and bloody, and was promptly split to his teeth.

Behind their monarch, the entire Norse army surged.

Suddenly the press of shields from the front was irresistible. Unferth and Rothgar found themselves stumbling backward. A throwing spear hurtled past, glancing the side of Unferth's helm, striking open his cheek, but travelling with such force that when it struck the lower belly of a housecarl behind him – Unferth saw that it was Gunwald, Letwold's father – it pierced his ring-coat, plunging deep into his innards. Gunwald gave a protracted, tortured gasp as he doubled over.

'*On me!*' Unferth heard his father shout. The earl had grabbed Wiglaf by his shoulder harness and was lugging him back from the initial melee, but only so they could rally. '*Swaledale... on me!*'

Athelbere retreated to his master's side, still swiping, laying Northmen left and right on a roadway slick with gore. Other carls joined them, Redwald chopping and cutting like a man possessed. Unferth went too. His body was numb with fatigue, his sword-arm aching, but the fight was on him. This was the only way. They formed a phalanx around the Blue Boar banner, hoping to stand firm as the Vikings flowed past. But axes rained blows upon them, hammers and darts smashed into the bulwark of their shields. The air now stank of sweat and guts and was riven by the most terrible dissonance, a hellish noise they could surely hear even in York. And still the invaders threw their might against them, Unferth stumbling and tripping as they were forced steadily back. He sensed the marsh again, now a morass of corpses as well as mud and reeds, but still capable of sucking an armoured man down should he venture too far into it.

'Father, the fen!' he tried to shout, but Earl Rothgar was distracted, and his son saw the reason.

Athelbere had broken formation to close with none other than Sigurdsson himself, the Viking ruler's teeth bared in his immense white beard, his eyes burning like fiery jewels through the slits in his face-plate as he launched blow after colossal blow. Athelbere, perhaps the only man there who could stand against this monster, this troll of the sagas, parried them all, but tottered with exhaustion, while his opponent seemed tireless, inhuman. Rothgar tried to fight his way through to his champion's side, only for a spear to strike the edge of his sword, deflect and catch him in the throat.

The earl stood stock-still, gagging, clawing at the wound.

'*Father!*' Unferth screamed, lurching toward him.

A Viking got in the way, so he slammed the iron boss of his shield, all that remained of it, into the grinning, filth-spotted face. Another came after the first, so he used the boss again, and then on the one after that, breaking noses and teeth, running each man through with his blade as they dropped. Just ahead, his father sank to one knee, head lolling, blood coursing through the fingers clamped on his throat.

A couple of yards beyond him, Athelbere fell.

A spear thrust from behind had skewered his back. He spasmed in response, opening his guard, and Sigurdsson weighed in, the scramasaxe shearing through the Englishman's shoulder, burying itself deep in his trunk. Unferth slid to an astounded halt.

For a brief moment, time slowed down. The lad stood rigid, paralysed, watching as the greatest warrior in his father's house, the swordmaster who'd taught him everything he knew, twisted to the ground, turning slowly in a crimson spray, the earth reverberating when he struck it.

Only laboriously, with monumental effort, did Unferth battle his way back to reality, blinking hot tears as he stumbled forward. His father was still upright at least, albeit sagging. But a Northman got to him before Unferth could, a Northman with a war-hammer. The two-handed swing to the earl's temple would have shattered a giant's skull, helmet or no. As Rothgar dropped, Unferth screamed his throat sore, smiting the Northman with a mighty blow of his own, slicing his gullet wide. He struck another behind him and another behind that one. His world now was a blood-drenched blur, a confusion of cries, shrieks and flickering, cavorting images of hatred and death. On one side, he saw Englishmen stricken in the marsh, overwhelmed by mail-clad beasts, trampled beneath stamping feet, pinned down with spears, drowning in mud, blood and offal. In the other direction, Edwald, Athelbere's son, wept as he defended his father's body, only for an axe to lop off his sword-hand at the wrist, and a seax to rip across his belly, his entrails boiling out.

Further into the field, the English shieldwall had fragmented, batches of the other earls' housecarls standing like rocks, with waves of Northmen engulfing them, axes striking in shimmering, blood-wreathed patterns, smashing helms, cleaving faces.

Too dazed to make sense of it, Unferth thought he spied Morcar Aelfgarson, dappled crimson, mounted on a horse that someone had brought him, but ranging helplessly about, his shield in pieces, his sword broken. When a javelin flew at him from close quarters, the horseman ducked low to avoid it, and then galloped for his life, riding down friend and foe regardless. The javelin thrower was none other than Tostig

Godwinson. Tostig the traitor, Tostig the devil, Tostig who had caused this carnage, now resplendent in gleaming ring-mail, his green livery and unscarred green shield embossed with the Golden Lion of Northumbria. It was as though he'd scarcely been involved up to now, though that didn't surprise Unferth, for he'd many times heard his father say that Earl Tostig would fight to the last of his hearth-men before surrendering.

His father...

'Father... *Father, FATHER!*'

Unferth yowled like a child, turning stiffly, sagging to his knees.

Rothgar lay motionless, the whole left side of his skull a crush of bone and metal. Other corpses, yet more of his slaughtered followers, were draped across him.

'Father...' More tears threatened, but suddenly Unferth's eyes were too dry, too sore. There would be a time for weeping, but that time wasn't now.

His gaze narrowed as it levelled on Tostig.

If nothing else, he would make *that* wastrel pay. He threw away the blood-slimed boss and hefted his sword. But before he could lurch forward, a mangled face swam into view, one eye-socket broken, the eyeball dislodged onto the cheek.

Wiglaf, the standard-bearer, was barely recognisable as he slumped against his overlord's son, mucus and vomit slathering his beard. He couldn't speak, yet even as he crumpled down he had strength enough to push into Unferth's hands the wooden pole from the top of which the Blue Boar banner of Wulfbury still billowed.

'Wiglaf? *Wiglaf...*' the lad stammered. Again, he swayed where he stood. 'Swaledale,' he said in a hoarse whisper. Then louder, lustier: '*SWALEDALE! TO ME!*' And he held the banner aloft.

But on all sides now, his household lay like butchered meat, limbs tangled, blood-streaked faces turned sightless to the sun.

'Swaledale,' he wept, his voice breaking. Just ahead, another wall of Viking shields came forward en masse, hacked, splintered, a forest of axes raised at their rear. '*Swaledale!*'

Lowering the banner till its spear-tip was level, Unferth Aelfricsson, new earl of Ripon, ran at his foes alone…

CHAPTER 10

The autumn evenings fell quickly in Swaledale, the steep hill-sides casting deep and early shadows into the dale's sheltered heart.

Cerdic stood alone on the palisade. Shreds of cloud were scattered across the ash-blue sky; underlit by the setting sun, they glowed like embers. Below him, lamps and candles flickered to life in Brackley-on-the-Water. The landscape, heated for so many weeks, exuded a comforting warmth. There was an odour of dust, wheat and sun-dried grass. But there was also, for the first time, a tang of autumn freshness. By late night it would be much cooler.

In only struck him how majestic a place Swaledale was now that it was under threat. For too long, Cerdic had taken these rich and verdant acres, this happy place that his father and fore-fathers had carved out of the northern wilderness, for granted. No one could look upon it, especially at moments like this, and attribute it to anything other than an all-powerful Creator. And not just that, a Creator with an eye for the exquisite. Of course, none of that meant it would be the Aelfricssons' forever, or even that it would or should remain in its current tranquil, cultivated state. Cerdic *hoped* that it would. Even as he stood there, he prayed that it would, firstly to the Holy Virgin, whom he imagined would have greater empathy with all things peaceful and pastoral, and then to the saints, Basil and Walstan, who were known respectively for a love of all living things and an admiration of those who worked the land. Of course, Heaven was doubtless assailed by such entreaties from all corners on a daily basis.

Dear Lord, protect this place, preserve this loveliness...

Speaking of loveliness, movement in the valley caught his eye and, peering down, he spied a familiar figure pushing a two-handed cart out of Brackley, heading eastward along the valley road. Even from this distance and with the day dimming fast, the slender, golden-haired shape of Eadora was unmistakeable.

Cerdic's boyish ardour had cooled a little since he'd seen her climbing so dexterously through the branches in Gonwyn's Orchard, her brown, firm-muscled legs exposed to the thigh, his groin twitching, his stomach twitching, everything twitching, even his heart. Now, she seemed more like a figure of pity. Her brother was gone, at least for the moment. Unferth, who'd admitted that his feelings for her were more than purely sexual, had also gone. All her protectors had gone; she had to be hurting both physically and emotionally. The villagers likely thought less of her. Even those who believed she'd been raped would now consider her soiled goods. And still she was expected to carry out her heavy workload, with no assistance and no certainty for the future.

She hated Cerdic, of course. Her family were somewhat richer because of his folly, but it was doubtful that Eadora would see any of that. Even if she did, what had she to be grateful to *him* for? And yet, Cerdic had promised Unferth that he'd look out for her, do what he could to ease her burdens, though it would hardly be straightforward, which perhaps explained why thus far he hadn't raised a finger on her behalf.

Briefly, he wondered if things were secure enough here at the burh for him to break away from his post for half an hour, ride down there, speak to her, even offer some kind of apology. He still had an eye for the lass. Which red-blooded male wouldn't have? But she'd been mistreated, partly with *his* involvement. It hadn't been purposeful where he was concerned, but it had happened nevertheless, and he didn't like that. He didn't want her to think that he was just another over-privileged young cockerel.

Not after his conversations of the last few days.

He continued to watch her diminishing form. She was probably completing the last of her daily chores. Afterwards, she would bar herself into her family's cottage and not emerge until morning. His opportunity to speak with her this evening, if that was what he intended to do, would have gone.

Well... so be it. He shrugged. But then again, he'd made *that* promise to Unferth.

He glanced around. Several of the fyrdsmen were watching from the gantry, eyes on different parts of the valley. Whether they'd been practising with weapons, as he'd requested, he wasn't sure, but at least if there was anything to see, they'd see it. As much as the dusk would allow them to. In light of that, he couldn't imagine it would do any real harm if he went down there. It might even be something his father would approve of: mingling with the people, checking all was well, reassuring those who were nervous.

Hurriedly, he descended the nearest ladder and ran across the burh, calling for a groom. Within moments, he was mounted on Fireflax and picking his way down the Keld Brae. He trotted through the village and took the road east.

Eadora was now out of sight, but Cerdic knew which way she'd gone. About forty yards past the last of the cottages, he diverted south along a narrow, beaten trail to the village mill, a circular stone tower on the very edge of the river.

The level of the river was low, of course, but the mill-wheel still turned, albeit falteringly, the creak and groan of the grinding stones inside sounding more laboured than usual. Thirty yards east of there, a timber landing jutted out into a deeper section of water known as the Mill Pool. Eadora's cart stood nearby, the six or seven metal pails she'd been transporting lined up on the landing. Eadora herself sat at the end of it. She'd removed her boots and was trailing her feet in the gentle current.

She seemed to be in a world of her own, humming some gentle ballad; clearly, she hadn't heard the approach of Cerdic's hoofbeats. He dismounted and walked his animal forward. When he got close, he saw that she had one of the pails under her left arm, and was picking small items out of it, tossing them into the Pool, where sleek, bobbing forms darted excitedly around.

'You're feeding the otters?' he said aloud, startled.

The girl went rigid, before scrambling to her feet. When she saw that it was Cerdic, she looked frightened. 'It... it's not really feeding them, my lord.' She showed him the pail and its odorous contents. 'It's only scraps from yesterday's dinner. Fish heads and fins.'

Cerdic looped his reins around a low branch. 'All the same, I can think of a few people in the village who'd object.'

She watched him nervously. 'Are you one of them, Lord?'

'I'll be honest... I've never considered it. If you wish to feed them, who am I to interfere?'

She relaxed a little, emptying out the remaining slops, a feeding frenzy commencing in the water. 'They're beautiful creatures,' she said. 'Little wonder Saint Cuthbert is their patron.'

Despite his many real-world concerns, Cerdic was astonished. 'They have their own patron saint?'

'Of course, Lord.' She looked shocked that he didn't know. 'They brought him fish when he was starving in his hermitage. They're an important part of our world, I believe. And very misunderstood.'

'Misunderstood? You're lucky they didn't take your toes off.'

She half-smiled. 'They wouldn't hurt *me*.'

'So, you do this often?'

'I...' She became serious again. 'I hate it when we treat them like vermin.'

Cerdic strode onto the landing. 'The trouble with otters is we have thousands of them. And they eat all our fish.'

'Better to give them a taste for our leavings, then, no?'

He had to chuckle. 'There's logic there, I suppose.'

She glanced around at him, curious, taking in his felt boots, his black woollen breeches and black tunic with its rich gold-and-silver embroidery.

'You're not girt for war, my lord?' she said. 'Is the danger passed?'

Up close, he could see that the small wound on her lower lip was already healing. Not that it harmed her looks in truth. She was still radiant.

'No,' he said, clearing his throat. 'I mean, I don't know. I doubt there's an imminent threat.'

She drew no obvious comfort from that, but now stood there, awkward and unsure. Belatedly, he realised that she was confused by his arrival here, and maybe becoming frightened again. What might his intentions be in this secluded place? Had he followed her here? This goaded him into action.

'I've come to, erm –' he made a quick but vague gesture '– to express my regret about what happened.'

She looked even more confused. 'You mean during Harvest Ales?'

'I'm sorry I hurt your brother. It was foolish and unbecoming of me.'

'Yes, well… I'm sorry too, Lord.' She turned and, one by one, dipped the pails into the Pool. 'Because he tricked you into that.'

'I should have seen it coming. Doesn't make it any better for you, though. You were hurt *and* shamed.'

She didn't look at him as she moved to and from the river, loading the pails onto the cart. 'It happens all the time, Lord. You shouldn't be concerned.'

'Yes, well… we are, I mean *I* am… I mean, well… we should all of us pull together in times like these.'

She loaded the last pail, pointedly not looking at him. 'What do you wish of me, my lord?'

'The truth is, Eadora... the truth is I'm here on my brother's behalf. He asked me to take care of you while he was away, to see if you needed anything.'

'Lord Unferth said that?' Though struggling to remain reserved, she still looked shocked.

Cerdic nodded. 'He knows that Haco beat you when he learned that you and he had been together. He doesn't blame you in any way for what happened after.'

She moved back to the cart. 'I can only say it again... I'm sorry my brother extorted money from your family. Maybe he will die in this war, and justice will be served. Forgive me, I still have work to do.'

She took the cart by its two handles, kicked away its support bar and manoeuvred it from the landing toward the path.

'Eadora, wait.'

She did, standing stiffly.

'None of us think that Haco should die for this,' he said. 'That would be ridiculous. But we're all now in the same situation. I mean the fear... the uncertainty. Maybe we should be friendlier than we are?'

Immediately, he realised what an obvious approach this must seem to her. Despite his denials, he could only want to tumble her. Take up where his elder brother had left off.

'Here...' He moved alongside her, grabbing the cart by its handles. 'Let me show you that I mean well. You can lead Fireflax. Don't worry, she'll come gently.'

Reluctantly, Eadora backed away. 'My lord, you shouldn't...'

'No one round here thinks I'm any use.' Cerdic started forward, straight away finding it awkward, the cart jolting and rocking, water sloshing. 'At least I can prove to *you* that isn't true.'

'My lord, this is unseemly.'

'You mean they'll laugh at me? Don't they do that already?' Clumsily, he pushed on, aware that, behind him, the girl had taken Fireflax by the harness and was leading the docile brute forward. He tried to follow the path through the dry, yellow grass, but it proved a challenge just keeping a straight course. 'This is tricky,' he laughed. 'Do you use this much water every day?'

'It isn't just for us,' she replied. 'With Haco away, I must collect for the forge. My lord,' she sounded increasingly uncomfortable, most likely because they'd now turned through the trees toward the road, 'why are you doing this?'

'I've already said… I've been charged with assisting you.'

'You mustn't do menial work. It's wrong.'

'Consider it a penance.' He threw her a swift glance, speaking as matter-of-factly as he could. 'Look… I'm clearly making a fool of myself. Again. But I behaved badly, Eadora. At the tavern, I mean…' He brought the cart to an ungainly halt. 'Damn.' Lowering the support bar, he mopped his brow. 'And I'm sorry about that.'

When she gave no reaction, he glanced around.

She stood a few yards behind, Fireflax waiting beside her.

'Doesn't that mean anything?' he asked.

'Lord Cerdic… why would you be sorry?'

He almost replied with a question of his own: wouldn't that be the done thing? But the complete non-comprehension in her face was all the explanation he needed. It illustrated more than words ever could the immense gulf between them. Because though any woman would rightly regard herself ill-used in this situation, by both her master and her own brother, she was simply too astonished by the mere concept that a nobleman might not just apologise to a peasant, but go out of his way to make things right by her. It was something she'd never have expected, most likely because it had never happened before.

He tried to push the cart on, but struck another divot, one of the pails slopping out half its contents. 'Damn and blast!'

Eadora moved forward to take charge of the vehicle. 'My lord, I need to get back.'

Cerdic took Fireflax's reins. Somewhere ahead, from the direction of the village, he heard raised voices. But it only distracted him briefly.

'At least tell me if there's anything I can do for you, Eadora.'

She pushed the cart forward, with far greater proficiency than he had shown. 'There's nothing you can do for me, Lord. Nor should there be.'

He followed, leading his horse. 'Nothing?'

'We've already had a purse of coins, and that was ill-gotten. I should ask *your* forgiveness for that.'

'Forgiveness freely given,' he said quietly, watching as she pushed on with her cart, taunted by her strong, slim body, her steady gait, the sensual sway of her hips even as she exerted herself. And yet somehow, any amorous designs he'd once had on the lass had faded even more.

She was in a tired, sad state. Her new confusion about the lowered status she now held in the village where she'd lived all her life clearly added to this. He could still have taken her if he'd wanted to. Unferth had given him permission in his absence, as if that was all that mattered. Even his father had mentioned that village girls like Eadora would never dare refuse when a brash young nobleman came gallivanting along, so again, it wouldn't technically be rape. But it seemed revolting even to contemplate a seduction now. And anything beyond the purely physical was impossible anyway. Oh, that dream was still there: the triumphant battle-lord parading amid his cheering warriors with a gorgeous wife or consort on his arm. Eadora would have fitted that bill perfectly, but like so many of his youthful imaginings, the realities of wartime life were hitting home now, reducing it to nothing more than a childish fantasy.

Abruptly, he was shaken from this introspection by an increased uproar from the direction of the village. A village that, half an hour ago, had been settling down for the evening. He saw Eadora pause on the path ahead, as if she'd heard it too.

He mounted up and urged Fireflax forward. Eadora turned to look at him.

'I think something's happening, Lord,' she said.

'I think you're right.' He broke into a fast gallop.

When he entered Brackley-on-the-Water, another rider was there ahead of him. Whoever he was, he'd halted outside The Corn Mother, and sat slumped over the pommel of his saddle amid a frenzy of gabbling voices. Cerdic rode into the village so recklessly that he had to rein Fireflax sharply to avoid ploughing through the crowd now cramming its narrow streets.

The other horseman was someone he'd seen several times before. His name was Ranald, thegn of Beckerthwaite, one of the earldom's westerly estates. He was flustered and covered in grime, his hair hanging in rat-tails. His ring-coat had been muddied and cut to shreds, and was streaked with blood from a gash on his left cheek, which was only partly healed. He had no weapons, either on his person or on his horse, which steamed after what had clearly been a furious ride.

'What happened?' Cerdic shouted as his animal shouldered its way through.

Ranald regarded the lad curiously. 'Who are *you*?' he asked.

'I'm...' It was a struggle for Cerdic to keep his voice level. His heart was banging. 'I'm Cerdic. Second son to Earl Rothgar.'

Ranald spat a mouthful of phlegm. 'Well, Cerdic, second son of Rothgar, the battle is lost. We fought hard at a place called Fulford, just south of York, but they overcame us.' He craned his neck around. 'For Christ's sake, bring that ale!'

Agnetha appeared from The Corn Mother, carrying a brimming tankard. Ranald drank thirstily, froth spilling down his whiskers.

'What of my father?' Cerdic asked tautly.

Ranald dropped the empty pot into the dirt. He shook his head and wiped his mouth. 'The earl was in the thick of it, but I didn't see what happened to him.'

Cerdic couldn't believe the icy cold that now sank through his body. His mind whirled as he hoped against hope that

Ranald might be mistaken. Perhaps he had left the melee before a final, more satisfactory outcome. But there was no uncertainty in the thegn's battered face, no doubt in his downcast eyes.

The lad spoke again, querulous. 'My... my brother was there, too. What of—'

'I don't know what happened to him, either. The only one I saw fall who I knew was your champion.'

'Athelbere?' That alone was a bitter truth to absorb. Already, a lump was forming in Cerdic's throat.

Ranald shrugged. 'I believe the Hardraada himself struck that blow.'

'How... how many others fell?'

Village folk now ringed the mounted duo. The silence as they awaited an answer to this question was ear-splitting.

Ranald eyed Cerdic closely. 'How many soldiers did the earl send?'

Cerdic shrugged. 'Hundreds. Thousands, counting the fyrd.'

'And how many have returned?'

'You're the first.'

'That must tell you something.'

A low groan passed through the crowd, followed by a whispering and sobbing.

Panting and red-faced, Aethelric arrived, holding the hem of his habit as he stumbled down the brae track, several others behind him. He thrust his way through. Cerdic climbed from the saddle and grabbed the priest by his shoulders, stammering incoherently as he imparted what he'd just learned.

Aethelric turned to Ranald. 'What of King Harold?'

'If he's coming at all, he didn't arrive in time,' the thegn replied.

'What... what do you mean if he's coming at all?' Cerdic asked.

The thegn shook his head. 'There was talk he's bringing an army north, but I don't know how true that is.'

'Surely he'll come now the northern forces are beaten?' Aethelric asked.

'It seems likely.' Ranald glanced up the brae. 'But until he arrives, you people would do well to shelter in your stronghold.'

The sobbing halted, replaced by mutters of fear.

'Surely they won't come this far north?' the priest said.

Ranald shrugged. 'It would be nice to think that, but some of them are already on their way.'

The mutters of fear became whimpers of dismay.

'I took thirty housecarls to York,' the thegn added. 'I emerged from the battle with four. The only thing possible was to head home. But we weren't alone. It soon became apparent there was a Viking company behind us.'

'How strong?' Cerdic asked.

'I don't know. We tangled with their vanguard, and that's why now I have no carls at all. Oh yes —' his eyes roved the pale-faced congregation '— my men died and I lived. Look at me as a coward if you wish, but only a man who's never faced the Norse would think in those terms.'

'Who are they?' Aethelric asked.

Ranald frowned. 'How could I know that?'

'I mean, do they come in force? Are they a break-away company?'

The thegn shrugged. 'They might be, I can't say. It's certainly not their whole army. Hardraada is still camped on the Ouse. But this particular group are coming *here*.'

'And when do you expect they'll arrive?'

'They were close behind me all the way. That's why I say shelter in your burh. And pray that God favours you. After what I saw at Fulford, you'll need Him.'

Ranald kicked his horse's flanks, but Cerdic lurched forward and snatched his reins. 'Surely you're staying?'

'Are you a madman?' Ranald said.

'What, you fled the battlefield and now you're fleeing us?'

Ranald snarled. 'I fled the battlefield, little earl, when I had nothing left. I told you nearly all my host was slain. My sword and spear were broken. When we met them again on the road, I had to fight my way out with *this*.' He presented his right fist, which clasped a bloodstained knife, its blade snapped halfway down. 'And you'll feel it in your neck if you don't release my bridle.'

Cerdic reached for Usurper's hilt, but of course the sword was back under his bed. Aethelric, meanwhile, yanked the reins from his grip, handing them back to Ranald.

'If I have to die, it'll be defending my home,' the thegn said, addressing the crowd in general. 'I don't wish to be the bearer of this news, but it's best you know the truth.'

'We need you,' Cerdic hissed.

'So does my family.'

'And your family is where you belong,' Aethelric added hastily. 'Go.'

Ranald said no more, turning his animal around and steering it through the crowd. Not for the first time, Cerdic felt helpless, ineffectual and numb all over.

This was it. The Northmen were actually coming.

He glanced around at the fire-lit faces, most wet with tears. They watched him expectantly. It was sobering, if not terrifying, to realise that the welfare of so many relied on the next decision that *he* made. Up until two or three minutes ago, his role here had been a pretence of mastery. He'd been these people's lord in name only.

He whispered into Aethelric's ear: 'Are we sure these people will be harmed? They're non-combatants.'

'Who can say?' Aethelric mumbled back. 'Sometimes the Norse destroy them as an example. Many they'll sell as slaves. Few of the women will be spared rape.'

'The Hardraada is a Christ-worshipper,' came a creaky but confident voice. 'In his own way, admittedly, but he has been baptised and has done good things in God's name.'

These words came from Father Brithnoth, a shrunken figure buried in his habit and leaning on a crooked staff. A white beard straggled from his chin, but his head was as bald and shrivelled as a nut. At present, he was talking as much to the people crowding around him as to their overlord.

Aethelric regarded Brithnoth with annoyance, and Cerdic knew why. The earl's chaplain considered the village priest a throwback, a man stubborn in some ways but lax in others. He'd read widely on the history of this land and its people, but his cell was filled with almanacs on ancient lore rather than monastic writings. He was tolerant of the older ways, so customs like the profane Nutting Day ritual, the Samhain fire festival and the woodland couplings on La Bealtaine persisted. Brithnoth didn't encourage these things, but he didn't deplore them as much as Aethelric thought he should. Even now, the village cleric wore heretical corn spirals on his rope-belt.

'The Hardraada may profess to follow Christ, but what of his warriors?' Aethelric argued. 'Do *they*? And if they don't, can he control them from his camp on the Ouse? Will he *desire* to control them? He needs their fury, Brithnoth.'

'Why assume that?' Brithnoth said. 'If the Hardraada's come with Earl Tostig, they'll seek to rule this population, not brutalise it.'

'That makes sense,' Cerdic jumped in, eager to grab at hope. 'Earl Tostig—'

Aethelric shook his head. 'Earl Tostig is likely the reason Hardraada came here, but by now he's probably a puppet. I'm sure he wants his earldom back intact, much as the king of Norway seeks also to be king of a happy England. But that latter is infamous for his butcheries. He'll kill as many as he needs to, you can trust me on that.'

'God help us,' someone wailed.

'We still don't know why they're coming *here*,' Cerdic said.

'No disrespect, my lord,' Aethelric replied, 'but you don't need to know why they're coming, you only need to know that they are.'

CHAPTER 11

Cerdic stared dumbly at his mentor, who waited for a response. The lad's stomach twisted till it hurt. He felt worse than nauseous. The villagers were still watching him, eyes wide as coins in blanched, bloodless faces. It was almost as if they expected him to wave a wand and magic the evil away.

'What to do next must be *your* decision,' Aethelric said. 'You're in charge now.'

Suddenly, Cerdic knew that he was going to vomit.

'Tell the… people,' he stammered. 'Tell them, if they wish… to go to the burh. Tell them… it's their refuge. Until the crisis is over.'

Aethelric nodded and shouted to the crowd. Brithnoth stood to one side, unsure that this was the correct course of action. He eventually objected, saying that he should talk to the Hardraada personally, as Pope Leo had done with Attila, in response to which Aethelric barked at him about 'nonsensical egotism'. The villagers meanwhile bustled, some toward the foot of the brae, others to their houses. In their midst, Cerdic stumbled around into a narrow passage on the river side of The Corn Mother, where his gorge rose. Slime spattered the pebbles at his feet. He heaved several times before his belly was empty, and then sank against the tavern wall, his body shaking. When he sensed a presence, he glanced left and saw Eadora. She'd run to the village after him, and had heard most of the news, because she was now white-faced and hugging herself even though it wasn't cold.

'Please tell me you didn't see that,' he said, straightening up.

If she had, she didn't comment on it. 'What do we face?' She hurried forward, frightened. 'Lord Cerdic, tell me... what do we face?'

He shook his head. 'I don't know.'

'You told me the threat wasn't imminent!'

'What can I say? I was wrong.'

'So what about my brother? He went with your father's army.'

'Eadora, I don't know.' He took her by the hands. 'They lost the fight, but that doesn't mean they're dead. They may even be able to reorganise...' He glanced across the river and saw a woman leave one of the houses, a bundle of blankets in one arm, a child in the other. From all other parts of Brackley-on-the-Water, panic-stricken voices rose on the air. He had duties to attend to. He hastened to the end of the passage, steering Eadora by her elbow. 'You should get to the burh with the others. Bring anything you need, but hurry.'

They re-entered the street together, splitting up. Cerdic grabbed Fireflax's reins. Villagers still darted back and forth. Large numbers were already streaming up the brae, and as dusk had now become darkness, many carried torches as they struggled toward the palisade gates. Others, by the sounds of shutters banging and bolts ramming closed, had chosen to remain in their homes. There were always some, he remembered his father saying after viewing many a burnt ruin and smouldering corpse, who refused to accept that danger was at hand, who gambled that it would not befall *them*.

His next thought was to ride three miles west of the village, and bring Oswalda, his old nurse, and her husband, Guthlac, to safety. They would not even know about the impending danger. But, looking at the frightened people around him, it quickly became obvious that this would take time he couldn't spare. The interests of one or two, much-loved as they were, did not outweigh the interests of the many. Aethelric alone did not wield the necessary authority to organise quarters up there for such a number. Cerdic had to go up as well. But who knew, he might still get a chance to send a message to them.

As he led Fireflax past a row of terraced cottages, Eadora emerged from one of them. She'd thrown a cloak over her kirtle and bound her hair in a linen veil, while the sack she carried was so full and heavy that it all but bent her double.

'Good Lord,' he said, 'are you bringing everything you own?'

'All the food we have, my lord,' she replied. 'Plus as much spare clothing as I could find…'

She stared at him desperately, hoping he wouldn't command her to leave it.

But he saw the sense in what she'd done. The point had already been made that if Wulfbury was put under siege, no one could say how long it would last, or how long the supplies currently occupying the burh's storehouses would hold out with so many extra mouths drawing on them. However, it would be a huge effort for her to carry this burden up the brae.

'Here…' He took the bag off her and loaded it onto Fireflax's back.

'Lord Cerdic?' she asked, looking him straight in the eye. 'Is my brother dead?'

'I can only say again… I don't know,' he replied.

'Who will defend us if the earl's walls are breached?'

'There are a few of us up there.'

She didn't respond to that but from her quivering lip he knew what she was thinking: those few deemed unworthy to have gone with the army.

He kept his voice level. 'The burh is highly defensible. They'll think twice before even trying to assault it.'

She nodded bravely, and a short while later he was leading Fireflax up the brae track, the sack of belongings draped over her saddle, Eadora walking alongside. It wasn't easy. The track was steep, stony, cluttered with struggling, load-bearing villagers.

'Thank you for this,' Eadora mouthed.

'I promised Unferth,' he muttered.

At the burh gates, a huge timber affair much larger than the doors to the dragon hall, Cuthred appeared on the parapet above, armed with a bow.

'How many in the compound?' Cerdic called up as he entered.

'Plenty, my lord. We'll soon be crammed to the stockades.'

Another voice sounded, snapping with annoyance. The refugees who'd already entered milled around confusedly, blocking the central thoroughfare leading to the dragon hall square. Osbert fought his way through them.

'Lord Cerdic!' he exclaimed. 'Lord Cerdic... who are all these people?'

Cerdic despatched a thrall to take Eadora to the hall, before turning to the steward. 'Who do you think? The people of Brackley.'

'But, my lord, I thought we'd agreed—'

'We agreed nothing, Osbert, but even if we had, the danger is upon us now... *right this moment*. I've no time to decide who lives and who dies.' Osbert's brow furrowed. His mouth dropped open as if, shocked though he was, he still sought to object. 'I'm sure,' Cerdic added, hoping rather than believing, 'this matter will be settled one way or the other in the next few days.'

'Even a few days will eat into our stores—'

'Lord Cerdic!' Cuthred called from the palisade. 'There's something happening in the village.'

Cerdic hurried up the ladder. The fyrdsmen assigned to guard duty had gathered on the gantry and were staring down-hill. Full night had fallen, so it was difficult to see what was happening, but lights now moved from one end of the village to the other, and yelps and shouts were heard. A weird, cawing, crow-like laughter wavered its way up to them.

Cerdic's hair prickled. 'What is *that*?'

Before anyone could answer, plaintive cries came from the brae track. Cerdic glanced down and saw that Osbert had marshalled a couple of thralls to help him close the gates. Many villagers were still outside, using the weight of their bodies to try and keep the gates open.

'Osbert, damn you!' Cerdic slid down the ladder and pushed the thralls away.

'Master Cerdic, I can't allow this,' the steward protested. 'We've nowhere to put everyone.'

'These people need protection.'

'And *you're* going to offer that?' Osbert's tone was haughtier than usual. Underneath, he clearly still regarded Cerdic as an unimportant pup who, once the authority of his father had been withdrawn, was little more than an irritant. 'With your *vast* experience? And your *handful* of men-at-arms?'

'Lord Cerdic!' Cuthred shouted.

'Osbert...' Cerdic replied, only to be distracted by a bellowing male voice beyond the palisade. It sounded something like: *Antan!* Another replied to it: *Vali!* A squeal of agony followed, and then a chorus of intense, terrified screams.

Cerdic shoved Osbert aside and moved to the gap between the gates.

Beyond it, he saw that three figures had now flung off hooded cloaks, burly, bearded men who'd crouched low to pass unnoticed in the crowd. All were dressed head to foot in grey fur. A figure lay at the nearest of their feet. Cerdic recognised him as Godric, the reeve. His shoulder had partly been severed from his torso, bone nubs glinting in the deep, crimson rent. With another guttural roar, steel flashed and a second man went down, a tottering white-beard who'd once served as the earl's herdsman. He'd been smitten across the throat, and his head went spinning on an arcing font of blood.

'Dear God!' Cerdic whispered. 'They're among us already.'

In a whirlwind of panic, refugees scattered from the track, many falling over each other, or tripping in the tussocky grass. Cerdic dragged at the nearest woman and her child, lugging them through the gates. Osbert was still at his shoulder, talking loudly.

'Close the gates!' Cerdic shouted.

'A wise decision,' Osbert intoned sarcastically.

With a *crack* of bone, another victim was felled. Red globules rained across Osbert's face and down the front of his tunic. His mouth dropped open in horror.

'Someone, help!' Cerdic shouted, trying to force the left-hand gate closed by himself, muscles straining against the huge timbers.

But the majority of those around him were women and children, driven by terror as they flooded further and further into Wulfbury burh. Osbert stood rigid, too shocked to react, as were the fyrdsmen on the palisade. Cerdic had just managed to push the left gate into place and had moved to the right, when the left one was buffeted open again, and a nightmare figure stood there. For a spine-chilling second, the lad was reminded of that poem Hoki the Skald had related: *Beowulf*.

It was a giant. His height and breadth, his frothing lips, straggling hair and thick, blood-drenched beard, made him look more a bear than a man. Mail glinted beneath his fur and he wielded a Dane-axe, a weapon Cerdic had only heard about in legend. Its ash haft was a seven-foot pole; the colossal blade on the end of it, now red and dripping, must have weighed fifteen pounds or more.

Fear almost strangled the lad as he realised that he was facing a *berzerker*.

'Osbert, the gate!' he stuttered. 'The gate!'

But the human beast had sprung through the opening and was upon him already.

Cerdic hadn't blinked before his feet were dislodged by the lower end of the Dane-axe haft. He landed on his back with such force that the wind exploded from his lungs. The next thing, the *berzerker* was astride him, drawing back his blade for a gigantic downstroke. The Northman howled, a sound so fierce and heathen that it evoked the icepacks, the frozen forests, the dark *wargs* of the north. And yet that howl was silenced prematurely as a fair-haired shape lunged across Cerdic's vision, striking with a spear, the broad point plunging into the Viking's exposed throat, tearing his gullet in a boiling mass of blood and spume.

When the Northman fell, the ground shook. It drew the attention of his two comrades beyond the entrance, who, having cleared a bloody swathe across the brae track, came shrieking at the burh gates, Dane-axes twirling. Cerdic scrambled to his feet, and ran for the left gate, which, with Osbert's help, he was able to push closed. The other gate was dealt with by a couple of thralls, the crossbar falling into place to roars of fury from without. Cerdic leaned against the wood as blows impacted on the other side. When he turned, Eadora was standing close, breathing hard but still clasping the weapon with which she'd slain the *berzerker.*

Their eyes met and she shook her head, white-faced. 'I... I *had* to do it.'

'Of course you did.' Without thinking, he grabbed her and hugged her, and she was too shaken to do anything other than reciprocate, dropping the spear in the process.

'I couldn't just hide.' She shuddered in his arms, voice quavering. 'I had to return.'

'Trust me, I'm glad you did.'

'But...' She pulled away, staring at the corpse. 'To kill is a terrible sin.'

'A sin?' Cerdic said, darkly amused. 'It was God who sent that monstrosity to us. All you did was send it back.'

'Cerdic!' Letwold called, now appearing from somewhere in the burh. Before Cerdic could issue orders to him, Aethelric arrived as well. 'How many villagers are trapped outside?' the priest asked, blanching at the sight of the body, and stepping gingerly around it.

Cerdic shook his head. 'The tail-end... but there are some who didn't come.'

'And in the other villages too,' Eadora added.

Aethelric glanced at her distractedly, before climbing the ladder.

'You should go back to the hall,' Cerdic told her. 'I don't doubt your courage. How could I? But there'll be people there who may need you.'

Eadora looked as if she wanted to argue, but then nodded and backed into the milling crowd.

Cerdic now scaled the ladder himself, Letwold and Osbert following, the former having armed himself with Eadora's spear. At the top, they moved onto the gantry over the gates and glanced down. A rock was hurled at them, which just missed Letwold's head, but the dead *berzerker*'s two companions were retreating, their rage cooling, their mission, such as it was, failed.

Not that this was much consolation, for behind them hundreds of Vikings carrying flaming torches ascended the Keld Brae. Thirty yards short of the gates, they halted, fanning out across the hillside. Clearly many of them remained in the village below. More torches could be seen moving down there, to the accompaniment of screams as the people who'd remained in their homes were hauled out. The bodies of those villagers killed outside the gates, ten or eleven in total, were dragged out of the way like sacks of rubbish.

A path now cleared down the track as several figures ascended on horseback.

Their mounts were fine animals: a piebald mare and two chestnuts, young, strong, their coats too glossy to have endured a sea voyage from Norway. Pain tugged at Cerdic's heart as he realised that these beasts had been seized from those thegns and housecarls lying slaughtered near York.

All the Northmen, including the three riders, were girt for war, wearing coats of heavy ring-mail, with circular shields on their arms, many battered and hacked as though they'd already seen much fighting. All of the Vikings, horseman or footman, wore elaborately fashioned helms, handsome head-gear, which, among the English, belonged only to men of rank.

The horsemen halted. Their foremost was massive across the shoulders and barrel-chested. He removed his helmet and shook out a wave of hair so red it was almost crimson. His dense beard and moustache were the same vivid colour, yet his face was an eerie ghost-pale, even in the golden light of the torches. Cerdic took note of this fellow in particular. He felt he was facing an underling, but an underling of high standing. The redhead's shield had a distinctive design, its brilliant purple field centred round a squinting scarlet eye with the iron boss, painted green, as its pupil. The single eye of Odin, the lad realised.

'English!' the redhead shouted, addressing them in their own tongue. 'Your power here is broken. Your new lord is Wulfgar Ragnarsson. He awaits below in your alehouse, enjoying his spoil of battle and the fruits of your labour.'

'Ragnarsson's battle is not over yet!' Cerdic shouted back.

'Cerdic,' Aethelric warned him.

'He should know that ealdormen remain in this place,' Cerdic whispered. 'Else he'll think that all he faces here are peasants and fools.'

'Who speaks?' the Viking shouted.

'I am Cerdic, son of Rothgar,' the lad replied. 'My father is master here, and you Viking dogs profane his lands. Begone, or his vengeance will fall on you.'

The Viking spoke to those around him. Then he turned back to the gates.

'Jarl Wulfgar is not a cruel man. He honours courage and rewards loyalty, as this horde of warriors must surely prove. But he cannot wait in a village hovel while some stripling boy dictates terms. We have among our prisoners a holy man, a shaman of your religion. He sought to ward us off by making Christ's mark and waving a sprig of mugwort...'

That would be Brithnoth, they realised. Only Brithnoth could make the sign of the cross and at the same time wave an ancient herb of healing.

'But, as always happens, when your craven Christ confronts the Allfather, our victory was assured,' the redhead added. 'We

114

hold your shaman in good health. But be warned... we have a halter round his neck. If you fail to deliver this stronghold, he will feel Jarl Wulfgar's wrath.'

Cerdic turned to Cuthred. 'Can you hit him with an arrow from here?'

Cuthred looked shocked. 'My lord?'

'Surely he's in range?'

'My lord, that will only enrage them,' Osbert hissed, horrified. 'They hold the upper hand. We must surrender.'

Surrender. That word again. Without having offered even a token amount of resistance?

'Impossible,' Cerdic replied. 'Cuthred, do as I say!'

Cuthred was a veteran of several campaigns, but he looked frightened by what was being asked of him here. He nocked an arrow to his string, but clearly had no intention of doing more.

'I warn you, boy,' the Viking called up. 'Defy us, and all your people will perish.'

'Cerdic, think on what we discussed,' Aethelric said. 'There are other ways.'

'Give up everything we have? At the first sign of danger?'

Cerdic had pondered much on the value of geld since the council meeting he'd called. He knew it would be useful, that it could buy them time, but now his blood was up, and given that one of these brutes' best men had already fallen, his impulse was one of defiance. Who did these upstarts think they were, anyway, coming to his father's gate in force, murdering his father's tenants, offering dire threats? Did he fear them? Of course – they numbered several hundred at least; they were almost an army in themselves – but they were still locked *outside*, and he was damn well not going to cower when he held an advantage like that. He glanced sideways. For all his words of admonition, Aethelric, who looked uncharacteristically pale and unsteady – he had been wrong too, of course – seemed wary about their next move, as if, having finally met these dogs face-to-face and seen local folk, maybe some he knew personally, reduced to lifeless, butchered clay, he'd been stricken with doubt.

He was only a priest, the lad was reminded. A wise old bird, well educated. But in truth, he likely knew nothing about war and its strategies, and probably very little about the souls of men who were vastly more evil than the peace-loving Swaledalers he was used to.

'Do your worst!' Cerdic shouted. 'We don't fear you!'

'My lord, please,' Osbert whimpered.

'Quiet!' Cerdic retorted. 'We can't show weakness.'

'At least *try* to negotiate,' Aethelric said. 'You don't have to offer them everything.'

'And you think they'll settle for that when they know we're too frightened to fight?'

'Cerdic, we *can't* fight—'

'We have to show some resistance, or they'll want it all!'

Down on the brae, the redhead had tired of the debate. Rather casually, he turned in his saddle, and signalled to a foot-warrior. The warrior produced a bizarre implement, a length of spiralling horn, two feet's worth at least. He raised it to his lips and blew a single, shrill blast. Down in the village, an upright object was set alight.

'Brithnoth!' Aethelric choked.

Cerdic leaned forward, looking harder. Surely that wasn't Brithnoth? They hadn't…?

As the figure commenced burning, it was yanked from its feet and hauled away along the valley road, evidently being drawn behind a horse. There was no sound as the blazing shape was dragged several hundred yards beyond the village, before being dragged back along the dale in the opposite direction. At length it vanished from sight.

'English!' the redhead called again. 'Your shaman has passed to his gods.'

Even those in the burh who hadn't witnessed Father Brith-noth's fate gibbered in fear.

For several seconds, Cerdic was too sickened to speak. Had *he* been the cause of that? No, of course not. It was the ones who'd done it to him… wasn't it?

'I now address the rest of you!' the redhead continued. 'As your boy-earl cares nothing for your innocent hides, look to Wulfgar Ragnarsson. He is rightful heir to these lands. Tear down this impostor, and Jarl Wulfgar will spare your lives. The seasons will roll by as normal.'

Cerdic glanced at Letwold, who regarded him worriedly. Osbert climbed down from the gantry, muttering under his breath. Further along the palisade, the fyrdsmen talked animatedly together. One of them said something like: 'The Norse ruled this land in our great-grandfathers' time.'

Another added: 'Aye. Half our traditions are Norse.'

The volume of dissent in the burh was also rising.

'If you won't pay them, say you'll surrender,' Aethelric advised. 'But only to the Hardraada.'

Cerdic was stunned. 'But why? You said he was a killer, a monster.'

'Yes, but maybe we can pit one against the other. The Hardraada is master of this jackanapes who calls himself heir. If you make such an offer, and Ragnarsson refuses it, he'll be defying his own king.'

'But the Hardraada will take everything too.'

'He can't rule alone. He may do as Canute did and keep most of the nobles in place, especially those who ease his accession.'

That was not a given, but Cerdic knew that this was no time for nit-picking. He turned back to the besiegers. 'I will surrender. But only to the King of Norway.'

A short silence followed, during which the mounted Northmen spoke together again. At length, the redhead shouted back: 'You must yield to me. I am Sigfurth Blood-Hair, and I am Harald the Hardraada's deputy.'

'Yet you haven't mentioned his name once,' Cerdic replied. 'You said that we should surrender in Wulfgar Ragnarsson's name, not the Hardraada's. I find that curious.'

'Try not to question their honour,' Aethelric advised.

But Cerdic's confidence was growing again. The Northmen looked discomforted. They exchanged doubtful glances. And so they should, perhaps. They were still stuck outside, their *berzerker* lying slain. Felled not by a warrior, but a girl…

'The Hardraada is busy elsewhere,' the redhead called up. 'We are charged with capturing this stronghold.'

'I don't believe you,' Cerdic laughed. 'If he's half the commander he's supposed to be, he'll be awaiting an attack by King Harold of England. How could he spare so many men? Does he even know you're here?'

'Cerdic!' Aethelric warned. 'Don't overplay it.'

But Cerdic laughed again. 'The Hardraada *doesn't* know, does he?' They weren't exactly squirming, but he knew he had them. These scum were profiteers and renegades. They'd gone behind their master's back, which surely gave him all the leverage he needed. 'While your king fights the real battles, you and your jarl have deserted!'

The redhead flung a spear. It happened so quickly that it caught them by surprise, the missile flying up and *thudding* into an object alongside Cerdic before he had any hope of ducking or dodging himself. His kneejerk thought was to mock the poor marksmanship, but when he glanced sideways, his spine froze.

The shaft stood quivering in Aethelric's chest.

The priest regarded his young master with harrowed eyes. He tried to speak, but pinkish froth bubbled from his lips. Then he dropped backward from the parapet.

Outside, the redhead spoke to his followers. It was in English and loud enough so that everyone inside the burh could hear it.

'Break the gates. Kill them all.'

CHAPTER 12

'*Aethelric!*' Cerdic screamed.

As he scrambled down the ladder, pandemonium broke out inside the burh. Villagers and servants ran in all directions. There was a mighty impact on the other side of the gates – then another, and another. In the maelstrom of his thoughts, Cerdic pictured more Dane-axes being wielded by men with bodies like oak trees and arms bulging with iron muscle. The heavy wood panels juddered as though they would soon shatter, but for now he had other concerns.

Aethelric lay alongside the fallen *berzerker*. The javelin still transfixed him, and one of his spindly legs was folded at a gruesome angle. Yet, somehow, he was alive. His chest, though penetrated by steel, rose and fell spasmodically. His eyelids fluttered; his mouth frothed with gore.

'Cerdic,' he gasped. 'I need Cerdic...'

'I'm here, old friend.' Cerdic dropped to his knees, his heart thudding in a frenzy.

'Cerdic... I... I can't see you...'

'Don't try to talk. You're hurt, but you'll recover...'

Aethelric reached out a twitching hand. 'Cerdic. Take... this.'

Cerdic gripped the hand, and realised that Aethelric was trying to pass him something. It was a golden ring, one of three identical rings, each carved with the Aelfricsson family crest and official seal, the boar-head insignia. Rothgar and Unferth already wore one each of these. Now Cerdic had one, too. Without thinking, he shoved it into his belt-pouch.

'Aethelric, I'm sorry. I caused this. I've failed you all...'

'Go... to the chapel...' Aethelric was struggling for breath, and Cerdic thought he had misheard.

'The chapel?'

'Those letters... your father's business...'

'The ones you said were private?'

Aethelric took the collar of Cerdic's tunic, twisting the embroidered material as tremors of pain surged through his body. 'Under the font. Cerdic... you must... take them. Don't let the Northmen...'

'Under the font, you say?'

'Under the...' The priest grimaced and gave a prolonged, inhuman croak.

'Cerdic!' Letwold called from the gantry. 'Cerdic, they're running! The cowards!'

Cerdic glanced up, and saw the fyrdsmen backing along the palisade, still brandishing weapons but retreating from the gates. It wasn't difficult to see why: all manner of missiles were being hurled up at them: javelins, throwing axes, rocks.

Cuthred came lithely down the nearest ladder.

Cerdic met him at the bottom, grabbing his arm. 'Where do you think you're running to?'

'You heard,' Cuthred jabbered. 'They're going to kill us all! And it's your fault! All *your* fault!' He tore free of Cerdic's grasp, and fled.

Cerdic pivoted round. There were more blows on the gates. The main crossbar was holding, but the timber panels were cracking; splinters flying.

Letwold shouted again from above. 'Cerdic, what do we do?'

'Hold them off as best you can.' Cerdic dropped back to his knees. 'Aethelric, talk to me... please.'

But their family's old stalwart would never talk again. His breathing had ceased, his eyes were glassy baubles.

'Aethelric...' Cerdic whispered in slow disbelief.

The sense of loss was sudden, irreversible and crushing, so immense it was almost palpable. The shock and horror surged through the lad's body like swift poison, burning his innards, blurring his vision. His very consciousness threatened to dissipate like smoke.

'*Aethelric...*' he stuttered. '*You... you can't go... I can't, I...*'

Letwold came hurriedly down the ladder, spear in hand.

'I told you to hold them off!' Cerdic shouted.

'With what?' Letwold also had to shout to be heard over the barrage of blows. 'There are hundreds more coming up the brae. They've even got a battering ram, a beam from one of the village longhouses. The village is on fire, by the way. They've torched every cottage.'

Cerdic got to his feet. All across the burh, doors and windows were being shuttered. Several folk had entered the dragon hall itself. With its heavy doors, that was the most obvious place to try and hole up, but it wouldn't be impregnable without strong men to defend it.

'Go.' He pushed Letwold in that direction. 'Protect Eadora.'

Letwold scampered off.

Cerdic reeled where he stood, head spinning, before grabbing hold of himself, looking first to the top of the palisade, which was unmanned, and then down at the gates, which shook with astonishing violence. One particular blow, dead centre, was landing again and again, much more heavily than the others. On the seventh or eighth impact, the crossbar fractured.

He glanced again, one last time, at the fallen priest, determined to try and be strong, to batten down his grief so that he could think clearly, before turning and walking stiffly along the central thoroughfare. It was important to remain calm and commander-like, to instil confidence through his composure if not through his mere presence. Behind him came a tearing of wood as the gates erupted inward. A thunder of enraged male voices followed. Cerdic broke into a run. As he crossed the dragon hall square, he glanced over his shoulder, glimpsing an inrushing tide of metal and muscle: roaring red mouths, flame glinting on ring-mail, on nose-guards, on the bosses of shields, the points of spears, the wicked edges of fire-hardened axes.

With howls of glee, the intruders began smashing doors and dragging shrieking women out by the hair, rending off their clothes, falling on them with animal gusto. The men they hauled out, they slew. Cuthred was one. He was thrown out through a workshop window. A laughing Viking grappled with him for his bow, snatching an arrow from the quiver and driving it through his neck.

Cerdic kept running, but also kept looking back, and thus collided with Osbert, who was standing at the foot of the dragon hall steps, dazed by the unfolding calamity. The sight of Cerdic seemed to bring the steward to his senses, and he grabbed the boy's throat with his flabby hands. Osbert's face was pork pink and speckled with sweat, his eyes wide and shiny with delirium.

'You should have given up Wulfbury without a fight,' he snarled. 'That would have been the sensible thing. Your father would have done that.'

'Father would have fought!' Cerdic wrestled hard, surprised by Osbert's strength.

'Not without his hearth-men. You fool! You wretched young fool!'

'Get your hands off me!'

The steward did as ordered, but then reached down to a scabbard he now wore at his waist – the first time he'd ever been armed, as Cerdic could remember – and ripped out a hefty broadsword. A broadsword notched with heathen characters, a broadsword whose pommel was surmounted with an enormous emerald.

Usurper.

'What the devil!' Cerdic spat. 'You went into my room to get that?'

Osbert rounded on him and, thinking he was about to be skewered with his own weapon, the lad leapt back. But Osbert didn't strike with it. Instead, he examined the inscription on its blade with an ironic expression.

Cerdic extended a palm. 'You damn thief! Give it back.'

Osbert eyed him narrowly. 'You're in no position to give orders. Neither you nor your hot-tempered brother will ever be earls now. And Lord Jesus be praised for that.'

'Osbert, this is no time for—'

'I surrender this burh!' Osbert shouted, pushing past him. 'In the name of Earl Rothgar, I surrender it!'

Cerdic watched in disbelief as Osbert marched across the dragon hall square, holding the sword aloft, one hand at its tip, the other at its hilt. The mob of Vikings might have rushed on him and hacked him to shreds, but there was something about his manner – the confidence, the pompousness, not to mention his affected finery – that perhaps made them think him a man of note. They circled him, blades drawn but making no attempt to attack.

'It's yours!' Osbert shouted. 'Take it, I beg you. But spare the lives of these poor Christians. I offer this token as a mark of our submission and your victory.'

Cerdic spotted the red-haired Viking emerging into the square on foot, leading his horse by its reins. But he too held back, for now, it seemed, the true master of the hunt had arrived. Another horseman appeared, one Cerdic hadn't previously seen.

He remained in the saddle, trotting slowly into the square. His mount was a magnificent grey stallion. This rider, too, was clad in gleaming ring-mail, but he also wore a full-head helm, its protective face-plates worked into the visage of a demon. A cloak made from several wolf-skins, still with various sets of paws and jaws attached, hung from his shoulders, while a silver torque with a snakehead clasp was fastened at his throat.

This could only be Wulfgar Ragnarsson, though Cerdic doubted that even King Harald the Hardraada would have decked himself so grandly. Again, the lad was reminded how

Viking armies often comprised disparate, jostling warbands, each minor chieftain with selfish ambitions of his own. This, Aethelric had always said, was the reason their empires rarely lasted.

Aethelric...

A terrible scream was lodged in his chest. He so wanted to unleash it, to let his anguish rip through the night, his hatred to break over the invaders like a wave, but for the moment at least their attention was elsewhere.

Wulfgar drew his horse up alongside Osbert. Compared to the portly steward, he was an immense figure; ripples of white-blond hair flowed from under his helmet, forked plaits of white-blond beard, stiffened with clay, jutted from his jawbone.

Osbert bowed solemnly, offering the prize weapon with both hands.

Jarl Wulfgar took it in casual fashion, turning it both ways, holding it aloft so that it shone with firelight. He paid close attention to the green gemstone set into its pommel, before nodding and grunting, and then flashing the weapon around and down, cleaving Osbert's skull in twain at a single stroke.

The rest of his dogs howled with glee and charged across the square, their eyes fixed on the final object of their assault: Wulf-bury Hall itself. Within, they'd been told, lay the plunder of their dreams: gold coins and jewels, tapestries, precious vessels, sacred icons.

Cerdic's yellow mane sprayed sweat as he crashed into the hall and threw the bar closed. When he turned and viewed the interior, it resembled any other autumn evening. Seasoned logs crackled on the hearth, the sweet smoke rising in a vertical column to the gap in the centre of the ceiling. Fresh rushes had been laid, the tables dusted, the crucks adorned with new-cut herbs; tallow lamps twinkled in the niches. Despite its many battle-standards and ancient carvings, it looked warm and welcoming. The small clutch of people cowering behind the seat of justice – Eadora, an ancient man and a young boy, and a pair of elderly sisters who worked for the earl as seamstresses – didn't detract from this.

Nor did Letwold, who was stacking benches across the room in a half-hearted effort to build a barricade.

Cerdic walked forward. 'We can't stay in here. We'll never hold it.'

A huge weight crashed against the doors.

'But won't King Harold come?' Letwold replied in a voice of restrained panic. 'Surely we won't need to hold for long?'

'Letwold, King Harold, if he's even come north at all, will have other things on his mind. Besides, if they can't get in, they'll burn it around our ears.'

'Surely not? They must *want* it, Cerdic, or they'd have burned it already.'

'Rebuilding Wulfbury may be a small price for them to pay.' Cerdic struggled to keep his voice steady; again, he *must* show leadership here, and that didn't mean mounting a futile last stand. 'What they really want is the earldom. The burh is only its symbol.'

He ushered them down the hall, out through a side-door and along a wood-panelled corridor leading between his father's and his brother's personal chambers. From here, they took the external door by which the earl and his family normally made their way to chapel. There was a narrow cloister beyond this, and a private entrance to the chapel itself. At which point they heard raucous laughter. Red flames flickered behind the chapel's narrow, cruciform windows, doubtless fuelled by Aethelric's collection of beautifully scripted prayer books.

Cerdic stopped dead.

'Why are we going to the chapel anyway?' Letwold whispered. 'There's nothing for us there.'

Silently, Cerdic agreed. The documents Aethelric had charged him to recover were lost already or would remain hidden. Either way, there was nothing to be done.

'This way.' He turned right.

Another passage led between the main hall and the kitchen. It was so narrow they could only travel in single file. At its end, they rounded a corner into a maze of animal pens and storage sheds. It was dark here, but always the sounds of pillage assailed them. The old man, the boy and the two sisters were soon separated from Cerdic and his band. Cerdic himself wasn't sure which way was which – this part of the burh was the domain of thralls – though he knew that if he kept pushing north toward the vast ridge of hillside called the Devil's Brow, they would find the perimeter and escape to the uplands. But now they had another problem, because on turning the first corner, they saw the moving glow of torches just ahead.

More harsh voices sounded, along with smashes and bangs as new doorways were kicked in. They doubled back, turning another corner, Cerdic drawing the other two at speed across a quilt-work of vegetable allotments, and into a shed smelling of soil and filled with hoes, spades and other tools.

'They're searching the entire burh,' he said, breathless. 'Working out what they've got.'

'Plus, they're probably looking for *you*,' Letwold said, his face a pale orb glimmering with sweat.

'Yes. Anyway, it's plain we can't just walk out of here. We need to hide. Until they're either asleep or so drunk on victory they don't know what's happening.'

'But that could be hours.'

Cerdic nodded. 'I know.'

Eadora indicated the flimsiness of the shed. Firelight shone in through its multiple chinks and fissures. 'This won't protect us for long.'

'I have a plan,' Cerdic said, 'but it may be a tight squeeze.'

Letwold shrugged, bug-eyed. 'For God's sake, we're all ears.'

'Do you remember when we were young boys? And that loose plank we removed from the base of the wall at the back of the barracks whorehouse? We slid through it, so we could lie underneath the floorboards and watch the women.'

Under normal circumstances, it might have been embarrassing to admit such a thing in front of a female, even a female of ceorlish stock, but none of them were concerned at present about boyhood puerility.

'We were youngsters,' Letwold said. 'Could we even fit in that crawlspace now? All three of us?'

Cerdic looked unsure. 'We need to try. It's the best place I can think of. No one even knows that space is there. If we kick that plank back into place behind us, we can hole up there until the early hours. These bastards will never know.'

Letwold gave it brief thought. 'And in the early hours?'

'If they've finished feasting, or rather *when* they have, we come out. And we get right away from this place. As far as we can.'

Letwold nodded. 'It may work. I suppose it's all we've got.'

Cerdic glanced at Eadora. 'It'll be dirty, I'm afraid. There'll be rats, beetles.'

'You think that's a problem for me after what I've seen tonight, my lord?' she replied.

Cerdic nodded. 'Then we're agreed.' He pressed his ear to the ill-fitting shed door. It had quietened down outside. He opened the door by an inch or so.

No immediate movement was visible. Beyond the vegetable patches, a passage led behind the armoury, which doubtless now would be empty and of no interest to the intruders. Ultimately, it led back toward the dragon hall, but there was a left turn before then, which would bring them to the rear of the barracks whorehouse, and the point where the loose plank was located.

'If the women haven't been taken out by now, I imagine they very soon will be,' Cerdic said quietly. 'We need to be wary as we approach. Keep our ears pinned back.'

The other two nodded, saying nothing. They set off like a group of mice, quiet, huddled together as they crossed the allotments again… only for a pall of orange firelight to come swirling down the passage ahead.

Cerdic slithered to a halt, Letwold and Eadora crashing into him.

'Back!' he hissed. 'Back!'

But already two Northmen had sauntered into view, one on a horse, harnessed in a coat of leather rather than ring-mail, the other on foot carrying a firebrand and a sack over his back that clanked, no doubt already stuffed with looted items. The horseman reined up, the footman halting beside him. They gazed at the youngsters with surprise, though leering grins soon split their bearded faces. The horseman kicked his steed to life and galloped forward.

'Run!' Cerdic shouted. He turned, pushing his two friends as hard as he could.

More by instinct than design, he then swung back, at the same time grabbing a shovel that stood upright in the soil.

As the horseman rode past in pursuit of Eadora, Cerdic spun in a circle, wielding the implement two-handed, striking the beast's forelegs. With shrieks of shock and pain, it stumbled and bucked its rider forward, throwing him clean over its head, so that he landed face-first in the dirt.

His friends already out of sight, Cerdic twirled to face the other Northman, only for a gauntleted fist to smash into his left eyebrow, bursting it like a piece of ripe fruit. The lad staggered backward, wafting his makeshift weapon. With a single blow of his seax, the footman sent it spinning away. Cerdic was left wide open, dazed and unarmoured. But instead of lunging with his blade, the footman grabbed him by his front collar and threw his helmeted head forward. Pain exploded in Cerdic's other eyebrow, and the next thing he was down on one knee, his vision filled with blood. A third blow landed, this time from the pommel of the footman's seax. It struck Cerdic's right temple and felled him flat.

As he lay in a stupor, all he could blurrily see was a dark shape standing over him. Another joined it, and another. They spoke together in Norse, and laughed.

CHAPTER 13

'You have cost me money, *vargrkind*... and that makes me unhappy.'

Cerdic looked up from where he sat chained against the thick timber post supporting the stable roof. In the filth and the stink and the darkness, he hadn't noticed that any of his captors had come in. On top of that, though it was now the early hours, the victory celebration in the dragon hall was still ongoing: the shrieks of women, the wild, harsh laughter, the banging of fists and axe-hafts on table tops as thralls raced around with kegs of beer and mead. It had drowned out all other sounds, but now that he blinked the sticky blood from his eyes, he saw an upright slat of firelight where the stable door had been partially opened.

The silhouette of a hefty man stood there, half-blocking it. Further glints of firelight added reddish tints to his unruly locks, revealing that it was Sigfurth Blood-Hair, though it wasn't the jarl's sidekick who had spoken this time. As Cerdic's eyes adjusted to the lesser dimness, he became aware that another had entered the stable too and now stood much closer to him; an even more massive figure, taller than most men, broad as an ox, his upper body naked and well-muscled, his white-blond hair hanging in long battle-braids, his beard forked. Unlike the martial finery he'd donned on first entering Wulfbury, the only clothing adorning Wulfgar Ragnarsson now were shaggy sheepskin breeches, boots with steel caps, the silver serpent-headed torque at his throat, and a sword-belt, in the scabbard of which Cerdic recognised Usurper's emerald pommel.

'You're a Northman,' the lad replied. 'Which usually means it wasn't your money in the first place.'

Ragnarsson chuckled. 'Spoken like a true son of nobility. *Your* thefts don't count.'

If anything, his command of the English tongue was even better than his underling's, his accent less noticeable. Cerdic was puzzled by that, but determined to remain defiant.

'I'm not the one standing on stolen ground,' he said.

'You think so?'

'I know so, brigand.'

'You have a fast tongue for a petty *vargrkind*.'

Cerdic didn't know what that meant, so he said nothing.

Ragnarsson flexed his huge left hand; it was clustered with jewelled rings, but on the middle finger Cerdic saw the Aelfricsson family ring that had only recently been stowed in his pouch. 'Your mistake was revealing to us that you are the earl's son.'

'Let me guess, because that means you have to kill me?'

The Viking chuckled again. 'I would have killed you anyway. You have nothing to buy your life with. I already hold your father's treasure. Eight chests, taken from under the floorboards in his private rooms. Even if I hadn't, all men offering resistance must be reckoned with. Especially you, who stood yourself above the others. That is not just my people's way. It is your people's, too.'

'That isn't true,' Cerdic retorted. 'Not since England became a Christian land.'

'Hah! Say you so? What is it your White Christ preaches? An eye for an eye?'

'He didn't say that.'

'It is written in your holy book, is it not?'

'Jesus was different. He said we should love our enemies…'

Blood-Hair snorted with laughter.

'Your father did not heed that message.' Ragnarsson sounded as if he was enjoying the conversation. 'He and his men fought hard. Sent many of us to Valhalla.'

Cerdic tried to sit up, but the manacles binding his hands behind the timber post were inflexible. 'Where is my father? Did he survive?'

Ragnarsson shrugged. 'Many died. The men wearing boars' heads on their shields and battle-coats fell in large numbers.'

Cerdic refused to consider the possibility. 'Do you have a prisoner called Unferth?'

'We took no prisoners.'

Even after what now felt like hours of horror, pain and grief, Cerdic was confused. 'But... aren't you here for booty or tribute?'

'We have what we are here for. And we had to move quickly to claim it. Why weigh ourselves down with men in shackles?'

Again, Cerdic tried to get a grip on his emotions, to think clearly. They had already emptied these stables, sharing the horses between them, but as he'd also seen, they'd acquired mounts earlier from fallen opponents. Even then though, they'd covered the fifty miles between York and Swaledale at great speed. That in itself showed a real determination to occupy Wulfbury before anyone else.

'You say this earldom was stolen from you?' Cerdic said.

'Does my name not mean anything?' his captor wondered.

'Wulfgar Ragnarsson... you are descended from Ragnar Lodbrok and his sons?'

He sensed the Viking smile in the half-darkness.

'Who were thieves and murderers,' Cerdic added, 'just like you.'

Ragnarsson smiled on, ignoring the insult. 'Descended from the Uí Ímair dynasty was my esteemed ancestor, Wulfric Eric-sson. One century ago, he was lawfully declared Hold of these lands by Eric Bloodaxe, who was King of Northumbria, this title to be passed in perpetuity to his descendants.'

Cerdic shook his head. 'There are no kings in Northumbria now. And Bloodaxe is long dead. Any promises he made died with him.'

Ragnarsson pondered that briefly. 'No matter. We hold this place now by force of arms. And that is how we will keep it.'

'For how long? Because King Harold will come here. Not your Harald Sigurdsson, our Harold Godwinson. And he will take it back, also by force of arms, and he will restore it to its rightful owners.'

Over by the door, Blood-Hair chuckled to himself. Ragnarsson glanced round at him, smiling, turning his body so that Cerdic saw the front of his right shoulder; it was marked by a single black tattoo, what looked like a wolf-headed staff crossed by a hammer.

'Alas that you put such faith in such undeserving men,' the Viking jarl said.

'Undeserving? And what of you? Your ancestor, you say, was Wulfric Ericsson. Yet you call yourself Ragnarsson. Which is it, my lord? Did you invent a connection to Ragnar and his sons? Did you give yourself a name of great renown that you'd never earned? Maybe to attract more freebooters to your banner?'

Even in the dimness, Cerdic saw the Viking's lip curl. White teeth glinted.

'And then you came to England in the guise of serving the Hardraada,' the lad said. 'Was that the only way to be safe? To come as part of a larger force, under the flag of a great commander? Whom now you have abandoned. How will that read in the annals of your people?'

In leisurely fashion, Ragnarsson kicked him in the face. His boot was made of thick, tool-worked leather, but the toe of course was steel, so the blow was heavy and brutal. With a stinging *crack*, Cerdic's nose broke, blood surging into and over his mouth. He slumped against the post, stunned.

'As I say, *vargrkind*, you are a special case.' The jarl spoke quietly but intently. 'Intelligent, for certain. Rather *too* intelligent. But it matters not. Your people must understand that a new lord governs these lands. That the old one is vanquished. As such, one month and one week from now, on the first night of *Vetrnætr*, our sacred feast of winter, I will summon all your people to the village below. And they will watch as we honour the Allfather with your blood.'

Then he turned and left the stable.

Blood-Hair ambled forward. 'The Blood-Eagle sacrifice, *vargrkind*. You know of this?'

Cerdic struggled to breathe, but at the same time was determined not to show fear or even discomfort. 'Yes.'

'It is a great honour.'

'If you say so.'

'But it never ends quickly.'

'Maybe. But it will likely be the only thing your master ever has in common with Ragnar and his sons. Did he fool you too with his lie?'

'One month, *vargrkind*.' Blood-Hair walked from the stable. 'And one week.'

The lad sagged down, head on chest, body shuddering. He could have shouted further insults, calling more doubt on Jarl Wulfgar's lineage, but what purpose would it serve? He'd read about the Blood-Eagle. Two hundred years ago, Ragnar's sons had inflicted it on King Aella of Northumbria. There were other stories from other times that mentioned its use. An abbot had died that way, he thought. Perhaps the abbot of Iona. Incredibly, it wasn't untrue that it was supposed to be an honour, because only men of rank were given such a death. A king, an abbot, and now the son of an earl. He still had a month and a week to wait, of course.

A whole month in this foul confinement, which would get colder and damper as the autumn worsened. But a month was still a month, and anything could happen in that time. Harold Godwinson might arrive, though Ranald the thegn hadn't held out great hope. Even if the king did come, with the northern army destroyed he'd have to defeat the Hardraada first, on his own, and if he managed that, how would he know that this earldom had fallen? Swaledale was far to the north of York.

More shudders racked Cerdic's body. He turned sideways and retched, what little sustenance was still inside him gushing out in a rancid, bloody stream.

He tugged at his manacles. The steel cuffs clasping his wrists had been screwed into place, so tightly they almost stopped the blood in his hands. There was no way he could loosen them on his own. His spirits flagged even further. He breathed slow and heavy, tasting more blood as he pondered the living nightmare of the Odinist sacrifice.

The splaying out of a naked prisoner face-down on a sacrificial block. The slicing of flesh and muscle down the length of his spine by use of a sharp blade. The peeling back of said flesh, and then the introduction of a serrated blade as, one by one, his ribs were sawn from his backbone. The wrenching open of his entire ribcage. The drawing out of his lungs and their arrangement over his shoulders like the wings of an eagle. And if the sacrificial priest and his assistants were skilled enough, those lungs would continue to inflate and deflate as the prisoner's semblance of half-life went on. At which point, he'd be hung up, most likely by his hands, garlanded with greenery, and left there to linger for the greater glory of the Allfather.

The horror of it flooded his mind. He grimaced in mental torment, twisted and turned in his bonds, the gore crusting his hair and face cracking open.

He could pray for a quick death, he supposed, an extinction of life the moment the first knife was inserted. But who could he request that from? The saints themselves had mostly suffered gruesome martyrdoms. Though it would be inflating his own importance hugely to consider this a martyrdom.

To start with, it wasn't as if he didn't deserve such a fate.

For all his conversations with his father and Aethelric about how best to manage a crisis situation, the moment the enemy had appeared he'd reverted to threats and defiance. That was the way a warrior would respond, he'd told himself. Draw steel, issue a fearless challenge. But that had been instinct talking, not intellect. He'd thought *his* battle had finally come, and that already, immediately even, he'd been on the front foot. But what had he been in truth? A little dog barking at a wolf, a boy waving a stick at a bear. He *could* have negotiated, as Aethelric suggested, tried to offer them a payment. Even his father had mentioned that sometimes sacrifices were necessary. Who knew whether they'd have gone along with that and refrained from using violence to try and avoid losing men. Either way, it would have been more sensible than waving that stick, than goading them simply for the sense of strength it gave him.

In the end, of course, they'd barely lost anyone because offering stout resistance had been no more than a bluff on Cerdic's part. Which only underlined his folly, and made its consequences all the more painful.

'Aethelric…' He leaned back against the rough wood, eyes blurred, unseeing. His mentor and tutor, his friend… still lying out there, broken and impaled. 'Forgive me… please.'

Even Brithnoth, that harmless old fellow with his muddled ideas, might have evaded his awful death had the stand-in earl actually readied them for a Viking attack instead of paying lip service to such, had he been at his post and not mooning after Eadora on some fruitless quest to improve his personal standing.

Somewhere inside, a small, sad voice told him that his predicament had been unprecedented, a surreal nightmare for which no one could have prepared. But if that was the truth, his own actions, his own arrogant bravado, had only made things worse.

Cerdic's bones now trembled. 'Sweet Jesus. Spare me a pointless death. I'm not a coward, but if I must die, let it be in the course of making up in some way for these errors—'

There was a sudden grunt outside. A heavy, chesty noise, cut off abruptly. He glanced toward the stable door, which still stood ajar. As he did, a shadow flickered past it. Then a hand appeared, curved around the edge of the timber, pushing it open slowly. The hinge squealed long and loud, though no one would hear it thanks to the din from the dragon hall.

Cerdic watched intently. Maybe this was it. Maybe they'd decided to kill him now.

He prayed they had.

A figure appeared.

Another Northman; that much was plain from the gleam of firelight on his ring-mail. But it was neither of the previous two, for his build was different.

Even so, Cerdic was bemused.

The fellow came forward at a slow, heavy trudge. He carried a spear in one hand, the butt end of which he lugged through the dirt behind him. Presumably this was a guard. When he was five yards away, he stopped, his face indiscernible in the gloom. And swayed. Cerdic watched, even more puzzled.

And then the guard fell, full-length onto his side. He jerked once, before rolling onto his face and lying still. Only then did Cerdic spy the cruciform hilt of a dagger protruding from his upper back, just above the collar of his ring-coat.

He jerked upright as much as he was able to, hope surging. As he did, two other figures appeared in the doorway. They were mere silhouettes, but he could tell from their shapes that they were male and female, and also that they were young.

'Cerdic!' a voice hissed. 'Cerdic?'

'Letwold!' he almost shouted.

The two figures scampered forward. He knew before they'd reached him that the female was Eadora.

'How?' he stammered. 'How is this possible?'

'We hid where you told us to,' Eadora said.

'Under the whorehouse floor?' Cerdic replied. 'I can't believe that worked.'

'It was perfect,' she said. 'They'd already taken all the women into the hall.'

They lapsed into brief silence, listening to the screams of pain and terror from the dragon hall, and the roars of wild, heartless laughter.

'These men are goblins, Lord Cerdic,' she said with feeling. '*Devils!*'

'Yes, and those poor women are now in Hell,' Letwold said querulously. 'It's all terribly sad. But in the meantime, we have to get Cerdic free before their man is missed.'

'Yes, yes,' Cerdic urged them. 'Get me free...'

Eadora moved to the stable door to watch while Letwold squatted behind his friend's back, though after several seconds of fiddling about with the steel fetters, it became apparent that releasing the captive wouldn't be so easy. He yanked at the chain, but it was useless; attempted to twist and turn the heavy post, but it was solidly buried in the hardpacked earth.

'Damn it.' Letwold stood and moved back to the front. He rubbed his jaw. 'I can't...' His tone had turned flat, almost fatalistic. 'Cerdic, I *can't*. Those clasps are screwed onto your wrists. I can't open them.'

'What about tools?' Eadora said from the doorway.

No one responded, because all of them knew the nearest smithy was down in the village. And while getting out of the burh undetected would be a huge challenge on its own, getting back into it again would be near-impossible.

Cerdic gazed up at Letwold, incredulous that even now he might not be saved. But then, Letwold and Eadora were also in peril here. Horrendous peril, which only deepened as they dallied.

And then a new thought struck Cerdic, out of nowhere.

'Just before Father set off for York,' he said, 'Redwald's horse was in here. It had partly thrown a shoe. The grooms finally managed to get it loose with a pair of iron pincers. Those pincers could still be around...'

'Cerdic, I'm sorry...' Letwold sounded defeated. 'It's pitch-dark in here and we can't risk lighting a torch. It might be better if we go to get help.'

'From where?'

'I don't know. Anywhere...'

137

'Letwold,' Cerdic spoke quietly but firmly. 'You *have* to get me out of here. And you have to do it *now*. Because if you don't, they are going to sacrifice me to their heathen gods.'

Eadora swung from the doorway, shocked. Letwold, who'd been stepping from foot to foot, went stiff.

'Yes.' Cerdic nodded. 'You'd think they'd be better served selling me and adding to their coin. But instead they are going to carve an eagle on my back and rip out my lungs. Not today, and not tomorrow. But soon enough. You go away from here now, for any reason, and you and I both know you won't be coming back.'

'I...' Letwold was lost for words, but Eadora came forward, brushing past him.

'Hurry,' she said. 'If those pincers are in here, we'll find them.'

Cerdic waited nervously. The pincers might not be here. And it was true, it was very dark. But at least someone was looking.

Torturous minutes passed as he sat against the post, his two friends searching through the blackness behind him, rooting with their bare hands amid heaps of stinking, manure-filled straw, or scrabbling along rugged shelves, no doubt picking up cuts and splinters. Then, somewhere out in the night, they heard a gruff male voice. It sounded as though it was calling the name 'Ketil'.

Letwold and Eadora froze. Cerdic did, too, his attention fixed on the lifeless shape lying a couple of feet away.

'Ketil?' the voice called again.

'God's bowels,' Letwold breathed.

'Quiet,' Cerdic hissed.

He watched the doorway, at any moment expecting the appearance of another dark, hulking shape. But that didn't happen. The voice didn't call out again even though several more minutes passed.

Behind him, Cerdic heard his friends stirring back to life.

'This is hopeless,' Letwold whispered.

'We haven't looked everywhere yet,' Eadora replied.

'But I can't see my hand in front of my face.'

'Wait, wait,' she said. 'I've found them, I've found them…
they were hanging from a nail.'

Cerdic craned his neck around to look. The girl was already
on her knees behind him, a pair of hefty iron pincers in her
hand. Letwold knelt alongside her to help, though even then it
wasn't easy. Initially, they pinched Cerdic's flesh.

'Christ!' he hissed through gritted teeth.

'I'm sorry, Lord,' she said. 'I can't see properly.'

When they finally made contact with the screw clamping
the steel to his left wrist, it required much twisting, turning,
grunting, sweating and side-to-side waggling of the pincers
before it finally came loose.

'Thank God,' Cerdic said, yanking his left hand free, jumping
to his feet and promptly going dizzy, his legs bloodless underneath him.

Eadora caught hold of him as he stumbled. As he righted
himself, she broke away and brought the pincers to his right
wrist. Now in the firelight from the open doorway, they were
able to loosen this one more easily.

'Can we go?' Letwold said in a pleading voice.

Cerdic met him eye to eye. 'You were going to go without
me.'

Letwold shook his head. 'I didn't *want* to.'

'But you would have if Eadora hadn't intervened.'

'There'll be time for squabbling later, my lords,' the girl said.
She moved back to the door, glancing outside. 'The way's clear.
We should go now while we can.'

'I came for you, didn't I?' Letwold said. 'Would you have
done that for me?'

'Would *I* have?' Cerdic thumped his friend's chest. 'I only
got caught because I was looking out for you!'

'I… I…' Letwold averted his gaze downward.

In daylight, he'd have been red-faced with shame. He couldn't deny that his courage had briefly failed him. Briefly, yes, but also near disastrously. Cerdic wanted to berate him further, to shout and bellow... but then his own performance of late had hardly been creditable, and if Cerdic himself could hide, or try to, behind the terrifying uniqueness of this day, then so could Letwold.

'My lords...' Eadora moaned. 'We must go *now.*'

Cerdic nodded, stepping to the door alongside her. 'What weapons do we have?'

'None,' Letwold muttered.

'Wait.' Cerdic scooted back inside, dropping to his knees alongside the Viking corpse. He yanked the dagger loose, wiping it clean on the dead man's hair, before searching the rest of the body. He found a hand-axe, which he slid into his own belt, and then stood up, handing the dagger to Eadora and the spear to Letwold. 'Time to show your father you're the warrior son he doesn't yet realise he has, yes?'

'Yes.' Letwold snatched it off him determinedly.

They went back to the door together, looking left and right. With no one in sight, they took another alley running beside a pigsty, then a passage between a grain-house and the burh buttery. The palisade was somewhere ahead of them. All they needed to do was climb up it and drop down the other side, and they were free. Even as Cerdic considered this, there came a fierce, angry shout from somewhere to their rear.

They stopped dead. More shouts replied to it, and more. And suddenly the entire burh was in hubbub.

'Keep moving,' Cerdic said. 'We're almost out of here. They won't know which way we've gone.'

But as they turned the next corner and sighted the palisade about twenty yards ahead, a light appeared on its gantry. They slid to another halt, one of them kicking a metal pail, which clattered away. The torch-carrying sentry, who was tall and helmeted, spun in their direction. And laughed aloud, before calling out to his compatriots and climbing down the nearest ladder.

'Not again,' Eadora said, sounding as though she was about to weep.

The sentry came along the passage toward them. With a rasp of steel, he pulled a sword from his hip. Cerdic felt for the hand-axe, but this fellow was already the size of a bear, and grew larger still as he approached.

'You two find another way,' Letwold said, pushing in front. 'I'll take care of this.'

'Letwold!' Cerdic tried to grab him, but Eadora clung to his waist, halting him.

'It's not just Father I've got to prove myself to, Cerdic!' Letwold said over his shoulder. '*I* need to know as well.'

'You damn fool! There's a time and place—'

'And this is it.' Lowering his spear to the level, Letwold advanced. 'Go while you can. Let me buy time for you.'

And he broke into a run, dashing the last ten yards and meeting his opponent head-on. In the twirling torchlight it was difficult to see, but almost immediately Cerdic heard fierce blows and gasps of shock and pain. The leaner shape of Letwold was already being flung from wall to wall.

'Letwold!' he cried again.

He strove forward, but Eadora clung to him, hauling him to his knees.

Letwold screeched like a panicked animal as the Viking took his hair and rammed his head into the rock wall on his left, the hollow impacts sounding again and again. When the lad slumped to the ground, the tall shadow of his assailant kicked and stamped at his face.

'*Letwold!*' Cerdic shrugged Eadora off and was about to lurch forward when the Viking, who had now snatched Letwold's spear, thrust it downward, leaning on it with all his weight. Letwold gave a single, piercing scream. The assailant then struck with his sword, massive two-handed strokes, one butchering blow following another.

'Letwold…' Cerdic choked.

'Lord Cerdic!' Eadora pleaded. 'Please… don't make his death pointless.' She tugged at his arm. In agony, he allowed her to take him, coarse laughter booming after them.

They headed back the way they had come, but saw more torches ahead and heard vicious shouts.

'Can we climb?' Eadora said.

They were alongside another storage house, and one of its shutters was loose. Cerdic nodded dully, making a stirrup of his hands, so that she could ascend. Seconds later, he'd scrambled up with her. They scaled the thatched roof on all fours, lying flat as heavy bodies passed below. They lay still for several seconds, drenched with sweat, lungs heaving. When they were sure it was clear, they crawled up to the apex and ran along it, keeping low. At the end, there was a short gap before the next building. They leapt it easily, the hot blood of terror reducing their fatigue so that they teetered along several more such roofs, each time jumping gaps below which torch-bearing Northmen rowdily passed.

The last jump would be the hardest, for it was to the palisade gantry. It was further than the others, almost six feet, so they backtracked to the middle of the roof. Eadora tied her skirts at her hip, as she'd used to when climbing for apples. Then, one after another, they ran forward, hurling themselves into space. In both cases the collision was heavy. Cerdic skinned his knees and cracked his injured forehead on the upright logs. Eadora barked her shins on the edge of the gantry itself. Yet they gave neither yelp nor whimper, for now they were beyond pain. Cerdic leaned over the palisade parapet, held Eadora by the hands, and at full stretch released her. She dropped the remaining seven feet with comparative ease. Before he went over himself, he glanced back into the burh. He could see little, but still heard bass shouts and wild laughter.

In truth, he was dizzied by the turn of events; he almost felt drunk. It was difficult to comprehend that only eight days ago they'd been celebrating Harvest Ales, with its fun and frolics. It was inconceivable that in so short a time the sun-dappled world of song and celebration had vanished into this nightmare.

From somewhere nearby, in an adjoining passage, a Viking voice sounded: '*Vargrkind!* Where are you, *vargrkind*?'

With new urgency, Cerdic vaulted over the parapet.

CHAPTER 14

'*Letwold*,' Cerdic mumbled, as they clambered northward through the rocks and thistles. He moved stiffly, sluggishly, but his hair prickled as full awareness of recent events seeped back to him, slowly filling his thoughts. 'I was... was only vexed with him for a moment. But I shouldn't have mentioned his father. I thought it would fire him, but instead it... it goaded him to—'

'He died doing his duty!' Eadora hissed, grabbing him by the tunic.

'His duty?' Cerdic was nonplussed.

'Defending his lord,' she said.

'But, but I never asked—'

'Why would you ask?' She shook her head, baffled that he didn't seem to understand.

He *did* understand, of course, but until this moment, the meaning of laying down one's life out of obligation had been nothing but barrack-room talk. His thoughts now hung on it with a new, terrible clarity. In the meantime, Eadora had stepped back and was pointing upward with a shaking finger. Cerdic looked up too, and went cold. Blazing specks of light were dotted along the precipice at the top of the Devil's Brow. Norse voices echoed down.

'They've circled up onto the high ground?' he said, incredulous. 'How? They must have camped extra men up there. There are even more of them than I thought.'

'My lord, we just need to get away from here,' Eadora replied. Her own resolve was cracking. She sounded tearful, frantic.

Just beyond the slopes of scree now facing them, a gully ran straight up the Brow's rock face like a chimney. Neither had relished climbing it in the moonlight, though Cerdic had felt it was the quickest route up to the higher moors. But this door was obviously closed as more and more lights appeared on the Brow itself.

'Believe it or not,' he said, 'this could be... useful to us. Maybe even a good thing. Jarl Wulfgar must have weakened the Hardraada's army by bringing so many men here before the war is fully won.' Cerdic's thoughts were finally piecing themselves together again. The shock of the last few hours, Letwold's death in particular, was receding in the face of necessity. Surviving this horrific event was all that mattered at present, and that meant assessing and evaluating it as his father would have done. 'Even though King Harold wasn't at Fulford, he'll have to engage them soon,' Cerdic said, 'and maybe it'll now be easier for him.'

'Does that matter?' Eadora said. 'We obviously have to go another way.'

Cerdic didn't hear. The thought of the larger game at play was almost comforting; Wulfbury was lost, but it might not have been lost in vain if the Norse horde was still defeated. Perhaps Letwold hadn't died in vain either. Eadora was correct; it could and should be written that he'd died doing right, a hero who was part of a bigger war. Though this brought no immediate comfort. The torturous truth was that Letwold had only behaved so recklessly because his best friend had provoked it from him. Unintentionally, but perhaps Cerdic's hardest lesson of all today was that some mistakes had bitter consequences indeed.

Eadora, meanwhile, was heading back downhill. The burh lay far below; it was partly obscured by rocks and treetops, but enough was still visible to show the compound filled with torches moving up and down its narrow ways. Despite this ominous sight, Eadora stumbled downward toward it, drunk with tiredness. Cerdic caught her elbow and veered her to the right. He too was feeling his hurts: sprains, twists, his split and swollen brows, his fractured nose through which he could still barely breathe. Their sweat-soaked clothes clung like second skins. It would be easy to surrender to sheer exhaustion, but Cerdic had no intention of doing that, or allowing Eadora to.

He pushed her down onto the steep pasture on Wulfbury's eastern side, which they called the Upper Meadow. A flock of sheep scattered in front of them. It wouldn't be long before these animals were rounded up; the Viking army would need to be fed. So he drove her even harder. Past this, they descended a rocky slope onto a broad ledge. This led several yards to an overhanging limestone scarp, below which spring-water gushed into a chasm. A sheer cliff covered in moss and hanging vegetation blocked any access to the other side, but Cerdic had spent his childhood romping on these fells and knew them very well. Taking a grip on a root, he swung his body beneath the cataract and was able to insinuate himself into a near vertical fissure, which led down to a network of similar fissures and grikes created by earlier torrents. This was the 'Elf Stair', as he and his friends had once christened it. He beckoned Eadora to follow. There were brief moments of horror for her as she clung to the side of what felt like an abyss, but Cerdic grabbed her skirts and pulled her in. Soon they were descending through the rocky recesses in relative safety.

Sixty feet down, they reached level ground, circled around the now thundering cataract, and clambered over mossy boulders surrounding its foaming plunge pool. Again, they headed downhill, but at a much gentler gradient.

'Isn't this Brackley Beck?' Eadora asked.

'The start of it,' Cerdic replied. 'Those trees – down there to the left – that's Gonwyn's Orchard.'

She made no reply. Despite everything, the business with Unferth clearly still embarrassed her.

He was about to say that he shouldn't have mentioned it, when his foot slid down a boulder into a pool, grazing his ankle.

Cursing, he limped away from the rocky stream, pushing into the dense vegetation on its west shore.

Eadora followed. 'My lord, where are we going? We can't just blunder through the night.'

'We're not blundering,' he retorted.

He didn't explain further because, though a partial plan was forming in his mind, he was concerned that it might bring peril to friends who, thus far, may have avoided it.

Oswalda and Guthlac had been well rewarded by Earl Rothgar for nurturing his second child. Their freehold farm, a gift from their overlord, sat midway between Brackley-on-the-Water and Tollering. They grew their own crops and owned their own livestock. They also had a horse and cart by which they delivered their produce to market. That same vehicle might carry them all to safety; not just Oswalda and Guthlac, but Cerdic and Eadora too. However, there were two questions. Firstly, had the Northmen already arrived at Guthlac's stead? Secondly, if they hadn't yet but were actively searching for Cerdic, would his flight lead them straight there?

He agonised over this second question as they battled through tangled thorns, but the awful truth was that, even if the enemy hadn't yet discovered his friends' freehold, they would in due course, with or without Cerdic's assistance. It would make no difference if he opted not to go there, except that he wouldn't be able to warn them in advance, or obtain any kind of help or sustenance.

In that regard, there was no argument really. They *had* to go.

At last, they came to the valley road, where they paused and hid in a blackberry thicket. Several moments passed as they listened. The only sound was the chuckling of the river on its bed of stones, and faint wind hissing on the heathery uplands, the only light was the pale luminescence of the moon. By Cerdic's reckoning, Brackley lay two miles to the east, Guthlac's stead about a mile to the west. Beyond that, by a further two miles, was Tollering village. He had an obligation to the folk of

Tollering, of course, to warn them about the Vikings – though what good it would do he couldn't imagine. In the first instance, he had to save himself.

'Lord Cerdic?' Eadora asked in a small voice. 'I've heard you mention King Harold more than once. Do you really think he will come all the way here?'

She sounded doubtful, which was perhaps inevitable given her northern upbringing. Harold Godwinson was respected as a great warrior and capable administrator, but he'd formerly been Earl of Wessex, and was virtually an alien to those born and raised in these northern dales. Though most folk here had never seen him, let alone met him, he was likened in gossip to his brother Earl Tostig, another southern stranger, and one who had been imposed on the north and had ruled it with a cruel hand. It was difficult to know for certain that King Harold would not turn out to be another such self-interested despot. Cerdic, also northern born, had heard this talk all his life, despite his father having engineered Harold's accession. But even if the new ruler of England turned out to be monstrous, things could always be worse. Cerdic hoped and prayed that when a king finally came to Swaledale, it would be King Harold Godwinson of England, not King Harald Hardraada of Norway.

'I'm sure he'll help us,' he said. 'Whether he's a good man or not, he won't want some Viking bandit setting up a private kingdom in the middle of his realm.'

They set off along the road, keeping to the verge, though soon the trees and undergrowth ran out and they were passing between water meadows. Cattle grazed in small enclosures. Fish traps were set along the river, none of which had been interfered with. This was encouraging. The farmstead at last hove into view, its steeply pitched sod roof coming almost to the ground. Light was visible through its gable-end window, smoke spiralling from its rock chimney. The dales folk rose early when there was work to do.

Cerdic broke into a run. After the depredations he'd witnessed during the night, he knew this was too pleasant a scene to last.

Oswalda herself answered the door. She was a hefty woman in late middle age, at present wearing a nightgown and a shawl. Her long grey hair hung loose. Her eyes lit up as soon as she saw them, though just as quickly she took in Cerdic's brutalised face, and his and Eadora's torn, dirty clothes and sweat-sodden hair.

'My poor dears,' she cried, shooing them inside.

'You have to leave!' Cerdic stammered, wiping his bruised eyes, using his sleeve to clean the fresh blood leaking from his nose. 'We all have to! There's no time to argue! Northmen are here!'

'Northmen?' Oswalda replied, pale-faced. 'What do you mean? What's happened?' Guthlac, an old but still solid man with a head of snow-white hair and thick, white whiskers, was already in his work clothes and seated by the hearth, polishing tools. He stood up, shocked.

As the lad stuttered out the story, Eadora stood wraith-like alongside him, eyes red. The elderly couple listened in stunned silence as he related the arrival at Brackley of Ranald the thegn, the villagers' flight into the burh, Jarl Wulfgar's attack, the rape and slaughter as his warriors broke in, the capture of Cerdic, their threat to put him to the Blood-Eagle, and the youngsters' eventual escape, costly though that was in terms of Letwold's life. By the time he'd finished, Guthlac stood grey-faced, while Oswalda had been forced to sit and put one hand on her ample bosom as though to steady her heart.

'Surely they won't venture this far along the dale?' Oswalda said.

'They will,' Guthlac replied, gruff but thoughtful. 'Why in God's name wouldn't they? Sacking Wulfbury Hall won't benefit them much. Nor will the small tithe of Brackley-on-the-Water. They'll want the entire dale, if not the entire earldom.'

'Their leader told me that himself,' Cerdic said. 'They're here to stay.'

Guthlac turned to his wife. 'I'll get the cart. Ready some food, and be swift.'

But no sooner had Oswalda taken two sacks from the wall than hoofbeats sounded outside. Guttural cries followed, and shouts of harsh laughter.

'God save us,' Oswalda breathed.

'Quickly!' Guthlac moved to a corner of the room. 'You two, over here.' Throwing aside a rush-mat, he revealed a trap-door. 'Down to the undercroft. Stay there and keep quiet. I may be able to persuade them you haven't been this way.'

'Uncle Guthlac,' Cerdic pleaded, 'these are real Vikings. They won't listen.'

'We've no choice, lad. They don't just want to make an example of you to cow peasant folk like us. It goes further than that. If Rothgar died in the battle, these lands are already theirs. Possession is all of the law. But they'll need to make that good with whichever king takes control, and if you still live as Rothgar's son that's a challenge they can't ignore.'

Cerdic nodded, swallowing his fear. He lowered Eadora through the trap first, and was about to jump down himself. Then he remembered something. 'Uncle Guthlac... what does *vargrkind* mean?'

Guthlac shrugged, puzzled. 'It's an old Norse word. Out of use in this country now. It means wolf-cub. But *vargr* means "bad wolf", a destructive wolf. One that *must* be killed.'

Cerdic nodded, having guessed something similar, though it was no consolation. He made to climb down, but now Guthlac grabbed his shoulder.

The old man looked hard into the youngster's eyes. 'Whatever happens up here, whatever you hear... you stay hidden, understand?'

Cerdic nodded dumbly.

Guthlac regarded him closely, the gaze bright in his leathery face. 'Flight, not fight, is the best route to survival. But you know what I always say... when you're in a battle, all that matters is emerging alive. Nothing else. So, if you *have* to fight, lad, you fight like the Devil.'

Cerdic nodded again, and swung down into the undercroft. The trapdoor lid was closed behind him, and rushes rustled as they were replaced over the top. It was dark and damp down there, with a rich, loamy smell. There were piles of turnips, carrots and apples, not to mention a mound of fleeces, which Guthlac had shorn from his small flock the previous spring and had planned to sell at the winter market. Cerdic grabbed a small one of these, tied its four corners together and stuffed fruit into it.

'What are you doing?' Eadora whispered.

He indicated a second trapdoor, this one leading out to the rear of the cottage. 'We have to go.'

'We can't leave Guthlac and Oswalda.'

'It's too late.'

As if proof were needed, there came a heavy, meaty thud overhead, a muffled scream and the sound of a body falling. The youngsters went stock-still.

The guttural tones of several Northmen could now be heard overhead. One of them was shouting: '*Vargrkind! Vargrkind!*'

Cerdic screwed his eyes shut.

'We don't know what you mean,' they heard Oswalda whimper. It sounded as though she'd fallen to her knees, probably beside her felled husband. Furniture crashed as it was kicked over.

Another Northman spoke, this time in English. Cerdic recognised the voice of Sigfurth Blood-Hair. 'They say you are the one who mothered him. You know why we believe them, Mother? We put them to the test. We twisted their limbs and washed their hands and feet with flame. So tell us... where is Aelfricsson... the *vargrkind* who defies Jarl Wulfgar?'

'We don't know,' Guthlac replied, his voice thick and slushy, as though spoken through blood and broken teeth. 'I swear on our Lord Jesus that we haven't seen him.'

'Blasphemy as well as lies,' the redhead said. 'Take the dolt outside.'

Oswalda wailed as a weight was dragged across the cottage. In the dimness below, Eadora's head dropped into her hands, tears streaming through her fingers.

'Cease your caterwaul!' the redhead said, his voice calm. There was a ringing *smack* of flesh. Oswalda yelped. 'You embarrass your god with your cowardice.'

'Where are you taking him?' she sobbed. 'He's an old man. He can't hurt you.'

'We don't fear hurt. But *you* should. Now tell me… Aelfricsson?'

Eadora reached for Cerdic's hand, but couldn't take it. His fists were clenched so tightly that his nails drew blood from his palms.

'He's not come here,' Oswalda insisted. 'He'll have run to the hills, where you and your foul tatterdemalion will not dare chase him.'

There was a pause. Then the redhead said something in his own tongue.

With another resounding *smack*, a heavy body fell.

Cerdic stood taut, but held his ground.

An eerie silence followed, finally broken by the progress of heavy feet across the cottage to its door. There was a low female groan, which rose in timbre until it became a piercing scream. Cerdic thrust the bundle of fruit into Eadora's hands, and spun around. At first she thought he was heading for the exterior trapdoor as he'd said, but instead he went to the one they'd descended through.

'Cerdic!' she hissed.

He didn't reply, but climbed the nearest pile of vegetables, drew the hand-axe and pushed the trap open with his head.

As the lid rose, the rush-mat rustled out of the way. Woodwork creaked as Cerdic hauled himself up and crouched low. But the sole Viking left inside the cottage was too preoccupied to notice.

At first, Cerdic wasn't clear what was happening. Peering across the hearth, he saw the Viking's mail-clad back as he knelt alongside a prone figure. There was another female groan, which rose to a frightful keening. The Viking turned and, using Oswalda's own metal tongs, extracted a red-hot coal from the hearth.

Cerdic rose to his feet.

What he then saw broke cold sweat on his brow.

Oswalda lay groggy, but she wasn't unconscious. Her mouth was bleeding, and she moaned again, loudly, as if sick with fever. Her assailant's dirty left hand clamped her forehead, his spread fingers holding her eyelids open as his right hand, still grasping the tongs, moved the glowing coal back and forth above her face, as though deliberating which eyeball to sear first. The brute had removed his helmet, revealing himself to be a younger fellow with a veil of greasy black hair hanging over a grin that grew progressively more demented as he prepared to do the deed. Only then did he sense the presence.

He twirled around, but it was too late.

Cerdic put everything he had into the blow, and his aim was perfect.

The axe split the Viking's cranium wide open, lodging several inches deep in the brain-matter beneath. With blood spurting down his face, the young invader's eyes rolled white, and he crumpled into a heap.

There was a disbelieving gasp.

Eadora had also climbed through the trapdoor. She scurried forward to where Cerdic stood trembling. The front of his tunic had been sprayed with a fine red mist. His face had blanched, and his teeth were clenched in a grimace. He kicked at the body twice to make sure it was dead, before retrieving the axe, for which purpose he had to place his foot on the Viking's face and yank with both hands. Even that proved difficult, the blade grating on shattered bone.

'Hel… help Oswalda,' he stuttered.

Eadora knelt at Oswalda's side, but could do little more than flick the hot coal away from her. Still insensible, Oswalda moaned and turned her head, but she wouldn't wake fully from what looked like a shock-induced stupor. Eadora glanced at the front door. It was open, and the other Northmen were surely waiting just beyond it.

'We have to leave,' she whispered. 'We can't do more for her.'

Cerdic knew she was right.

He lurched to the door. Eadora went with him, and they glanced outside together.

The cottage faced toward the river; there was fifty yards of open ground before the water's edge. Much of this had been squared off into vegetable allotments, their rich black soil already cleared of rubble and tilled in straight furrows. A central path ran between them, at the far end of which two other Vikings were visible. Like the one inside, both had relaxed and removed their war-helms. The redheaded one had his back turned, while the other was crouching over another victim.

It was Guthlac. The hoary old dales man lay face down, his head forcefully submerged in the shallows.

'Oh my God,' Eadora breathed.

Cerdic said nothing, just set off along the path with a heavy trudge, unconcerned that the sound of his boots on hardpacked earth might alert them. When he was five yards away, it did. The redhead was the first to turn, but the axe was already in motion. It hit him in the mouth with a *clunk* of metal on bone. The redhead fell sideways, striking the ground hard. Cerdic would have struck him again and again, had the second Viking, an older, paunchier fellow, not jumped up and made a wild grab for him. The lad stepped aside and, with a single backstroke, caught him across the temple, sundering it like a knife hacking cheese.

The older Viking plunged backward, his scalp flapping, and landed in the river, where, alive or dead, the current carried him for several yards before the weight of his ring-mail dragged him under.

'Cerdic!' Eadora screamed, running down the path.

He turned partly toward her, but was distracted by Guthlac, who still lay face down. His wrists were bound behind his back and his white hair rippled around his head. When Cerdic turned him over, the wise old face, which had been beaten until it was black and blue, had hardened into a rigid mask. The old eyes that had seen the passing of sixty winters and more, that had roved for so long over the green hills and rolling northern vales of this land, that had gazed fondly on Cerdic as he'd squalled and kicked and fed from Oswalda's bountiful breasts, were glazed and swollen. When Cerdic tried to open Guthlac's mouth, river water trickled out.

'I'll kill them for this,' the lad intoned. 'To take our hearth is one thing. To take the roof from over our heads, the food from our mouths… but to take… I swear, when I return I'm going to kill them *all*!'

'Yes,' Eadora agreed, 'yes, but now we must go.'

He ignored her, lowering Guthlac's head, then standing and lurching around to chop again at the prostrate shape of Sigfurth Blood-Hair, but the burly figure lay unmoving, and Eadora now grappled with him frantically, pointing back toward the road, where some distance away a dark knot of horsemen was approaching.

Hurriedly, Cerdic led her down into the river. There was no ford at this point – the only ford in several miles was at Brackley-on-the-Water – but they waded out regardless. Again, the river's level was low, but the flow was still strong. It rose past their knees, past their thighs, past their waists. The soft mud and loose stones shifted beneath their feet. Eadora hung onto Cerdic's arm, but he was equally unsteady. Soon, they were chest deep, the water fiercely cold, the current even stronger. It was all they could do not to be swept away. Both could swim, but to be washed down to the Viking-infested village would be a worse outcome than drowning. They clung together, bracing themselves. When Cerdic trod on a slippery stone and almost toppled, they shouted in unison. But at last the far shore emerged through the gloom. The water-level receded, and they floundered into the shallows.

It was swampier on the other side, and covered in marsh marigolds. Exhausted, they crawled through these on all fours, tottering to their feet when they reached firmer footing. The south bank was not cultivated at this section; its ground was damp and deep in meadowsweet. A hundred yards ahead there was a line of trees, and beyond that the rapidly steepening slope of the dale's southern flank.

'We're almost there,' Cerdic said, as they lurched forward.

Eadora nodded weakly.

He felt sudden overpowering warmth for her. Only now did it strike him how steadfast this everyday village girl had remained throughout their ordeal, showing courage when his own had flagged, urging common sense when he'd given in to wildness. He saw that she still carried the bundle of fruit, cradling it across her belly. It touched something inside him that went far deeper than simple affection. More than ever, he understood what Unferth had seen in Eadora, and he envied him for it, as well as loved him. She was so much more than a mere object of desire, than the Golden Girl of Swaledale... Then there was a *swish* of air and a *thunking* impact.

Cerdic turned. Eadora had come to a standstill and was regarding him strangely, a half-smile on her lips.

'Eadora?'

She sagged to her knees.

'Eadora!'

She fell face down.

He saw a gleam in the grass just to one side. It was a Norse throwing axe. Then he saw the dark stain spreading through the flaxen hair at the back of her neck. He dropped down next to her, groping the bloody locks aside, and for several seconds tried to deny the evidence of his own eyes as he beheld her cleanly severed nape.

'Eadora!' he laughed, taking her shoulder. She didn't respond. 'Eadora, it's not serious. Come, don't joke!'

He shook her, with increasing force. But still she didn't respond. Finally, he grabbed her up and cradled her in his arms. He kissed her milk-pale cheeks, her lovely eyes. She didn't blink. Her head lolled, a lifeless weight.

It was some small solace for Cerdic that, when he finally lowered her, the corners of her white-lipped mouth were turned upward as if she was smiling. And in truth, why shouldn't she be? Because now she was spared all this darkness, this misery, and the even worse darkness and misery that would follow.

He looked back to the far side of the river. Sigfurth Blood-Hair was back on his feet, watching. From this distance his expression was unreadable, but the lower half of his face was running with gore. Behind him, three Viking horsemen were drawing up. One dismounted and hurried forward, just in time to catch their wounded comrade as his legs gave way and he fell again. Quick words were spoken, and the two still mounted urged their steeds into the water. Immediately they ran into difficulty. The more forceful the current, the more their horses became frightened. The riders were soon compelled to dismount, only to find themselves in trouble with their heavy mail.

Cerdic continued to stare across the river, his eyes locking with those of the redhead, who was lying on the grass but still facing him. The two horsemen bypassed the river's mid-point and, with much shouting and spluttering, were finally closing on the south bank. Cerdic wanted to say a prayer, but found it difficult to assail Heaven when Heaven had turned its back. Instead, he brushed at Eadora's eyes with his fingers, closing their lids. He kissed her again, this time on the forehead, and laid her in the meadowsweet.

He glanced again, one more time, at the wounded Blood-Hair.

'You call me a bad wolf,' the lad shouted. 'You don't know the half of it. Tell your jarl I'm coming after him. This, I swear! Him! You! *All of you!*'

Then he grabbed the bundle of fruit and ran for the treeline.

PART TWO

LIKE THE DEVIL

CHAPTER 15

The wind over the British Isles changed. The warm, gentle airflow from the west abruptly halted, replaced by a cooler turbulence from the east. Though the greater population of the land barely noticed, the new breeze also filled the sails of all those craft whose planned cross-Channel excursions had been delayed for so long, and as such would soon prove a harbinger of the most terrible darkness the kingdom of England had faced at any time during the one hundred and thirty-nine years of its existence.

It also, finally, brought the autumn.

At first it was merely fresher, damper, greyer. But then it became cold, with a promise of worse to follow. In the first instance, particularly over the hills and valleys of the north, when the chill spread to the warm rocks and the high, sun-dried moorlands, it created mist.

And in the mist, everyone knew, there were *things*.

–

Cerdic was immersed in the mist, though it only partly concealed the hellish landscape around him, a landscape now alive with wolves; the dirge of their howls a cacophony of screaming demons. Worse still, when he glimpsed them through blood-red vapour, they weren't wolves of the natural sort, but upright hybrids, twisted and two-legged, with jutting snouts and ears erect. Fenrir's children, drooling and spattered with gore as they loped about amid fog and fire. One had a cloven throat and gullet, another a gash across its mouth, which split it to the back of its skull. Yet they lived and snarled and slashed at each other, and picked with raking claws over the corpses of men and women strewn so thick there was no ground, gibbering at a moon that burned crimson in a sky the colour of ash...

Cerdic's eyes snapped wide open. He was cold and stiff, and lying at an awkward angle amid sharp-edged rocks and damp, grassy hummocks. Some twenty yards away, on slightly lower ground, there was a treeline, and in the midst of that treeline, a single wolf.

A majestic silver-grey. Watching him without blinking.

Jolted to life, Cerdic stumbled to his feet, drawing his axe from his belt.

The beast was sleek, well-fed after the long summer. Its ears stood pointed, but its ruff hadn't risen. It regarded him with curiosity, sniffing the air, before turning and rippling away between the trunks into the rags and tags of morning mist.

Cerdic stood helpless as he watched it, legs shaking, dazed by the ferocity of his nightmare, though as the memory of the previous day spilled over him again like a pail of ice-cold water, his breathing slowed. He lowered the axe, shoulders sagging, head drooping, finally slumping backward against a hefty, stone-built wall and sliding down it to the ground.

Only now did he realise how much he ached, how stiff he was, how torn and wet his clothing. He was sure he'd pissed his breeches, while vomit and bile slathered the front of his tunic and burned in the pit of his throat. He'd clearly pushed himself hard during the night, though he had very little memory of it. Half his face was numb, and when he touched it, puffy and bruised. He sneezed, and a wad of blood flew out, the fractured cartilage of his nose stinging abominably.

Belatedly, it struck him that he was leaning against a building. He got painfully back to his feet to look, and was surprised to see the old Roman fort of Cataractonium. Though nothing more now than a large, square structure, mostly tumbled down and overgrown despite its elevated position a few hundred yards from the York road, it was a noted landmark and located several miles further south than he'd come the day before, so he had indeed been pushing himself during his first night's flight, especially considering that he was on foot. He backed away from the ancient edifice, eyes searching its decayed upper parapets. He'd known about it since childhood, vaguely aware that it represented the southernmost boundary of Earl Rothgar's domain, though he and his friends had long believed it haunted, and on those few occasions they'd travelled this far south, had steered well clear. Little wonder he'd seen such horrific visions in his sleep, he told himself.

Hunger gnawing his insides, he now found himself a block of fallen masonry, sat down on it and unravelled the bundle of fruit. It was mostly apples, but they were well-tended, fresh and plump.

'Oswalda,' he moaned, the agony of what they'd done to her chewing at his heart.

He barely tasted as he ate. Hunger had hollowed him, but after a couple of pieces he spat out a mouthful of pips and pulp, and wrapped the remainder of the bundle up again. He stood. He was weak, groggy, and as for the first time in months, the air was genuinely cold, it bit him hard through his damp rags.

Then he heard a voice.

He stiffened, went even colder.

'*Vargrkind!*' It sounded far off, perhaps even was borne on the wind. But there was no mistaking it when it sounded again. '*Vargrkind!*'

Cerdic listened carefully. It had been closer the second time, though still a good distance off. He listened on, but aside from the dawn chorus, heard nothing else. He rubbed his eyes, which were gritty and sore. Though he'd slept deeply, probably through sheer exhaustion, he'd lain among stones and been tortured by feverish dreams, and so weariness still infested him. But he couldn't wait around here. Clearly, they were still looking for him.

They had to.

He'd been promised to Odin.

—

It was fifty miles from Wulfbury to York, but a straightforward journey if one followed the king's highway. Very soon, however, it occurred to him that he knew nothing of the new politics in this region. If the Northmen genuinely had routed the English at Fulford, did that mean they controlled everything now? Had York and its hinterlands fallen? The road passed through countless towns and villages before it reached the northern capital. Were they all in the hands of enemies? Had he escaped one band of murderers, only to risk falling victim to another? An added threat was still Jarl Wulfgar. Cerdic had heard his men shouting for him, presumably trying to spook him from his hiding place, so it didn't seem unlikely they'd also send mounted patrols south along the York road, looking for him.

The obvious thing was to stay off it, but that brought its own difficulties, especially as the weather had turned. Pushing south through trackless woods, first of all in heavy rain, which turned the mulch of the woodland floor to sucking mud, and then when the rain had eased, through rank mist, was a vastly more trying process than Cerdic had envisaged. It wasn't just physically challenging, it was also a matter of which direction to take. He'd hunted and hawked all around Swaledale and knew every pathway. But half a night and half a day south of there, with the hills and vales behind him, it looked and felt like a different country. Thanks to the cloud cover, he couldn't even locate the sun.

All he could do was follow his broken nose, pressing doggedly onward through an alien landscape, and all the while the question nagged at him: what was he doing?

Wulfbury was now occupied; it was highly likely that York was, too. It made no sense to go that way. Except that, whatever happened next, he knew he wouldn't survive alone. Though he'd been reliably informed that Athelbere was dead, nothing of any certainty had been said about his father or brother. Thegn Ranald had survived the battle, so they might have as well, and the only way to find the truth was to go to the battlefield himself and look.

But, without sight of the road, he did not know the way. Deciding the only solution was to avoid the road itself, but not veer too far from it, he ploughed on. But forcing his way through the brambles, thickets and tangles of undergrowth required constant exertion, all while a perfectly clear road lay so close on the right that he could see it through the trees. It was beyond frustrating. That first afternoon, exhausted again and famished, still damp from the rain and shivering with cold, he gave in to temptation, drifting back toward the highway. Yet he hadn't even emerged from the road's boundary treeline when he heard the muffled thuds of approaching hooves, the jingle of harness, the clink of mail.

Diving down, he rolled in the wadded refuse of the woodland floor, covering himself over, and when he heard the voices, lay very still. For half a hopeful second, he thought they were English; his heart leapt at the possibility the tide of the war had turned and the soldiery of Swaledale were heading home, maybe with his father among them. But then, just as quickly, he recalled that Tostig the traitor was also English. And then, when the horsemen, who numbered ten or twelve, came parallel with him, he realised they were speaking Norse.

He even heard the word '*vargrkind*'.

Only several minutes after their hoofbeats had faded did he tear free of the rotted leaf litter and scamper back into the gloom of the woods.

The next night of his journey south was as much an ordeal as his first.

He slept restlessly, seeing more fire, more blood, hearing more screams of the dying. He even envisaged Eadora lying alongside him. She was a corpse now, and looked like one, but that didn't prevent her putting an arm around his neck, nuzzling at his ear with a mouth that smelled like sewage. He awoke with a near-scream to find that it was still the darkest part of the night, rain hammering through the tree canopy. His legs and lower body were drenched. A fortuitously located bough had sheltered the rest, including his face, but that hardly reduced his misery.

Having now eaten what remained of his fruit bundle, he spent that second day foraging for food rather than continuing south. He ate what berries and mushrooms he could find, and even discovered a wild apple tree, though, save for a few wormy remnants, someone else had already pillaged it. He had neither rod nor net for fishing, and though he plunged repeatedly into brooks to chase the darting, silvery forms with his bare hands, he never succeeded. Other game proved equally elusive. He saw rabbits and squirrels aplenty, but though he'd hunted all his days, that had only ever been with horse, hounds and bow.

He prayed regularly, every few hundred yards in fact. And he prayed hard, feverishly even, usually while kneeling. Praying hadn't helped much up to now, but he told himself that he had no other recourse. Even then, it soon became a chore that he found tiresome. The truth was that, in the same way he knew no one who'd ever seen a dragon, he knew no one who'd ever witnessed a miracle, and no matter how much he yearned for it, he knew in his bones that a roasted boar's head with all the trimmings was not going to descend to him on a beam of celestial light.

He also felt that praying constantly for assistance was taking up time that could be better spent trying to make some progress south. The trouble was that he rarely had much clue which direction he was meandering in, and resolved the problem every so often by working his way back to the road, which also felt like a monstrous waste of time and energy. At the end of the second day, he had no idea how far he had come or how far remained, and he was desperately hungry.

As such, on the third day, the nobleman's son was reduced to begging.

Hugging the road again, he came to villages and outlying farmsteads. But all were closed to him. Stockade gates were barred. Doors and shuttered windows refused to open. Even countryside chapels were locked. In one village, the few folk who did show their faces called him a vagabond, threw faeces and set their dogs on him. Bitten and freshly bloodied, with his feet two solid blocks of blisters, Cerdic now limped his way south rather than trudged.

On the fourth day, he became a thief.

And, irony of ironies, for now he was sure that he hated the Norse robbers more than any other creatures on Earth, it was this that saved him.

He came upon a rock-built barn with a sod roof. When he forced it open, seeking shelter from another impending downpour, he discovered chickens. Confined in there, they were unable to escape him, and so he captured and killed two. Later, elsewhere, he kicked his way into a second woodland shack, this one abandoned, and there plucked the birds, cleaned them, built a small fire and cooked himself his first proper meal that week. Only while he was eating did it strike him that, though he'd always enjoyed hunting and had shot and speared much game, this was the first meal that he'd ever prepared for himself. Athelbere had given him lessons in woodcraft in case a time ever came when he was on campaign and needed to live off the land, but neither of them had taken the possibility seriously. It was fortunate though, Cerdic realised, that he'd still paid some attention. He also felt humbled by the experience. At one time, surviving on the proceeds of begging or theft would have been inconceivable. In addition to that, even if it had been gladly given rather than stolen, he could never understand how so many got by on such scant fare. The mere thought had been repugnant. Yet now, not even a week after fleeing his home, he felt neither guilt nor revulsion, while the food, raw in some parts and overcooked in others, was as good as a feast, or so it seemed.

Feeling stronger after this, and more purposeful, Cerdic bathed in a forest stream, before dressing again and following the course of the water, which finally brought him to a washerwoman's cottage on the outskirts of another village.

Sundry items of clothing warmed on the rocks here. When the washerwoman emerged, a crone of lean but wiry build, he told her that he was an honest traveller who would work for food. Taking pity on his reduced state, she set him to cutting wood and picking vegetables from her small garden.

Working for food, and at his own suggestion.

He was literally living like a ceorl. Again, the lad was astonished that such a thing had come to pass less than one week after he'd been deputy earl of Ripon. Yet once again, whether he liked it or not, he felt no revulsion at his new status, no sense of shame at being degraded so. It was keeping him alive, just as it did that vast multitude of other unwashed souls who made up the population of England. It was wearying, of course, but probably not as wearying as dying from hunger or exposure. And it was honest labour too. That much, he felt glad about. He remained guilt-free about the chickens he had stolen – that had been needs must – but it was still better not to steal. He could hardly condemn the Viking wolves if he felt otherwise.

At the end of his afternoon's work, she fed him a bowl of turnip porridge, followed by fried eggs and ham, which he ate voraciously.

When she asked him who he was, he lied that he was the son of a thegn who had died in defence of Wulfbury. Fear that she might be in league with the enemy prevented him telling her the absolute truth, though at least he was sincere about his destination.

'I'm bound for York,' he said. 'I have relatives there.'

'That's another day on foot, at least,' she replied. 'And beware, for Danes are marauding in the land.'

He nodded, scratching his stubble.

'Are these the ones who killed your father?' she asked.

'Aye.'

'It's the same reason no one will talk to you. They fear all strangers at present. They'll think you a spy or scout for these pagan dog turds.'

'But you don't?' he asked.

She cackled. 'What have I to lose? A few bits of garb that don't belong to me. A basket of turnips and carrots. The Danes that destroyed your home came through here already, several days ago.'

Again, she referred to them as 'Danes', even though these new invaders had come under the flag of the King of Norway. It had been the same with Guthlac and Oswalda, and was often the way with old Northumbrians haunted by folk memories of the Danish chieftain, Ragnar Lodbrok, and the ravages unleashed by his sons.

'They took what they could,' she added. 'Stripped a few orchards, sacked the church. But they didn't tarry long. Left our grain, our animals.'

'They were in a hurry to get to Wulfbury,' Cerdic said.

'A greater prize by far,' she replied. 'We were saved by their greed. Who'd have thought it?'

Her home was little more than a hovel, its interior clean but basic, with only the crudest furniture but a central hearth comprising a bed of glowing coals. Cerdic was told he could sleep there that night.

'You haven't got very much, grandmother,' he said, moved by the offer. 'And yet you seem more than willing to share it with me.'

169

'For all your troubles, you've worked hard. The least I can do is reward that.'

Her own bed was a small cot in a corner, heaped with blankets. Cerdic would have to use the floor, but she bade him lie close to the hearth where he'd be warm, and gave him an old sheepskin cape to wrap himself in.

Such selfless generosity reminded him of Oswalda, and that worried him.

'Grandmother,' he said, 'if the Northmen come back, don't assume that just because they had business with Wulfbury they won't also have business with you.'

'Do you suggest I run?' She bedded down comfortably in her corner. 'Where would I go?'

He was about to suggest hiding in the forest, but he'd experienced that for himself, and even though he was younger and stronger than she, it had nearly killed him.

'There's nowhere I can go,' she answered the question for him. 'So whatever will be will be. At least I know that at my age I'll fetch them precious little in the slave market.'

She cackled at that. Cerdic tried to laugh too, but couldn't. Oswalda wouldn't have fetched them much either, but look at her now.

'Maybe they won't come back,' he said, attempting to sound as if he believed it.

'Oh, they'll come back,' she replied. 'They always come back. Their goal these days is to rule this land, not raid it.'

–

Cerdic cut away from the road again, this time on its other side, taking a forest path the washerwoman had directed him to. As well as the sheepskin cape, which his hostess had allowed him to keep, he now carried six golden apples in a knapsack: as payment for his having spent the first part of that morning clearing a new area of ground so that she could plant more vegetables in the spring.

But now he wondered about her other comments. About the Danes seeking to rule, and Jarl Wulfgar's claim to ancestral ownership of Wulfbury. If the English had truly been destroyed at Fulford, and King Harold was forced to sue for peace because the Danes, as she'd called them, again held the north, perhaps his own family's claim to the earldom would be deemed illegal.

Perhaps?

He laughed at his own naivety.

'Perhaps nothing!' he spat.

Another bastard Viking on the new throne of Northumbria would give nothing to anyone save the edge of his sword. Not if they dissented. Especially not if they were English. Wulfgar Ragnarsson might have broken from the Hardraada's army to fight his own private battle, but the Norwegian king would need strong men to control his new realm. Even if it wasn't that simple and King Harold was able to impose conditions on the Norse, if the Ragnarssons had a genuine claim to the earldom of Ripon, a court might uphold it.

Cerdic had felt better on first leaving the washerwoman's home. He'd eaten well, and now knew that his journey was almost over. But the more he brooded on it, and the less muddled his thoughts, the more it felt like a fool's errand.

Barring a miracle, he feared his home was lost.

CHAPTER 16

As he approached the environs of York, Cerdic veered into the woods to the southwest. Partly because he knew the battle had taken place on the south side of the city, but also because he didn't yet know if the Vikings were in possession of the capital itself or not.

Even then, circling around the city at such distance that he couldn't see its outer walls didn't feel like a sensible plan. The fight had occurred at a place called Fulford, and Cerdic had no real idea where this was. Pressing blindly in a vague direction meant there was a chance he'd miss it entirely. But it wasn't long into the sixth day of his journey from Swaledale when he saw a sky filled with carrion birds. He hastened toward them and before long the odour of death was in his nostrils, tempered only slightly by the smoky, heathery scent of purification fires.

As the trees thinned out, a hideous droning of flies assailed him. The year was waning, but every bluebottle left in the Wolds, it seemed, had come here for a final feast. He heard voices before he saw anything, but now he was running, barely thinking straight. Only as he emerged from the woods did it strike him that the voices were English.

It scarcely mattered. Because what he then saw brought him staggering to a halt.

He'd emerged on the edge of a broad highway, so hardpacked that though rain had fallen in recent days, its surface still looked firm. Laid out in straight lines along both sides of it were dead men. More than he had ever imagined possible in one place.

He held back, agog, wafting half-heartedly at the swarming insects.

It wasn't so much the stink of these former warriors, more their condition. They lay encrusted with blood and ordure, many of them sundered by axe or sword-stroke. In numerous cases a head or limb was missing, or both. Broken hafts of spears still jutted from some; arrows pin-cushioned others. Several had been dismembered and then pieced back together like sections of an ogre's puzzle, not always correctly. Scavenger birds hopped among them, strands of meat dangling from beaks. One of these, surely the largest, ugliest raven in all Creation, fixed Cerdic with so malign a gaze that he imagined he'd seen it once before, on the hewing block back home in Wulfbury.

He turned, still dumb-stricken by the ghastly array, which he now saw led on along the road for several hundred yards to a point where the curve of a river was visible on the right, and not too far beyond that, the straw roofs of a village. At that far point lay a more chaotic strewing of the dead. Figures moved among them with staffs, attempting to separate one from another. Mainly, these appeared to be monks, no doubt from the chapter houses of York.

'Who are *you*?' someone asked belligerently.

A small group of monks stood close by, scarfs wrapping their lower faces, sleeves pushed back to the elbows on habits stained with unimaginable filth. Cerdic realised it was one of these who'd spoken to him. They regarded him with open hostility. He noted dazedly that clubs hung from their belts.

'Well?' another snapped.

'I'm... Cerdic,' the lad said. 'I'm looking for my father and brother.'

The first monk who'd spoken nodded. Up close, Cerdic saw that he wore a black cassock with a brown chasuble belted over it, rather than a habit, indicating that he was actually a priest, though these holy vestments were also smeared with human grime. The priest was younger than the others, tall and very lean, his hands and forearms particularly caked with gore. He still seemed suspicious, but now ventured forward, drawing down his scarf, revealing features equally as long and thin as his body.

'My name is Aethelbald,' he said. 'You're among the first of many who'll come, I imagine, now the news is spreading that the Northmen are slain.'

Cerdic glanced at him distractedly. 'Slain?'

The priest frowned. 'You hadn't heard?'

'I've...' Cerdic shook his head. 'I've come from Swaledale.'

The monks muttered in disbelief. The one called Aethelbald eyed him up and down, taking in his sheepskin cape, his ripped and dirty garments.

'When the news travels widely,' he said, 'we expect many to come seeking their menfolk. It's our custom to lay the dead out in a respectful way. We have lost brothers here too, and several holy fathers, so we understand the pain.'

Cerdic glanced back toward the village. A horse and cart were approaching slowly, the back of the vehicle heaped with corpses. A limping monk led the animal by its harness, an old, tired-looking priest walking alongside, singing prayers.

'You say you're looking for your father and brother?' Aethelbald prompted.

Cerdic nodded. 'My father was... Rothgar, Earl of Ripon.'

The priest's eyebrows arched. 'Earl of Ripon!' He again surveyed the lad's ragged clothing, his worn-out boots. 'And yet you came on foot... without a bodyguard?'

His voice was cultured; he sounded better educated than was the norm.

'The Northmen destroyed our home,' Cerdic said. 'They killed... everyone.'

There was a touch more understanding in the priest's face now, but dislike lingered. Presumably, because men of his vocation believed in the sanctity of human life, while the lords of this land, of all lands, in fact, held the opposite view.

'In that case, you'll be doubly glad that the Northmen are slaughtered,' he said.

Still dazed, Cerdic looked around. 'Slaughtered? I heard they'd won.'

'They won this battle. But four days ago, the king arrived with his southern levies. Ten miles east of here there's a crossing on the River Derwent… Stamford Bridge?'

Cerdic shrugged.

'The Vikings mostly died there,' Aethelbald said. 'King Harold slew them. All of them. Including his own brother, and that bear of a Northman, the Hardraada.'

Cerdic could scarcely believe it. 'Earl Tostig… the Norse king too?'

'All of them.'

'The invasion…?' The lad still thought he'd misheard. 'It's over?'

'Ended as quickly as it began,' a monk added. 'Those few left are being hunted as we speak. When King Harold's messengers returned to York, they said he'd spare none of them. Told us to tell anyone who asked that the Viking menace to England has ended *here*. Once and for all.'

The hope now kindling in Cerdic's breast was something he'd hardly dared dream. 'If I can find my father and brother, and our housecarls are in condition to fight—'

'You'll find none of them here,' Aethelbald cut in. 'Not if they're still alive. Archbishop Ealdred arranged for a hospital camp. It's a mile back from here, on the way to the city. But it will be crowded. The victory on the Derwent was costly. The wounded are still coming in.'

'Which way is York?'

Another of the monks pointed right. Cerdic hurried off.

'Wait!' Aethelbald called.

Cerdic glanced back.

'You should tarry.' The priest regarded him sombrely. 'At least until you've satisfied yourself your kin are not among these dead. In another week, we must cremate all those remains not reclaimed. It's against our custom, of course, but God will understand. If we don't do it, it will poison the whole land.'

Cerdic came slowly back, unnerved by the mere prospect of searching through the dead closely. The face of one nearby was completely cloven in two. Another lay disembowelled, flies glistening green and blue on his exposed innards.

'We try to arrange them in households where possible,' Aethelbald said, 'but it isn't always easy. What were your father's colours?'

'My family crest was a blue boar's head on a field of white.'

Aethelbald shook his head. 'I haven't seen that sigil myself, but if you go down to the village… that was the main scene of the battle, there are many as yet unmoved.'

Cerdic nodded, and headed in that direction.

'Cerdic!' Aethelbald called again. The lad turned back, and caught a spare scarf the priest had balled up and tossed toward him. 'Take this.'

Cerdic tied it around his face and continued on his way, again passing more dead than he'd ever seen gathered in a single place. Every fifty paces or so, a brazier contained a fire crammed with herbs as well as kindling so that it issued pale, sweet-scented smoke, though neither these nor his scarf made much difference, his stomach roiling at the overarching stench. He halted briefly when, under a glutinous mask of gore, he thought he could distinguish the shattered features of Eadwig, a thegn from the northern reaches of his father's earldom. But short of scraping the blood clots away with his own fingers, it was difficult to be sure. Even so, he checked the bodies laid out on either side, relieved to find that none of them was anyone he recognised.

He pressed on, and ahead now saw the gate to the village of Fulford more clearly, as it occupied raised ground. Several figures, also with scarves muffling their lower faces, kept watch from the palisade, but the gate was wide open, the cowled shapes of monks moving in and out, or standing with groups of villagers, talking.

Immediately in front of the village, the road broadened, rugged ground on the right tilting down to the river, while on the left lay an expansive stretch of marshland. As he'd been told, this was clearly the site where the most intense fighting had occurred, for though another cart creaked past, laden with jumbled bodies, a tired-looking priest intoning prayers alongside it, the majority of the dead still lay tangled together.

Cerdic stopped in the middle of them, barely able to breathe the foul air. When he peered over the marsh, hundreds of bone-white faces were visible under its glassy surface. One dead form appeared to be sitting upright, though it soon became clear that a spear had transfixed him and propped him above the water.

More movement now caught the lad's eye.

A troop of lean, dirty figures was picking its way around the far edge of the marsh toward dry ground. So dingy and cadaverous were they that, for half a hideous second, it was as though several corpses had risen and were trying to find their way back to their companies. And then an angry voice commenced hurling abuse at them, and the beggarly band came to a halt.

Their abuser was another priest, older and heftier than Aethelbald, foursquare in shape. He'd hurried to the marsh's edge and yanked his scarf down, exposing a face of sun-toughened leather. He'd even drawn the club from his belt.

Now Cerdic understood why the monks were carrying such weapons. Something he'd heard about but had never imagined possible in a Christian land was happening in front of him. Even as the dead lay unburied, human buzzards were descending on them. Though the Northmen had likely stolen anything significantly precious – swords, torques, jewelled brooches and cloak-clasps – there were ring-coats still on show, leather gauntlets, buckled belts...

'Away with your damned hides!' the hefty priest shouted, waving his club. 'God's blood, I'll make you pay!'

The line of dirty figures retreated, vanishing through the sedge and bullrushes into the deeper greenery of the woods.

'As if these days aren't bad enough,' the priest added, partly to himself and partly to Cerdic. 'It's harvest time for rogues like that.'

Cerdic grunted, mainly because he felt some kind of answer was expected. Then he pulled his own scarf down and asked: 'Where are the Viking slain?'

The priest glanced at him. 'Already claimed, I'm told. Pagan devils left our dead for the crows, of course. Now the boot's on the other foot.' His mouth crooked into a humourless smile. 'They burn together... all of them... along the banks of the Derwent. Seems fair enough to me. Good preparation for the eternity they'll spend in Hell.' He looked thoughtful. 'Anyone you're looking for in particular?'

'The housecarls of Ripon. Earl Rothgar and his men.'

The priest pondered. 'Blue boar? White background?'

Cerdic nodded tautly. 'That's it, yes.'

'Over there.' The priest pointed across the road, to a clutch of trees just north of the bend in the river. 'Some of them. There are probably more.'

Cerdic trudged that way reluctantly, doubts and fears churning.

It would not be possible, however well-intentioned, for these religious folk to find and lay out *all* of Wulfbury's fatalities. They ought to be identifiable from their household livery. Not only did they wear the boar's head device on their surcoats but on their shields as well. And yet, how many shields remained intact on the anvil of battle? How many sigils of any sort could be seen on surcoat or mantle under such a tarring of blood and filth?

So, even if Earl Rothgar didn't lie here, that meant nothing for certain.

The lad halted, stunned, stricken by the sudden reality of what he'd feared.

In front of him, sixteen corpses lay on their backs in a tidy row. The two in the middle were of notably larger stature than the others.

A sob caught in Cerdic's throat.

He saw straight away that the one on the right was Athelbere. Like so many others, the marshal of his father's house was steeped in blood, but his features, though brutally gashed, were discernible. Which meant the one on the left, who matched the marshal for height, the only man at Wulfbury who did, could surely only…

Cerdic swayed. The left-hand body had been covered with a cloak, but the lad knew what he would find. With a strangled scream, he tore the cloak away.

There lay his father, Rothgar Aelfricsson, Earl of Ripon.

He too had suffered severe head traumas. His whole face was lacerated, yet it was unmistakeably him from the grey, blood-sticky straggles emerging through rips in his coif. It was anyone's guess which wounds had proved most fatal, for as Cerdic rose back to his feet, gazing numbly at the duo, he saw bodies carved by many blades, broken by the multiple blows of clubs and mattocks.

'You went down hard, didn't you, old warhorse?' he whispered, a deathly cold enveloping him. 'I'll wager you made the beasts pay. And you, Athelbere.'

He managed to steel himself a little longer, just adequately to walk up and down the rest of the line. It was a consolation of sorts that Unferth was not among them, but as Cerdic had already told himself, that didn't mean anything. Not really.

Thoughts tumbling, he turned dizzy and slumped to his knees. Finally, after so many days of numbness and disbelief, with head drooped to chest, he wept, hot tears gushing forth, for the fall of Wulfbury, the end of the family Aelfricsson and the untimely fate of all those friends and companions he would never see again in this world.

CHAPTER 17

The hefty priest, whose name was Osric, helped Cerdic carry Earl Rothgar, now wrapped head to foot in his cloak, back along the road. Rothgar was still mailed, of course, which, added to his natural bulk, made him a killing weight.

'He was a strapping fellow, your father,' Osric grunted.

'He was,' Cerdic sniffled.

'They all were. To stand up to those devils, the way they did. I'm sure it'll be no consolation to you, but we lost some of our own too.'

'I heard.'

'Several of my brothers from the Minster School…'

Cerdic eyed him as they lumbered along. 'You're from the Minster School?'

'Yes. I… I taught rhetoric.' Osric reddened in a way that had nothing to do with the unaccustomed exercise. 'Don't laugh. I know I look nothing like a teacher.'

'I won't laugh.' Even in the midst of his grief, Cerdic wondered if he should mention that he himself had been bound for the school, but he quickly decided no. He wasn't bound there now; at present, he was little better than destitute. 'I doubt I'll ever laugh at anything again.'

'You'd be surprised,' Osric replied in an affable, encouraging manner, the exact opposite of the thundering tone he'd hurled at the party of scavengers.

Feigning anger on demand like that seemed to Cerdic a very teacherly talent. He couldn't help wondering if missing out on the Minster School meant that he'd missed out on something valuable. But there was nothing to be done about it now.

Once they'd passed the river and the marshes, they diverted a short distance into the wayside woods, and there the lad used his axe to break up the sod and his cupped hands to scoop out the soil from underneath. Aethelbald, who had seen them, came into the trees at their rear. He rubbed his hands on a towelling rag and pulled his scarf down.

'You found someone?' he asked.

'The lad's father,' Osric replied.

'My condolences, Cerdic. That's a grievous loss.'

Having vented his sorrow so copiously alongside the corpse, Cerdic was determined to stay dry-eyed now. He nodded his gratitude. 'He died defending his country. I take solace from that.'

'Is there no sign of your brother?'

Cerdic shook his head and continued scooping.

'He can't take his father back to Wulfbury,' Osric said. 'I've suggested that, if we get the earl below ground here, and mark the spot, he can be reclaimed at a later time… perhaps receive a grander ceremony. In some place more to his family's liking.'

'Even a shallow grave will take the two of you the best part of what's left of today,' Aethelbald replied. 'But I think I can help.'

He departed, returning a few moments later with a barrow and three shovels, which he distributed between them. Then he dug, too.

'You don't need to help me do this,' Cerdic said, again feeling humbled by the unhesitating assistance he was receiving from ordinary people.

'We don't need to,' Osric replied, 'but we will.'

'I suppose you'll be doing a lot of this in the days to come.'

'Not so,' Aethelbald said. 'As I've already explained, we can't bury everyone.'

'Then my father would be flattered that you consider him worthy of this honour.'

The tall priest shrugged. 'You've travelled fifty miles on foot, with no guards, scarcely any food by the looks of you… he must have been a special father.'

'I don't think we'll see his like again. Not in Wulfbury.'

'That remains to be seen,' Osric replied.

'I know it to be true,' Cerdic grunted.

'Only God knows the future,' Aethelbald said. 'No man has an inkling what plans He has in store for us.'

—

Later that afternoon, with Earl Rothgar's interim grave covered by leafage, they heard angry shouting, and Cerdic went back onto the road with the two priests. Immediately, he saw the difficulties they'd be facing that night.

Other bands of scoundrels had come to rob the dead.

Though the monks, now with several village men under pay, repeatedly saw them off, frequently administering beatings, the scavengers were persistent as rats, and their numbers grew. But as dusk descended, even worse threatened.

'Once it's properly dark, wolves will come,' Osric said, huffing and puffing after having chased one tattered, spindly fellow who'd run with the wind at his heels.

Cerdic listened sourly. He'd stayed as the night drew on, mainly to rest but also to eat, Aethelbald giving him a loaf, a jar of honey and a flask of cider from a supply cart, where several of the other churchmen had now gathered to rest and talk quietly together. It occurred to the lad that if wolves really did venture this far from the hill country – and they almost certainly would, as the stink of death had to be noticeable now for many miles – then one foot down would not be a deep enough resting place for his father. Not even temporarily. He didn't mention this though, because even as a lord, and Osric and Aethelbald nothing more than priests, they'd already done more for him than he could have asked. It was frustrating though, that his father might now be dug up and devoured by a wolfpack that wasn't even especially hungry, and all because these holy men would be too busy chasing away two-footed predators.

'We should hang them,' he said firmly. 'Why do you merely beat them? What they do is indefensible.'

Osric smiled to himself and ambled away, then began jogging when more angry shouts sounded in the dimness along the road.

'You haven't seen enough death?' Aethelbald asked, leaning his elbow against the cart.

Cerdic found the priest's intense grey eyes unnerving.

'I just... I mean... what if...?'

'What if we hanged every person who was starving?' Aethelbald said. 'There'd certainly be fewer people in the world, Cerdic. I'm not sure there'd be many fewer criminals. Don't be too quick to judge those who have so much less than you.'

'So much less than me?' The lad bridled. Maybe it was time to remind this low-level prelate about the ranking structure here, about who had lost the most, and suffered the worst. But Aethelbald now mentioned that very same thing.

'You, of all people, Cerdic, should know what it's like. Didn't you get a taste of it on the road between here and Swaledale?'

Cerdic clamped his mouth shut, remembering the chickens he'd stolen, which he'd justified to himself because his belly was so empty, and how, even though they didn't know he'd committed any offence, the villagers had called him filthy names and pelted him with turds and offal.

'It might be a kindness to hang some of them,' Aethelbald added. 'Who knows? But even that isn't our decision to make. Not mine, certainly. And not yours... yet, little earl-in-waiting.'

–

Clearly, Aethelbald was one who spoke his mind, regardless or not of whether those he admonished were supposed to be his betters. But Cerdic had reached a point now where he was too deadened by events to take offence easily. And anyway, it was true what the priest had said. These last few days he'd wallowed in the pit of human experience, and at the end had been rewarded with the mangled corpses of loved ones. And of course, he wasn't alone in that. Who knew how many families were bereaved thanks to this one battle? Who knew how many more would suffer because of the war in general? It wasn't just that. The journey down from Swaledale had almost been the death of him. He'd only managed it through the kindness of a stranger, yet as Aethelbald said, there were countless others who were ragged and penniless and endured such torments daily, whether there was a war on or not.

Thus, when they prayed together later, saying first the Requiem Aeternam as they knelt close to Earl Rothgar's grave, Cerdic, who'd become slightly less enamoured by prayer since the loss of his friends, recited it loudly, word for word in correct Latin, which Aethelbald looked impressed by. When Osric came back to join them, they switched to English, the priests extending their entreaties on behalf of all those other souls cruelly taken, and the lad implored Heaven just as heartily, and he even felt good about it, and useful – for the first time in several days.

Afterwards, in repayment for their help, he offered to stand with them that night, and guard the battlefield against scavengers of all ilks. But Aethelbald advised against this.

'At the moment you are the sinned-against, not the sinner,' he said. 'Why reverse that situation?'

'You fear I'll take lives?'

'It was you who said it, not me.'

'Then leave the wolves to me. You can deal with the rest.'

An amused smile touched Aethelbald's lean face. It wasn't an unpleasant sight. 'You won't be breaking any wolves' heads tonight, son. You try that and they'll tear your throat out. But you come from the northern hills. You already know this.'

'What would you have me do?' Cerdic protested.

'Find your brother instead.'

'There's no hope of that now, it's too dark.'

'Try the hospital camp on the road to York. There's light aplenty there. The sick need tending whether it's day or night.'

With no better plan in mind, Cerdic thanked the priest again and set off walking.

In some ways, Aethelbald was right to have worried about his temperament. They'd certainly have been suspicious if they'd seen him remove one of his father's gauntlets and from underneath that, the golden ring with the boar's head crest. Which was why he'd done it quickly and surreptitiously before Osric could help him wrap the dead nobleman in his cloak. They'd possibly have accepted that it was his by right, that having lost his own official ring to Wulfgar Ragnarsson he currently had no proof that he was son and heir to anyone. But given that they'd initially thought him a thief, it wouldn't have been ideal.

He turned the ring over in his hands as he trod the highway, before slipping it back under his clothes. It would have been ostentatious to wear it in this situation, not to say completely and utterly stupid.

But at least now he could show men who he was, if they demanded to know.

–

The hospital camp covered extensive acres of open land. It comprised candlelit tents of many shapes, including rickety frames lashed together hurriedly, with sailcloth roofs stretched over them. Access through the camp was via a rabbit warren of well-trampled footpaths, many of them impassable with injured men standing around glowing braziers, or sitting in rows, leaning on each other as they slept. Most were swathed in bloodstained bandages, or leaned on improvised crutches, while the more seriously wounded were under cover, lying side by side, groaning, or if they were gruesomely mutilated, raised above the rest on collets so that orderlies might attend them. Again there were flies everywhere, clustering on the wounds of those too weak to brush them off, on the unblinking faces of those who'd died without anyone noticing.

Whereas down near the village of Fulford it had primarily been priests and monks dealing with the dead, here, among the living, it was mostly nuns and sisters. And it wasn't the atmosphere Cerdic had anticipated. These men had survived the war. More importantly, the invaders had been annihilated. He hadn't expected laughter and celebration, but he was surprised by the air of doom. Some wept and others wailed. Most simply brooded, staring wordlessly into the night.

He threaded among them, oftentimes cursed or pushed. He saw no one wearing the livery of Wulfbury, though in truth there was next to no livery on show at all. In many cases mail and leather undercoats had been removed too. Despite the deepening cold of the autumn night, some wore only loincloths, while one poor fellow, who stumbled past in a state of near-somnambulance, his left arm ending in a gangrenous stump, was completely naked. The stench inside the tents was particularly repulsive, though this time it wasn't the putrid sweetness of decay. Instead, it was blood, vomit, spent bowels. He'd never have believed how much more foully the living could smell than the dead.

Several times, he asked if anyone knew the fate of Unferth, the young lord of Wulfbury. But again he was either cursed or shoved.

'What's it to you?' a yellow-tinged face croaked up from what looked like a deathbed. 'Did you serve him? I hope so. And I hope he's here. It would do my heart good to see a servant live while his master—'

Cerdic tried to retort that he was no one's servant, but the wounded man's face creased horribly as he commenced choking up wads of black-brown mucus. A diminutive sister shouldered through to assist, but the patient's eyes had already turned to glass. More disconsolate than he'd ever been, Cerdic went outside again into fresher air. Not that it really was fresh.

The humours of the nine-day-old battlefield were noticeable even here. Not quite as pervasive, but noisome enough.

'Watch where you're going, you damn country lout!' a housecarl snarled.

Cerdic hadn't actually collided with him, had merely wandered close, but the carl leaned on a broken spear shaft and ran with sweat; under his woollen jerkin, the wrappings binding his chest were bright with crimson blossoms.

Cerdic said nothing, though the fellow spoke with an accent he didn't recognise. Probably, he was a southerner. The lad remembered Father Aethelbald's words, that the wounded from the fight on the River Derwent were now coming in. Most of these would be the king's soldiers. How many there'd be, he couldn't imagine, but it was little wonder this encampment had already filled to capacity and beyond. The little hope he had left when he'd arrived here sank even further. He walked on quickly, turning corners at random. What hope was there of finding Unferth in this sprawl? And why was everyone so bitter? Yes, they were hurt, but they'd done right by their country. They'd answered its call. The red they wore was their badge of courage.

More angry voices sounded, two in particular. He was in a broader central thoroughfare, and now saw a press of men approaching quickly. So quickly that he had to step aside. The two at the front were in particularly heated discussion, when a young thegn forced his way toward them.

'Earl Edwin, Earl Edwin! A message! I believe it's important.'

The older and burlier of the two men came to a halt. He had a mass of tawny hair and a shaggy beard and moustache, and wore a stained orange surcoat over his ring-mail, emblazoned with a black eagle. A great many of those behind him, mostly housecarls, wore similar colours. They, too, halted.

Clearly, this was Edwin of Mercia. Older brother to Earl Morcar of Northumbria, who'd been Cerdic's father's own liege-lord. The fellow he'd been in dispute with, who looked similar but younger, and now had one arm in a sling and a sutured sword-slash in his left cheek, was most likely Morcar himself.

Earl Edwin opened the scroll he'd been handed.

Cerdic waited with interest, listening.

'It's from the king,' Edwin finally said. 'He bids us attend him in York.' He rolled the scroll and thrust it under his belt. 'You know what this'll mean?'

Earl Morcar looked worried. 'He's aware half our host is lost? The rest exhausted?'

'He'd probably say the same about his own.'

'When duty calls, I suppose...'

'Duty?' Edwin shook his head. 'How about survival? You consider that less important?'

Morcar couldn't answer.

'*Bring us our damn horses!*' Edwin roared.

'We're for York, then?' Morcar asked.

'We're for York.' The earls stormed forward, their followers crowding behind. 'Just leave the talking to me.'

Cerdic had been toying with the idea of making himself known to them, but already the chance had gone. Frustrated, he swung around, shouting aloud that he needed to speak to men from Swaledale, that if any housecarls from Wulfbury were here, or even any fyrdsmen, they must present themselves to him. It drew only scowls of irritation, but he persisted, barging along several passageways and into one of the larger tents, still shouting.

'Lord Cerdic!' a voice suddenly responded. 'Lord Cerdic, is that you?'

Cerdic spun around. 'Who is that?'

'It's me!' Whoever he was, he was close by. He sounded desperate, full of hopeful pleading. 'Haco.'

'Haco?'

At first, Cerdic held back from the figure close by him on the ground. Though whatever sly trick the young blacksmith had played during the Harvest Ales festival now seemed a hundred lifetimes ago, fate had paid him back a dozen times. He sat slumped against a stout wooden pole, one of several supporting the cloth roof. If he'd had any armour, he was only in rags now, and filthy rags at that. His face had been grotesquely injured, and while the whole section above the middle of his nose was bound round and round with tight bandages, blood had still seeped through, leaving two fiery red blots where his eyes ought to be.

Cerdic's former enemy reached out imploringly, his grime-encrusted hands groping at the air. 'Forgive me, Lord,' he begged. 'I know we parted on evil terms. But yours is the first voice I've recognised in more days than I can count...'

Cerdic stood close by, but not close enough to touch, though this was more through horror than loathing.

'What happened?' he asked in disbelief. By rights he ought to be stern and unforgiving, still indignant about those events at home, but the fellow at his feet was a broken, mutilated wretch. What purpose would anger serve here?

'It was the battle near Fulford, my lord. We were holding our own, but then the Northmen seemed to throw extra forces in—'

'I know about the battle. I mean what happened to you?'

'I was close to your father when he fell. I couldn't get to him to help.'

I wonder how hard you tried.

'When our banner came down, most of our company broke and fled.'

'Were you one of them?'

'No, my lord. No. I was in the rear-guard.'

It wouldn't be unusual for someone like this to cast himself in a heroic role, of course, but Cerdic didn't necessarily disbelieve the story. Back in Swaledale, Haco was known as a brute and a bully. But he'd shown sufficient courage to go and fight.

'It didn't save those who went ahead of us, though,' the blacksmith added. 'Some of the Northmen had circled round the marsh. They came through the woods onto the road, into the path of those retreating. There weren't enough of them to completely blockade the route back to York, and it wasn't just our men, but many of us by this time had thrown down our weapons and taken off our ring-coats so as not to be encumbered. These unprotected, they chopped down like grass…'

'And yet somehow *you* escaped?'

Haco hung his head. 'If you can call it that.'

Cerdic realised that he was being overly harsh. Whatever this man's faults, he'd fought and he'd suffered. If everyone else had chosen to depart the bloody field, was he supposed to have remained there alone?

'It's… a ghastly tale,' Haco stammered. 'The Norse are more demon than man. I had my blacksmith's hammer. I accounted for many, but their love of blood-fray is something I've never seen. In the chaos of that final fight, when all our leaders had gone…'

Yes, Cerdic thought, *the earls Edwin and Morcar, for example, the former of whom has clearly come through the battle without so much as a nick.*

'…even the rear-guard broke. By then though, more and more Northmen were flooding onto the road. I tried to fight my way through. I struck and struck with my hammer… it was a strength born of terror, you understand. I'm no Alfred, no Athelstan. I'm far from being a hero… I didn't even see the blow that caught me in the face. It was a sword, I was later told. Hit me edge-on. Across the eyes.'

Cerdic swallowed bitter spittle. 'How bad is it?'

'I'm blind, my lord. I know it for a fact. When I finally got someone to look, he told me I'd always be blind. He said that, though he didn't much like me, he was sorry for me and would try to help me if he could.'

Cerdic was puzzled. 'This was after the battle, of course?'

'Two days after.'

'Where?'

'In this camp. Apparently, other comrades brought me here when I was half-dead.'

'And who was this fellow who told you he'd help you and then left you to the tender mercies of others?'

'My lord...?' Even with his mangled, rag-wrapped face, Haco looked surprised. 'It was your own brother, Lord Unferth.'

CHAPTER 18

Cerdic gripped him by the shoulders. 'Unferth is alive?'

Again, Haco seemed surprised. 'You weren't aware?'

'Just answer the question...'

'He was alive after the fight at Fulford, but that's all I can say for certain. There's been another battle since then. I can't help wondering if this one on the Derwent is the reason he didn't return when he said he would...'

Cerdic clutched him by a handful of tattered clothing and led him out through the camp, taking one crowded passage after another, until they hit open space, where, in a wooded glade on the outskirts, he sat him on a fallen log.

'Tell me what happened, exactly,' Cerdic said.

Haco shrugged. 'Your brother fought with uncommon valour, my lord. I know there's been trouble between my family and yours—'

'Get to the part where he survived.'

The wounded man cast his thoughts back. 'It was after your father fell. And that huge fellow... the captain of your house...'

'Athelbere.'

'Yes, yes... he'd fallen too. Most of your carls were dead by then, I think. But Lord Unferth made an attack on the Northmen all by himself. He fought like an enraged wolf. They couldn't put him down. But then, as all lines broke and the flight began, he was called to his senses by those few left. They cut their way through to him and then together, they cut their way back.'

'All this you saw?'

Haco nodded. 'I lost track of him then, but he must have made it off the field. Because, when I regained consciousness in this camp, he was speaking to me. I recognised his voice. He made it clear that he didn't like me. But anyone from Swaledale who'd come through the fire... those were his words, "come through the fire", was to be praised. And protected, if possible. This wasn't purely for me, of course. I got the feeling he'd spoken similar to most of our survivors.'

Cerdic was frustrated. He still had no clear picture of what had happened. 'You have any idea how many others there were?'

'Few, I fear. It was a brutal contest, but we gave them a fair mauling. They didn't come after us... they stayed at Fulford, licking their wounds. Later, they moved across country to join their comrades on the Derwent.'

'And Unferth hasn't been back here since? You're sure of that?'

'If so, he never spoke to me.'

'And no one else from Wulfbury has been here? No one since that second battle?'

Haco shook his head.

'Have you looked around this camp to see?'

'My lord, I can't *look* for anything.'

'No, of course.'

'But all of those here are in a poor state,' Haco added. 'Many will die or be crippled. I'm not sure even you can round up a company from these tents.'

Even me, Cerdic thought, bitterly amused. *What in God's name have I done to command the loyalty of soldiers? I wasn't even here.*

Not that he took the sentiment too seriously. It was evident that Haco of the sneering lip and mocking voice, Haco the bastard who'd outwitted him so easily in Brackley, was only offering this flattery because he needed a friend.

'My lord?' Haco said, as though he'd read Cerdic's mind. 'You won't leave me here? When you return to Wulfbury, you'll take me with you?'

Cerdic stiffened. A cool breeze rustled through the damp autumn leaves.

'At some point they'll turn me out,' Haco explained. 'I'm clearly not going to die. Even though I'm blind, there are folk all across England so afflicted. But at present I'm all alone in a land I barely know. I'll struggle to *sniff* my way home.'

'I'm afraid there is no home, Haco. Not anymore.'

An astonished silence greeted this.

Cerdic explained as best he could. About Jarl Wulfgar's assault, about the numbers slain. The cruelly disfigured face grew progressively longer, eventually registering what could only be described as slack-jawed horror.

Cerdic didn't detail what he considered to be his own failures, but he didn't gild his role, either. What was to be gained from that? So, he offered the basic facts. There'd been too many attackers, too few defenders. The assault had come from nowhere. No one had foreseen it. Of course, there was no way to gloss over Eadora's death.

Haco hung his head for several moments, his body visibly juddering. When he finally looked up again, his mouth quivered. He'd probably loved his sister in his own way, despite the harshness with which he'd dominated her.

'If our home has gone, my lord,' he stuttered. 'What... do we do?'

What do we do? Cerdic thought. Were they a duo now? A partnership? The very idea came as a sobering shock. How could he be lumbered with someone like this? Clearly, Haco needed a helper, if not an actual nurse. Most likely, he'd need such for the rest of his life. But how could Cerdic provide that? He didn't know how much of a life he himself had left.

'I... I.' He struggled to find an adequate response. 'Look, before anything else, I need to find my brother.'

'My lord, if he went to fight in the second battle—'

'He may have died there. Yes, I understand. But I can't do anything on my own.'

'You'll have *me*.'

The voice sounded ridiculously hopeful. A desperate, beseeching smile carved itself on the damaged features. When Cerdic didn't reply, Haco said: '*You* aren't going to leave me as well, my lord?'

Cerdic still didn't know what to say, let alone do.

'What will the future hold for me? I'll be nought but a blind beggar at the minster gates. You wouldn't condemn me to that?'

'You don't have family anywhere else?'

'Nowhere.' Haco lurched forward, grabbing Cerdic's sheepskin. 'My lord, listen… your brother. He said he would protect me. Those were his exact words. He would protect me because I'm one of you.'

'One of *us*?'

Cerdic could scarcely believe what he was hearing, though mainly because of the difficulty looking after such an invalid would entail rather than because it wasn't true. The ruined face in front of him was the only one he'd seen here that he actually knew. In a time of murder and massacre like this, there was some degree of kinship there, whether he liked it or not. And Haco, for all his foxy ways, had indeed answered Earl Rothgar's call and been maimed in his service. But, good God… how could the lad do any of the things he felt he needed to do, or anything at all in fact, while carrying such an encumbrance?

'Do you have bedding?' Cerdic asked.

'Bedding?'

'It's the middle of the night, Haco. I'm worn to the bone. I need sleep.'

The blindman shrugged. 'Only a dead man's cloak, which I managed to steal before they took his body away. But in the morning, where will we go?'

'To York. I imagine all survivors will be gathering there. If we have no success then, it'll be on to Stamford Bridge, to see if Unferth lies among the riverside fallen.'

Haco nodded on hearing that, relieved that, whatever plan it was, he apparently was part of it.

Cerdic scrubbed a hand through his matted hair. It was almost too awful to imagine having to pick his way through another host of eviscerated corpses. But what other option was there? In fact, he'd probably need to go there quickly. As Aethelbald had mentioned, no one wanted mountains of the dead polluting the land for long. Soon there'd be burial parties among them, mass cremations.

He led the tall, stumbling wreck that had once been his father's assistant-blacksmith back into the camp by his hand.

'Many here, I've heard, sleep standing,' Haco said. 'So long as they can get close to warmth. I'm told they crowd the braziers all night, snoring on their feet.'

'Marvellous,' Cerdic muttered.

He was so tired himself that he fancied *he* could probably sleep on his feet if it came to that. But it didn't. They slipped through an entrance to one of the larger hospital tents, curling up in a corner so far from the nearest candleflame that the dimness provided cover. All night though, the sounds of suffering assailed them. Gasps, coughs, whimpers, stuttered prayers as dying men begged for forgiveness. The sisters – weary, unsmiling women all – worked continually with sleeves pushed back on bloodstained forearms, but there was only so much they could do. Every so often, a priest came in, a young-looking man who seemed exhausted himself, to say the Last Rites over some poor soul before the broken body was carried out and the cot washed down with a bucket of river water.

Cerdic huddled with his head under his sheepskin cape. His thoughts drifted on the great battles of the past, those occasions he'd heard about in songs in his father's hall, when his ancestors had showed heroic courage against the invading Northmen:

Brunanburh, Tettenhall, Ethandun, Ashdown... even Maldon, where the English were defeated though they'd fought courageously to the last.

But where was heroism to be found *here*?

Where was the glory?

And while they were on the subject, where was God?

He knew that he was asking too many questions like this at present, and that one could never be so presumptuous as to expect God to deliver victory on the battlefield simply because the opponent was heathen. That had never been the way of it. Battles had to be won by men. But this snake-pit of suffering was scant reward for those hardy souls who'd come out here and sacrificed so much to draw steel against Christendom's foes.

Cerdic told himself that England's history had been ever this: victory followed by setback followed by victory followed by setback. The only difference now was that he was seeing it with his own eyes, and he found it ugly. Horrifically ugly. The weakness therefore lay with him, not the Almighty. If he was to survive this, he needed to find more mettle... and for that he needed the Lord. Thus, far from refusing to pray purely because he hadn't seen the outcome here he'd wanted, and remembering how steadfast the faith of Osric and Aethelbald, the lad vowed to pray harder, particularly during the loathsome night that he knew lay ahead.

And he did so, for hours, half-in and half-out of sleep, mumbling his pleas to Heaven, only gradually becoming aware that somewhere beyond the tent, he could hear a steady and repeated clink and thud. As of men on the move. Men carrying arms.

Soldiers?

Cerdic sat upright, pulling the sheepskin from his face.

Daylight flooded the tent, though it was no less a hive of misery and pain.

He jumped to his feet regardless, listening hard.

'What is it, Lord?' Haco wondered.

Cerdic glanced absently down at him. Saying nothing, listening on.

He could definitely hear tramping feet, clinking armour.

He hurried outside.

'My lord!' Haco shouted, also clambering to his feet.

It had rained overnight, because when Cerdic entered the thoroughfare between this tent and the next, it was thick with mud. Peering lengthways along it through the ghostlike figures of the wounded, he saw the York road, and what seemed like an endless procession of levies moving along it, footmen and horse mingled together. The early morning light glinted from helmets and ring-mail coats.

It was a relief to see so many Englishmen still in harness, but Cerdic was bewildered as to why they were heading south. He pushed his way through the camp. Haco followed, grabbing at his sheepskin.

'My lord, my lord… what's happening?'

'Get your hands off me!' Cerdic tried to yank himself free. 'At present I'm lord of nothing. Why can't you understand that?'

'We're Wulfbury men… that makes us kin!'

'*Kin?*'

'You can't leave me here.'

'It won't be for long.' Cerdic strove on. 'But I can't help you on my own.'

'You said you'd try, damn it!'

The blacksmith's voice became truculent. His grip on Cerdic's sheepskin tightened, his hands still strong from his years on the forge. Cerdic glanced back, frustrated. He didn't want to just abandon the helpless oaf, but what other course was possible? It occurred to him to send the fellow to the Minster School and ask for Father Osric, but would the priest be there? Was the school even there? Cerdic swore aloud. If he'd had money he could have paid one of the monks or sisters to look after the casualty until he returned, but he had nothing. And all the while, that army was marching past.

'Look... I won't forget you're here!' he said, struggling to get free. 'I'll come back for you. But I *must* go... our last hope is heading away from us.'

'Come back for me?' Haco's teeth bared yellow. 'Promise that! Swear it.'

'Wait here.' With no more time to disentangle the claw-like grasp, Cerdic threw off the sheepskin, leaving it in the blindman's hands while he pushed on.

'I'll remember that promise, Cerdic Aelfricsson!' Haco called behind him. *'You can't just abandon one of your own!'*

Cerdic shook his head as he emerged from the camp onto the roadside.

Several of the men passing by returned his gaze, but all looked tired and dispirited. Again, he saw horsemen and footmen mingled, as if this departure from York, if that was what it was, had been arranged too hastily. There was no particular order to the rank and file either, bands of thegns or housecarls riding alongside trudging fyrdsmen. Already, the procession snaked far into the distance, the banners of many districts and households, none of which the lad recognised, visible along the line. Every man was girt for war, but shields were still gashed and spattered with dried blood. Helmets were dented; several of the men carried noticeable wounds.

'Why are you leaving?' he shouted, though no one bothered to reply.

He ran alongside them, shouting louder. One or two spared him the odd, disconsolate glance, but no one spoke.

'Listen to me, please!' He put himself in the way of horses, but they shouldered past or around him, their riders uninter-ested. 'Stop... please! Don't go. What's the matter with you all? There's a Viking army still here in the north. It occupies Wulfbury... that's in Swaledale. In Christ's name, you're going the wrong way. *Don't go home yet!'*

'Out the way, boy!' A mounted thegn whose bridle he tried to get hold of slashed down at him with a riding crop. 'Out the way, damn you!'

'In God's name, what're you doing? You can't go south again… not when the Northmen are still in the field!'

He approached a clutch of village infantry, pleading with them nose to nose. Most didn't even look at him. One who did, a burly type wearing an iron cap and a leather hauberk, pushed him away.

Frantic and helpless, Cerdic felt the fear and anxiety of the last few days bubbling up inside until he couldn't contain it. This was a considerable force, for though the king's army had an air of defeat, he couldn't yet see its farthermost end. It could easily retake Wulfbury, but it was still fifty miles from there and adding more distance by the minute.

'In Christ's name!' Again, he ran next to them, now far from the hospital camp. 'You have to stop! This is madness!'

But the road had narrowed, trees closing in from either side, and his voice was lost under the clanking of swords and mail, the thumping of hooves and boots.

'I'm Cerdic of Wulfbury!' he shouted. 'Son of Earl Rothgar. If you don't stop, I'll stop you myself. You can't run from this battle. Run from this next fight and these pagan murderers will never leave us!'

He drew his axe from his belt and moved to a stand of roadside silver birch.

With wild grunts of effort, he set about cutting the first one down. Working at its base with his blade, hacking and hacking like a madman. Ten minutes in, his sweat flew, foam flecked his lips. His strength was ebbing, but he drove himself on, chopping again and again at the gaping wound in the bark, woodchips spraying.

'What in the name of God?' someone demanded.

Cerdic saw that a grizzled, grey-haired thegn wearing a black-and-orange surcoat had detached from the main column and cantered up on his horse.

'We must stop them, my lord,' Cerdic replied. The thegn looked utterly bemused.

Cerdic hacked on, more splinters flying. 'If you won't stop them, my lord, I will...' He was breathless now, drenched with sweat. 'I'm closing this road.'

When a hand grasped his shoulder, he looked round again. The thegn had dismounted, his face graven in stone. 'You village idiot! You think we haven't troubles enough without lunacy like this?'

'All I know is—'

Cerdic never saw the punch coming, a bone-mallet fist in a thick leather gauntlet smacking the side of his jaw with such force that he tottered sideways, dropped his axe and fell. He lay blinking in the mud, all coherent thought lost. For which reason, he also failed to see the steel-capped riding boot when it flew at his face.

He saw nothing at all after that.

CHAPTER 19

'Cerdic... you need to sit up.'

Cerdic tried, but turned giddy and slumped back onto his elbow. The rough jolting of a wagon turned his stomach. Retching, he leaned over the side of it and spewed a stream of frothy mucus.

'Just in time,' Unferth said. 'Uther Pendragon, they say, choked on his own vomit.'

Unferth...?

Cerdic jolted upright – as much as he was able to – knocking himself giddy again in the process. He was in the back of an open-topped cart or wagon, propped against sacks of what felt like war-gear. A white Wulfbury cloak, much besmirched with grime, was laid over him. More important than any of this, Unferth was also in the cart, at the opposite end, about five feet away. He appeared to have been packed under furs and flax, but he too was propped up, and he regarded his younger sibling with a wan smile.

'Unferth, I...' Cerdic tried to sit up properly again. 'Thank Christ, oh thank Christ!'

'Don't thank Him too quickly,' Unferth replied.

'I... I...' Cerdic was so relieved that words had simply failed him.

Now he looked around, and saw that he was in the midst of a moving army, almost certainly the same army he'd attempted to waylay. The woodlands they travelled past were reddening quickly as the autumn came on. Overhead, the lowering sky was a dingy slate-grey. Overcome by grogginess, he slumped back. His head still spun, his face aching abominably. When he fingered it, there was a swelling the size of an egg under his left eye. He had masses of other bruises, not to mention a broken nose, but that particular socket was so tender that he could barely touch it.

'Your cheekbone is fractured,' Unferth warned him. 'In normal times I'd say you should rest the next few days. Alas, I don't think that will be possible.'

Sensing the weariness, not to say the pain in his brother's voice, Cerdic appraised his sibling properly. Unferth looked thinner than he remembered and was pale as ash, a long cut crusted with scabs on the right side of his face. Under his fur coverings, he still wore his ring-coat, but it was rent in many places, and Cerdic caught glimpses of bloodied bandaging.

'You're wounded,' he stated.

'In more than one place.' Unferth used his teeth to pull off his gauntlet, to show his left hand, where two digits had been lopped off, only blood-sticky stumps remaining. Cerdic winced. 'It's nothing,' Unferth said. 'I got this at Fulford. I didn't even know it until later, when I was free of the melee. More serious is this one, which I had at Stamford Bridge.' Very cautiously, he felt at his left side. 'Broadsword thrust. A torrent of blood came out. They've stitched me, but I think it's cut through the two lowest ribs on that side. I could still die, or so I'm told.'

Not for the first time, Cerdic sat in awe of his older brother. 'You lost the fingers on your left hand, and yet you went and fought in the second battle too?'

'No choice,' Unferth replied. 'At Fulford, we feared the Vikings would pursue us back to York. Those of us able put a skirmishing line across the road... to try and protect Archbishop Ealdred's hospital.' He became pensive. 'It was a strange thing, Cerdic. Suddenly, I was the most senior man there. Thegns were jumping to it when I issued orders. But then, only Viking spokesmen came, not their army, offering Hardraada's terms for

203

sparing the city. A fantastical sum. More gold than the average man could imagine, to be delivered promptly to their camp on the River Derwent. I sent word to York and held the line. Our scouts reported that the Northmen were indeed moving east to the Derwent, though we still didn't trust them. And then, within a day, gallopers reached us from the south. Another armed force was approaching. It was the king. I wasn't the senior man anymore. But I tell you, lad, it didn't worry me.'

'You were happy to go with the king to Stamford Bridge?' Cerdic asked. 'Even though you'd already fought?'

'Again, no choice. We could man the city, under leadership of the earls Edwin and Morcar, or ride with Harold against the main bulk of the Viking army.'

Cerdic wasn't at all sure that he'd have taken the second option. It would be typical of Unferth, of course; though the brash, self-assured Unferth from before the campaign rather than the meeker, more humble-seeming Unferth who confronted him now.

The elder brother spoke on. 'From the beginning of this war, Father expressed concern to me...' He broke off warily. 'You know about Father?'

Cerdic nodded. 'I buried him myself by the roadside.'

Unferth considered this for a long moment. 'You can tell me *your* story in a minute.' He continued with his own. 'Father had doubts about the willingness of their mightinesses, Edwin and Morcar, to fight. They had large forces and were respected across the north. Doubtless you've heard that?'

Cerdic nodded.

'But Father knew them better than most,' Unferth added. 'He was glad they were here, but was unsure about their loyalty to King Harold.'

'You mean they were more interested in saving themselves than in saving England?'

Unferth gave a weak but wry smile. 'That sums it up nicely.'

Cerdic nodded for him to continue, not bothering to mention that this was the same conclusion he himself had drawn when he'd glimpsed the aforesaid earls of Mercia and Northumbria in the hospital camp the previous night.

'When we arrived in York, the king held a quick council,' Unferth said. 'He agreed that Edwin and Morcar… because they'd suffered severe losses already, would hold the city while he and his main army advanced to the bridge on the Derwent. As I say, Cerdic, we had a choice… stay or go. Remembering Father's uncertainties, we went. Of Father's ninety carls, and my twenty-five, we had forty-eight and nineteen. Now, those numbers stand at thirty-three and fourteen.'

Cerdic glanced around again, this time properly, wondering if he might see old friends close by. The army moved on as wearily and morosely as before, passing through woods and meadows flatter than anything he'd seen back home in Swaledale. Several housecarls kept pace close by on horseback. Some, he recognised as members of Unferth's hearth-troop, particularly Redwald, who now carried the Blue Boar banner. There were others behind them whom he thought he recalled from his father's retinue, Aeschmund and Hodda, for two, though their numbers overall looked alarmingly small.

'We *won* that battle,' he said, confused. 'I know we lost at Fulford, but the big one was on the Derwent, and we *won*.'

'Even victories can be costly,' Unferth replied. 'When we reached the Derwent, many of Father's housemen were burning for vengeance. Most had quit the field at Fulford without knowing that Father and Athelbere were dead. They were deeply ashamed, and to atone they threw themselves at the Hardraada and his *drengr* with suicidal courage. It was one of ours, I think, who actually slew the bear-king. "A greeting from Earl Rothgar!" he apparently shouted as he disembowelled the bastard, only to be speared down himself a moment later.'

Cerdic sniffled again, the shock of so many losses coming over him anew.

'Someone bring this boy a drink,' Unferth said. 'And something to eat.'

One of the housecarls, having rummaged in a saddle-bag, offered Cerdic a leg of cold roasted chicken with only a few fragments of dust adhered to it. Cerdic was hungry but knew that he wouldn't be able to keep it down. He waved it away, but accepted a flask of mead, which he gulped thirstily.

'So how do *you* come to be here?' Unferth asked.

In a dull monotone, broken only by further sniffles, Cerdic told him everything, leaving out no detail this time, not even his own failings.

Unferth listened, nodding now and then, and making no comment.

When it was over, and Cerdic reached the part where an angry thegn kicked him unconscious by the roadside, Unferth leaned backward as though he needed sleep, but instead stared at the sky. 'I wonder if God will ever smile on us again,' he said.

'He gave Lord Cerdic back to us,' commented Redwald, who'd ridden close enough to overhear.

'Yes, that was fortunate,' Unferth agreed. He glanced at Cerdic. 'Before you ask, a fyrdsman of ours witnessed the altercation you got into by the roadside, and thought he recognised you. After you'd been felled, he went over to have a proper look, and yes, it was indeed *you*. We were doubly fortunate, I suppose, in that he was far ahead of us. Had he been far behind, he might not have been able to catch up with us in time.'

'We were also fortunate,' Redwald told Cerdic, 'that he saw you in mid-brawl. Had he passed by *after* it had happened, well... one more body lying in a ditch would likely have gone unnoticed.'

Cerdic probed gently at his battered, aching face. 'It's a kind of luck, I suppose.'

'At present, any kind of luck is good,' Unferth replied.

Cerdic regarded him curiously. 'You seem different, brother.'

Unferth nodded again. 'Sadder, obviously.'

'Wiser too... I mean no offence.'

Unferth half-smiled. 'I think the two go hand-in-hand.' The smile faded. 'You say Eadora died as well?'

'In my arms. I'm sorry…'

For a second or so, Unferth's tired eyes were moist, but no longer than that. Whatever his feelings for Eadora, the village lass, and they clearly went deeper even than Cerdic had realised, they were still scattered like twigs in the howling wind of this overwhelming tragedy. So many had been lost, so many valued people, that it was difficult to pinpoint one in particular to be heartbroken about.

'The one thing about very dark times,' Unferth murmured, as much to himself as to his sibling, 'is that better times often follow.'

'But they won't this time,' Cerdic blurted. 'Not if we keep heading in the wrong direction. There are more than enough men here to recapture Wulfbury… so why are we going south?'

'I've already told you our losses, Cerdic,' Unferth said. 'I'm sure the king would cut us loose from his army, if we asked him. But on my own I don't command nearly enough men to confront this Viking lord. You must see that?'

'But will the king not come himself? I ask again, why are we heading south?'

'You haven't heard, Lord Cerdic?' Redwald looked surprised. 'You surely know of William the Bastard?'

Cerdic frowned. 'The Duke of Normandy?'

'He's here. In England. He invaded the south coast only two days ago.'

'Surely you heard about this possibility?' Unferth said.

Cerdic shrugged. 'There was some minor talk. But Father regarded the Hardraada as the bigger threat.'

Unferth nodded. 'I suppose, at the time, he was.'

Cerdic remained puzzled. 'Why should an invasion in the south be of concern to us northerners?'

'The south is as much a part of Harold's kingdom as we are,' Unferth replied.

'It means more to him, Lord,' Redwald said. 'His own earldom lies in the south.'

'But I don't understand why his southern levies can't deal with it,' Cerdic said. 'He didn't bring the entire male population of Wessex to the north, did he?'

'We only know what messengers have told us,' Unferth replied. 'But by all accounts, this isn't a raid. This is an army of conquest.' He coughed, which seemed to hurt him, and wiped a pinkish trickle from the side of his mouth. 'Father *did* mention this before... that the Duke of Normandy had his eyes on the English throne. But then it was only a remote possibility.'

'He has a claim to it through distant family ties to old King Edward,' Redwald offered. 'He also says the late king promised it to him.'

'So now you must fight your third battle in a month?' Cerdic told Unferth in a voice of angry disbelief. 'I'll wager you can't even stand up.'

Unferth shrugged. 'So long as I'm there, there's more chance the king will send soldiers back north with us afterwards.'

'This king asks an awful lot of his loyal subjects,' Cerdic said bitterly.

'An awful lot may be required, my lord,' Redwald replied.

'But surely there are enough men here to defeat these Normans?'

Unferth mused. 'Maybe.'

'Maybe? What are they, devils in human guise?'

Unferth glanced at Redwald.

'Well?' Cerdic demanded.

'Redwald is your man,' Unferth said. 'He's visited Normandy. He stayed there for a time. He knows the Normans.'

Cerdic glanced at Unferth's captain, who reddened behind his whiskers.

'My lord, it's not a view everyone shares,' Redwald said. 'But in my opinion, they are the warrior elite of Christendom. Their best men are called "knights", and they serve their masters in return for land and status.'

Cerdic shrugged. 'Like our thegns.'

'It is similar, yes, but there are many more of *them*. In Normandy, the knights form the majority of the military force, not just its officers. A Norman knight's training is long and hard. It commences when he is very young, when he starts an apprenticeship to another more experienced knight. These younglings they call squires. When a squire is deemed fit, he is promoted to knight through a sacred ceremony—'

'It's not just a Norman thing,' Unferth cut in. 'Didn't you tell me this was the new fashion across all the lands of the Franks?'

Redwald nodded. 'It is, my lord. Its originator was a duke of the Franks called Charles Martel. He first employed the system several centuries ago, against a Moorish horde from Spain. Up to that point, these pagans from the south had been all-conquering. But Martel vanquished them in a single battle.'

Vanquished was quite a word, Cerdic thought. It had an air of finality, it implied that not a single enemy remained. And yet this was a Moorish army they were talking about, the arch-villains of so many bedroom stories told to naughty Christian children even far into northern England, where men with brown skin were almost never seen.

'And the Normans, you say, are better even than this Charles Martel and his Franks?' Unferth asked.

Redwald nodded soberly. 'They've had centuries of practice since then, Lord, and have developed many new skills. To begin with, they mostly fight from the saddle. That's how they train, and they've become masterful horsemen. Plus, they wear chain-mail, a thick iron mesh, but lighter than our ring-mail and yet harder to penetrate with a blade. When they aren't waging real wars, they have what they call tournaments. The knights fight each other in mock-battles so fierce there are many deaths and injuries...'

'We can still beat them,' Cerdic interrupted irritably.

Terrible as they supposedly were, these Normans weren't their problem. All that mattered now he'd reunited with Unferth was ridding Wulfbury of Wulfgar Ragnarsson.

'I think we can, my lord,' Redwald agreed. 'But through tactics, not brute force. If the Norman cavalry catches us in the open field, we are doomed. When the day comes, we need to find a position of strength and hold it.'

'Then tell all this to the king, for God's sake.'

The housecarl smiled, amused. '*I* can't advise the king, my lord. I'm only a servant.'

'The king already knows,' Unferth put in. 'He fought alongside Duke William, himself. Years ago. You know this tale?'

Cerdic shook his head.

Unferth adjusted his position, again seeking greater comfort and, from his sickly grimace, finding none. 'This is why the Bastard is here. When Harold Godwinson was Earl of Wessex, he was taken hostage in Normandy after being shipwrecked there. He served on one of Duke William's campaigns and acquitted himself well, but he only bought his freedom by promising to support the duke's claim to the English throne if King Edward died without issue.'

'But he's not English, he's a Norman...'

'Who go by that name because they are descended from Northmen,' Redwald said. 'As is King Harold, on his mother's side.'

'But King Harold is here,' Cerdic protested. 'In England. A great nobleman, beloved by all—'

Unferth shook his head. 'None of which counts for anything if you're the pope in Rome and you need Norman sellswords to counter the Germans in the north of Italy and the Moors in the south.'

Cerdic was shocked. 'The pope has given the Normans his blessing?'

'The story is that Duke William has arrived in England with a papal banner. The Keys of St Peter.'

'But Archbishop Ealdred...?'

'Archbishops Ealdred and Stigand are supportive of King Harold for the present.'

'For the *present*?' Cerdic wasn't so much shocked now as stunned.

'Stigand of Canterbury's an opportunist,' Unferth said. 'While Ealdred is… ancient. Whatever he says, it may not count for long.'

'Carrying that papal banner has made an already strong opponent even stronger,' Redwald said dourly. 'It means that William the Bastard hasn't just come here with his army of elite knights… it means the cutthroats of Europe have come too.'

'Why would a holy war attract cutthroats?' Cerdic asked.

'Because when you're waging holy war, you can do anything you want, and it isn't a sin,' Unferth said. 'It is guaranteed to attract the worst elements in Christendom.'

'If we can destroy the Vikings, we can destroy scum like that.'

'We won't need to,' Redwald said. 'Duke William will destroy them. Once he's made use of them.'

Unferth chuckled. 'I wish I believed that. Famed though he is, Duke William will never bring enough knights to hold down this land. Even if he defeats us, he'll have to send forces across the whole country. The only way to summon such numbers and keep them in harness is to offer lands and properties to every man-jack of them. That'll mean lordships for some of the worst people in this world.'

'Don't worry,' Cerdic said. 'The Hardraada brought thousands upon thousands of seasoned warriors, each one promised an earldom, no doubt, and he didn't even capture York.'

'I'd still feel more confident if God was on our side,' his brother retorted.

'Is Pope Alexander really the voice of God?'

For half a moment, Cerdic was shocked that he'd uttered such words. As recently as two weeks ago, to have questioned the authority of the pope would have been unthinkable. It was discomforting to do so now. Even though he knew the political reasons for Rome's allegiance and found them depressingly unspiritual, this was still the Holy Father they were talking about, the head of the Church, the heir to St Peter. And yet in these days of turmoil, all Cerdic's certainties about this world and the one beyond had gone. The notion that life was complicated but that God's will would always prevail seemed hollow. The absolute belief that, if all else went wrong, a celestial host of saints and angels was watching, eager to reward the righteous and hinder the wicked, had first started to diminish when he was tired and starving in the forests between Swaledale and York.

But what did you believe in once that kind of certainty had failed you? Nothing at all. Which was even worse. So, despite all, you struggled to keep believing…

'Don't blaspheme, Cerdic.' Unferth's words cut across his thoughts. The older lad winced in pain again; there was a trace of blood at the corner of his mouth. 'This is a tired army. Many of these men are hurt. They're not showing it, but they are. The last thing we need now is the Lord of Hosts against us.'

CHAPTER 20

The city of London was actually three cities. Cerdic had never been there before, and only knew what his father had told him, though on the ninth day of the journey down from York, he finally saw it for himself.

First of all, there was Thorney Island, on the north bank of the River Thames. It wasn't really an island, more a flat mass of open ground, about a mile and a half in diameter, separated from the main riverbank by two rivulets formed from a stream called the Merfleot. This was the same spot where, twenty-four years earlier, the marshland had been drained and vegetation cleared so that King Edward might replace the small, semi-ruined chapel to St Peter with a great abbey-church of his own. And there it stood now, towering into the dull October sky, the kind of basilica Cerdic had only read about in Aethelric's missals. They called it the West Minster and it was a monumental sight, built from stone, with towers, pillars, thick walls and round arched windows filled with stained glass. It stood within a stockaded enclosure, which also contained many elaborate, timber-and-daub townhouses belonging to senior churchmen and other local dignitaries.

The second town, which was the Port of London, more commonly just referred to as London, also stood north of the river, some three miles east. This one was walled too, though in this case by ancient stone ramparts first erected by the Romans. Parts of these were in visible disrepair, even from a distance, though in places whole sections of replacement masonry had been added. It was the same at York, though according to

Redwald, these battlements were far sturdier. Needless to say, all along the road between the two settlements, clusters of shanties had appeared, hastily erected shop stalls and open-fronted huts, selling everything from religious trinkets to hot pies, from roasted chestnuts now the winter was coming to fresh beer and wanton women. The third town, meanwhile, was the most distant, certainly from Cerdic's perspective. This was Southwark, and though filled with shops and housing of its own, was mainly a fortified landing stage on the south side of the Thames directly opposite London.

The River Thames, though, was perhaps the most impressive thing to greet the lad's awe-stricken gaze. It was easily the broadest waterway he'd seen in his life, a vast glassy sheet, more like an estuary than a river, flowing slowly east, its far shore hidden under great swathes of rushes. Sheep grazing on the far side were little more than tiny white blots. It also, though, presented a huge problem. At least, as far as Cerdic could see. Because all the way across the section lying between London and Southwark, black stumps of burned timber jutted above the surface: relics of London Bridge, which King Aethelred had burned in Cerdic's grandfather's time, to prevent two Viking armies joining up. The problem with that, of course, was that even now, over fifty years later, it meant the River Thames was still uncrossable at this point, even for a lone traveller, never mind an army, and yet somehow the army needed to get over there. When Cerdic raised this matter, Redwald replied that King Harold would have something in mind. And, most likely, it would involve ships.

The army veered off the road midway between the West Minster and London, pitching on a broad stretch of meadow to the north. By the time Unferth's party arrived, a huge encampment was already half-built, tents erected, hammers clinking, blades grinding on whetstones. On all sides, men threw down their arms, heavy kits were unloaded, horses treated to nosebags of fodder.

From this point eastward, the river was filled with sails of many sorts, particularly around London itself, but none of them belonged to any kind of craft that Cerdic would describe as a ship. Mostly, they appeared to be fishing boats, traders, goods barges and skiffs. But even had the royal fleet been present, he couldn't see how King Harold's host, which had swelled notice- ably since they'd entered the southern half of his kingdom, could be transported easily to the river's far shore. At the very least, he'd have expected it to take weeks, and the word was that those spies who constantly updated the king on the invaders' manoeuvres were becoming ever more agitated. William the Bastard's army was immense, they reported, and had already ravaged many towns and villages, acquiring themselves a huge supply train of stolen goods in addition to the one they'd brought over from Normandy. They'd even constructed what they called a 'castle', a great fortification of their own.

'He's still camped on our south coast, though,' Cerdic said, climbing down from the cart. 'He has a toe-hold, that's all. It surely won't be hard to push him back into the sea.'

'Which is why he'll try to parley,' Redwald replied. 'It will buy him time so that he can move inland.'

'Will King Harold fall for that?'

Unferth, who seemed so much weaker and paler now that he remained in the cart, seemed indifferent. 'Whether he falls for it or not, no general can ignore parley. If he can avoid a fight, he will. He may even try to buy the Normans off, though the cost of their enterprise already must be colossal. To answer your question though, Cerdic, he will want to get south as soon as possible. Speed has always served him. Certainly, it did on the Derwent. Though I agree with you, how he intends to get us all across this great river...' His words petered out.

'You fear he can't do it?' a new voice asked.

They looked around.

A horseman had reined up. He and his mount were spattered with mud from the road, yet there was much about both to admire. The horse was a fine grey mare, sleek and muscular, tossing its head proudly. The man was broad across the chest and shoulders, with a stout neck. Having pulled back the hood of a richly embroidered cloak now turned ragged and dirty from battle and hard travel, he was possessed of a large head with a mass of tawny curls and a tawny beard and moustache. He wore ring-mail under his cloak, and over the top of that a mantle of red displaying a single golden dragon. It may have been this device that Unferth recognised rather than the man himself, but he instantly jolted upright.

'Lord King!'

Cerdic went rigid with surprise.

Harold Godwinson had a fierce, leonine countenance, but he was handsome too in a rugged, imperfect sort of way. A number of other horsemen reined up next to him. They too sported heavy cloaks and ring-mail, and wore notable crests on their mantles: a white horse on red, a trio of golden crowns on blue. Unferth, meanwhile, was attempting to clamber from the cart, only to grimace again and twist into a ball of agony. The king raised a hand, indicating that such subservience was unnecessary, though the rest of the men dropped to one knee.

'I said... do you fear he cannot do it?' Harold asked again, though without anger.

'Sire,' Unferth stuttered, head bowed as he knelt in the cart. 'If I feared anything about your plan, my brother and I, whose homes are far to the north, would never have come all this way to serve you.'

A smile touched the king's lips. He glanced up at the Aelfricsson standard, which Redwald had planted in the ground. The boar's head symbol fluttered on the autumn breeze. Slowly, he seemed to recognise it.

'You are Earl Rothgar's troop?' he asked.

'My lord,' Unferth replied. 'I am Unferth, his eldest. This is Cerdic, his youngest.'

The king's smile faded. 'Where is Rothgar himself?'

'Dead, my king… at Fulford.'

There was a long, thoughtful silence. They knew that Harold Godwinson and their father had been more than acquaintances. Friends and military allies, in truth, a remarkable turnabout given that only one year prior to that the two had met each other at Northampton on opposite sides of Tostig's rebellion, but a turnabout so genuine that it was Rothgar whose voluble support and persuasive tongue had later paved the way for Harold's accession.

'So you,' the king asked Unferth, 'are the new earl of Ripon?'

Unferth glanced awkwardly at his brother.

'What ails you?' Harold demanded.

'My lord,' Unferth said, head even lower. 'Forgive us, but Ripon is lost. A Northman called Wulfgar broke from the Hardraada's host and claimed it as his own.'

It took a long while for the king to absorb this, though outwardly at least he remained unperturbed. The other horsemen with him glanced uneasily at each other. Cerdic understood why. It meant there was yet more work to be done in the north. The battle at Stamford Bridge, however costly, had not resolved the issue.

'How many of you remain?' the king asked.

'Enough to stand with you when we meet the Bastard, sire,' Unferth replied.

The king nodded, again thoughtful. 'Your plight won't be forgotten.'

They bowed again as he wheeled his horse around and rode in the direction of London, the other horsemen cantering after him.

'That's as good as we can hope for, I'd say,' Unferth muttered. He turned to Cerdic. 'When we return to Wulfbury, how many will we need?'

Cerdic was still a little dazed by the encounter. In recent times, his father had said nought but good things about Harold

Godwinson, praising his intellect and courage, but above all the influence he wielded. Even those who opposed him politically, the earl had said, liked him as a man. He had a natural air of command, but was also affable and even-tempered, someone you could trust to show wisdom and mercy. Cerdic felt he'd sensed that for himself. There hadn't been much that was obviously grand about their sovereign-lord, nothing in terms of splendour or finery, but he'd effervesced strength and intelligence. Simply seeing him at a time of crisis like this, battle-scarred but clearly unafraid, was reassuring, encouraging...

'Cerdic!' Unferth said. 'I asked you a question.'

'Oh, erm... probably more than we can field ourselves,' the lad said.

Unferth considered. 'It went hard for the king at Stamford Bridge. The story is he slew Earl Tostig himself.'

Cerdic was astonished. 'His own brother?'

'It's only a story. Probably grown with the telling. But Tostig died and Harold and he were once close.' Unferth settled back onto his bed of furs. 'The north will hold only hateful memories for him.'

'He said our plight wouldn't be forgotten.'

'He did,' Unferth agreed, grimacing in pain. 'But brother now slays brother. The world's on its head, Cerdic. I don't know where any of us will finish up. I doubt King Harold knows either.'

–

The following noon, with many of the men so fatigued they were still sleeping, Cerdic, yawning, rubbed his eyes and walked down through the jumble of shops and sheds on the south side of the London road to the shingle beach, and saw for himself how the king planned to transport his army across the Thames.

At first he didn't notice anything particularly different. He was still groggy with sleep, his eyes fixed, without really seeing, on a raven hopping about in the sludge on the waterline, picking at the bones of a rotted fish, but then he became aware of a great commotion, and he looked up properly.

About a quarter of a mile to his left, ships had arrived overnight. A great number of them. They were cogs and knorrs for the most part, but there were longships among them too, and all were clearly in the hands of expert helmsmen, for they'd mostly now lined up side by side all the way across the river, from what appeared to be a jetty built out of new timber to a similar construct on the far shore, though carpenters and their labourers were still clambering all over this second structure. Teams of such artisans were busy on the ships too, nailing down a roadway of recently sawn planks, which, once it was complete, would lie across the water in its entirety.

A hundred bemused thoughts hit the lad at once.

All these ships would be moored, but this river was affected by currents, and presumably the tide. What was to stop the craft drifting apart a little way? Even small distances would cause problems. But then he realised that the bridge itself, once fastened in place by those long, steel spikes that carpenters used when erecting scaffolding, would behave as an anchor in its own right.

Would the ships be able to take the weight of the army passing over them? What if a section of bridge collapsed, or a vessel went under? Everyone using it was mail-clad. They'd never be seen again. Well, he supposed that was a risk they'd have to take. At least it opened the road south.

Redwald joined him. Even he seemed heartened by the sight.

'I never considered this,' he said.

'The king's well ahead of us,' Cerdic replied.

'Maybe we'll catch these Normans unawares after all.'

'When do we make the crossing, do you think?'

'No point putting this wonder together so quickly just to sit on our arses, Lord. I'd imagine at the first opportunity.'

Redwald was correct.

The camp was breaking up by mid-afternoon. Royal marshals traversed the host, issuing orders for a staged assembly on the riverbank. Each household commander was given his own time to attend, and strict regulations for the crossing. Men were to march in orderly groups, no more than two abreast. Horses were to be led and not ridden and carts were to be taken over without passengers, though an exception was specifically made in the case of Unferth, whom the king had seen for himself was grievously wounded.

It was the Wulfbury contingent's turn shortly after sunrise the following morning.

On the way over, the ships dipped, tilted and creaked, but the footway felt solid enough. Cerdic walked alongside one of Unferth's older housecarls, a man called Ceolweard, who claimed that these same ships would later sail out of the estuary and around the coast, so they could block off any attempted retreat across the Channel.

'There'll be no going home for the Norman Bastard now,' he said with grim pleasure. 'Him and his men are going to die in England.'

For a brief time, with the river flowing gently beneath them, the sky an unbroken blue, it seemed more than possible that this would be the outcome. But once they were back on dry ground and had passed the great log palisades that guarded Southwark burh, the sky turned grey again and the shadows of heavy clouds darkened the land.

It struck Cerdic now that there was nothing between them and their enemy, just empty countryside, much of it comprising deep, autumnal woodland. And indeed, there was an odd silence, even a tension, as the army slogged south. Groups of mailed outriders, spears levelled and shields high, performed a flanking guard on either side, while the main army advanced in denser, tight-packed formation. They scanned the trees and undergrowth for anyone who might be lurking there.

Cerdic found himself saying protection prayers under his breath.

'Christ with me, Christ before me…' he mumbled. 'Christ behind me, Christ within me…'

It was the old Breastplate prayer the Britons and the Irish had incanted before battle. It was said to have a soothing effect on a warrior's soul, and it did, a little, but even so, at times like these, it was difficult for Cerdic to believe that this was their own country. The Normans surely couldn't know it well enough to be preparing ambushes here, but he wondered what they might actually now be doing, fifteen days after they'd landed. He thought again on the many tales he'd so far heard about William the Bastard, the hard-bitten ruler who, having inherited numerous foes from his infamously brutal father, had learned his trade the hard way, mostly in the saddle, nearly always at war.

According to Redwald, two battles in particular had seen him secure his title. At Val-ès-Dunes in 1047, the duke and his ten thousand knights outfought a rebel horde some twenty-five thousand strong, while at Varaville, ten years later, he'd personally led charge after charge against the massed shields of a French invasion force three times his own army's size, finally inflicting a gory massacre.

Redwald explained that the Normans had devised new ways of fighting that would be completely alien to the English. It was considered demeaning to their knightly rank to use missile weapons, except for throwing spears and javelins as these required training and skill, so mostly they fought with lances. Again, these were spears, but extra-long and sturdy. The Normans carried them horizontally as they rode, couched under the right arm, so they could drive en masse into their opponents. A moving hedge of lethal steel tips, with a colossal weight of armour and horseflesh behind it, was often sufficient on its own to break the strongest infantry.

Even their swords were different from those used by the English and the Vikings. Their blades were longer and narrower, so they could be wielded more effectively from horseback. Longswords rather than broadswords, and because this made them heavy they required hours and hours of additional training, which turned the Norman knights into specimens of huge physique. Their upper-body strength in particular was something to behold.

Cerdic found it difficult to believe these Norman knights could be more imposing than the English housecarls. When he made this point, Redwald mused that it would be an even match, but said again that, while the housecarls were the elite corps at the heart of every English army, the mounted knights who served William the Bastard were more widespread across his forces. At the same time, the Norman duke could field battalions of heavily mailed infantry, crossbowmen, archers and spearmen for the most part. Unlike the knights, who fought for land and honour, this section of Norman arms was fully professional. It lived in barracks wherever Duke William was located and fought exclusively for pay. When their two armies finally met, it was still the case that there'd be more English slingers and bowmen among the fyrd, but the Norman archers, because they were well-organised, could make devastating work of opponents who were not.

Cerdic was reminded of Redwald's earlier words: that if King Harold wished to win this encounter, he would need a strong position and as solid a shieldwall as he'd ever stood behind. He also pondered the crossbow, a weapon he'd never actually seen, though he remembered hearing that various churchmen had issued writs against its use when the foe were fellow Christians.

And yet somehow it would be permissible here?

'Is all of Christendom against us?' he asked on the third day of their penetration into the great southern forest known as the Weald. 'Just because one pope among many has branded us evil? I mean, you told us why he did that, Unferth. But will the rest of Europe not see the truth of it?'

A half smile stole over Unferth's ashen, sweat-beaded face. 'You mean will anyone come to our aid if the battle goes badly?'

'I didn't quite mean that.' In truth, Cerdic hadn't considered the possibility they might lose.

'They won't,' Unferth said. 'Most likely because Duke William is a fearsome opponent. But also because Pope Alexander would disapprove.' Several seconds passed while Unferth physically struggled. 'Holy war is… a new thing in our world.'

Briefly, his eyes fluttered closed. He seemed even weaker than he had when they'd crossed the Thames. Several times that day alone, Cerdic had seen him mop blood from his lips. But at present, the younger of the two Aelfricssons had other concerns.

This notion of 'holy war' had been discussed much during the journey south. Just wars had always been fought, against the Vikings for example, but no man present ever remembered the Church actively seeking to unite the Christian world against the Norse in a single holy endeavour. In the East, it was supposed to be common. The Moors frequently declared holy war on the kingdoms of Spain, or so he'd been told. This had never worried the Spanish, as the Moors were heathens anyway, but Cerdic couldn't help wondering what it might mean for those who resisted a Christian holy war.

Damnation? Hell?

'Remember, Cerdic,' Unferth said, as though reading his thoughts. 'Our own priests have said that it's… it's deeply presumptuous to second-guess the mind of God.'

'Only the Almighty decides who is damned, Lord Cerdic,' Redwald added. 'And it's a good and honourable thing to defend one's country.'

Cerdic was reassured by this, though not greatly.

He felt he'd glimpsed Hell that night in the grim shadow of Cataractonium and had no desire to experience the real thing. It made it more important that, when they finally confronted these Norman interlopers, they defeated them. In fact, didn't just defeat them, destroyed them, put them all to the sword. He hoped the anger this stirred in him would bolster his courage.

Later that same day, a rumour worked its way back through the column. Namely, that Harold's scouts, having ridden ahead to assess the Norman disposition on the coast, still about ten miles away, had found no Normans there at all, save for a small garrison manning their castle at Pevensey. The majority of the Bastard's army was less than a day's march ahead of them.

Redwald rode forward to seek verification, and returned an hour later, grave of expression. It was true. The Normans, who numbered some thirteen thousand, had not, as many had hoped, dug in around their temporary fortress to receive the English onslaught from a well-defended position.

They'd gambled on advancing northward, at speed.

As Cerdic had guessed, Duke William had not risked sending skirmishers into the Weald to try and harry the native forces. Instead, he'd brought his whole army.

CHAPTER 21

The priests in the camp had attempted to deal with concerns that the pope was against them by reiterating the position of archbishops Stigand and Ealdred, namely that the Holy Father had his own valid reasons for supporting the Norman cause, but that he didn't endorse violence and killing as a means of bringing them victory. Cerdic tried not to question this too much, though in his eyes one simply contradicted the other. You couldn't take anything from someone else when they didn't want to surrender it without at least a threat of violence. Again, the lad wondered if the pope, once the most revered of all their mentors, could seriously be considered the mouthpiece of God when he'd adopted this amoral and ridiculous stance. Surely God did not advocate the destruction of one Christian realm by another purely so the other could be satisfied? But if he did, what kind of god was he? And what would he have in store for them all on the morrow?

'You'll find it easier in the morning if you get some sleep,' Unferth said.

Cerdic glanced around, surprised. He was hunkered on the edge of the plateau, gazing down its grassy south-facing slope. Though it was relatively shallow, it still ran downhill for hundreds of yards before levelling off into open meadow and then deep tracts of woods, which now that evening was falling, were blue and dim and spangled with fires. English troops milled about on the flat grassland behind him, most just restless, but some looking to pitch their tents there, even though their official camp was about eighty yards back, sheltered amid clutches of gorse and thinly spread trees. That was where the wagons and pack-animals had been left, so he hadn't expected to see his brother come wandering all the way over here on foot, even using a spear as a crutch and shivering in his swaddle of furs.

'Is that even possible?' Cerdic wondered as his sibling, awkwardly and with much wincing, lowered himself onto the turf. 'I ask a genuine question. *You've* done this before.'

Unferth steadied his breathing. He was sweating again, hard, his left hand ungloved but bound tightly with blood-stained bandages. More blood, fresh blood, could be glimpsed under his fur wrap. 'Aye, I've done it before.'

'And is it possible?'

'Not easily. For men like us.'

Cerdic frowned. 'Men like us?'

'We've *ridden* here. The fyrd have mostly marched. They'll sleep, you can be sure. Their bodies won't allow otherwise.'

Suddenly aware that his insistence on riding the cart all the way from York might be viewed by some in the army as less than comradely, had any of them even noticed, Cerdic felt a twinge of shame, though only briefly; there were other, bigger matters to contend with now.

He looked downhill again. 'There seems to be more than we anticipated.'

The evening gloom had deepened even in the last few minutes, and all that could be seen of the Normans were their campfires, which flamed in the depths of those woods for what seemed like miles in every direction.

'We were told they numbered thirteen thousand,' he added. 'It looks more like fifteen. Maybe more even than that.'

'You can't tell from here,' Unferth replied. 'But even if that's true, we still match them. We'd have more men yet if the earls Edwin and Morcar had brought their forces south. Apparently they're on the move, but in no great hurry.'

Cerdic shook his head.

For a moment neither said anything. They were still ten miles from the south coast, and remained shaken by the speed with which their enemy had come upon them. No one had been prepared for the shock news that the Norman host had advanced inland with such pace that if the king hadn't immediately located a suitable place, they might have found themselves facing charging cavalry while still on the march. But they'd been fortunate. Harold's scouts had immediately directed him to this excellent piece of high ground, known locally as Senlac Ridge, which lay directly in the path of the advancing Normans.

The position was so good that Unferth was surprised the Normans, who'd appeared below within hours of the English arriving, were even contemplating an assault. If they did press one, and it looked now as if they were going to, most likely in the morning, the English would have an open range on which to hit them with every missile they possessed. There was no cover; only a single tree occupied the ridge, about ten yards to the left of where Cerdic now sat, a long-dead apple tree, hoary and sun-bleached, a twisted white sentinel to mark the top of the slope.

'Uncle Guthlac...' Cerdic glanced at his brother. 'Oswalda's husband...?'

'I know who you mean.'

'He fought many times in his younger days. He always said all that mattered in a battle was emerging from it alive, not who'd won.'

'And what do you think about that now you face your own first battle?'

'I know what he meant. Because all I can think now is how unsuited for combat I am... or so you used to say, when we sparred together.'

Unferth snickered. 'I was deliberately provoking you, because I always felt you were capable of more. For what it's worth, I still do.'

Cerdic's gaze remained glued on the fire-speckled darkness downhill. 'This will be a test of *all* of us, won't it. William the

Bastard has clearly earned his reputation. Confronting us while we were still on the march, that's an audacious move.'

Unferth smiled weakly. 'You didn't really expect him to sit on his arse on that beach, did you? He'd have been pushed back into the waves in very short order.'

'I understand that. It was common sense to come inland. But to have advanced this far in full battle-order, in a hostile land... that seems reckless. On top of that, they say he's pillaged every town and farm from here to Wight, which will surely only galvanise the locals into resisting.'

Unferth shrugged. 'It's a more standard tactic than you may think. The Hardraada's Vikings did the same, though they had to leave half their forces to guard their anchorage at Riccall. That weakened their forward thrust. Duke William has no such worry. No one can sneak along and burn his fleet without being seen when it's moored on the coast.'

'So, he's an all-round better general than the Hardraada was?'

'We'll know that by the end of tomorrow.'

Cerdic frowned. 'There's something about him, isn't there? William the Bastard. We haven't even seen him yet... I've called him reckless. And yet the mere fact he's here makes him a force to be reckoned with.'

'It does no harm to consider your opponent strong, as Father would say. There's less chance you'll make a mistake.'

'This is what I mean, though.' Cerdic tried not to sound nervous. More than anything on Earth at this moment, he didn't want Unferth to know how frightened he was. Not after all the complaining he'd done when he'd thought he was bound for the Church. 'If we lose tomorrow, who is there to stop him?'

'Edwin and Morcar.'

'That's not funny, Unferth.'

'Oh, they'll fight if they have to. They're proving slow to get here. They want the king to fight the battle for them. But they'll be recruiting as they travel. They've no choice in the matter.'

Cerdic huddled into his cloak. 'All the way down here, all I could hear were those words of Uncle Guthlac's: "All that matters… emerge alive". And it made me resent every mile we travelled, because all I could think was that *this battle* didn't mean anything and that somehow we just had to live through it, so we could go north again and fight the one that counted. And now…' He shook his head. 'Well, I wouldn't say I know better, but at least I can see that even if we were back in the north, you and me, rousing what paltry forces we could, and even if we managed to throw Jarl Wulfgar out, if Duke Bastard is victorious tomorrow, *this battle* would come to our doorstep too. Eventually.'

Unferth considered this. 'Have you heard the phrase, "the new *wyrd*"? That's also something Father would occasionally mention. It's the reason he was able to persuade the rest of the witenagemot to vote Harold Godwinson onto the throne…'

Almost on cue, they heard the bass tones of the king.

He'd dismounted some thirty yards to their right, and led his grey mare to the ridge to view the Norman dispositions. On foot, he looked even more impressive. He was tall as well as broad, with long, strong limbs and an agile gait. A warrior's build, for certain. He had others with him, the marshals of his royal house, giants like their master, but also two noblemen, less imposing physically, though Redwald had already explained that these were his brothers, the earls Gurth and Leofwin. The former, whose fair locks were unshorn and hung down his back, wore a blue mantle bearing the Three Crowns of East Anglia, the latter, whose hair, like his older brother's, Harold's, was bushier and mane-like, wore the White Horse of Kent on a field of red.

'This life we all lead,' Unferth said, 'or *did* lead… an England at peace, a land of great halls and prosperous farms, where there are feasts and festivals, where the people lead contented lives… that was England at the end of Edward's reign. The England our father sought to preserve. That, I'm afraid, was the old *wyrd*.'

Cerdic was briefly puzzled. *Wyrd* was an archaic word, associated mostly with the pagan era, and seldom spoken now. It meant destiny, though not destiny in the sense that it was a future shaped by good or bad fortune, but in the sense that it had been chosen, or rather woven as though on a loom, by one of those mysterious elder beings the Vikings referred to as *norns*. Assertive Christians like Aethelric held this to be superstitious nonsense, and so if his father *had* used such a term, it would be purely illustrative.

'Old *wyrd*,' he said aloud. 'You mean, as opposed to *this*, our new one?'

Unferth shrugged. 'Father always knew that things could change quickly. He'd lived a full life. He saw powers rise and fall, and their people fall with them. Macbeth, Gruffydd... he sought to prevent that here, and so he pushed the strongest man in the realm toward the throne. But he always said to me, in case it didn't work out... prepare yourself, if necessary, for a sharp shock, for everything to change. Stay lithe and alert, and if you must, adapt quickly to the new *wyrd*.'

'I don't know where this is leading,' Cerdic complained. 'If it's supposed to bolster my courage, it needs some work.'

'Your old *wyrd*, Cerdic, yours personally, was the Church. But that isn't your new one.'

Cerdic said nothing in response. He'd never have believed it a few days before these calamities began, but he now had mixed feelings about this. For all that he'd dreaded a future in the cloister, he'd suddenly, with no 'by your leave', been thrust into a warrior's role instead, and already he was finding it a harsh, unforgiving world.

'Our other new *wyrd*,' Unferth said, 'mine and yours, is that Wulfbury may be our past... not our future.'

It was a second before the lad fully comprehended this. 'You mean even if we win tomorrow?'

Unferth shrugged again. 'Harold's highest priority will not be to reclaim our lost earldom. It may be one battle too many for him.'

'But he said—'

'He said our plight wouldn't be forgotten. That was no kind of promise.'

'But a couple of days ago, you said he might allocate some soldiers—'

'It depends how many he's got left. It depends what this Jarl Wulfgar offers in parley, because he will certainly parley. His Viking friends are slain in such numbers I doubt they'll darken these shores for a generation. But the earldom of Ripon is an anachronism.' He glanced around. 'You know what that means?'

Cerdic nodded.

'Its purpose had ceased to matter even when Father was alive,' Unferth said. 'But it suited whoever sat on the English throne that Father was their right-hand man, their wise old owl, their trusted presence in the turbulent north. Do either of *us* fulfil that role, Cerdic? It may just be easier to make this Jarl Wulfgar swear an oath.'

'But the murders, the rapes…'

'Oh, I'm sure Morcar will impose a hefty fine. He'll want his cut of Father's estate, one way or another.'

Cerdic slouched on the grass. Briefly, he dreamed about his home again. And then was startled that he considered it a 'dream'. As if the place was no longer real. The green and purple summits basking in sunshine, the deer running in the forest, the salmon leaping in the river. The roars of thegns feasting in the dragon hall.

'Whatever happens,' Unferth said, 'it will be altogether easier if tomorrow we can slaughter these foreign rodents. You've already accepted, Cerdic, that you're here now to fight for England and the English way of life. And if you're to do that you can't do it in these ragged, stinking clothes that you haven't taken off for days. Redwald's been around what remains of the troop. He's put together some proper gear for you.'

Cerdic realised that Redwald was now approaching, carrying a bundle of items, which he laid down alongside them. As

Unferth said, it was war-gear: a coat of gleaming ring-mail; a ring-mail coif complete with aventail, lined inside with wool; thick leather gauntlets and a buckled leather belt and scabbard, both tooled with images of serpents and wyverns; a polished chieftain's helmet with hawk's beak nosepiece, cheek-guards and a secure chinstrap; a fine-woven cloak, dyed white and blue in the household colours, which fastened across the chest with a silver chain and intricately carved clasp. When he threw off his own garb and put the outfit on, it was slightly large, but comfortable enough for him to move around in easily.

Unferth nodded, sweating again, weary. 'Now… you look the part.'

Cerdic had to admit that he did, but increasingly he felt troubled. 'Don't lie to me, Unferth, you didn't cobble this together from the backpacks of the hearth-men.'

Unferth waved it away. 'It's important that men can see you on the field, so they'll know who you are. Father believed that absolutely.'

'But whose was this? And, for God's sake, don't say Father's. He was much taller than me. None of *his* arms would fit.'

'Mine, if you must know. My secondary kit, the one I reserve for ceremonial duties.'

Cerdic was shocked. 'Then you should wear this, yourself. I'll take the stuff you're dressed in now.'

'You think I'd gird you with ring-mail and gauntlets slimy with blood clots? What kind of brother would I be?'

There was no riposte to that. It was true, Unferth's current mail wasn't just hacked full of holes, it was bloodied beyond belief, most likely inside as well as out.

'Cerdic,' Unferth became serious, 'if the worst happens tomorrow, you won't be able to throw yourself on their mercy. They know none. But you might be able to throw yourself on their greed. Even use it against them.'

Cerdic felt a stab of unease. 'That's why you've clad me in finery?'

232

Unferth adjusted his position. 'Tell him, Redwald.'

Redwald spoke up. 'The Normans aren't just here for plunder, Lord Cerdic. They're here for land. But you'll need to play it carefully. William the Bastard considers himself a pious prince. But in truth, he's a rapacious pirate—'

'If he's victorious tomorrow,' Unferth cut in, 'he *won't* be negotiating. You understand that? The same goes for his great lords. So you'll need to be clever. Very clever.'

'And won't *you* need to be clever too?' Cerdic replied.

'It doesn't matter about me.' Unferth offered his arm so that Redwald could help him up.

'Doesn't matter?' Cerdic protested. 'You talk as if you won't be there.'

'First of all, we'll win tomorrow, so it's a pointless conversation.'

'Unferth, what are you—'

'Cerdic!' Unferth wobbled on his feet. Fresh sweat dripped from his sallow face. 'I don't know how much longer I'm for this world. My chances of survival, even if we win, are slimmer than yours. Surely you can see that?'

Cerdic stood up too. 'If you don't make it through tomorrow, then I won't either. I'll see to it. I won't have it any other way.'

Unferth shook his head and smiled weakly. For half a moment, Cerdic thought he was going to reach out and ruffle his hair, as he'd used to. Maybe he was but lacked the strength.

Instead, the older Aelfricsson lumbered away, Redwald supporting him. 'As I say, you'll need to be clever,' he said over his shoulder. 'You'll certainly need to be cleverer than *that*.'

CHAPTER 22

It was early, a dank, grey mist covering the land when they took their positions on Senlac Ridge. They couldn't see anything below them; it was a swirling abyss. But no enemy, it seemed to Cerdic, no matter how bold, could seriously challenge the force that King Harold had mustered.

They might be depleted in numbers after Fulford and Stamford Bridge, but there were still at least fifteen thousand men here, maybe more. And to see a company of that size, almost every man helmeted, girt with mail, multiple weapons slotted in belt and harness, was formidable. Following the strict orders of the king and his two brothers, they were formed up in rigid ranks, the thegns and the housecarls manning the shieldwall at the front, the lesser men behind but no less ready. Even the men of Wulfbury, though they made up only a fragment of this incredible fighting machine, and now were stationed under their own banner some thirty yards left of the king's position, had the air of an indomitable rock upon which waves of enemies might break.

Cerdic had slept fitfully, woken constantly by nightmares and nausea, but now that they were here, in this place together, a solid part of the king's force, he felt fresh, invigorated. His nerves tingled, though rather to his surprise it was more with excitement than fear.

As well as the new armour, he carried a broadsword and shield, and a twelve-inch hunting knife, honed to lethal sharpness, which he wore in a sheath under his right armpit. All three had previously belonged to one of Unferth's carls, a certain

234

Grimwald, who'd emerged alive from the Fulford bearpit, but died from his wounds later. The shield was dented and gouged, but still serviceable, the sword unblemished as Grimwald had preferred to fight with an axe.

Silence hung, eerie, as they watched the roiling mist on the downward slope.

Unferth swayed. Cerdic glanced at him, concerned.

He'd remonstrated with his brother all the way from their camp, insisting that he'd done enough, that his presence here was noted, that there was no need to fight.

Unferth had simply nodded in the direction of the royal banners: the Golden Dragon of Wessex, the Fighting Man of the Godwinsons, the White Dragon of England, the Three Golden Crowns of Earl Leofwin, the White Horse of Earl Gurth. The king himself was encircled by a ring of heavily mailed housecarls, with whose colossal captain, Aelfrith Eagle-Eye, he was now exchanging quiet words. He wouldn't have noticed if Unferth had quietly withdrawn, but his brothers and marshals had a roving commission on the field. Mounted at the rear of the royal position, their task was to gallop up and down the line via a route specially kept clear for them, to issue orders and, if necessary, reprimands. *They* would notice.

It hardly seemed fair, given the severity of Unferth's wound. But then, as the young earl himself had said that very dawn, war was never fair.

Below them, the mist veils were clearing.

For the first time, Cerdic saw them.

The Normans.

They, too, were a multitude. The differences between figures he'd heard quoted – thirteen thousand, fifteen thousand – barely seemed to mean anything when confronted by the actual thing.

They filled the lower slopes and the flat ground lying in front of the woods, scarcely an inch of grass visible. But this was no roaring Viking horde.

There was no blasting of horns, no wild shouting or chanting. These opponents had the air of quiet organisation.

They were drawn up in neat companies, horsemen interspersed with footmen, innumerable flags and banners flying to indicate who was who. Cerdic had heard tell, mainly from Aethelric, about the Romans. How they'd fielded the finest soldiers on Earth: the best trained, the best armed, and how they'd marched and fought in disciplined regiments, their formations unbreakable, their purpose implacable. More than anything else, these Normans reminded Cerdic of that, and yet the majority of this force was mounted, which added a whole new level of threat. Never had the lad seen so many horses arrayed in one place, and these weren't palfreys – he could tell that even from a distance. These were battle-steeds. High at the withers, huge in chest and shoulder, many clad in hooded trappers to protect their hides against spears and arrows.

For minutes on end, the two forces regarded each other, the Normans ranked in silence, the English shouting and catcalling. Cerdic strained his eyes to locate anyone down there who might be Duke William, but they were still too far apart. He glanced toward King Harold's position, but it was impossible to see him for the forest of spears and raised axes. The mounted earls Gurth and Leofwin were only just visible, the pair of them sitting tall in the saddle, watching and waiting.

'Don't they plan to hold talks first?' Cerdic wondered aloud. 'Wasn't that the way last year at Northampton? Weren't there peace talks between Father and King Harold, when he was Earl Harold of Wessex? Wasn't the battle averted?'

'Apparently, there were talks last night,' Unferth replied, ashen-faced, sweating again. He leaned on his shield, which he'd jammed rim-down into the grass. 'The king sent emissaries to the Norman camp, but the Bastard wouldn't even receive them. Instead, he conveyed a message through his brother, the Bishop of Bayeux.' Unferth gave a grim smile. 'A bloated human toad, or so it's been reported. The message went something like this… if we seek to live through this day, Harold must forfeit the crown and disband his army. In that event, all will be spared. And that was the entirety of it. No guarantee was offered that titles would be respected or earldoms left with their rightful owners.'

'They can't give any such guarantee, can they?' a voice on the left mumbled. It was one of the few remaining members of Earl Rothgar's original hearth-troop. A rangy, dour-faced housecarl called Sigmund. 'The Bastard has already promised those lands and titles to his followers, else he wouldn't have been able to bring so many.'

Cerdic was reminded again that this would be an all-or-nothing struggle. He'd come south angry, sulky, convinced the real battle lay in the north.

Not so, it seemed. Not so at all.

–

With hooves rumbling, the Normans came uphill, though they didn't come in a single mass but as individual horse companies. Cerdic watched intently, the ground shaking under his feet, the hairs at his nape pricking, moisture trickling and itching beneath his woollen under-garb.

Again, he was terrified to the point of nausea, but breathless with excitement at the same time. His first battle… his very *first*.

He was also bewildered.

This was a piecemeal attack, not a full charge. A mistake, surely? That said, the horse companies were at least a hundred riders strong each. Little wonder the earth quaked as they galloped faster and faster up the slope, looming ever larger, ripped turf flying, the air now reeking of horse sweat.

Then, he saw *who* they were.

Knights. Duke William's special strike-force.

They were everything Unferth and Redwald had said they'd be in terms of armour and weaponry, wearing hauberks of chain-mail rather than coats of rings. Some sported colourful livery over the top of this, while others wore additional layers of steel-studded leather. Their helmets were conical, with stout nose-pieces and chain-mail aventails. Their shields were similar to those of the English, in that they were heavy, most likely made from wood, rimmed with steel, faced with ox-hide or leather, yet they were larger, kite-shaped rather than circular, which offered more extensive protection. Their longswords they wore in scabbards, either at their hips or on their backs. As they drew nearer, Cerdic saw their faces for the first time. They were clean-shaved and close-cropped, no straggles of long hair poking out from helmets or coifs. Again, he thought of the Roman people, whose faded images he had seen in frescoes in the overgrown ruins of country villas. Again, he remembered what he'd been told about the iron command exercised by Duke William over disciplined troops who did nothing but fight and train.

As they came in striking range, the horse companies veered left, riding across the face of the English line rather than charging into it. Their first flight of javelins was not launched at the shieldwall but over the top of it, the heavy, steel-tipped shafts driving deep into the unsuspecting ranks behind. Men screamed as they were impaled. The second volley sought the same mark, Cerdic turning his head to look, and seeing men dancing and tottering to avoid those colleagues already grovelling on the grass in blood and bowels, clutching at the thick, wooden staves transfixing them.

'Hold the line!' Earl Gurth called, cantering by at the rear. 'Hold the line! No one goes forward, no one backward.'

By Cerdic's estimate, twenty such squadrons of cavalry rode past, hurling thickets of javelins, before their strategy changed. New contingents advanced uphill, blocks of infantry, men-at-arms, well-mailed but carrying shorter shields and, in some cases, broadswords, axes or maces instead of the longswords favoured by the knights. As they ascended the slope they, too, kept tight formation. Professional infantry, Cerdic realised, in the duke's direct pay. Before they entered the range of King

Harold's missiles, they halted and additional ranks formed up in front of them.

Cerdic went cold when he saw that these were cross-bowmen.

The infantry advance recommenced, this time with the crossbows at the front. Twenty yards further on, they halted again, the first rank of crossbows dropping to one knee, weapons levelled at the shoulder, the rank behind them standing but also taking aim. The feathered volleys, which they loosed alternately, hurtled uphill, travelling so fast they were all but invisible.

Shrieks sounded all along the line.

On bellowed instructions from King Harold's marshals, the English responded. Their own missile men had extensive reach, and indeed crossbowmen now sagged to the ground, struck by spears, darts and slingstones, but their own volleys remained organised, the hail of death hitting the English front line again and again, the bolts, when they didn't embed themselves in flesh, thudding into shields, their bodkin points punching clean through, gathering there until the shields became heavy and cumbersome. Cerdic wasn't in the first rank, but as the men in front of him dropped, he soon found that he too was exposed, numerous shafts lodging in his shield.

More messages were relayed from the king and his party, that their position must hold at all costs, that the crossbowmen would in due course be out of quills, and when that happened, the English must still be here. But then the tactic changed again, the Norman marksmen lowering their sights to their targets' legs. More shrieks sounded, more men dropped gasping as shins and knees were pierced.

Cerdic wore stout leather boots and thick woollen breeches, an overlay of wolf fur bound up to either thigh with leather cross-garters, but this was for comfort on the muddy march, not protection. He was easily as vulnerable as the rest. But then, yet again, the Normans changed tactics, the crossbows now aiming high, fresh flights whispering over the helms of the front ranks, arcing down into the companies behind, striking chests, necks, shoulders.

This would be the time to surge down on them, Cerdic thought. Significant numbers had already been hurt or killed by this one tactic alone: Cerdic and Unferth were now in the front line. But before any such decision could be reached, the crossbows withdrew. As the king had said, they only had a finite number of missiles. They'd wreaked some bloody havoc for certain, but now it was the rest of the Norman infantry's turn. They came uphill in a jaunty battle-march, calling what sounded like the names of saints, even the Virgin Mary. Cerdic felt sweat freeze on his brow as he saw the red of their faces, the glaring orbs of their eyes.

With echoing belly-roars, they charged.

But it was their undoing, for the tight-packed phalanx of English, though they'd spread under the crossbow hail, drew together, and when the two storms of blades broke on one another, any advantage gained from that airborne assault was lost.

The cacophony was unbelievably loud.

Cerdic's shield was smitten again and again, each impact a jolt to his shoulder. A broadsword sang over its rim and smote his helmet. It knocked him dizzily to one knee. Only instinct made him loft his shield, creating a roof. More blows rained down, pounding his skull through the wood and steel. And then, with a *swoosh* of air and a *thunk* of meat, Sigmund swung his axe through the horizontal, shearing the lad's opponent's neck with a stroke, a gallonage of blood exploding.

'Back to your feet!' The carl grabbed Cerdic's collar, hauling him upright.

Emerge alive... No sooner had the first foe gone down than a second appeared, but this one's shield was already split. Cerdic parried his initial blow, then thrust his blade through the breach, driving all his weight behind it, feeling its tip penetrate the

Norman's hauberk and breastbone. Hot ruby droplets sprayed as his opponent sank downward.

Cerdic tottered backward to get a breath, surprised at how quickly his nerves had loosened again. Now they were into the fray, it was all about doing his work.

Glancing left and right, he saw that the infantry assault had made no more headway than the last one. Innumerable corpses strewed the English front line, many the enemy's. Additional numbers slithered away on sluglike crimson trails, dragging innards and half-severed limbs.

'Hold!' came more furious shouts along the English line. 'Do not pursue! Let them die slowly... like the rabble they are!'

Cerdic watched incredulous as the Norman infantry fell backward, cursing and shouting, pointing at those they intended to get even with.

'Do not pursue them!' came another pealing voice. 'Hold the line!'

Belatedly, Cerdic glanced left. Unferth still stood in close proximity. His shield was gashed and battered, and he leaned on his upright sword, the entire length of which smoked with gore. His shoulders heaved as he sobbed for breath. Then he sensed Cerdic looking and glanced round. Though he was ghost-white and drenched with sweat, he winked.

Yet more shouts now went up, calling on the shieldwall to re-form. Cerdic stared downhill again and saw sizeable bands of mailed archers advancing. Not crossbows this time, but war-bows and hunting bows combined. Some sixty yards short of the English, they halted and commenced raining down showers of arrows, flight after flight falling widely across the main body of the army, many skipping across helmets and shield-rims but others finding their mark, as multiple cries of pain and anger attested. In no time, Cerdic's shield was too heavy to manage. He chanced lowering it, to break off the numerous arrow husks buried in it, only for more shouts to split the air.

Downhill, the arrow companies had ceased shooting and hunkered down. Weaving through them, hooves drumming, more squadrons of cavalry galloped uphill.

This time, straight-on.

The Norman steeds were as well-trained to fight as their riders, rearing at the cliff-face of interlocked linden wood, hacking and smashing with their hooves, crushing the helms and faces behind it, driven even madder by the spears that gouged them. At this range, the knights in the saddle looked titanic, thrusting downward with lances, cleaving with their longswords. The housecarls fought back in a brutal rage. When horses dropped, the knights thrown over their heads were assailed with every kind of weapon. Even in their fine, strong mail, limbs were lopped, skulls sundered. Blood and brains flooded the grass. The din of battle was fantastic, the shattering blows of steel on wood and bone resounding like thunder, the screams of men and mounts affrighting the very air.

The stink of sweat and torn turf swamped Cerdic's breathing. His teary vision was filled with slashing blades, blood spattering, dirt and spittle flying. The impacts on his shield were incredible, hooves smashing wood as well as maces, swords, mauls. Even he, who'd suffered every kind of indignity as his home fell, was briefly transfixed by the manic eyes under the Norman helmets, by the brutish foreign faces.

They were here to vanquish the world he knew, to kill everyone in sight, to burn and desecrate. So, yes, he struck back with a fury he'd never previously known.

Emerge alive… fight like the Devil!

With a single blow of his broadsword, he bit through a horse's skull. When the beast collapsed to its knees, screeching, and the rider was flung forward, he hewed the fellow, and hewed him, and hewed him until a mangled mockery was all that remained. Another horseman hove in from the side, his sword sweeping in a backhand. Cerdic parried, before ramming his blade through the trapper and into the horse's ribs. It bucked madly away, its rider falling head-first to the bloodied ground. Again, the lad hacked crazily, chopping through the thrown warrior's shield and arm and then through his face-guards, reducing the features beneath to crimson pulp.

He staggered backward, gasping, and ten yards to the front, spied Redwald.

Somehow his brother's captain had been drawn out of position, and now was in full engagement with two Norman knights who'd both been unhorsed. Cerdic watched, helpless, as the housecarl cut his way around them with skill. One crumpled down, his left thigh slashed to the bone. The other struck at Redwald all the harder, smashing his already broken shield to pieces. The housecarl drove him back with ruthless strokes, and when his blade clove the Norman's left shoulder, the fight was almost won, had a third knight not ridden up and lunged down with a broad-bladed spear, striking the nape of Redwald's neck, severing the spinal column beneath.

The great warrior flopped to the ground, a puppet without strings, a jumble of unconnected limbs.

It seemed an age before Cerdic realised that he was the one screaming.

CHAPTER 23

It took two slaps to the face from Unferth to bring Cerdic back to his senses. 'This is war! Men die! Resume your place, the fight's not over.'

It was for the youngster's own good that his sibling had briefly dragged him out of the line. He'd turned rigid as a pole, dropping his guard as he stood there, blinded by tears, screaming and shouting.

Unferth might have been visibly enfeebled, but he'd dredged up some last vestige of strength and authority to impose himself sufficiently to shock Cerdic out of his horror-stricken trance. Though he almost toppled with the effort, the older brother shook the fevered sweat from his brow and pushed Cerdic back into place.

The latest Norman assault had failed inasmuch as it hadn't broken the English defence, though the knights who'd led it, having finally committed to the melee, were reluctant to withdraw and regroup. Cerdic saw one particularly huge individual cantering back and forth through the battling men. He wore a huge bearskin cloak and a longsword on his back, and over the top of his mail a black tabard bore the shape of a rearing white leopard. He also carried a chain-mace, which he spun around his head in a continuous blur. Whenever he struck with it, and in each case a single impact was all it took, another Englishman died, helmeted or not, his cranium shattered. Even as Cerdic watched, the huge horseman must have accounted for eight men, one after another. Enraged, the lad scrabbled for a throwing spear, determined that this one would be his, only for a horn to sound through the tumult: the Normans called to retreat. This time, it was a scene of chaotic disorder. Riderless horses, neighing hysterically, collided with horses on whom the riders were slumped sideways because they'd had limbs lopped or heads and bodies gouged. Others lay crushed and broken beneath their equally mangled mounts. Those who'd managed to hack their way through the English shieldwall had been pulverised by those ranked behind it, their chopped corpses now flung out on top of the others.

To Cerdic's eye, the entire upper section of slope swam with blood, the mounds of fallen men and beasts, the broken spears, the sundered helms, forming an additional rampart of their own behind which the English could stand.

But Harold's army had suffered, too.

As well as Redwald, Cerdic saw Sigmund stretched on his back, his throat slashed to the gullet. Hodda lay next to him, face down, a spear standing upright between his shoulders. The air itself stank of open bowels and seething sweat. More and more figures had joined the English front ranks who looked like fyrdsmen rather than carls. There were weapons aplenty for them to pick up, so they threw down their scythes and cleavers, and brandished swords. But though they roared as lustily as the rest, there had to be questions about these amateur warriors' actual skill.

As Cerdic pondered this, a frantic shout went up. It hooked his attention to the far right because, for the first time that day, there'd been a new note in it. Anger certainly, desperation understandably, but also, possibly, maybe... *fear*.

And he saw why.

On that far right flank, contingents were advancing down-hill.

'Stupid damn fools!' someone bellowed.

Cerdic fancied it was Earl Leofwin, for the younger Godwinson had detached from his brother's personal troop, and now rode pell-mell along the line.

Memories stole into Cerdic's numbed thoughts. Of Unferth saying that the Kentish fyrd, most of whom had only joined them the night before – Earl Leofwin's own peasant militia – had seen their homes and families suffer severely at the invaders' hands, and so had been purposely stationed on that flank because the king's scouts had told him they'd be opposed by companies of mercenaries, mostly Breton, and it was these sellsword scum who'd been the worst burners of Kentish property, the worst despoilers of Kentish women.

From the looks of things, the Bretons, notable for their poorer arms and armour, had already suffered grievously. Their dead and wounded littered that section of slope thicker than leaves, and the men of Kent, vengeful and defiant, were now breaking rank to finish them. Flails and reaping hooks rose and fell as they butchered first the maimed, then further downhill the walking wounded, and then farther downhill yet those mercenaries who weren't injured but limped away in shock. It was a sight to stir English guts. The invaders staggering and tottering, flopping to their knees, hands clutched together for mercy. Receiving none.

The whole English line should charge, an inner voice told Cerdic. They had them on the back foot. Even the knights in the middle had retreated far downhill. But raging voices from the English commanders demanded restraint.

And very soon, he saw the reason for this.

There were still numberless mounted knights below, all now turning their animals round and riding westward, hitting a furious gallop as their lances lowered. At their forefront was one who stood out clearly thanks to the scarlet surcoat he wore over his mail, and the scarlet cloak billowing at his rear. And because he'd removed his helmet and lofted it on high, on the tip of his lance.

As if that wasn't reckless enough, he made additional efforts to draw attention to himself, sitting high in the saddle rather than hunching, shouting at the top of his voice: '*C'est moi,*

Guillaume, votre duc! Vous me voyez, guerriers! Je ne suis pas mort! Je vis! Je vis! Je vis!'

Cerdic felt a prickle of awe. This was surely him. Duke William the Bastard. Presumably now seeking to cancel out some rumour that he'd been slain. But not only that, leading the centre of his army against the English right, which had descended the hill and now was scattered, unable to regain the high ground quickly.

The duke replaced his helmet a handful of yards before careering into them, dropping his lance to the level as his stallion ploughed a bone-crushing trail, spitting a staggering fellow on his spearpoint before discarding the weapon and drawing his longsword. His knights copied him. Again, their steeds rose to the fight, rearing up, the steel-clad hammers of their hooves splintering skulls, tearing faces, their swords and chain-maces whirling. Those Kentish footmen who stayed to fight were outnumbered, the knights bounding back and forth, striking them down at will. Even those who tried to scuttle uphill were overhauled.

The English on the ridge shot arrows and slung stones. Several Normans were struck, but it was too little. The fyrdsmen fell under the invaders' blades en masse.

On the English army's now depleted west wing, Earl Leofwin, overlord of Kent, sat despondently on his horse. Only the Kentish carls remained with him. In what had seemed no time at all, the majority of his part of the army was a pile of butchered meat.

Duke William, meanwhile, cantered casually back to the centre.

'Shouldn't we have gone down to help?' Cerdic said tightly.

'And meet the same fate?' Unferth replied.

If it was possible, even more colour had drained from his milk-grey features. He still used his sword to support himself, and now Cerdic saw with alarm that fresh blood was streaming from under the ring-mail on his left side. If his wound had ever properly closed, it was open again now.

Duke William himself led the next charge.

Cerdic had watched him continuously for the last hour, not losing sight of him once. At first, the scarlet-clad figure had waited in the middle of his force, the bulk of his knights around him, while his arrow companies re-assaulted the army at the top of the hill, persistent showers of missiles falling from on high, lodging themselves in wood, mail and flesh.

It was a wearing-down tactic, the lad realised. With each flight, men dropped, either wounded or slain. Given enough time and materials, this strategy alone could win the battle, or at the very least provoke King Harold to abandon his position of strength, which was why Cerdic was still astonished to see yet another sudden, reckless action by their foe's commander-in-chief; Duke William breaking out from his protective ring, another lance lowered, cloak flowing, the entire devil-horde of horsemen advancing behind him.

English missiles rattled down. Several glanced from the duke's blood-streaked shield, a couple from his helmet. But he bore through, roaring '*Ha Rou!*' as he urged his fearsome mount up and over the heaps of corpses, his lance breaking on the battlement of shields, hacking on all sides with his longsword. From behind him, the host of knights drove in. Sparks flew as blades clashed, men swore and choked, axes sliced mail and flesh, spearheads drove into bellies, scythes carved skulls. Those who'd lost their weapons fought on the ground like dogs, clawing at eyes, ripping out hunks of hair and scalp, working with their teeth at noses, cheeks and throats.

Yet another Norman knight was flung over his animal's head, somersaulting, landing with force alongside Unferth. Unferth, too weak to engage nose to nose, stumbled forward for a quick kill, but the knight sprang swiftly to his feet. Cerdic lunged at him, pushing Unferth aside. The knight dealt the lad a backhand with his mace, catching the side of his helmet. Lights dazzled Cerdic. A downward stroke, and his sword was knocked loose. Had an English thegn not grappled with the Norman from behind, wrapping an arm around his throat, yanking his head backward, the lad would never have had time to pull his hunting knife and slam it to its hilt twice through a breach in the knight's hauberk, a crimson fountain erupting. As the lifeless form dropped, Cerdic saw that the thegn who'd saved him was a grizzled oldster, ingrained with filth, but clearly wearing a surcoat of black and orange.

The thegn seemed to recognise the lad he'd felled on the road from York. His wounded mouth split into a gap-toothed, blood-glutted grin.

And then was smashed to raw meat by the single blow of a spiked ball swinging from a taut chain. Cerdic spun as another Norman horseman reared over him. Another one bearing the emblem of a rearing white leopard. Only the lad's youthful vigour saved him this time, for he ducked under a second wild swipe, and as he did, dragged his knife along the horse's belly, laying open its trapper and the matted, sweaty hair beneath, severing the leather girth. The Norman turned in his seat, but he was slow and heavy – he was an oldster too, it seemed – and his saddle shifted with him. The next thing, he'd tipped off and landed headfirst on the carpet of corpses. Cerdic would have fallen on him, stabbing, stabbing, stabbing, had he not been knocked aside by a housecarl forcing his way past with axe in hand. Treading in guts, Cerdic's foot slithered, his legs splaying apart. He dropped down, a spear missing him by inches. The housecarl's helmet had come off in the melee. He ducked and dived, but a slashing blow caught the side of his skull, splitting the bone wide, his brains spurting.

Cerdic scrabbled away, for a riderless horse now came madly through the throng, its nostrils slathered with crimson mucus, its flanks torn by spearpoints. Men were pounded beneath its hooves like soggy bread. Only by sheer instinct was Cerdic able to evade it. Close by, meanwhile, the knight in the white leopard design was being helped to his feet. He clutched his shoulder as he was assisted to the rear. A younger Norman, a squire maybe, sprang forward to protect his escape. A broken-off arrow hung from his left cheek. He fought on, his teeth visibly clenched on its steel head. There was no time to try and remove it, but then a thrown maul struck him between the eyes, dropping him to his side, multiple axes raining chops on his gibbering, twitching form.

Again though, the Normans were backing off. The English yelled and roared and waved their blades, and showed their shattered shields.

Only ten yards downslope, a single Norman knight, clad in scarlet livery, had refused to retreat. Instead, he removed his helmet again and sat astride his horse, and glared at the English in disbelieving frustration.

For half a crazy second, Cerdic fancied the two of them had locked stares.

As was apparently the fashion in Normandy, Duke William had shaved his dark hair to a mat of sweat-spiked bristles. His features were pale rather than tanned, but full and rounded as though by good living, his mouth small and set like a trap, his eyes livid and strangely overlarge.

He cannot believe that he hasn't broken us, Cerdic told himself. *He's assailed us for most of the day. His best soldiers have died. But try as he may, he cannot dislodge us. And yet he must, he must...*

With an enraged shriek, the duke replaced his helmet and spurred his horse forward, intent on attacking the English alone. Inevitably, shamed and horrified, his knights flooded back uphill.

Again, the collision was unimaginable, shields exploding, blood misting the air. Within minutes, the Normans were retreating again, only for their duke to bellow and scream at them, and goad them into new charges. It happened a second time, and a third, and each time Cerdic saw their elite warriors fall like cattle. He himself was in the thick of it again until he saw Unferth on all fours, a few yards away. He disentangled himself and hastened over there.

'Are you alive?' he said, shouting to be heard over the din.

Unferth laughed in response.

'They surely can't keep this up?' Cerdic said, hefting his brother to his feet.

Unferth shook his head. His helmet was battered out of shape, his nose bled profusely. His whole left side was bright crimson.

'Christ!' Cerdic exclaimed.

Unferth's knees buckled. He slumped down, and Cerdic had to wrap his arms around him. 'Redwald!' he cried, only to remember that Redwald lay slain.

Panting hard, he hauled the casualty back toward the apple tree, no longer hoary white now, but hacked and cut and daubed with red.

Somewhere close by, he heard an intense Norman voice crying out.

'Tuez-les avec des flèches!'

Without looking, he knew that it was Duke William.

Without understanding the Frankish tongue, he knew their tactics again were changing.

Glancing back, he saw the Norman archers jostling forward, loading their bows en masse, eager, hungry, like packs of ravening wolves.

CHAPTER 24

The arrows sleeted down with venom.

There were fewer men now to raise shields, so they struck home more often, into bodies, shoulders, heads, thighs. Each time eliciting curses and shrieks. With the Norman archers much closer, it was now the loins of the English army that were decimated. Cerdic glanced back again and saw vast open spaces where once there'd been serried lines of warriors; saw upturned faces, tearful and slathered with gore where previously there'd been defiance; saw the rearmost ranks, the fyrdsmen with their mallets and polearms, attempting to close up and advance, but hampered by the corpses of thegns and their carls, falling themselves as they too were struck once, twice, even thrice by the arrows of the enemy.

'What... what happened to... Eadora?' the semi-conscious Unferth had grunted, as Cerdic laid him beside the apple tree and commenced covering him over with the shields of the fallen. 'Did you... you say...?'

'She... erm, she's safe,' Cerdic had replied, only thrown by the question briefly. With effort, he'd smiled. 'Of course she's safe, we got her away...'

A similar smile had creased his brother's lips as Cerdic placed a final shield over his face, then found that he only had seconds to grab up another shield with which to protect himself.

Again, what seemed like a dozen arrows lodged in it before the Norman archers moved aside and their cavalry rumbled back up the slope, the infantry close behind.

'*Saint Ouen! Notre Dame!*'

Cerdic ran to join the line without thinking, even though there were so many gaps there. The enemy lowered their lances, to exploit these, at least one knight bearing down on him straight away. Cerdic ducked, missing being skewered by inches. The Norman sped past, veering left to ram his steel-tipped pole through the back of another target. Cerdic cavorted round as a footman came at him, and caught him in the midriff with a two-handed sword-stroke, driving it with such force that it opened the footman's belly, its entire vile contents bursting out.

The next one threw an axe. Again, Cerdic ducked it. He bounced back to his feet, but a fyrdsman wielding a heavy stone crushed the Norman's skull.

This was the way of it now.

Massacre. Murder.

Two formerly rigid lines of opposing troops tangling in a frenzied, gore-drenched enmeshment. Everywhere Cerdic looked, men were being put to the sword.

Or the axe. Or the hammer.

Only a matter of yards away, he saw Aeschmund fighting furiously. The big carl cut his opponent down and roared in triumph, only for a javelin to hit his throat. As he collapsed to his knees, gargling, hands clawing at the gouts of blood, a Norman man-at-arms came up, wrenched the shaft free and plunged its steel head into his chest, driving him backward to the ground, pinning him there. Screaming, Cerdic threw himself forward. They swapped blows brutally, until Cerdic struck clean, incising his foe's shoulder from the neck, leaving a crimson chasm.

He stepped back, dazed by his own proficiency.

I always felt you were capable of more...

These were only common footmen he was now killing one-to-one, but even so his confidence soared. When a horseman ranged forward, longsword drawn, Cerdic parried two strokes, then ripped his steel across the animal's haunches, slicing muscle to the bone. As the beast collapsed, screeching, the rider was trapped underneath, his right thigh cracking like a branch. Cerdic smote him as he lay writhing, again, again, again.

Like the Devil…

When he staggered back, the entire front of his body slicked with other men's blood, the enemy was falling back downslope.

Surely this was it? Surely?

He looked to the royal banners, still flying proudly. The mangled forms of Norman retainers lay deeper around the king's position than anywhere else. He had the mightiest house-carls, of course. The king himself, bloodied head to foot, lifted his dripping axe and shouted his defiance downhill.

Cerdic shouted with him, and then was struck heavily on the helm. As he reeled to his knees, he saw a broken arrow land alongside him. He wasn't so groggy that he couldn't scrabble around in the blood and ruin for the nearest shield – a Norman's, he realised – and swing it over his head. And just in time, for fresh torrents of goose-fletched shafts spilled over them, this time relentlessly.

It seemed a deadlier hail this time. He saw men stitched to their own shields, to each other, to the very ground. When he risked a glance, Duke William had brought his archers much further upslope than previously. They stood again in blocks, amid ranks of crossbowmen, all now loosing feverishly.

He manoeuvred himself onto one knee, finding that, with this larger shield rather than the circular linden wood of the Saxons, he could shelter his entire body. He wasn't sure how many barbs had plunged into it before he rose to a crouch, edging back toward his brother. Unferth, under shields of his own, was protected, but how long could he leave him lying there?

Then Cerdic was dealt a tremendous buffet from the side, such a battering-ram blow that his mind blanked as he hit the floor.

Seconds seemed to pass as he lay insensate. Only slowly did he realise that he'd been ridden into by a horse. As he got to his feet, the animal blundered against him again, sending him staggering. He raised his shield to ward off the expected sword-stroke. But it never came. When he glanced up, Earl Leofwin peered down at him, seemingly puzzled, confused. Cerdic then saw the barbed arrow-head protruding from the front of the nobleman's ring-coat. Dark blood seeped from the side of Leofwin's mouth. When he toppled from his horse, his whole back was clustered with feathered shafts. Cerdic swung toward the royal standards. The Golden Dragon, the Fighting Man... he could see them all clearly. He could even see where the poles had been set into the ground, because the milling thegns and carls that had blocked his vision now lay in heaps. He could also see the frenzied action around the king.

Aelfrith Eagle-Eye, his mouth a torn, bloody hole where a mailed fist had dashed out his teeth, was busy with two other housecarls, lowering a slumped shape to the ground. Behind them, Earl Gurth reared on his horse, helmetless, shield thick with arrows, long, flaxen hair rippling in the wind. Cerdic's eyes flickered back to the fallen figure, whose helmet was being levered off by aides, and then saw it for himself.

A length of goose-shaft jutting from their lord king's left eye.

But jutting only three or four inches, which showed how deeply it had sunk.

Voice cracking with emotion, Earl Gurth called on God and wheeled his horse around the small group, spurring it into a manic, downhill gallop.

Cerdic stared after him. The arrow showers had ceased, for the Normans were ascending the slope again, cavalry and infantry together. The king's brother twirled his battle-axe as he rode, but the first one he met was the hefty knight in the bearskin cloak, who'd replaced his chain-mace with a longs-word, and struck at the earl brutally, slicing into his shoulder. The earl replied with a blow of his own, his axe embedding in the knight's shield, before sliding sideways from his mount. Even with gore jetting from his wound, he landed on his feet, only to be set upon by six or seven more. Drawing his broadsword, he parried a few blows, and even stabbed one in the chest, but then the knight in the bearskin rode up again and clove the crown of his head.

A half-second later, dozens of feet and hooves were trampling him in the filth.

They were all coming now, Cerdic realised. The whole Norman army.

They'd used up their arrows and had thrown caution to the wind. He turned, expecting a counter-wave of Englishmen to meet them. But his gaze roved numbly over blood and corpses extending too far back to see. Some of those English remaining advanced, in small and wounded groups. But others, mostly ragged shapes from the fyrd, many pierced through arm and leg by arrows, now stumbled backward toward the Weald.

Fresh cries drew Cerdic's attention to the royal standards, around the base of which Aelfrith Eagle-Eye and his final two housecarls swung their axes at those Normans who tried to close in. One fell quickly, struck from overhead by the longsword of the knight in the bearskin cloak. The two remaining carls hacked and chopped madly, the second of them going down with a seax sheathed in his chest. The final one, Eagle-Eye, swept two heads from shoulders before he was speared through the back.

Even as that last Englishman fell, further blows rained down, biting timber, the royal banners crashing to earth, the Golden Dragon of Wessex intermingling with the Fighting Man of House Godwinson.

Cerdic stood frozen.

Overhead, the sun, a single cyclopean eye, sank crimson through the autumn miasma. Below it, packs of Normans crossed the field, stabbing with spears and swords at any English who twitched or groaned. Jeering cries drew his eyes back to the royal position, where the jackal-like victors had pulled King Harold's body free of the corpses of his last three men and now sheared at it with their blades, cutting away his ring-mail, gibbering with laughter as they reduced his noble form to a dismembered ruin. As they did, they spat on him, again and again.

Of this immediate group, only the knight in the bearskin cloak took no part, sitting astride his horse, holding aloft the fallen king's Fighting Man banner.

Alongside him, one of the others hurled a lump of shapeless, bloody tissue, another swatting it away with the flat of his sword. A chill struck Cerdic's very bones when he realised that these were the king's severed genitals.

For all the violence of that day, this was the moment that most sickened him. Not just the sheer, visceral savagery of it, but the thought that these bestial fiends were to be the new rulers of England. These slavering, demented curs, these snorting, drooling trolls were the fellow Christians whom Unferth thought might be fooled into behaving like civilised men if Cerdic was 'clever'.

Which reminded him of his brother.

He lurched back across human flotsam toward the apple tree and the form lying prone under a pile of arrow-filled shields.

'Unferth... we have to go.' Frantically, he threw the shields aside. 'We have to go *now*, we—'

The words died on his tongue.

Unferth lay as before. None of the arrows had touched him. But his face was the colour of tallow, the empty orbs of his eyes fixed motionless on the darkening sky.

Cerdic had known that his brother was dying.

All that torturous journey from York, he'd watched him weaken daily. It had only been a matter of time, and yet somehow he'd kept the knowledge at arm's length. As though, if he didn't dwell on it, or even admit it, it wouldn't happen.

Wolf-like snickers sounded behind him.

He rose stiffly, before turning.

A posse of footmen approached, stumbling and slipping over the human debris. At first, he imagined they hadn't really noticed him, were maybe too mesmerised by the destruction all

257

around. Except that one of them carried a crossbow, took casual aim at the lad, and loosed. The quill flew straight, thwacking into the last remaining chunk of Cerdic's shield. He tossed it aside and stood waiting with sword-in-hand. Leering grins broke their sweaty, steel-rimmed faces.

One of them was a mercenary type, bushy bearded, wearing a leather corselet and a helmet lacking nose and cheek-pieces. He was only here for money.

Cerdic ran at *him* first, screaming.

Like the very Devil…

The charge caught the mercenary by surprise. He parried the sword but was caught in the groin by the knife, which Cerdic wrenched upward until it stopped at the ribs.

The others weighed in with blows of their own.

He stabbed a second in the throat, sent him staggering, gurgling. Sliced a third at the knee. Split the skull of another who'd thrown off his helmet… split him to the chin. Screaming, froth spraying, the lad spun to look for a fourth. Found the crossbowman, who rammed Cerdic's face with the stock of his weapon, knocking him several feet back into some vast, immovable object.

Slimed with ordure, fuddled by agony, the lad twisted around.

It was a horse. On top of it sat the knight in the bearskin cloak.

Cerdic drew back his sword to drive it home. But the knight struck first.

CHAPTER 25

Cerdic wasn't sure how long he'd been conscious. Somehow, without noticing, without having any grasp of time at all, he'd emerged from the deep, muffled blackness of insensibility into this world of noisome smells and debilitating pain. He was aware that he lay in the midst of catastrophe, but he wasn't entirely sure how. He could smell the blood and bowels of slaughtered men, but he wasn't certain who they were. Even with his eyes part-closed, the twisted apparition of a hoar-white tree, hacked and slashed, filled with arrows, hovered on the edge of his vision. More worrying than that was the fire suspended above him, the fist-sized lump of searing bright pitch. Its acrid stink penetrated his nostrils; it dripped fresh pain onto his battered, tortured form.

Worse than that, though, were the three hulks standing over him, faceless in the crimson night. They snickered to each other as they prodded and poked at his ring-mail coat. One bent over and swooped something up. Firelight glimmered on the blade of Cerdic's sword. There was more conversation as another hunkered down and tugged at the silver chain and the finely worked clasp, then took the lad by the chin and turned his face side-to-side.

The fellow rose up and said something else. The rest of them seemed to find it funny.

With sluggish horror, Cerdic realised that when, on first returning to consciousness, he'd scraped the blood from his eyes, but had left the rest of his face, he'd inadvertently made it obvious that he was still alive. A foot now struck the side of his helmet. It was only a light kick, but pain lanced his skull like fire. He couldn't prevent himself twitching and gasping.

They laughed.

From all sides, feet toed at him. A gloved hand slapped his face. Once, twice when he didn't respond, then three times, this last time much harder, the hand grasping his jaw again. Cerdic jerked up, the knife still clasped in his left fist, striking at the arm, making good contact. With a bellow of anger and pain, the arm was withdrawn. Shouts and curses sounded as more boots flew in. The first one to catch the side of his head properly pitched him straight back down the river of oblivion.

–

'You're awake at last,' a despondent voice said. 'Good thing. I doubt there'll be much tolerance of shirkers in this place.'

Cerdic glanced groggily around, bewildered by what seemed to be a woodland glade. He was on the ground, because it was damp, but slumped backward against the bole of a tree. Autumnal smells filled his nostrils: fungus, decayed leafage. When he tried to shift position, blinding pain shot through his head. He gasped and grimaced, a mask of what could only be dried blood cracking apart on his throbbing face.

His helmet had gone, but glancing down at himself, he still wore his mail, though it was filthied beyond recognition. He also saw that his wrists were manacled.

He tried to sit upright, but went dizzy again and felt sick.

It was several seconds before he was able to adjust his position more slowly.

Not only were his wrists locked together, it seemed he was shackled by a single chain to a large block of stone about ten feet away and set with iron rings. Other chains radiated out from it, each one connected to another prisoner sitting or lying curled on the ground. There were ten of them in total, all sullied and bedraggled, several wounded, as he undoubtedly was; the blood clots now dried all over him could not have come solely from the men he'd slain.

'How do you feel?' the same voice asked.

They were sitting in a circle, the great stone in the middle, but it was the fellow on Cerdic's right who spoke. A gangling specimen, he was, all knees and elbows, also wearing mail, though bloodied, dirtied and chained, his bearded face cut deeply down the left-hand side.

'I… I…' Cerdic shook his head, still disoriented.

He glanced leftward through the trees, and saw how quickly they thinned out, giving way to meadow and then the great upward sweep toward Senlac Ridge. In bleak daylight, and from this low angle it resembled a mountain of corpses, the only movement among them the odd pennon fluttering on a broken spear, the crows and buzzards hopping back and forth.

He glanced at the other captives. None would look him in the eye. They sat with heads hung. Bleary-eyed, broken, more straw-stuffed dummies than living men.

Cerdic turned to the one who'd spoken. 'Where am I?'

The man rotated his neck slowly as though to straighten it. 'In the camp of Cynric FitzOslac. The so-called Leopard of Tancarville.' He glanced round. 'You're a prisoner of the Normans. Surely you realise that?'

'I… I…'

'They dragged you in during the early hours of this morning. Who are you?'

'Cerdic Aelfricsson. Second son to the earl of Ripon.'

'Earl of Ripon?' If it was possible, the other prisoner looked amused. 'You're far from home.'

'It's a long story,' Cerdic said, trying to look past the circle of chained men, and now seeing the smoke of fires and what looked like numerous tents among the trees. The mail-clad forms of Norman knights and men-at-arms were also visible. Amid the browning, trampled undergrowth, he saw other prisoners seated in their own shackles.

'Long or short,' his new companion said, 'it's over now.'

'Who are *you*, anyway?' Cerdic asked.

'Eadhelm. I *was* thegn of Tenterden, in service to the Earl of Kent. Now I'm just Eadhelm.'

Cerdic looked him over again. As well as the wound on his face, the man called Eadhelm had many gashes on his arms and hands. He might be a beanpole, but he'd fought hard for his master, Earl Leofwin. The lad's eyes roved again over the others. None were armed, of course, but it seemed strange they remained girt for battle.

'You say we're the prisoners of Cynric…?'

'Of Tancarville.'

'Not William the Bastard?'

'Duke William is their overall commander,' Eadhelm said. 'But there are many warlords under his banner with minds of their own. Count Cynric, like most of these Norman nobles, I'm led to believe, doesn't trust his overlord to be generous once England finally falls. So, they're getting their share while they can. They seized you, I imagine, because of your quality coat. No fyrdsman ever wore such ring-mail. Me, I just plain told them who I was… said that my family would pay a ransom. That ransom, I now fear, will be everything we have.'

'How do you know all this?'

'One of them speaks English… when he deigns to converse with us. The rest though… you have to be careful, young Cerdic.' His gaze speared through the trees to a place on the left. 'Watch *that one* in particular.'

Two Norman horsemen were riding past. Neither wore helmets, the one at the front a squat but scowling individual with a standing thicket of greasy red hair.

'That's Count Cynric's son,' Eadhelm said. 'Joubert. For whatever reason, the hatred he harbours for us wasn't discharged on Senlac hill. And he likes to make examples. Look over there.'

Cerdic followed his nod, and about twenty yards away saw a ragged figure, hands manacled like the others, but swinging by the neck from a creaking bough, a neck that had extended by several unnatural inches.

Eadhelm grunted. 'A few hours ago, that fellow, whoever he is, or was, refused to look at Lord Joubert while being addressed. That was all, refused to look at him. *That* was his reward.'

'Welcome to the new England,' the man sitting chained on the other side of Thegn Eadhelm said. He wore only blood-stained rags and hugged himself in the cold.

The new wyrd, Cerdic thought, with a pang of disbelief. *Hanged for looking at someone the wrong way? Or for not looking at them?*

'We need to escape,' he muttered.

'Escape?' Eadhelm shrugged. 'Can you even stand?'

Cerdic attempted to struggle up to his feet, but promptly went groggy and landed hard on his backside. He felt sick again as he sat there, head drooped.

'Am I badly hurt?' he eventually asked.

'I think you are,' Eadhelm replied. 'Your face looks as if it's been danced on by a man in clogs, but more important, you have a head injury. It's in the very middle of your scalp. Looks like a sword's edge did that. No doubt your helmet saved your life, but the blade bit clean through.'

A vague memory surged to the front of Cerdic's fuddled mind. The mounted knight. The one in the bearskin cloak, who'd accounted for so many during that terrible melee on the hillside. The one Cerdic had attacked.

Only to receive a sword-stroke in return.

A sword-stroke to his head, after which he remembered nothing else.

He probed at his scalp. His hair felt as though it was plastered with dried mud, though doubtless it was congealed blood. When he fingered the wound, even though he was careful, it stung agonisingly.

'It should be stitched,' Eadhelm said. 'But don't hold your breath for that here.'

'Will I die?' Cerdic almost felt hope in asking. Death would be one quick way to relieve this misery, though on reflection, it was hardly the warrior's way.

'If you don't die, it'll be nothing to do with our captors,' Eadhelm replied. 'No one here cares one way or the other. If they can't get coin for *you*, they'll get it for your armour, and cut their losses.' His eyes narrowed as he focused on something beyond their immediate vicinity. 'Speak of the Devil.'

Now that his stupor was fading, Cerdic saw further into his captors' camp, to one tent in particular, which stood out among the others. A virtual pavilion, firelight shimmering inside, next-door to which a distinctive standard flew atop a tall pole: a rearing white leopard on a field of black.

Two figures had now stepped outside from it. The first was a pale-faced young priest with thin, sombre features, his hair shaven into a painfully severe tonsure. Even under his maroon cassock and cloak, he was long-bodied and spindly-limbed, like an insect. The fellow with him was far more impressive, not least because the guards at either side snapped immediately to attention.

Count Cynric, Cerdic suspected.

More interesting still, though, this was possibly the same Norman knight he had seen thrown from his horse at the height of the battle, who'd then been led to safety. Not only because of the White Leopard coat of arms, but because he now wore only boots, leather hunting breeks and a cloak, his left shoulder padded and bandaged, his left arm strapped across his naked chest.

Cerdic still sought clarity. 'That's the count?'

'None other,' Eadhelm replied.

Cerdic appraised him. Unlike his son, who was of solid, stocky build, the nobleman was tall, about the height of Earl Rothgar, but leaner. He had a mop of white hair, and different to the rest of the Normans, a scraggy white beard and moustache. His features were gaunt, and his exposed physique, while not emaciated, was not muscle-packed either. A man in his mid-sixties, at the youngest. It was impressive that he'd ridden to war, let alone fought, though of course, if he'd not had loyal men around him, he'd never have left the field alive.

'He doesn't look like the Devil,' Cerdic said.

Eadhelm snorted. 'The worst ones never do.'

CHAPTER 26

It rained for much of that first morning, and the prisoners sat without shelter, chained and shivering. While the majority of the Normans withdrew into their tents, the captives remained under the guard of a single man-at-arms leaning on his spear, huddled in his cloak, watching them, feral-eyed, as though it was their fault that he was out in the cold and the wet.

Cerdic stuttered a few prayers, those he was clear-headed enough to remember, but after all this turmoil, none of them seemed to mean much anymore. He thought on Osric and Aethelbald, who had partly restored his confidence in petitioning Heaven, but you could only ask for divine assistance for so long and receive none, before your doubts that anyone was listening became overwhelming. Aethelric – poor Aethelric – had always preached that God moved in unfathomable ways, and that Man should never presume to understand his motivations. However, there were some things Cerdic *did* understand, better now than ever before: pain, squalor and utter, abject despair.

After a couple of hours, when the rain had eased off, their captors reappeared, but gingerly, glancing with disgust at the lead-grey English sky. A camp-boy brought a bucket of what looked like pigswill into the circle of saturated men, a single wooden spoon indicating that it was for them. A bucket of water was also delivered, most likely rainwater, this with a single iron cup.

Cerdic didn't remember the last time he had eaten, or at least the last time he hadn't eaten and promptly vomited, so he partook of the repast hungrily. They all did, passing the two buckets around until they were empty. Afterwards, though he was certain he'd consumed nothing but filth, the lad felt better. He certainly felt that he was thinking more clearly. He also probed at his scalp wound and found that the rain had washed it clean.

'How many men did we lose?' he asked Eadhelm.

'See for yourself,' Eadhelm said. 'Most of them are still up there.'

Cerdic glanced through the trees again, and up onto the moonscape of the dead. The ghostlike figures of women and girls had now appeared, looking for missing husbands, lovers, sons. Those who found someone promptly set up a wild wailing, dropping to their knees and cradling the tragic remains.

He watched this with a slow rekindling of his youthful rage. For a moment, he was about to blurt out that this war wasn't over yet, that England's northern earls were not present, that still there were English armies in the field. But then he recalled how he'd seen for himself that Edwin and Morcar had possessed no stomach for this fight even when King Harold was alive. Now that he was dead, he doubted they'd come anywhere near the south of England.

Instead of making a fool of himself, he leaned back against the tree trunk. He'd been unconscious the night before rather than sleeping, and was deeply exhausted, his joints and muscles aching from his efforts in the battle, his bones throbbing where he'd been pummelled, his head thumping. The laceration in his scalp burned as though hot coals sat in it.

But it soon became clear that there'd be no time for rest.

Before Cerdic knew it, the young Norman called Joubert had ridden up through the trees and reined in his steed. He shouted something unintelligible and the man-at-arms on guard duty came quickly to attention, two or three others hurrying forward from the nearest ring of tents, fitting their helmets in place.

Hurriedly, they unfastened the chains tethering the prisoners to the central block, and with much shouting and kicking, got them to their feet. None of those captured found it easy. Eadhelm in particular struggled, his wounded face pale and twisting with pain.

'Where are you hurt?' Cerdic asked, trying to help him.

'It's nothing,' the thegn hissed. 'Horse kicked me in the base of the spine. It sounds bad, I know, but it only knocked the wind out of me. I'll live.'

Joubert reddened as he watched all this from the saddle, his thick lips curling with irritation. With a curse, he took a coiled whip from his saddlebags and rode around the circle, lashing down with it. Stinging cracks were dealt to backs and shoulders already bent with pain. Any exposed flesh was laid open.

Cerdic still wore his ring-coat, but sometime between now and when he'd been pulled down from Senlac Ridge, he'd not just lost his helmet, but also his cloak with its precious chain and clasp, his tooled leather sword-belt and his gauntlets. A single blow from the whip cut him across the back of his left hand, a second across his left cheek. He glared up at the young noble, who at this proximity he saw was probably no more than two or three years his senior, and Joubert glared back with a hatred so livid it was like a whip-stroke in itself. The Norman spat out two or three phrases, none of which Cerdic understood, before laughing, rearing his mount onto two legs, and galloping away again.

'I told you not to aggravate him,' Eadhelm said. 'I told you what he's capable of.'

'If *this* is to be our life from now on, I can think of better options,' Cerdic replied.

Though they remained manacled individually, they were coerced into single file and kicked and pushed into a stumbling forward march.

'You mean death?' Eadhelm said, having fallen in behind him. 'And what control will you have over the manner of it? That fellow hanged. Lord Joubert threw the rope over the branch personally. Hoisted him up there himself, taking his time all the way. It was the slowest execution I've ever seen, but I imagine there are slower ones he could think of. Don't provoke him, Cerdic. When his wrath falls on you, it might fall on the rest of us too.'

'Were you really a thegn?' Cerdic asked him.

'Ah, you mean my unwillingness to die foolishly is unsuited to high office?'

'Even in all this shit, we should remember who we are.'

'And who are we?' Eadhelm said, quite seriously. 'This region is called Haestinga. It was named many centuries ago, after a great leader of the pagan Saxons. There's a town on the coast not too far from here, which also bears his name.'

'I know nothing of that,' Cerdic said.

'Precisely my point. Princes rise and fall with indecent speed in this land of ours. Be wary... lest this earl of Ripon from whom you draw your own greatness is not already forgotten by the time our new king is crowned.'

Cerdic wanted to reply that Eadhelm's attitude was cowardly, pathetic, that they weren't beaten yet, that they could over-whelm these dogs. But that wasn't even close to being true. As they trudged through the woods, they passed more and more Norman encampments, each one delineated by a different crest on the flags flying beside the central tent, and in all cases they saw knights and men-at-arms, well-armed, heavily mailed, standing by smoky campfires, talking and laughing as they drank and ate, while all the prisoners he spotted – each house-hold seeming to have captured its own quota – sat grizzled, bedraggled, shattered of spirit.

A short time later, they were pushed out onto the open meadow. Even here, on this lower, flatter section, there was evidence of slaughter. Lone corpses lay untended in the grass. Most likely individuals who had withdrawn from the fighting when wounded, only to die later. Further up the slope, of course, the refuse thickened.

There were now even more members of the bereaved up there, all weeping piteously. Astonishingly, though, Cerdic also heard laughter. Looking harder, he saw Norman men-at-arms, or maybe Breton mercenaries – it was difficult to distinguish between them from this distance – rooting among the dead, seizing boots, belts and weapons. His blood might have boiled, but he could hardly expect these lowest-level vermin in the whole Norman army, this literal gutter-trash, to behave any differently when their duke had ordered the same, and even worse, for the King of England.

–

In a short time, they'd reached a part of the field where certain Norman lords had erected their pavilions on the meadow itself, including one particularly huge one: a virtual canvas palace, dyed a deep regal purple, flapping and bellying on a sturdy frame of scaffolding, warm fires burning within, three huge gonfalons billowing from mast-like poles alongside it. The first portrayed the Golden Lions of Normandy on a field of scarlet. The second was also scarlet, but with the inverted Cross of St Peter emblazoned on it in black, and the golden Crossed Keys of the Papal States, while the third was a simple black cross on white, the time-honoured Holy Rood.

Due to the small phalanx of men-at-arms standing guard at the entrance, and the preponderance of knights, rather than lesser men, who seemed to be camped nearby, it seemed likely that this was the abode, at least temporarily, of Duke William.

However, there was no sign of the Bastard now, and they halted about forty yards short of it, again in response to shouts and kicks.

Other slaves had arrived ahead of them and were already at work.

Slaves, Cerdic wondered in disbelief. *Is that what we now are?*

This time yesterday, he'd been second-in-succession to a great title and a vast estate. One defeat later, he was a slave.

The other slaves, or 'prisoners-of-war', as he tried to tell himself, had been equipped with spades and picks, and were engaged in digging what appeared to be a trench or lengthy pit. Norman men-at-arms, acting as overseers, stood and watched, cajoling, barking orders, occasionally striking them with staffs or whips.

Cerdic was bewildered as well as horrified. He now understood what Eadhelm had meant when he'd referred to 'shirkers', but why such brutal treatment of men who had fought with honour in defence of lord and land? He couldn't understand. Weren't these fellow Christians who'd made them captive? Weren't they functioning here under a papal banner, which made them warriors of God?

He then saw something else, which partly answered his question.

Only a short distance away, further onto the meadow, he saw similar trenches, these now filled in. But also, he saw bodies being laid out in reverential rows, much as the monks had done with the English after Fulford. Many wore only loincloths or shifts, but they were clearly Norman, for each had the distinctive close-cropped hair. Even as Cerdic watched, more arrived, brought downslope over the backs of the horses of grim-faced colleagues, the majority steeped in blood, their bodies torn horrendously.

It was the price of war, the cost of conquest.

Though it still shouldn't have fostered this visceral hatred of an enemy who'd done nothing more than defend his home.

A backhand to the mouth brought Cerdic out of his reverie.

He tottered, eyes watering. When he tasted fresh blood, his gaze narrowed on a hump-backed, brown-toothed man-at-arms thrusting a spade into his hands.

'*Prenez-le, cochon!*' the stunted monster shouted, foul spittle spraying.

Scowling, Cerdic took the spade, and was directed with much pushing and kicking to join the line of trench-diggers already sweating and groaning as they worked.

The ground comprised thick, heavy sod. Not yet water-logged by winter, in fact firm-packed from the long, hot, rain-less summer, it was going to be back-breaking work even to dig a couple of feet, never mind the six or seven required to bury men permanently. But from the stony expressions on the faces of their captors, this made not the slightest difference.

Despite the difficulties of having to dig in heavy ring-mail and with hands fettered, the prisoners were forced to work for the rest of that morning and most of the afternoon. Rain fell over them intermittently, the stiff October wind cutting like a sword. For all this, they managed to deepen the first part of the trench, which had been measured out to around two yards in width and seventy yards in length, to about five feet, before they were ordered to down tools and rest, at which they slumped, gasping and panting, onto the great heaps of soil.

On the other side of the trench, knights and men-at-arms continued to bring down the bodies of fallen comrades, camp-boys then respectfully undressing them. The bodies, once semi-naked, were at least washed clean of blood and filth by the rain. Water dripped steadily from the nose-pieces of the helmeted guards standing by. Even they were so affected by this duty now that they'd ceased to direct hostile glares at the prisoners and simply looked weary and haggard.

Lord Joubert rode up again, halting to assess what progress had been made. As always, he seemed dissatisfied. He hawked and spat, then issued some casual orders to the overseers. The prisoners, expecting to be put back to work after only a few moments' respite, hung their heads with exhaustion, but instead, they were nudged and tugged back to their feet, and then their tools were taken off them and they were pushed back toward the treeline and hopefully Count Cynric's camp.

It was truly a wonder, Cerdic thought, that a muddy wood-land clearing, with no shelter and a central stone to which they'd be crudely chained, now seemed as desirable as a bed in a fire-warmed chamber.

'*Pas lui!*' Joubert shouted, a cruel smile splitting his already pig-ugly features.

Needless to say, he was pointing at Cerdic.

'*Il doit continuer à travailler!*'

Indifferently, the overseers pushed Cerdic back toward the edge of the trench, and his spade was handed to him again.

'*Vous devez creuser!*' one of them instructed, pointing at the section of pit still to be cleared out.

Cerdic watched Joubert's diminishing figure, rent sod flying at his heels. Then saw Eadhelm glancing back pityingly as he and the others limped away.

The hatred he harbours for us wasn't discharged on Senlac hill...

Clearly his fellow slave's warning was true, even if somewhat perplexing.

Fear of working the prisoners to death before their value could even be ascertained had perhaps prompted the unexpectedly early finish on the burial site. But losing the odd one was maybe unavoidable. Lord Joubert, as Cerdic had been advised, had clearly decided it was time to make another example. But again, the lack of any sense that they were all brothers in Christ was astonishing.

Cerdic dug again, fresh sweat beading his brow, but he was determined not to show pain or despair. If the slaughter of his friends and family couldn't crush him, then this definitely wouldn't. He was the son of an earl. But not just any earl. A fighting earl. An earl who'd played his own key role in bringing down the tyrant, Macbeth, in defeating the fiery Welsh warlord, Gruffydd ap Llywelyn. That was Cerdic's stock. He wouldn't be broken by this.

'You must have done something special to annoy him,' a Frankish voice said.

Cerdic glanced briefly around. It seemed that of all the grave-site supervisors, only one now remained: a huge fellow standing close to a glowing brazier. One of them could speak English, Eadhelm had said, though he rarely bothered. Cerdic was clearly honoured. He dug on, spading out the thick, sludgy soil, his sweat running in rivulets, each motion a jolting stab to his shoulder and elbow joints. He would empty this entire trench on his own rather than fail in the eyes of his enemies.

'You need to be careful, boy,' the fellow added. 'He'll kill you without a thought.'

'Not if I kill him first,' Cerdic couldn't resist grunting back.

There was a snort of laughter. 'You'll have trouble getting it done. I saw you fighting up there on the ridge. You didn't lack heart. But you have no skill.'

Cerdic straightened up and looked around properly. For the first time he realised that the man by the brazier, who wore a hooded green tunic and green braies cross-banded from knee to ankle, was clad in a heavy cloak of what looked like bearskin, with a longsword suspended over his back. The lad recognised the cloak if not the man.

This was the same knight he'd engaged with in that final, desperate struggle.

On reflection, it hadn't been a wise choice. The fellow was half a foot taller than Cerdic's father had been, and Earl Rothgar had had three inches on Cerdic. What was more, his physique was immense, his shoulders as broad as an ox. The rain appeared to ease off, so his shrugged back his hood, revealing a thick bullneck, a square head and hair shaved into very fine, dark bristles. His face was lean and chiselled. Handsome enough, though scarred and nicked in many places.

'Why don't you just kill me now?' Cerdic said. 'You tried to do it before. And see...' He released his spade. 'I've downed my tool. I won't work for you anymore. You *must* kill me.'

The knight ignored that. 'You should know that many of those English who fled the field... they formed another line later, behind a...' He struggled to find the word. 'We would call it a *fosse*. A ditch, yes? Very deep, which we didn't know was there. A lot of us fell into it. They killed us as we lay broken.'

Cerdic sneered. 'They should have taken prisoners instead. Thrown you into a ditch of their own. Filled it in while you were still alive.'

The knight mused. 'They *should* have taken prisoners, you are correct. Then they could have exchanged them for those *we* have taken. Such as you. *Non?* Instead, they ran into the forest. The *fosse* prevented us pursuing. We didn't know if other ramparts awaited us in the dark. I tell you this so you'll understand that your king's army wasn't entirely destroyed.'

'Unlike my king's body,' Cerdic said.

'Ah. You witnessed that?'

'Does it make me a danger?' The lad held his arms out. 'Then strike me down, as I've requested.'

The knight rubbed at his clean-shaved jaw. 'Could you find the place... where it happened?'

Cerdic was puzzled. 'Couldn't *you*? You were there.'

The knight made a gesture. 'And all I remember is piles of dead men, streams of blood. One chopped corpse looks much like another, *non*? Especially in the dark.'

'Especially when your idiot comrades cut away all his distinguishing armour and clothing.'

By his expression, the knight didn't disagree with that sentiment. 'The question is simple, my friend. Could you find the place again?'

Evidently, they hadn't been able to retrieve King Harold's body. Cerdic pondered this. Not that it posed much of a threat to them. All he remembered once they'd finished with it was a gutted, gelded husk. Even so, he had no intention of finding it for them. Even if he thought he could identify it, which he was sure he couldn't, he wasn't going up that hill of carrion again. Not so they could put his eviscerated master on display like some grisly hunting trophy.

'Well?'

Cerdic shrugged. 'I've had half my brains knocked out since then. How could I?'

The knight nodded, as if he'd expected this response. Then, surprisingly, he said: 'They shouldn't have done that to him.'

Cerdic watched him carefully. The fellow seemed genuine. 'Why didn't you stop them?' he asked.

The knight half-smiled. 'I might be Turold de Bardouville, Count Cynric's champion-at-arms' – Cerdic could easily believe that; the fellow had it written all over his huge form – 'but in rank I am landless. A knight in service. Count Eustace, my master's friend, led the charge on the dying king. Who was I to interfere? But Godwinson deserved better after the way he fought.'

Cerdic picked his spade up again. 'None of this makes any difference to me.'

'It means your king didn't shame you.'

'I'm ashamed just to be alive.'

'When you fought so hard to live?' The knight called Turold sounded sceptical. 'Your spirit is wounded, I understand. But it will heal. Until then you keep your head low and you say nothing. You understand that? At least… say nothing you don't need to.'

Puzzled by that final comment, Cerdic looked around again. The knight, having warmed himself on the brazier, was walking away toward a single-man tent.

'Wait! You say your name is Turold? That's not English. How do you speak our language?'

Turold looked back. 'An intelligent question at last. It shows there is hope for you.'

'Why are you helping me?'

The knight shrugged. 'I'm not. I am guarding you. You are property now. A possession. But it is better than death. So, heed me well when I tell you, say nothing you don't need to.'

CHAPTER 27

Cerdic dug on into the evening alone, but it was easier now. The knight called Turold didn't re-emerge from the overseers' tent to engage him in further conversation, and there was no one else around to kick or whip him.

As the rain eased off, a dank, grey dusk set in. Fires and torches sprang to life in the Norman camps, while out on the meadow an eerie mist arose. It lay along the ground, pouring into the trench like murky liquid. The overall effect was more than unsettling. Across the lower section of the battlefield, all he could soon see were the upright shapes of broken lances and limp pennons. Here and there, a twisted claw jutted from a corpse now mostly hidden. Meanwhile, the lamentation on the hillside had grown, for there were many up there now, whole families searching for their loved ones.

And then something happened, which briefly made Cerdic think he was dreaming.

A small procession came west-to-east across the flat, two monks at the front riding horses, one hefting an oil lamp, the other a two-handed crucifix. Behind them were two more riders, the first a young woman wearing a russet cloak, cut square and tied with a cord over her white kirtle, and a white linen veil draped loose around her shoulders. The other was also a woman, well-dressed in a tighter-fitted white gown but with a hooded coat of thick white wool over the top, the hood drawn up. Behind these, a burly manservant drove a cart, in the back of which lay an open, man-sized casket. The group approached in silence, all but gliding through the low-lying mist.

Cerdic stopped digging to watch. Whichever Normans were out and about, they also paused, fascinated. Even Turold seemed to sense the change in atmosphere, emerging from his tent and standing alongside the prisoner.

Thirty yards short of the duke's pavilion, the new arrivals halted, the monks and the two women dismounting. The monks, who looked cowed and uneasy, remained where they were, the one with the crucifix holding it ever more determinedly aloft, while the two women advanced a few more yards, the one with the hood now folding it backward, a cascade of flaxen-blonde hair falling over her shoulders. Clearly she was the older of the duo, though even from a distance of twenty yards, Cerdic spotted that she was a rare beauty.

The guards at the front of the tent had stiffened to semi-attention, unsure what they were seeing here. Their captain finally came forward, one hand on the hilt of his sword. The younger woman, who wasn't much older than Cerdic, approached him and they conversed in French, during the course of which the captain threw several guarded glances at the beautiful older woman waiting a few yards away. Eventually, still unsure, he retreated, turning and walking into the pavilion.

A brief mumble of voices sounded inside, before the captain reappeared with another man, a holy man, or so it seemed. He was of shortish, plump stature, wearing a purple cassock belted at the waist, a golden cross and chain at his throat, and a purple skullcap. In looks, he vaguely resembled Duke William himself, but his face was fatter and mottled, his eyes even more protuberant, his nose and mouth broad and flat. All he lacked were warts, for this was surely Bishop Odo of Bayeaux, the duke's brother and deputy, and the man Unferth had described as 'a bloated human toad'.

At first, the bishop seemed intrigued by the unexpected guests, though he took only one glance at the blonde-haired woman, standing fay and lovely in the mist, and a look of contempt crossed his face. He didn't speak harshly to the younger girl, but his voice was loud and thick with arrogance. Whatever he said was incomprehensible to Cerdic, though not to Turold.

'Interesting,' the knight muttered in English. 'The Lady of Walsingham herself, Edith Swan-Neck... the fairest of all. Or so we were told. Godwinson's mistress.'

'I thought they were married,' Cerdic replied.

'Only after the Danish fashion,' the knight said, again happy to converse with his prisoner. 'You will find that unacceptable to the Church of Rome, of which Bishop Odo is a keen advocate.'

'Aye,' the lad said. 'He looks it.'

The girl spoke again to the bishop in fluent French.

'Hah!' Turold said. '*They* want your king's body too. Lady Edith is here on behalf of his mother, Gytha Thorkelsdóttir, who seeks to bury her son in the family vault.'

'*Non!*' the bishop said firmly, adding further dismissive words, which left the girl visibly upset.

When she turned and spoke to her mistress, it was in perfect English, though her own accent was Norman-French. 'My lady, his grace, the bishop says it is not possible. He says that his brother, Duke William, who is soon to be King of England, cannot accept the creation of a shrine to... to a perjurer and a usurper.'

Bishop Odo watched them defiantly, but Lady Edith barely flinched.

'Ask his grace, Yvette,' she said calmly, 'if I may speak to Duke William directly. We have travelled a long way.'

'*Non!*' came the bishop's sharp response. Another diatribe followed.

The girl turned again to her mistress. 'The fact we have travelled a long way is no one's fault but our own, my lady.'

The bishop followed this with more belligerent advice, which this time the girl looked too embarrassed to repeat.

'Translate for me, Yvette,' Lady Edith said. 'Every word.'

The girl called Yvette hung her head before mumbling: 'You are known as a sinful woman.' She glanced up, teary-eyed. '*His* words, my lady.'

Lady Edith nodded. 'I understand that.'

Bishop Odo spoke on. Again, the girl translated.

'Even were it possible to hand over King Harold's remains, which it is not, for the duke intends to have them buried in a hidden place, *you* would be the last person he would consign them to.'

'Please remind his grace,' Lady Edith said, 'that I came here on behalf of King Harold's elderly mother—'

The bishop cut in with another tirade, as though he'd half-understood. Again, Yvette looked crestfallen.

'Translate, Yvette,' Lady Edith instructed her.

'Bishop Odo says you are foolish and deluded. The same applies to Gytha Thorkelsdóttir, whose wits must be scattered by the bitter winds that always blow on this island to think that before the war is even concluded, his mightiness Duke William would be so incautious as to hand over anything that might be used as a totem around which your remaining warriors can gather.'

The bishop added more, now with a degree of consolation.

'When the duke buries the king, full religious rites will be observed,' Yvette said.

The bishop spoke on.

She translated: 'We have the bishop's own word as a father of the Church.'

'I accept the bishop's word, of course,' Lady Edith replied, a single tear glinting in her lashes. 'But might I at least see my husband's remains before I depart this place, so as to bestow one last kiss on his cheek.'

Yvette was halfway through translating this, when a figure wearing scarlet over his chain-mail came furiously out from the pavilion, several attendants behind him.

Duke William had clearly been listening and had finally had enough.

All those knights and men-at-arms in the vicinity, including Turold, dropped to one knee, sword points in the dirt. Cerdic gazed at them as he leaned on his spade. Those who'd emerged with the duke included Count Cynric and several others who, from their swagger and superiority, were of similar high rank.

The duke came forward until he stood ahead of his brother. On foot, he was not a physically impressive man, squat and barrel shaped, though slightly taller than the bishop and lacking his excessive girth.

He too struck Lady Edith with a fierce tirade, which again Yvette was reluctant to translate, though, very gently, her mistress bade her proceed.

'What you see here, my lady... is all you need to see. So says Duke William.'

The duke ranted on, pointing toward the darkling ridge.

'See what your lover's vanity has led us to,' the girl said. 'This host of the slain.'

The duke spoke again.

'*Your* people as well as ours.'

He added more.

'He broke a vow,' she said. 'He betrayed all our trust.'

Turold happened to glance up and noticed to his dismay that Cerdic was still standing. Swiftly, he grabbed the lad's shoulder and yanked him down to one knee.

'Because of that, God has smitten us both,' the girl translated.

Duke William's rage was cooling, but he continued to pin the Lady Edith with his odd goggle-eyed stare, and to lecture her hard.

'We estimate that five thousand of our followers lie dead here,' the girl translated. 'Of your own people, it is twice that number at least. Maybe more.'

He added a footnote.

'This is all you need to see, madam. This is the price of your lover's treachery. There is nothing for you here. So, depart this place… with my blessing. While you still can,' he added with a cold smile.

Bishop Odo clearly felt it time to add further thoughts of his own.

'The bishop gives his word, madam,' the girl translated, 'in the name of His Holiness, Pope Alexander II, that Harold Godwinson will receive all due respect.'

Again, Cerdic was reminded what it was they'd been fighting. Not just some puffed-up brigand from Normandy, but the word of Pope Alexander, the mouthpiece of God himself. A mouthpiece, which on this occasion, whether God knew it or not, was lying through its teeth. Because they didn't even have the king's body.

Unable to constrain a sigh, Lady Edith signalled to her translator that it was time to leave. However, before the girl could move, one of Duke William's counts stepped forward. Like many of his fellow Norman soldiers, he was well-built, his hair dark and cut to the bristles, but his features, which might once have been handsome, were odiously pock-marked, and when he smiled, his mouth hitched strangely to the left, as if the nerves in one side of his face had been damaged.

When he spoke to Yvette, it was unintelligible to Cerdic, but delivered in a tone that was only superficially friendly. For her part, the girl regarded him as though terrified.

'Yvette?' Lady Edith queried.

'My lady…' Yvette's voice was tremulous. 'This is Count Eustace of Boulogne. He bids us stay awhile.'

Count Eustace walked around the young translator, speaking airily, gracing her with another lopsided smile that was patently fake.

'Yvette, what is happening?' Lady Edith came forward. She looked to Duke William, who now was listening to Count Eustace. 'My lord, you granted us safe conduct away from here.'

Count Eustace ignored her, addressing his overlord.

'Yvette,' Lady Edith said. 'You must translate my words for them.'

'My lady, I—'

'What is happening here?' Lady Edith demanded.

Count Eustace smiled again, speaking in gentle tones as he placed a forefinger under Yvette's chin, and tilted her face upward.

'Duke William, you have everything you could possibly want from us,' Lady Edith protested. 'I beg you... do not besmirch your honour with unseemly acts. Yvette, you must translate this.'

'My lady...' The frightened girl shook her head. 'I can't...'

Count Eustace then said something else. First of all addressing the duke, his expression hardening, and then turning to Lady Edith herself.

'That message was for *me*, girl,' the woman snapped. 'You must translate *that*, at least. I command you.'

Yvette swallowed hard. 'My lady, Count Eustace thinks he has recognised me.'

Lady Edith looked perplexed. 'Please explain.'

'My father, you may recall... Count Rodric of Hiemois, was in arms against Duke William only nine years ago. He sided with King Henry of France, a combined force that was crushed...'

'At the battle of Varaville,' Cerdic said half to himself, remembering Redwald's potted history lesson about the Norman state.

Turold glanced down at him.

'Your father is still exiled in Anjou,' Lady Edith said.

'That's correct,' the girl replied. 'But I am *here*.'

'And now they've recognised you?'

'I was only eight years old at the time, but... I've often heard it said that Count Eustace has an eye for *very* young girls. I must have made an impression.'

Duke William, suddenly looking tired of the business, issued fresh orders.

Yvette hung her head. 'Duke William says I must stay here. As his guest.'

'You mean his hostage!' Lady Edith glared at the Norman potentate. 'That is unacceptable. Tell him, Yvette. You were sent to me by your father when you were only a child. You lived under my roof and my protection. You are no possible threat to any plans he may have for the conquest of this country...'

The girl explained as best she could to the duke, who shrugged when he responded.

'Duke William says that at some point, he will need to make truces with his enemies at home. He cannot rule here if wolves are stalking his borders in Normandy.'

Lady Edith shook her head. 'And you are to be a bargaining chip?' She addressed Bishop Odo. 'Your grace, I beg you... this cannot be allowed.'

The bishop waved her away, spouting some further venom.

Yvette coloured pink. 'The bishop says don't talk to him with your...'

'Go on,' Lady Edith urged her.

'With your scheming harlot tongue.'

The lady fixed the prelate with piercing eyes. She no longer looked mournful. 'And what of our Holy Mother Church, whom he claims to represent? What of our Holy Father in Rome? What will *he* say on the matter?'

The bishop chuntered in response, as though it was inconsequential.

'The papal mission here is to supervise the reclamation of England's soul from a wayward Church and apostate practices,' the girl translated. 'Duke William's affairs with his nobles are his concern alone. The Holy Father will not interfere.'

Cerdic, still an enthralled observer, felt like shouting, 'What did you expect? They've already permitted the invasion of one Christian state by another. Murder and arson are only sins if they're committed by people they don't like.' Common sense forbade it, but he thought it nevertheless.

Try as he might, Cerdic now knew for certain that he'd never forgive those churchmen, of whom Pope Alexander was the foremost scoundrel, who'd endorsed this travesty of God's will. It couldn't be the Lord Himself; the lad refused to consider that. God was love, God was the Father who oversaw all things good. Yes, it was the case that many requests for assistance had failed during the unravelling of this catastrophe, but God knew better than His supplicants. Not all prayers could be answered with seeming beneficence. Cerdic *had* to believe that, because without it, what else was there? This though... this was different. This *man*, Alexander II, claimed to be the vicar of God, but on this evidence alone – the darkness, the dirt, the pain, the stony duke in his glimmering scarlet brocade, the gloating bishop with his poisonous words, the young woman seized while petitioning for kindness, the ghastly aura from that mountain of slaughtered men – he was more like an agent of Satan.

Again, Duke William issued orders.

'His Highness, the duke, will allocate trusted men to escort you to safety,' Yvette said. 'Meantime, I must remain here.'

'Tell him we need no escort,' Lady Edith replied in a tone dripping with sarcasm. 'I trust implicitly in the famous honour of his knights.'

When the girl told the duke this, he merely shrugged.

Now, Count Eustace spoke again, fondling Yvette's shoulder, entwining his gloved finger in the dark brown tresses emerging from under her veil. Before she could translate, the duke issued another order. Whatever it was, it didn't seem to please the count, who stepped back with a peevish expression. As Duke William re-entered his pavilion, it was Count Cynric who stepped forward, pointing the girl to where Cerdic and Turold had now got back to their feet beside the burial pit.

With a final, mournful glance at her mistress, the girl called Yvette trudged toward them.

'You are House Tancarville?' she asked, when she reached them.

'We are,' Cerdic replied. 'Welcome.'

She looked him up and down, scarce able to believe the cuts and bruises that covered his face and arms, the grave-filth that caked him, the open raw wound in the middle of his rank, ratty hair.

Count Cynric called over to them, this time addressing Turold, who listened attentively and nodded. Cynric then went back into the duke's pavilion. Count Eustace, throwing one last, dejected glance at Yvette, followed him. Turold turned to the girl. 'You're now under the protection of Count Cynric of Tancarville—'

'I heard, you dolt!' she hissed. 'You think I don't understand my own tongue?'

Turold, big as he was, tinged red as he lumbered away to make arrangements.

'Better Count Cynric,' Cerdic said, 'than Eustace, the lover of little girls, eh?'

'Please...' She sat on the mound of grave-dirt. 'Just... don't speak to me.'

'Forgive me,' he replied, stung. 'I thought you could have appreciated a friendly thought. Clearly I was wrong.'

She glanced at him again, then dropped her head into one of her hands and wept.

Immediately, Cerdic felt awkward and sorry. There'd been no call to take umbrage like that when the girl had just been abducted.

'Listen,' he said. He glanced around to see if there was anyone nearby who might understand English, and spotting no one, added quietly: 'If you can manage to speak with Lady Edith before she leaves, I can tell you where you'll find the king.'

It took a moment or two for that message to strike home. When it did, the girl looked up sharply, eyes wet but suddenly bright with hope.

'How... how could *you* know that?' she whispered.

Cerdic glanced around again, specifically looking for Turold, but the big knight was fifty yards away, conversing with some men-at-arms.

'I saw him die,' he said. 'I also saw what they did to him afterwards. I warn you, it's not pretty.'

The girl nodded as if she'd perhaps anticipated this. 'Where are they keeping him?'

'They don't have him. He's still on the ridge.'

She looked even more startled.

'They've searched,' he said, 'but they can't identify him.'

She stood up. 'Whatever state he's in, I'm sure my mistress will. There are certain marks on his body—'

Cerdic motioned for quiet. He glanced again toward Turold, who'd been on his way back, but was now drawn into a second conversation with a different underling.

'You'll still need a lifetime of luck,' he said, 'but at least I can direct you. In the middle of the ridge there's an old apple tree. You can't miss it, it's the only tree there. The king was slain thirty or so yards to the west. Close to the point where the land tilts downward. That's as much as I can tell you...'

She nodded. 'That should be enough.'

'I warn you again, it's a trail of woe getting up there. And when you do...' He shook his head, grimly.

'The choice will be my lady's.' Yvette glanced across the trench and the rows of half-naked bodies, to where her mistress, with the assistance of the two monks, was about to re-ascend to her saddle. 'The least I can do is give it to her.' She raised her voice to one of despair. 'Madame! *Madame!*'

As fast as her feet would take her, she scurried around the trench and across the wet turf, throwing herself into the arms of Lady Edith, the pair of them weeping volubly. The captain-of-the-guard snapped something in French and lurched forward. But a barked command from Turold, now returned to the gravesite, brought him to a halt. The knight stood beside Cerdic as the women hugged each other and sobbed inconsolably, offering their low-voiced farewells.

At the same time, there was renewed wailing from the hill-side. Another family had discovered their lost one.

'My congratulations to your duke,' Cerdic told his captor. 'Since he arrived here, England's never been happier.'

CHAPTER 28

They saw nothing of the female prisoner that first night, nor in the morning, though word spread that Count Cynric had made special provisions for her. She wouldn't be chained, and would sleep in the back of one of the supply wagons, a covered cart, wherein she'd at least have privacy and shelter from the rain.

'Maybe Cynric's feeling guilty,' Eadhelm said, as they were marched out again.

'More likely it's on the Bastard's orders,' Cerdic replied. 'He wants to trade her to her father for some renewed pledge of loyalty. And it wouldn't do to hand her over in a ruined condition.'

Eadhelm thought on this. 'Maybe. But I've been watching them, Cerdic. I think I might have been wrong about the count. He's clearly not his son.'

'Just because he hasn't hanged anyone out of spite yet, that doesn't mean he won't.'

Nothing else needed to be said, and they got to work under the same arduous conditions as before.

The mass burial was almost complete by the middle of the day. Clearly, Count Cynric was only taking responsibility for his own contingent, for by Cerdic's estimate, they'd laid about one hundred and eighty corpses in the makeshift grave before the thin, pale priest he'd seen previously came to the trench side, wearing a stole.

Whoever the priest was, he had next to no constitution, rocking on his feet as though ready to faint while attempting to sing his way through a hurried Latin mass. There were many unburied corpses around, of course, other prisoners still working as personal grave-diggers for the Norman households that had captured them, so the air was increasingly noxious. Cerdic noticed that the priest's gaze strayed all around him, but mostly into the sky. He never once looked down on the lumps of lifeless clay whose souls he was despatching to eternity.

'Count Cynric could have found himself a chaplain with a stronger stomach,' Cerdic commented, wondering how Aethelric would have coped but suspecting he'd have made a better fist of it than this. 'What did this feeble specimen expect would happen on a military campaign?'

'That's Father Jerome,' Eadhelm replied. 'He's some relative of Cynric's family.'

'Came here hoping for his own bishopric, did he?'

'The rumour is it's not his stomach that's at fault, but his heart. Supposedly, he believes in the goodness of man.'

Cerdic struggled not to laugh.

Once Father Jerome had stumbled away, they shovelled the soil in.

'I wonder how many men he has in total, our new master?' Cerdic said as they walked tiredly back to camp. 'Not counting the fyrd, my own father left Wulfbury with a compliment of four hundred fighting men. Of those, only ninety or so, his housecarls, made up his personal hearth-troop. The rest were carls in the service of tenant thegns.'

'And you wonder if Count Cynric's war-band was of similar size?' Eadhelm said.

'If it was, it's surely smaller now.'

'And what is the point of all this rumination?'

Cerdic lowered his voice. 'At the very least, Eadhelm, we need to appraise our enemy, work out something of their strengths and weaknesses.'

'You're going to get yourself hanged, Cerdic. Excuse me if I make every effort to avoid standing beside you when that happens.'

Cerdic supposed he understood his fellow prisoner's fatalism. Any attempted escape was likely to fail. They were too hungry, too tired, too wounded. And from what he'd seen, the consequences could be dire, and not just for those who'd made the attempt, but for those who'd known about it and done nothing to intervene. It was a hellish predicament, but surely no man could simply accept it? Not unless he was completely broken in spirit, and Cerdic was adamant that he wasn't. There had to be some way out of this that didn't lead to death, but it wasn't going to be an obvious one.

He wondered again about those cryptic words of his brother's.

You'll need to be clever. Very clever.

For the first time Cerdic tried to break that down, to work out what it actually meant.

King Alfred had been clever by playing dead, by pretending to be defeated and then rounding on the Danes when they'd least expected it. Clearly, that option was not available at present, but these bastards had to have a weakness somewhere. And maybe, just maybe, it was their greed. Because that was something else Unferth had alluded to.

You won't be able to throw yourself on their mercy. But you might be able to throw yourself on their greed.

Another snippet of homespun wisdom, tossed out in passing. But it had rung true. The Normans had only spared him on the battlefield because of his ring-coat, having assumed it meant he was descended from wealth. And he *was*, of course, even though he no longer had access to it. The real question therefore was how long could he fool them into thinking that he was worth keeping alive without actually having to prove anything?

Cerdic gave a wry smile.

That would certainly require him to be clever.

-

This time, they didn't return to the trampled, faeces-scattered clearing that had become their home. Instead, they were diverted into an open space in front of Count Cynric's pavilion. Here, a heavy, richly carved chair had been brought out, the count's own seat of judgement, no doubt. The count himself was now reclined on it.

For the first time, Cerdic got a proper look at his new master.

He had the sort of features the lad had only seen before on the stained-glass panels at York Minster. Gaunt and long, noble too, and yet somehow lacking. He made Cerdic think of saints who'd been martyred: perfect beings from long ago, so perfect they were always depicted ramrod-straight, eyes to heaven as though unaffected by pain, fear or even joy. Yes, Count Cynric's cool, blank features could easily sit on a saint from the past, had Cerdic not already seen him participate in butchery.

Turold de Bardouville, the count's household champion, stood to one side of him, while on the other was his knight-seneschal, a man called Roland Casterborus. Cerdic had had no contact with him yet, but had seen him around the camp. He was dark-haired and, like the count, affected a beard and moustache, though in his case they were very trim. Like his master, he had what Cerdic considered 'priestly' looks, meek, solemn, though like Turold he'd been marked by battle; a hard, white scar bisected the left side of his face from nostril to earlobe.

Both elite knights now stood fully mailed, longswords drawn but pointed down. The rest of the household encircled the space in interested groups.

One by one, the English prisoners were brought forward by Joubert, usually by the scruff of their necks or with his fist clamping a hank of hair or beard. Each time he made them stand in the middle, doused them down with a bucket of water, to wash off the worst of the filth and sweat, and then left them facing their captor-in-chief.

The count never addressed them himself, but conferred quietly and constantly with Roland Casterborus. It was Turold, who spoke English, who conversed with the prisoners, in each case demanding to know their name and rank, relaying this information to his count, and then interrogating them about their land, property and other valuable possessions.

Cerdic waited in line, watching tensely. As he'd been told, Count Cynric was looking to make good on his overlord's campaign without waiting for that overlord to bestow some reward on him. One after another, eager to please and to save their skins, the captives listed the goods and properties they'd happily sign over should they and the lives of their families be spared. Cerdic couldn't help thinking that none of it amounted to much. There were some forty prisoners in total, and mainly they were thegns, in several cases sub-tenants of other thegns. They had homes to call their own, and small plots of land, though as these men came from a variety of locations, such holdings were scattered widely across England's earldoms. It would not be within Count Cynric's power to claim them until Duke William had decided who the new earls would be.

Eadhelm, for instance, held several farms in the earldom of Kent, but it was rumoured that this prize had already been claimed by Bishop Odo. It seemed unlikely that anyone, even Count Cynric, could successfully horse-trade with *him*.

'I just hope my moveable wealth will interest them,' Eadhelm said, when pushed back to rejoin the others. He looked unnerved by the experience, his teeth clenched. 'I have precious heirlooms, horses, good weapons… I've offered them all.'

'I heard,' Cerdic replied.

'You think they understood?'

'Turold seems to speak our language very well.'

'Turold… the big knight? Maybe, but Count Cynric looked unimpressed.'

'Count Cynric looks permanently unimpressed.'

'I hope that's what it is,' Eadhelm conceded.

'You'd better *had* hope,' whispered the prisoner who had gone before him, another lean and wounded individual, caked in blood and grit, whose name they'd learned was Elfrid. 'You better had indeed. Because they're going to kill those of us they see no use for.'

'That's ridiculous,' Cerdic said. 'It would be plain murder.'

Elfrid gave a bitter laugh. 'They don't see it that way.'

'*It's ridiculous!*' Cerdic said again, perhaps more in hope than certainty.

'You think so? Why did they wait till we'd dug all those grave pits before they started these interrogations if not because they needed all of us for that, but don't need all of us now?'

Cerdic couldn't answer. He didn't even like to ponder it.

'You think they'll just release those they don't want?' Elfrid said. 'So we can go and join partisan bands and resist them all over again?'

Eadhelm, who, perhaps even more fuddled by pain than previously, remained firm in his new thinking that the count was noble of spirit as well as birth, shook his head. 'We're prisoners of war. We're owed some degree of respect.'

'We're dead men walking once we're no use to them,' Elfrid snorted. 'Why would they even bother keeping us in chains? It'd be a pointless waste of their supplies.'

'Supplies?' Cerdic replied. 'So far, all they've fed us on is swill.'

'Even that could be better used in the eyes of these murderers.'

Again, Cerdic struggled to resist such bitter logic. He looked around, and for the first time noted that several of the men-at-arms watching – in fact *more* than several, ten or eleven – were hefting crossbows at their shoulders.

Why would they be carrying crossbows when they clearly weren't on guard duty?

Especially as some of those bows were loaded with bolts already.

Then, with a whipcrack shout, Joubert grabbed him by his collar and hauled him out into the open space. In Cerdic's case, it took a couple of buckets of icy water to wash him down, to much snickering from the spectators. If this was meant to show him at his best, it didn't work. All the others had been left shivering with cold, which was hardly the way a warrior wanted to appear when bargaining for his life. Cerdic determinedly resisted, shaking himself like a dog, mopping back his wringing hair. If nothing else, the water had cleared much of the grime from his ring-coat, which shimmered in the weak noon sun.

The snickers fell quiet. These human jackdaws recognised valuables when they saw them. And so did Count Cynric, it seemed, because for the first time now he spoke aloud. It was in Norman-French, but Turold again translated.

'What are you called?'

'Cerdic,' the lad replied.

The knight nodded. 'His excellency wishes to know where you come from.'

Cerdic heard Unferth's words: *Be clever*. But he also recalled Turold's own curious advice. *Say nothing you don't need to.*

He teetered, unsure how to respond. None of these other prisoners, who had promised their captors everything they had, who'd told them where their treasures could be found, who'd promised to give them accurate directions, had received anything in return. Not a smile, not a nod, and certainly nothing so outlandish as a guarantee that they'd be spared. But on the other hand, to actually say nothing, as in nothing at all, might be construed as meaning that he had nothing to offer.

Was that what Turold had meant: give them something, but hold other things back?

Would that be the *clever* thing to do? Taunt them?

No. But use their greed against them.

Already distracted, he was then transfixed by the sight of three crossbowmen making their way around the circle of onlookers, to join another group. One loaded a bolt onto his weapon as he walked.

'Where do you come from?' Turold said again. 'It is Count Cynric of Tancarville who asks this. You must answer.'

'The north,' Cerdic replied.

'Whereabouts in the north?'

'A vast estate. Centred on a great green valley.'

Interested mutters greeted this.

'It is what we English once called a "hold",' Cerdic explained. 'Now, it is an earldom in its own right.'

The count asked a further question.

'If it's a northern earldom, who is the earl?' Turold said. 'Edwin or Morcar?'

'Neither.'

The muttering ceased. Count Cynric spoke again.

'Don't play games with us, boy. Who is the earl?'

'My father was the earl, your excellency,' Cerdic replied. 'But he is dead. My brother inherited the title after him. Now, he is dead too.'

There was another brief silence. The count eyed him, intrigued, before posing yet another question. 'Which means *you* are the earl?'

'In name, your excellency, yes.'

'Earl of what? Where is this place?'

Cerdic could now taste the bile brewing in his belly. This was the critical moment Turold had been referring to, the balancing act that he knew he had to get exactly right. Say too much and they wouldn't need him and might kill him. Say too little, and… he glanced sideways, at the crossbowmen, all now with weapons at the ready, being quietly addressed by their captain.

'I can't tell you that, my lord.'

'Can't… or won't?'

Cerdic hesitated. 'I won't.'

Joubert capered up and punched him in the side of the head. Cerdic was flung to the ground, where the count's son kicked him around like a bundle of rags. The others watched dispassionately. When Cerdic finally got back to his feet, he was dizzy and his ribs throbbed. Very fleetingly, his eyes fell on a gap amid the encircling Normans, and he glimpsed the face of Yvette, watching horror-stricken from the open rear-end of a covered cart.

'My lord, I mean no disrespect to you or House Tancarville,' Cerdic said. 'But if I give you the keys to my own kingdom, there'd be nothing to stop your son here beating me until I die.'

Joubert, detecting criticism of himself, struck out again, slapping the prisoner's head fiercely. Count Cynric watched and said nothing, so his son struck the manacled prisoner again, kicking him to the floor a second time, all the while ranting in French. Only when bleeding from the nose and mouth, was Cerdic allowed back to his feet.

'Lord Joubert says that he doesn't believe you come from a noble house,' Turold said. 'He says he thinks you found this ring-mail on the corpse of some great warrior while scavenging on the battlefield.'

'It's a remarkably good fit if that's the case,' Cerdic responded.

Joubert punched him again, and again. All Cerdic could do was duck and twist, but the blows rained down... until the count raised his voice and brought a halt to it.

Joubert stepped back, red-faced, sweating.

Count Cynric put more questions to the captive via his champion.

'My son thinks you are a common thief. How do you refute this?'

'It's not true, my lord. I fought at the head of my father's hearth-troop on Senlac Ridge. I was there when you yourself were unhorsed. It was right in front of me. I saw your men help you away. I hope your shoulder is not hurting you too much.'

The count's eyes narrowed. Surely he would know that only England's elite were stationed at the front of their army? Or would he be angered to hear it said that he'd been led from the field while his men fought on and died?

Now Turold spoke, addressing his master first in French, and then turning to Cerdic. 'For what it's worth, boy, I've told him that I saw you fighting up there. That I was the one who felled you. That I felt you'd had good men around you. A hearth-troop perhaps, as you've said.'

Count Cynric made another statement. Turold translated.

'My master understands why you're reluctant to provide further information about this mystery earldom. But you must realise that we can't just take you at your word.'

'There's something I can show you that will prove it,' Cerdic said. 'If someone will remove these shackles.'

Joubert hooted with laughter, but Cynric regarded the prisoner with sober deliberation. Then he nodded, and called one of his men-at-arms. The guard produced a key and Cerdic's steel bracelets were opened. He twisted and kneaded his wrists, before unbuckling his ring-coat at the waist, reaching inside it, and retrieving the ring bearing his family's crest from the pouch attached to the belt of his breeches.

Joubert snatched it, examining it suspiciously, before taking it to his father. Casterborus took charge of it first, turning it over in his gauntleted hands, to ensure it was in no way dangerous, before passing it to his master, who studied it with interest.

'My family's seal,' the lad explained. 'If you were to ascend the ridge, to the hoary apple tree, there are many lying dead there who bear that boar's head crest on their shields and surcoats. Those were our... *my* housecarls.'

Another thoughtful silence greeted this. It was highly possible there were many here, and maybe that included Count Cynric himself, who remembered that crest for themselves. As always, the nobleman's expression was inscrutable. But it was Casterborus who posed the next question. Turold translated it.

'You said before that you are the earl of this mysterious place... "in name". What did you mean by that? You are only earl in name because you are our prisoner? Or is there something else you haven't told us?'

Cerdic tensed again, unwilling to respond. This was a question he'd hoped he wouldn't have to answer, because all along he'd determined only to tell the truth in this situation. To lie, and to be found to have lied, would be a death sentence as they'd never believe him again. But it would be a difficult truth to impart all the same.

'My lords,' he said, now turning where he stood, addressing the count's followers as well as the count himself. 'I am earl in name only because there is currently a cuckoo in my nest.'

Turold translated. No one replied, but they were listening attentively.

'It's a cuckoo I can't possibly evict on my own,' Cerdic added. 'My earldom's capital was taken by a Viking usurper called Wulfgar Ragnarsson. He broke from the Hardraada's invasion force while our own men were at Fulford. Seized my home by force of arms.'

It was Turold himself, looking amazed, who finally responded to this. 'And you think *we'll* oust him for you?'

'I'm saying that if you want my earldom, you'll have to fight for it,' Cerdic replied. 'I'm not pretending it will be easy. But it's a rich prize indeed, and so far from here that if you manage to capture it, it will *all* be yours. You won't need to share it with anyone. Not even your duke.'

The household champion continued to regard him with a mixture of disbelief and fascination, before relating the conversation to his master. There were immediate mutters from those watching, some indignant, some sounding amused by the audacity of it. Joubert swore under his breath, but even he seemed so taken aback that he didn't come rushing forward with another clenched fist.

For his own part, Count Cynric continued to eye the captive, thinking long and hard. Again, he looked singularly unimpressed, but he was also deep in thought. Before he could say anything else, there was a sudden consternation on the edge of the camp. Voices were noticeably raised, several more men than before talking at the same time, and then one of Cynric's knights forced his way through, genuflected in front of his overlord, and handed him a scroll.

The count opened it and read. He then spoke quietly to Turold and Casterborus, though it was overheard by others, the message passing quickly among the ranks as Cynric got to his feet. He issued a quick, curt order to Joubert, who, grinning almost fiendishly, passed it on to the crossbows captain, then stalked across the open space, hauling certain individuals out from among the prisoners, eight in total – Elfrid among them, his head hanging – all of whom were taken by the cross-bowmen. Wailing and weeping, they were marched roughly away, the onlookers stepping aside to form a passage leading out of the camp and into a deeper part of the wood.

Cerdic stood watching, his skin ice cold, his stomach lurching. He started with shock when a hand grabbed a hank of his hair and yanked his head sideways. It was Joubert again, still grinning. He spoke to his father, clearly putting some kind of question to him.

Count Cynric gazed at Cerdic pensively but without emotion for several long seconds before replying with no more than two or three words, and then turning and walking away, Casterborus hurrying after him. Joubert clung onto Cerdic with a claw-like grip. The lad felt sure the gurgling contents of his belly were about to explode from his mouth.

And then he was released.

Joubert slapped him once, hard across the head, and then strode away in pursuit of his father.

'All you others!' came the voice of Turold in English. 'Remove your war-harness. You too, Cerdic.'

'Why?' the lad asked, shuddering, unsure whether or not he was out of the fire.

'It's served its purpose. It's brought you to the count's atten-tion. Whether for good or ill remains to be seen. But it won't be seen today.'

Sensing that the rest of the prisoners seemed relieved, Cerdic unbuckled the remainder of his ring-coat and handed it to a man-at-arms. As soon as he did, his fetters were reapplied.

Well done, he could imagine Unferth saying.

Well done? he thought bitterly. It might have been clever but it had been damn painful. Not that he was necessarily out of harm's way yet.

'What happened over there?' he asked Turold. 'What was that message the count received?'

'A summons from Duke William,' the knight replied. 'We've been awaiting a deputation from your remaining leaders. Mainly your archbishops Ealdred and Stigand. We anticipated they would send us the crown.'

'And?' Cerdic asked.

'They've refused.'

CHAPTER 29

The Norman camp broke before cockcrow, a great straggling procession of men, horses and wagons heading east.

On one hand, Cerdic wasn't unhappy. It was now three days since the battle, and a fetid stink had settled over the whole land, which he'd have done almost anything to escape. On the other, he was disheartened and confused because they were headed east. He'd anticipated that they'd be going north, to strike London itself, and they evidently weren't, at least not by a direct route. And that was going to make it doubly difficult for the prisoners as their fate was to walk. Their manacles were removed, but each had then been tied by the wrists with stout rope to the rear of a different cart or wagon. These were already loaded with weapons, supplies, loot, camp-boys taking breaks from their arduous daily chores and, in some cases, maimed and groaning Normans, so progress would not be swift. But even so, it would be an exhausting plod for the already hard-pressed captives who'd have no hope of stopping to rest, even briefly, until the wagon-masters said so. By good fortune, Cerdic found himself tied to the back of the cart which, for the time being at least, had become home to Yvette. It was covered by an arched awning, with an opening at the back, but at the start of the journey he neither heard nor saw her because she'd hung up a modesty cloth.

They followed an old Roman-made road, but it was in poor condition, the paving lost beneath layers of mud and mulch, the scabrous undergrowth on either side closing in until it was no more than a narrow track. The trees closed in too. It was mid-October and the leaves were falling freely, water dripping continually from the branches overhead, while the air was rank with autumn and cold with sea-wind.

'Why did you not tell me you were of noble blood?' a female voice suddenly asked.

Cerdic looked up with surprise. Yvette had lifted the cloth. She wore a shawl in addition to her cloak, but had removed her veil, her brown hair hanging long and lustrous. Up close, she was at least the equal of her lovely mistress, with brown doe-eyes, fine cheekbones and full lips.

'Every prisoner here is of noble blood,' he replied. 'You think they'd waste pig-slops and ditch-water on commoners? I'm only surprised they wasted crossbow bolts on those poor wretches who couldn't pay their way.'

She seemed sad rather than shocked to hear this. Of course, she'd already seen the ragged relics of men chained in the Norman camp, not to mention those the previous day who were marched off to face summary execution for the crime of being paupers.

'They're inclined to be cruel conquerors,' he added, 'these countrymen of yours.'

'I would apologise,' she replied, 'but what difference would it make? None of this happened at my command.'

'I know.' He lowered his voice. 'Did your mistress find her husband?'

'How could I know that?'

'You seemed confident she would.'

'I hope she did.' The girl considered. 'If she did, no one will hear of it.'

With a thudding of hooves, Turold came up behind. He laughed. 'So you and our pretty little Norman maid have become friends?'

Cerdic scowled. 'Don't confuse us English with you Franks. We don't hate people simply because of who they are, but because of what they do!'

'Franks?' Turold laughed again. 'You have much to learn about Normandy, boy.'

'Why would I wish to?'

'Then wallow in ignorance.' The knight spurred his horse forward. 'In time, it'll be your death.'

–

For someone as underfed, underwatered and as generally brutalised as Cerdic, the first part of the journey that day was every bit as punishing as he'd expected. They'd travelled only a few miles, but his body was beaten and weary, and now his feet were sore too, his knees ached and his wrists chafed from the tight-knotted ropes.

Once again, he tried to pray. Not so much for divine assistance now, but simply for the strength to endure and the will to keep going, though toward what end he didn't entirely know. It seemed a humble enough request, and yet – and this was happening increasingly as evil overran his world – even these half-hearted attempts to commune with the Almighty now felt pointless and monotonous, and gradually they petered out of their own accord.

Instead, he recollected something else, also taught to him by Aethelric, but relating to an entirely different culture. It was about the Greek writer Aesop, of whom Cerdic struggled to recall very much in this pained and exhausted state, though one of his pieces of text, which the lad had been required to translate, still stood out.

The gods help those who help themselves.

Aethelric had explained that Aesop was likely an atheist who held no patience with belief in the deities of Mount Olympus because they were false gods if not outright fiction. Strangely though, and Cerdic couldn't imagine where this thought had come from at a time like this, he now disagreed. It struck him that Aesop might have meant something else, namely that whoever the gods are, and wherever they reside, they are more impressed by men who seek to solve their own problems, to fight their own battles, to stand up and be counted even in their darkest times.

That wouldn't explain everything that had gone wrong this last month – had it only been a month? It was probably less than that, which seemed incredible – but it would explain an awful lot.

They halted around noon, pitching no actual camp, simply stopping on the road. Those Norman footmen he could see – there was a company close behind – sat by the wayside to regain their breath, camp-boys rushing about with pails of water and sacks of fodder. The men were fed as well as the horses, even, somewhat to Cerdic's surprise, the prisoners, though it wasn't what he'd normally have called food. A boy handed him an iron bowl containing a meagre portion of pottage or gruel, with a few dried cabbage leaves crushed into it, and a cup, the contents of which smelled and tasted suspiciously as if they'd been scooped from a puddle. It was better than nothing, of course.

Cerdic didn't know how long they'd be waiting here, and so slumped down alongside the cart's rear right wheel. Even though he was sitting in wet and filthy muck, at least he could lean on something and rest. As he did, messages travelled back and forth along the column, mostly borne by men on horseback. At one point, he looked on with interest as three important members of Count Cynric's retinue, the count himself, his son and Roland Casterborus, reined up to confer with a rider who'd come from the opposite direction and wore the scarlet livery of Duke William's personal household.

The usual incoherent doggerel was exchanged, and perhaps it would have been more sensible, for that reason alone, if Cerdic had simply looked away or feigned sleep, but as it was, he watched them through his sweat and his grime, only to attract the sudden attention of Joubert, who swung his animal around and over the road, halting it alongside the cart, barking out a single harsh command.

Cerdic didn't understand, but he assumed it meant that he had to get to his feet. He did so, sluggishly, every part of his body hurting. And was greeted with a ferocious slash from Joubert's riding crop, which left his right cheek striped with blood.

The count's son smirked down at him and said something else unintelligible. This time though, unexpectedly, someone intervened. It was Yvette. She'd appeared at the back of the cart, having overheard, and though she didn't speak angrily to the horseman, she clearly rebuked him as much as she dared to. He in his turn treated her to a long, cold stare, before replying curtly, then wheeling his animal back across the muddy lane.

Once the small group had broken apart and gone their separate ways, Yvette spoke to Cerdic, who stood close by, feeling gingerly at his face. 'Are you all right?' she asked.

'I'm fine,' he replied.

She watched him worriedly, visibly distressed by yet another display of casual and unnecessary violence from one of her countrymen.

'What did he say?' Cerdic asked.

'Erm...' She struggled to recall. 'He... he said I'm to tell you that eavesdropping on conversations that don't concern you is a folly you'll come to regret.'

Cerdic snorted disbelievingly. 'He *is* aware I don't understand a word of your language?'

'He knows that. But he's one of the worst of them.' She lowered her voice. 'You must avoid angering him... *Cerdic*? That is your name, yes? I think he is the sort who kills for pleasure.'

'I *know* he is. On that score, his actions speak louder than his words. But...' Cerdic paused, pondering. 'But words are important too. Can you tell me what they were talking about? He and his father, and that messenger from the duke?'

She glanced around nervously, in the unlikely event that someone who understood English might overhear.

'For God's sake,' he said, 'I'm hardly likely to pass this information on. I mean, who to?'

'We are heading east, all the way along the coast,' she said quietly. 'They intend to capture your fortress at Dover.'

'I suppose that makes sense.'

'And any other of your great ports they encounter on the way.'

He nodded. 'So your duke can bring in reinforcements more easily. He knows what he's doing, I'll say that for him.'

With much shouting and cracking of whips, the column jerked into motion, rolling slowly but steadily forward again. Cerdic groaned as he plodded in pursuit of the cart. He was attached to it by five or six feet of rope, which, fastened to a steel ring on the vehicle's tailgate, gave him about four feet of clearance. This meant he had to move smartly or he'd be yanked from his feet, and after that it would be a struggle to get back up.

'He's not *my* duke, by the way,' Yvette said testily. 'You must realise that by now.'

'Forgive me… in the course of these bone-idle days, with nothing else to occupy my mind, I forgot.' In truth though, Cerdic hadn't forgotten. 'Your father, my lady… is he powerful?'

She eyed him warily. 'He is one of Normandy's greatest barons.'

'Barons?'

'Counts, viscounts… our nobility. What you would call ealdormen.'

'If he's…' He floundered through deep runnels of liquid mud, which soaked his legs as high as his knees. 'If he's so powerful, why are you now a prisoner? Why is he in exile?'

'Duke William is more powerful still,' she replied. 'But though Father's forces are scattered, he is not defeated. And the duke knows this.'

Cerdic considered. 'Did they mention why they aren't marching on London? I'd have thought that was the obvious target.'

She glanced around again, warily. 'They will, or so they say. But first they will storm Canterbury.'

'I see.' That also made sense, Cerdic supposed. Attacking the kingdom's religious capital. The archbishop had refused to bring the crown to the Normans... so the Normans were going to the archbishop.

'This, they say,' she added, 'will also see them avoid the great forest, where your broken men reside.'

Cerdic nodded. This was a wise option, too. By 'broken men', Yvette no doubt meant the survivors of Senlac Ridge, who, for all Duke Bastard's boasting, would still be significant in numbers. With so many of their leaders slain, they'd be a weary, unruly mob, but in the denseness of the Weald, they could stage ambush after ambush. Arrows would fly day and night from unseen bows. Every morning, sentries would lie with throats cut. No, to march first on Dover and then on Canterbury, at the same time evading the dark tangle of southern England's deepest woodland, was a sensible strategy. But as he'd already realised, it would take extended time to get to London by that route, weeks rather than days.

'What ails you now?' she asked, noting his sour expression.

'Going via Dover, we'll be covering a much greater distance,' he explained. 'That'll be hard on us prisoners, who'll be walking the whole way.'

Her expression changed as the reality of this dawned on her. She hadn't exactly been haughty with him, though she'd been frustrated and angry as well as upset for herself, and though she'd been distressed by the condition of the duke's captives, only now did she seem to look on them as actual human beings and understand how truly dire their predicament was.

'Can you... can you survive it?' she asked.

Cerdic shrugged. 'With the weather worsening? My clothes are wet through, my boots full of water. None of my wounds have been treated.'

'Lean forward if you can, let me look at your head.'

He complied. 'I suspect it's not a pretty sight.'

Her face wrinkled in distaste. 'It's clean, at least. I think it will heal.'

308

'That's good to know. But our main problem here is the food. Or lack of it. Rations like ours wouldn't keep a rat alive. Not all the way from here to London.'

'Perhaps I can share some of my food with you?' she said. 'But only you. There isn't enough for all the others.'

'Why would you help me?' he asked. 'You won't be eating like a queen, yourself.'

She seemed unsure how to respond. 'You've been...'

'Don't say "kind". All I've done is be civil to a fellow captive.'

'In which case, we're on the same side... are we not?'

He eyed her curiously. 'You sure of that?'

'Cerdic!' She seemed surprised he should ask. 'You and your friends are prisoners of war, which is a joyless state. I am a hostage... but I'm of Norman blood, and they know I'll be useful to them. I won't be harmed or neglected as you will. But even so, at present I'm probably more of a danger to the duke than you are.'

Cerdic pondered this as he ploughed along another lengthy stretch of road that was more like slurry. He'd been mildly suspicious of Yvette for the very same reasons she now gave. Could the daughter of a Norman count, even a count currently at odds with his duke, really be considered a friend? He knew from having watched events in his father's world how the great men of the realm could change allegiances as often as their underwear. But all that said, there was something about Duke William the Bastard, even from the little Cerdic had seen, that gave him the impression this was one potentate who rarely forgave or forgot.

'To share your food would be most generous,' he finally said. 'But if you seek a genuine alliance with me, my lady, there's more you can do.'

'Such as?'

'Teach me your language.'

She looked startled. '*La langue Français?*'

'Why not?'

'What purpose will it serve?'

'To start with, I'll know what my enemies are saying. At present, I rely on you or Turold to tell me. Wherever we're headed for, ultimately, there's no guarantee you'll both survive. Then, what will I do?'

She seemed both unhappy at the prospect and unwilling.

'Look,' Cerdic said. 'We're a long way from either London or Canterbury. We'll be many days on these roads. A month at least. It's not as though we lack the time.'

'You want to learn while you're walking behind?' she asked.

'Sometimes, yes. Other times, I might be able to ride in there with you, I don't know.' He glanced over his shoulder. The next group along, the footmen, were trudging sullenly, seemingly completely uninterested in anything the youngsters in front might be planning.

'I've never taught anyone anything,' Yvette said. 'I wouldn't know how.'

'How did you learn to speak English so well?'

'I was a child at the time. There was a Benedictine sister, in Lady Edith's house...'

'Think what she did for you. The way she went about it. And do the same for me.'

Yvette shook her head again. 'In a month? I don't see how it's possible.'

'I have a gift for languages. Or so my late tutor said.'

By her doubtful expression, she clearly found that hard to believe.

'*Scio ut incultus esse videor, sed non barbarus sum,*' he said. '*Filius magni domini sum.*'

'I know you're the son of a lord,' she retorted stiffly. 'You wouldn't be alive otherwise.'

'*Ten megalen machen hen pollous tethnakasi epezesa. To tou Iesou Christou pragma estin.*'

She was blushing by the time he'd finished. 'I don't know any Greek,' she admitted.

310

'At least you recognised it,' he said. 'I doubt anyone else here would. I said that I survived the great battle in which many died, and that this is the work of Jesus Christ.

'There must be a reason He saved me. I believe He must have great things in store for me. But for that, I must be a greater man than I am now. I must be the equal of your leader. I must understand his language if I am to destroy him.'

Again, she looked bewildered. 'How will you destroy him? Duke William is lord of everything now.'

'Maybe "destroy" is a touch ambitious. But don't be fooled by appearances, my lady. This war isn't over. At least, *mine* isn't.'

'What can *you* do? You even need Count Cynric to help liberate your own earldom. Or so you told him.'

Cerdic smiled. 'Set one enemy against another... how can that be a poor plan?'

At this, she looked frightened. 'Don't underestimate my people, Cerdic...'

'I can hardly underestimate them if I don't know their language. Their own household champion told me that unless I come to know them better, it'll be my doom.'

'But if they find out what we are doing...'

'Won't they appreciate it? Then they'll be able to insult me directly to my face. Even when they're kicking and punching it.'

She still seemed unhappy. 'I... I can try, I suppose.'

'Good.'

'When do you want to start?'

'How about now?'

'Now?'

'What else have we to do?'

She glanced further afield, seeing on all sides only a vista of empty, leaf-strewn desolation. A cold wind blew, threatening more rain.

'I don't even know why my people coveted this country,' she said.

'There are some who'll covet anything if it belongs to someone else. Until they are stopped.'

She glanced at him again. Pitying his condition, but also deeply worried. 'Maybe I *should* teach you. Our customs as well as our language. I understand your hate, but I fear it will burn you.'

'And maybe burn some others as well?' he ventured.

'Maybe.'

'And you seek to prevent that?'

'Of course. This tide of deaths must turn at some point.'

'And who are you, Canute?'

'Don't joke about this.'

'Who's joking?' He smiled again. 'Shall we start?'

EPILOGUE

'He is clearly not his son,' the man called Eadhelm had said of Count Cynric.

He'd spoken it more in hope than knowledge, of course. Even then, there'd been an element of near comedic naivety in such a viewpoint. Because, three days into the march along England's south coast, fed on scraps and watered little, he finally succumbed to his fractured vertebrae, collapsing onto the road and dragged by the hands, face in the dirt, for many miles, until someone thought to cut him loose and kick him aside.

'*Le corbeau est... un présage de malheur,*' Cerdic said in faltering French.

'What's that?' Yvette asked.

Cerdic still trudged at the back of her cart. 'The raven is the harbinger of death and destruction...'

'I know what it means. I ask why you say it?'

He nodded to the wayside ditch, where the shrivelled, broken wreck that had once been Eadhelm of Tenterden passed them slowly by, and at the monstrous feathery beast, black as tar, its beak like a curved blade, perched on his face, pecking at the sightless eyes.

'A three-way war is waging,' Cerdic said. 'For the soul of England.' He glanced again at the raven, which gazed directly back in return. 'I wonder which side *he* aims to feast on first.'

'That talk is foolish,' Yvette replied. 'Birds have no understanding of such things.'

'This one, I think, does.'

TO BE CONTINUED…